The
Turncoat's Widow

The
Turncoat's Widow

A Revolutionary War Mystery

To my parents, Claire and Win

Praise for THE TURNCOAT'S WIDOW

"Meticulously researched and excellently written, *The Turncoat's Widow* is exactly the book that any enthusiast of historical fiction would want to have in their hands immediately. A deeply rewarding slice of American history, mingled with romance and adventure." – Lyndsay Faye, International bestselling author of *Jane Steele* and *The Gods of Gotham*

"An exciting Revolutionary-era thriller with a twisty mystery, great characters, and historical accuracy to boot." – Eleanor Kuhns, author of the Will Rees mysteries

"With immaculate research and a deft historical touch, Mally Becker paints the compelling story of two reluctant spies for General George Washington as they face deadly stakes and endeavor to solve a mystery that could topple the American Revolution." – Michelle Cameron, author of *Beyond the Ghetto Gates* and *The Fruit of Her Hands*

"*The Turncoat's Widow* reminds readers that treachery from within and without to our republic was real, and those early days for American independence from the British were fragile, the patriot cause, unpopular. This is a rousing debut novel with insights into the hardships of colonial life, the precarious place of women in society, while giving fans of historical fiction a tale with suspense, surprises, and an outspoken and admirable heroine in Becca Parcell. Mally Becker is an author to watch." – Gabriel Valjan, Agatha and Anthony-nominated author of *The Naming Game*

"*The Turncoat's Widow* has it all. A sizzling romance, meticulous research, and an exhilarating adventure. Becca Parcell is too independent for both 18th-century Morristown and her feckless English husband.... Becker balances the ruthlessness of George Washington and the underhanded charm of Alexander Hamilton with the excesses of the British, as part of a detailed picture of how the colonies were governed during a war that was far from a simple fight between two opposing nations. But historical exactitude is balanced by dashing romance between Becca and Daniel Alloway, the escaped prisoner charged with protecting her, and plot full of bold escapes and twists. A great series debut. I can't wait for the next installment." – Erica Obey, Author of *Dazzle Paint* and *The Horseman's Word*

Prologue

Rebecca's laughter floated above the symphony of clinking chain and creaking wood as the British prison ship rocked gently at anchor.

Strange he would dream of his wife's laughter. He'd heard little enough of it during their brief marriage. Her affection had amused at first, then merely bored him. And it had taken all his skill to hide the truth from her. A lady of genteel birth would not have exhibited his wife's curiosity nor her persistence. But his wife was neither genteel nor a lady.

Philip Parcell drew in a thin breath, laboring to ignore the barbed pain that snaked through his chest. They would leave him to die whether or not he told them where he hid the list.

So he didn't tell them. Not when they broke his ribs and his breath grew watery. Not when the knife carved bloody tattoos across his flesh. Philip squeezed his eyes shut to erase the memory of his torturer's smile, his small, wide-spaced teeth.

Each morning, the redcoats gathered the poor sods who'd died overnight and dumped them overboard into the shallow waters off the coast of Brooklyn. The skulls of the ship's dead lined the beaches as thick as pumpkins in an autumn field.

Parcell accepted the inevitable. Dying would be the only way he'd leave the ship.

He'd have the satisfaction of leaving the redcoats to wonder: Did the list really exist? Would it find its way to General Washington? His silence was his revenge.

He swiped at the swarming flies, and the shredded sleeve of his shirt fell from his arm.

All he'd wanted was enough silver to buy back his family's estate, or, at least, the London townhouse. He'd only wanted to go home. To England. Anyone would have done what he did.

He could still beat the men who called loudest for freedom and silently sold information to the British. Men like himself. Men like his friends.

He'd offered to sell their names to Washington.

Within a week, British soldiers had ambushed him in the Neutral Ground, the sliver of land that hugged the Hudson River's western shore. They'd tightened the rough rope around his chest. The pain had sliced his ribcage as they heaved him on to the horse.

No. The pain was real. It dragged Philip back to the present. Back to Rebecca.

What if she didn't look for the list? What if she didn't find it?

Philip strained to turn. The prisoner lying next to him looked strong enough to survive. His breathing was deep and regular. And there was something alert about him, as if he was ready to run if the opportunity arose. He would do.

Philip grasped the man's wrist.

"Go somewhere else to die." The prisoner shook off Parcell's hand. Then he hesitated, pushing a small tin cup of water across the narrow space that separated them. "Here. Drink this if you can."

Philip reached for the unexpected gift. Prisoners were only allotted one cup each day. His hand shook. He spilled more than he drank.

He was thirsty all the time now, but at least the hunger that had haunted him for the past few weeks was gone.

"I hid something. Not on this ship." Philip gasped for air with short, shallow breaths that made him dizzy. "Find my wife. She has it." Stop. Breathe. "Get it to Washington." Something rattled in his next breath. "He'll pay good money for it. Sterling. Not paper."

"Next you'll be bragging you and King George go drinking together." Bright green eyes peered out from the mask of dirt that covered the prisoner's face.

The clack-clack of boot steps grew louder. A British guard sauntered by. The two men stopped speaking until he was out of earshot.

"What could you know that's worth money to anyone?" White teeth gleamed through a sardonic grin.

"Spies. In Washington's midst." Punctuated by coughs and shuddering breath, Philip told his story.

The other prisoner was silent as if sifting for the truth in what he heard. Finally, he asked, "What's her name? How do I find her?"

Philip thought he heard Rebecca laugh again. Then the pain took him, and his eyes closed. Sometime later, he whispered, "Her name is Rebecca Parcell. She lives in Morristown. Tell her I'm sorry."

Chapter One

Morristown – January 1780

There was a nervous rustling in the white-washed meeting house, a disturbance of air like the sound of sparrows taking wing.

Becca Parcell peered over the balcony's rough, wood railing, blinking away the fog of half-sleep. She had been dreaming of the figures in her account book and wondering whether there would be enough money for seed this spring.

"I didn't hear what...." she whispered to Philip's mother.

Lady Augusta Georgiana Stokes Parcell, known simply as Lady Augusta, covered Becca's hand with her own. "Philip. They're speaking of Philip."

Becca couldn't tell whether it was her hand or Augusta's that trembled.

"The Bible says, if thine eye offend thee, pluck it out and cast it from thee, does it not?" The preacher's voice was soft, yet it carried to every corner of the congregation. "They're here. Amongst us. Neighbors who toast the King behind closed doors. Neighbors with no love of liberty."

Philip was a Patriot. He had died a hero. Everyone knew. Minister Townsend couldn't be talking about him.

The minister raised his eyes to hers. With his long thin arms and legs and round belly, he reminded her of a spider. She twisted her lips into the semblance of a smile as if to say "you don't scare me." But he did.

"Which of your neighbors celebrates each time a Patriot dies?" Townsend's voice rose like smoke to the rafters, took on strength and caught fire. "Their

1

presence here is an abomination."

He rapped the podium with a flat palm, the sound bruising in the quiet church. "Then cast them out. Now."

Men pounded the floor with their feet.

Becca flinched. It wouldn't take much to tip the congregation into violence. Everyone had lost someone or something to this endless war. It had been going on for almost five years.

Townsend's thin arm rose, pointing to her.

Becca's breath caught.

"And what of widows like Mrs. Parcell? Left alone, no longer guided by the wise direction of their husbands."

Guided? Becca pulled her hand from Augusta's. She rubbed her thumb along the palm of her hand, feeling the rough calluses stamped there. She had learned the rhythm of the scythe at the end of the summer, how to twist and swing low until her hands were so stiff that she'd struggle to free them from the handle. She'd fallen into a dreamless sleep each night during the harvest, too exhausted even to dream of Philip. She, Augusta and their servant Annie were doing just fine.

"He hardly slept at home, as I hear it," a woman behind her sniffed to a neighbor.

Becca's spine straightened.

"No wonder there were no babes," the second woman murmured.

Becca twisted and nodded a smile to Mrs. Huber and Mrs. Harrington. Their mouths pursed into surprised tight circles.

She'd heard them murmur, their mouths hidden by fluttering fans: About her lack of social graces; her friendship with servants; her awkward silence in company. "What else could you expect from her?" they would say, snapping shut their fans.

Relief washed through Becca, nonetheless. This was merely the old gossip, not the new rumors.

"Some of you thought Mr. Parcell was just another smuggler." The pastor's voice boomed.

A few in the congregation chuckled. It was illegal to sell food to the British in New York—the "London Trade" some called it—but most turned a blind eye. Even Patriots need hard currency to live, Becca recalled Philip saying.

"He only married her for the dowry," Mrs. Huber hissed.

Becca's hand curved into a fist.

Augusta cleared her throat, and Becca forced herself to relax.

"Perhaps some of you thought Mr. Parcell was still a Tory," the minister said.

The chuckling died.

"He came to his senses, though. He was, after all, one of us," Minister Townsend continued.

One of us. Invitations from the finer families had trickled away after Philip's death.

"We all know his story," Townsend continued. "He smuggled whiskey into New York City. And what a perfect disguise his aristocratic roots provided." The minister lifted his nose in the air as if mimicking a dandy.

"The British thought he was one of them, at least until the end." The minister's voice swooped as if telling a story around a campfire. "He brought home information about the British troops in the City."

Becca shifted on the bench. She hadn't known about her husband's bravery until after his death. It had baffled her. Philip never spoke of politics.

Townsend lifted one finger to his chin as if he had a new thought. "But who told the British where Mr. Parcell would be on the day he was captured? Who told the redcoats that Mr. Parcell was a spy for independence?"

Becca forgot to breathe. *He wouldn't dare.*

"It must have been someone who knew him well." The minister's gaze moved slowly through the congregation and came to rest on Becca. His eyes were the color of creosote, dark and burning. "Very, very well."

Mrs. Coddington, who sat to Becca's left, pulled the hem of her black silk gown close to avoid contact. Men in the front pews swiveled and stared.

"I would never. I didn't." Becca's stays gouged her ribcage.

"Speak up, Mrs. Parcell. We can't hear you," the minister said in a singsong voice.

Townsend might as well strip her naked before the entire town. Re-

3

spectable women didn't speak in public. *He means to humiliate me.*

"Stand up, Mrs. Parcell." His voice boomed. "We *all* want to hear."

She didn't remember standing. But there she was, her fingers curled as if they held the hunting bow she'd used since she was a child.

Becca turned back to the minister. "Hogwash." If they didn't think she was a lady, she need not act like one. "Your independence is a wickedly unfair thing if it lets you accuse me without proof."

Gasps cascaded throughout the darkening church.

From the balcony, where slaves and servants sat, she heard two coughs, explosive as gun fire. She twisted.

Carl scowled down at her in warning. His white halo of hair, fine as duckling feathers, seemed to stand on end. He had worked for her father and helped to raise her. He had taught her numbers and mathematics. She couldn't remember life without him.

"Accuse? Accuse you of what, Mrs. Parcell?" The minister opened his arms to the congregation. "What have we accused you of?"

Becca didn't feel the chill now. "Of killing my husband. If this is what your new nation stands for—neighbors accusing neighbors, dividing us with lies—I'll have none of it. Five years into this endless war, is anyone better off for Congress' *Declaration of Independence*? Independence won't pay for food. It won't bring my husband home."

It was as if she'd burst into flames. "What has the war brought any of us? Heartache, is all. Curse your independence. Curse you for...."

Augusta yanked on Becca's gown with such force that she teetered, then rocked back onto the bench.

The church erupted in shouts, a crashing wave of sound meant to crush her.

Becca's breath came in short puffs. *What had she done?*

"Now that's just grief speaking, gentlemen. Mrs. Parcell is still mourning her husband. No need to get worked up." The voice rose from the front row. She recognized Thomas Lockwood's slow, confident drawl.

She craned her neck to watch Thomas, with his wheat-colored hair and wide shoulders. His broad stance reminded her of a captain at the wheel.

4

He was a gentleman, a friend of General Washington. They'll listen to him, she thought.

"Our minister doesn't mean to accuse Mrs. Parcell of anything, now do you, sir?"

The two men stared at each other.

A minister depended on the good will of gentlemen like Thomas Lockwood.

The pastor blinked first. He shook his head.

Becca's breathing slowed.

"There now. As I said." Lockwood's voice calmed the room.

Then Mr. Baldwin stood slowly. Wrinkles crisscrossed his cheeks. He'd sent his three boys to fight with the Continental Army in '75. Only one body came home to be buried. The other two were never found. He pointed at Becca with fingers twisted by arthritis. "Mrs. Parcell didn't help when the women raised money for the soldiers last month."

A woman at the end of Becca's pew sobbed quietly. It was Mrs. Baldwin.

"You didn't invite me." Becca searched the closed faces for proof that someone believed her.

"Is she on our side or theirs?" another woman called.

The congregation quieted again. But it was the charged silence between two claps of thunder, and the assembly waited for a fresh explosion in the dim afternoon light.

With that, Augusta's imperious voice sliced through the silence: "Someone help my daughter-in-law. She's not well. I believe she's about to faint."

Becca might be rash, but she wasn't stupid, and she knew a command when she heard one.

She shut her eyes and fell gracelessly into the aisle. Her head and shoulder thumped against the rough pine floorboards.

Mrs. Coddington gasped. So did Becca, from the sharp pain in her cheek and shoulder.

Women in the surrounding rows scooted back in surprise, their boots shuffling with a shh-shh sound.

"Lady Augusta," Mrs. Coddington huffed.

Independence be damned. All of Morristown seemed to enjoy using Augusta's family title, her former title, as often as possible.

"Lady Augusta," she repeated. "I've had my suspicions about that girl since the day she married your son. I don't know why you haven't sent her back to her people."

"She has no 'people,' Mrs. Coddington. She has me," Augusta's voice was as frosty as the air in the church. "And if I had doubts about Rebecca, do you think I'd live with her?"

Becca imagined Augusta's raised eyebrows, her delicate lifted chin. She couldn't have borne it if her mother-in-law believed the minister's lies.

Augusta's featherlight touch stroked her forehead. "Well done," she murmured. "Now rise slowly. And don't lean on me. I might just topple over."

"We are eager to hear the rest of the service on this Sabbath day, Minister Townsend. Do continue," Thomas Lockwood called.

Becca stood, her petite mother-in-law's arm around her waist. The parishioners at the edges of the aisles averted their eyes as the two women passed.

As they stepped into the stark, brittle daylight, one last question shred the silence they left behind: "Do you think she turned her husband over to the British?"

Someone else answered. "It must be true. Everyone says so."

Chapter Two

Provost Marshall William Cunningham hummed as he examined the bloodied knife. Every muscle in his heavy frame felt effervescent, as if at any moment he would rise and float above the ice-choked harbor.

Sharp slivers of light pierced the portholes, nailed shut and covered like all the windows on the British prison ship, the *Jersey*.

By the stingy glow of the oil lamps, Cunningham marveled at the way the blade slid smoothly through layers of skin, as if the body welcomed the assault.

Cunningham always ignored the screams.

But now his mouth tightened into a moue of dissatisfaction. He rarely misjudged the depth of the cut nor a prisoner's tolerance for pain. This American soldier fainted before he could describe the troops that the usurper, Washington, had sent to Sandy Hook.

He'd finish the interrogation later.

As commander of all the prisons on the Island of Manhattan, and the floating prisons that hugged its shores, he had killed more Rebel vermin than General Howe ever would. He was a precise man, a neat man, and he kept a close count of his dead. More than twenty-five hundred so far. Most dead of starvation or disease.

Not much of a surprise, that, since he sold off the prisoners' food and pocketed the profit.

Cunningham lifted off the stained work apron he wore to protect his clothes from blood spatters, and "tssked" in disgust at a small, dark stain that marred the linen at his wrist.

He heard a knock at the half-open door of the forecabin. Shuffling footsteps. Cunningham didn't turn.

"Your Excellency, Mayor Matthews requires your presence. He asks that you attend him. He's waiting on the dock."

Cunningham's chest tightened with irritation. One day, he wouldn't be at the beck and call of oafs like Matthews. Oafs who paid him well to do the work they didn't have the stomach for.

His grip tightened on the knife. He'd seen the way Matthews and the others sneered at him. Some pretended they didn't know what methods he employed. *They don't have the strength of character to do what's needed.*

"Hand me a towel," he said.

The young, blonde guard fumbled with one of the cloths hanging in perfect order on a hook near the door. He snatched his hand away the second Cunningham touched it.

Cunningham stripped the blood from his knife, stroking the towel along each side until the blade gleamed. He dropped the rag to the stained oak floor, then poked the unconscious man's limp foot with the tip of his boot.

"Do something with this." He brushed past the guard to meet the mayor.

Cunningham stepped from the deck of the prison ship to the gangplank and squinted. His eyes watered at the sharp northeast wind sweeping across the Brooklyn waterfront. It was a rare sunny day.

Mayor Matthews pounded his brass-tipped walking stick onto the weathered gray dock as he waited.

"And a good day to you, sir," Cunningham called, opening his arms wide. "Welcome to the *Jersey.*"

Halfway down the gangplank, he noticed Matthews' eyes travel the length and breadth of his clothing. The two men wore similar fine navy wool capes with identical gold trim.

Here I am, Cunningham thought with satisfaction, *the son of an Irish soldier, and the mayor and I wear clothes from the same tailor.*

His collection of pounds, shillings and pence had grown like a garden of silver since he began selling the food meant for the prisoners. He had pocketed more than enough to pay for the finest tailors in the city.

"A pleasure to see you, Your Excellency." *You sod.* Cunningham smiled broadly as he reached the base of the gangplank. He lifted and tightened his cheeks to make his expression appear sincere.

Matthews cautiously twisted to see his guards standing near his waiting carriage, then straightened his shoulders. The nasal voice bleated: "You let Parcell die, damn you." His walking stick pounded the dock.

"Ah, yes, most annoying. But we've discussed this before, Your Excellency." Cunningham smiled. "'Tis a pity you told me to take care of Parcell before you knew you still needed him alive."

The shadows under the mayor's eyes were the color of weak tea. "How was I to know?" Matthews stopped, seeming to realize he'd just admitted his own fault.

Cunningham kept his voice cheerful. "You were outside the room when I questioned him. About a list, wasn't it? You didn't object when I ended it." His eyes narrowed. "Pain doesn't unlock every secret, Mayor. There was nothing more he was going to tell us."

"Where's the prisoner who spoke to him? Where's Alloway? I asked you about him weeks ago. You said you'd find him." Matthews' voice was querulous.

Cunningham lifted his sandy-colored eyebrows. "Alloway?" He had not, in fact, forgotten Alloway. How could he? Each American death was a gift to his King and every escape–the few there had been–a personal failure.

"You know damn well who he is." Matthews face turned a dangerous shade of red. "You let Parcell die and then you let the only man who spoke to him escape."

When none of the guards offered information about Alloway, Cunningham began to lash his own men, one at a time, six lashes each. Punishment had a remarkable way of sharpening memory. Two guards described the tall, green-eyed man to stop the pain.

"Hard to recall prisoners' names. So few survive." Cunningham's hand rose as if slapping away a fly. "His bones are littering the shore of Brooklyn with all the others." Cunningham squinted in the direction of the nearby shore as if searching for the missing man's skeleton.

"Don't lie to me. You don't know what's happened to Alloway. If you'd found him, alive or dead, you would have demanded money for the information," Matthews growled.

Cunningham's chest tightened. *Steady now.* "Ah, Your Honor. You know me so well. And haven't we done fine work together these past three years? I only mean to say that Alloway most likely died before reaching shore. We've searched." The provost's voice hardened. "This happened months ago. Why do you need him now?"

"There's a deadline," the mayor said.

"A deadline?" Cunningham's interest sharpened.

"We need to confirm that Alloway is dead or produce him before February 23."

"Whose deadline?"

Matthews leaned into Cunningham's face, his breath sour. "The man who paid us to take Parcell and question him. Did you think your payments came out of my pocket?" He lifted his gloved hand and swiped a spot of spittle from the corner of his mouth. "The man I write to. The Correspondent."

Cunningham wasn't surprised. Matthews would name a prisoner aboard the *Jersey* and whisper the questions to be asked. Cunningham used his special skills to extract the required information. Soon thereafter, the small, heavy velvet pouch would arrive filled with the welcome weight of British silver.

Cunningham never thought the money could have come from the mayor, who, the gossips said, was always in debt.

Matthews twirled his walking stick faster and faster. "The Correspondent says there are others who will take his money if we fail. He says there are great rewards for success and great penalties for failure."

He's panicking, Cunningham thought. *That's interesting.*

Both men hunched against a new blast of wind and turned to face Manhattan.

Cunningham watched the ice floes race down the East River. "My men will find Alloway. And you'll pay me twice the usual fee, even if he's dead."

He held his breath and waited for Matthews' usual explosion over price. It didn't come. *How interesting*, he repeated to himself. He wondered who was paying the mayor and how much more he might earn if Matthews were out of the way.

Matthews propped the walking stick against his hip and rubbed his gloved hands together for warmth. "Why on earth did your men take him to begin with? He wasn't a soldier. He wasn't part of the Americans' new government. He wasn't anyone."

"Our soldiers move back and forth to the Neutral Ground all the time. You know that." Cunningham envisioned the small ribbon of land along the Jersey side of the Hudson River, the Neutral Ground, where skirmishes between the Americans and the British army never ended.

"They bring back whatever they find of value, food, animals, prisoners. Half the residents applaud our men when they come through. They have no love for Mr. Washington. One day they came back with Alloway." Cunningham spat on the dock.

Matthews slid his foot back. "Keep me informed of your progress. And, Cunningham...." His drawling voice grated with sarcasm. "If you find Alloway alive, keep him that way, won't you?" Then he strode toward the carriage waiting at the end of the pier.

Cunningham considered, not for the first time, cutting Matthews' throat. The thought of slashing a necklace of blood across the mayor's neck brought a secret smile to his face. Would Matthews' blood run thick or as thin as his courage?

Despite his fine clothes and his title, the man reeked of fear.

Chapter Three

Daniel Alloway walked into the soot-stained room. The tavern hardly deserved the name. The remains of last night's dinner littered the dirty straw that carpeted the floor. The place smelled of too many men waiting too long for something better.

The tavern owner—a thin man who looked like he refused to eat his own cooking—put down the empty plates he carried.

"Is there something you're looking for?" He squinted at Daniel's right hand, which was stiff and bent inward.

Daniel tried his most charming smile, the one that had helped him build a printing business out of thin air when he first came to Elizabethtown.

The tavern owner didn't smile back.

Daniel cleared his throat. "I'm Daniel Alloway and I'm looking for the Parcell place."

The men sitting at the one occupied table quieted, listening, though not one of them looked up.

"Parcell's not there," the tavern owner said.

"I know he's not. I was with him when he died."

From behind the tavern owner, Daniel heard "Let him in, Tom. We want to know about Parcell."

Daniel waited. This wouldn't be the first tavern owner to show him the door.

Tom wavered, then stepped back.

Daniel found himself sitting with three strangers. They introduced themselves as Isaiah, Wesley and Hopper.

"Hopper?" Daniel asked, thinking he heard wrong.

"Just Hopper," the man said, and they all grinned. There was a story there, and if Daniel had brought enough money to buy a round of drinks, Hopper might tell it. But Daniel didn't have enough money. That was why he was here.

Tom slapped a glass of ale on the table in front of him before he even asked for one. The glass displayed the prints of all of the hands that held it and a few of the insects that landed on it, too. Daniel lowered the glass of ale below the table and used his shirttail to clean the rim.

Never before a fastidious man, dirty glasses and plates bothered him now. He'd had enough of dirty water, dirty pails and maggot-infested food on the *Jersey*.

Hopper spit on the ground. "Parcell died a hero, damn the British." His hair, faded to a yellowish gray, was held back in a tight ponytail bound by a frayed black ribbon.

"He was a brave one, one of the best," Wesley said.

They waited. Daniel thought they wanted him to confirm the story they told one another, that there was a reason for this war, glory in the disease and the mud and the death.

What would it hurt to lie? "He died a hero," Daniel said. "I came to let his widow know."

The men leaned back in their chairs, looking satisfied.

In that moment of silence, memory overtook Daniel. Some people set your teeth on edge just by opening their mouths. Parcell had been one of them. The man had wasted his breath threatening the guards, bragging about his British roots, claiming to be a British spy and cursing the redcoats.

But the morning before he died, Parcell turned to him. He explained how he came to the prison ship and why the British needed him dead.

The proof of what he'd related was in the whiskey. At least that's what Daniel thought he said. Parcell said his wife had that proof.

So he told Parcell that he'd find the woman. The promise was meaningless. *Why not comfort a dying man?* Daniel remembered thinking. He was used to shedding promises like a too small skin and moving on.

But there was the promise of money. And Daniel needed money. Badly.

He felt the now-familiar tug of the scar on his hand when he tried to stretch it and tamped down the customary regret. Within weeks of escaping from the prison ship, he knew he'd never work again as a printer.

He'd left Cornwall years ago and washed up ashore in Philadelphia. A distant relative found him an apprenticeship at the *Pennsylvania Gazette*. He hadn't expected to love the work. His right hand had flown as it placed metal letters into the composing stick, then from the composing stick to the galley. He felt as if each writer's thoughts traveled through his fingers and spoke to him on the page.

Daniel couldn't afford to purchase his own press, not even after five years in the colonies. But his former master had purchased it, and Daniel regularly sent him a portion of each month's profits.

That was over. There was no such thing as a one-handed printer. No such thing as a one-handed farmer, deck hand, or dock worker, for that matter.

After escaping the *Jersey*, he had traveled through one town after another like this. Fear surrounded each village like some ancient siege wall without a gate. Near the shore, Tories questioned his loyalty to the King. Here, in the north, they doubted his loyalty to independence.

He looked for work all fall and ran out of money and friends by early winter.

With no way to earn an honest living, there was no choice. He'd keep his promise to the dead man.

* * *

Hopper banked the fire, pushing logs close together to maintain a low flame for as much of the night as possible. He'd offered Daniel a place to sleep.

"Been in trouble a few times, meself. Come on then, Mr. Alloway." Hopper was just about slurring words by then. In the dark one-room cabin, he flung a thin quilt toward Daniel and pointed to the floor.

His host was snoring by the time Daniel wrapped the blanket into a cocoon around himself.

Promises. Daniel didn't believe in them. Not anymore. He closed his eyes and listened to Hopper's rhythmic breath until the night disappeared into memory.

He'd sworn he'd take care of Amelia and their son, Silas. He hadn't.

"The midwife says all you need now is sleep," he had told her on that last morning. "You'll be fine when you awake. I promise." He'd stroked her cheek, then pushed aside her now-lank blonde hair. She'd burned with fever.

"Liar." Amelia smiled, her lips dry and cracked. His petite, delicate wife had been in labor for more than three days.

Her expression would have broken his heart if it wasn't already shattered.

"Promise you'll take care of Silas." Her voice was barely a wisp of air.

He leaned toward her and smelled death. "I promise. With my life."

Silas had entered the world reluctantly as if he knew his stay would be short. He wouldn't feed from the wet nurse. Daniel had slipped his hand beneath his son's, marveling at the perfectly formed fingers and miniscule nails. Daniel's son had died an hour earlier.

Now, Daniel cupped his hand beneath Amelia's and held it.

He buried his wife and son together.

"You didn't die with her," his gruff father said months after the funeral. "So stop trying." He scraped together enough money for Daniel's fare to America. "Go make something of yourself. Do it for her. Get gone."

Daniel had meant to. Truly. To the sound of Hopper's breath, his eyes fluttered shut.

Chapter Four

On most days, Becca lost herself in the numbers and her accounts. No. That wasn't it. She found herself in them.

But this afternoon, not even the neat lines of credits and debits settled her. She raised her head from the household account book resting on her lap. "Who started the rumors?"

"What does it matter, dear. It's all anyone talks of." The thin afternoon light trickled into the sitting room through the wavy glass panes and highlighted Augusta's sharp profile, the planes and hollows of her patrician face, her perfectly coiffed silver hair.

The two women sat in matching white upholstered wing chairs by the frost-framed window as they had each day since the unfortunate event–that was what Augusta called it–at church last week.

Both women had avoided going into town since then.

Becca went straight to bed after the unfortunate event. Since Philip's death, she hardly felt anything besides weariness or anger. At least anger let her know she was still alive.

Augusta told Becca once that grief took some people that way, and her eyes were so haunted that Becca knew her mother-in-law must feel the same, though she hardly allowed her feelings to show.

Now, Becca pushed aside the account book and rose, smoothing the front of her maroon-colored gown with its low-cut bodice.

Her gaze swept Philip's sitting room. That was how she thought of it. Weeks after their wedding, her new husband commissioned the round cherry table and matching chairs from the finest Philadelphia craftsmen.

By the end of their first year of marriage, he had added a coat of robin's egg-blue paint to the sitting room, as well as a fine kitchen and a second story to the house.

"Almost fit for a gentleman now," he'd said with a querulous note of disapproval. Whatever demons drove her husband never left him entirely satisfied with the house nor, she thought, with her.

By the beginning of the second year, he spent the last of her dowry on the tall clock in the corner. He purchased it from a Loyalist eager to return to London.

"The minister's accusations—" Becca began.

"Are hogwash," the older woman finished.

"Language, Lady Augusta." Becca grinned.

Augusta harrumphed.

"I don't mean his accusation against me." Becca's smile trickled away. "What if the minister is partly right? What if someone else led Philip into a trap? Who wanted to hurt him?" The questions gnawed at her, whispering, then screaming.

"Have you heard the term 'strategic retreat,' my dear?" Augusta asked. "General Washington's temporary retreats have been quite effective."

The window rattled with the wind. A queasy feeling gripped Becca's stomach. "What does war strategy have to do with…."

"Pardon, madams." Annie bustled into the room with a tray holding tea, last night's leftover apple pie, a sharp silver letter opener bearing Philip's initials in script, and a creamy vellum envelope.

She thumped the tray onto the tea table near Augusta's wing chair. Her broad hands were bright red from a morning's work scrubbing laundry and an afternoon's cold walk into town. The smell of dried apple slices, sugar, and ginger scented the air. "The coach brought that letter you been waiting on, m'lady." Annie squinted at the envelope. "Good quality paper, too. The British still have real money for fripperies like this."

British? Becca narrowed her eyes, studying one woman, then the other. "What are the two of you plotting?"

Annie's fists rested on her hips. "Something for your own good."

Annie was a comfortably heavy woman with a rosebud mouth and a nose flattened by her father's long-ago beatings. Only a few years older than Becca, she'd never married. She had worked as a servant for Augusta since she and Philip arrived in America ten years earlier.

Becca's eyes flickered to her mother-in-law, who uncharacteristically failed to chastise the servant for her familiar tone.

Augusta slid the letter opener into the envelope and pulled out a single sheet. Two lines appeared between her eyebrows as she read. She raised her eyes to Annie and nodded.

The cups and dishes clattered as Annie poured tea.

"What is this about?" Becca said with frustration.

"A strategic retreat," Augusta said. "A very temporary strategic retreat." She raised the sheet of vellum. "Philip's cousin Samuel in New York has invited us for a visit."

"Lady Augusta sent Mr. Samuel a letter two weeks ago," Annie explained.

"Enough, Annie," Augusta said sharply.

"Two weeks? But that was before I stood up in church."

Annie stared at the ceiling. So did Augusta.

Becca crossed her arms. "Should I be impressed at your foresight or hurt that you wouldn't tell me you'd written to Samuel?" She was hurt.

"Impressed would do," Annie said.

The formality between Annie and Becca had crumbled the day they'd wept in each other's arms when a sudden hailstorm ruined the field of rye they were about to reap. They had worked side-by-side after Philip's death to harvest the corn, cabbage, and other crops that fed them.

"I was hoping it wouldn't come to this," Augusta said. "The war isn't going well, and, when people take fright, they look for someone to blame. They've chosen you, Rebecca. You won't be safe here much longer."

"The British hold New York City." She struggled to sound reasonable and only half -succeeded. "Everyone will think that the minister was right to call me a traitor. They'll think I ran to the redcoats for protection."

"Many Patriots visit their British relatives in New York," Augusta countered.

That was true, Becca knew. Spies and smugglers crossed the Hudson River too easily. It was a crime now to travel to New York City without permission from the authorities.

At the thought of leaving the farm, she felt herself grow transparent, as if she could disappear in moments. She would become another widow without property, a will 'o the wisp subject to charity or forced to marry. "Please thank Philip's cousin when you and Annie see him. I'll stay behind." Everything would be all right. She would make it all right.

"Annie will pack. We'll leave in the morning." Augusta continued as if Becca hadn't objected. "Philip would want us to be safe."

* * *

Becca met Philip the day before their wedding. He was twenty-nine; she, nineteen, practically an old maid. The front door of the Parcell house had swung open and her husband-to-be's perfectly formed, long English face drooped in disappointment.

"She looks like an Indian," he had said, scrutinizing Becca's wild almost-black hair, broad cheekbones, and her skin, which darkened with the least exposure to sun.

Becca whirled to her father to say that she would rather live in a cave than marry a man this rude. But at the look of hopelessness and entreaty in his eyes, she held her tongue. It was an expression she had never seen on his dear, beloved face.

Augusta stood next to Philip inside the doorway. She cleared her throat. Forcefully.

Philip's voice warmed immediately. "Yes, she—you—look like a beautiful, exotic Indian."

His light blue eyes met hers and her breath caught. He winked as if they shared a joke, as if she was not to take anything he said too seriously. First impressions could be misleading. Perhaps she had misinterpreted his initial outburst.

"Please. You are both welcome here." He swept his arm back, inviting

Becca and her father into the house.

She fell in love with his voice first, the crisp consonants, his slightly rolling "r's." Words she'd never heard tripped off his tongue as he read the *Philadelphia Evening Post* and *Boston Gazette* to her by the fireplace that winter. Her interest in imports and exports, news of the war and Congress seemed to amuse him. At least at first. He laid at her feet a world she never knew existed. She loved him especially for that.

He was beautiful, although that was not supposed to matter in a marriage. She made a study of his face, the way his lips tightened or relaxed with his moods, the flush of excitement that stamped his cheeks as he described the next new business that would make his fortune.

And Philip was kind. At least at first. She was awkward in society. Even the thought of the minuet made her squeamish. He had let her miss the balls, grand occasions hosted by the town's finest families. They intimidated her.

"They are not good enough for the likes of you," he would say during the first year of their marriage, then kiss her cheek before leaving without her for dancing parties and balls.

Later, Becca would wonder whether Philip was relieved to slip away from her even then. He wasn't faithful, she learned. He took little enough care hiding his affairs after her father died.

She knew he had married her for the dowry; yet his indiscretions hurt. There weren't many men of property willing to wed a blacksmith's daughter, even if the blacksmith had discovered enough iron ore up north to make him wealthy. Philip had accepted her and her dowry, perhaps not in that order. She'd been grateful, nonetheless.

She didn't know then that her father was dying when he arranged the match, despite the constant cough that bedeviled him. He'd only wanted to ensure that she was taken care of. That's what he told her at the end.

The sound of Annie and Augusta discussing which gowns to pack pulled Becca back to the present. She would miss them when they left to visit Cousin Samuel. She would stay behind.

Chapter Five

D aniel woke to the hiss of the fire.

Hopper flung a few more twisted branches onto the logs. "Free ale for all, the minister says. At the meeting house. Later. You're coming?"

Daniel breathed in the novelty of waking to warmth then lifted his head to squint at his host. "Ale? Is it a holiday?"

"Who questions free drink?" Hopper waggled his eyebrows, and both men chuckled.

Daniel insisted on carrying firewood into the house as payment for the night's lodging. He only noticed the deep splinter embedded in his bad hand on the walk to the meetinghouse. He casually picked it out, feeling nothing.

A wall of sound greeted them at the door. Knots of men already filled the dark room with laughter. Two men danced a jig in the middle of the room to music only they heard. The foam in the mugs each held arced in the air and spilled.

Hopper's forehead furrowed. "Hope there's enough left." He disappeared into the crowd.

Daniel kept his back to the wall. He jammed his bad hand into his coat pocket and waited. He knew what would happen next.

First one man turned to study him, then a few more.

Someone whispered to a neighbor and jutted his chin toward him. The two men stepped forward, forming a human wall in front of Daniel.

"I don't know him," one said. "I ain't seen him ever."

The second one spit on Daniel's shoe.

Daniel slowed his breathing. The faces might be different, but the suspicion he found everywhere was the same.

"'Scuse me, boys." Hopper shimmied through a gap between the men. He held two full tankards capped with foam, shoving one in Daniel's direction. "To liberty."

Daniel would give the crowd what it wanted: proof that he believed what they did. He raised the mug in his good left hand. He shouted to be heard above the din, "To liberty!"

He could have sworn the room fell silent. Then one of the two men flanking Daniel slapped him on the back. Another man roared, "To liberty!" The crowd echoed the toast and the noise level rose again.

The pox-marked man who'd spit on Daniel's shoe retrieved his glass of ale. "The minister's never this generous. I thought he'd be serving Parcell's whiskey."

Hopper snorted a laugh. "I hear there's a barn full of it, if you're desperate enough."

"A friend of Hopper's is always welcome." A short, stout man angled to Daniel's side. Deep-set shadows were stamped beneath his eyes as if he had trouble sleeping, but his smile was friendly.

"God bless you, Minister Townsend, for your ale," Hopper said.

Townsend's smile evaporated.

"And for your kindness," Hopper added.

Daniel coughed to cover his laughter.

"You'll excuse our suspicion," Townsend said. "It's difficult to know who supports the British these days. There are so many. What brings you to Morristown, Mister...?"

"Alloway," Daniel said.

"He knew...." Hopper began.

"Searching for work, like half the colony." There was something about the minister. Daniel didn't want Hopper to mention Philip Parcell.

"Work? In January? It's too early to plant and too late to harvest." Townsend's eyes darkened. "You might have better luck west of here."

Daniel grinned. "That's as polite a 'farewell' as I've heard."

"No need to hurry. Enjoy our hospitality for the day." He moved on.

Curious, Daniel thought, to find a minister so inhospitable. He tracked Townsend's path through the crowd.

The minister clasped one man's arm, then another. Daniel heard snippets of his conversation "God's will...Your loss...Poor fatherless bairns...You haven't heard from your son? I'll pray."

Everywhere he stopped, he left behind pockets of silence and men with hollowed out eyes.

A thin man, brittle as ice, stumbled away from Townsend. "Damn the British," his voice slurred, a low grumble. "Damn them."

A tankard slipped from someone's hand and shattered. A fight broke out in one corner.

Daniel wondered whether the minister's comfort always left misery in its wake. The room had been full of drink and good cheer. Now it wasn't.

Hopper tugged nervously at Daniel's arm. "We should go."

He feels it, too, Daniel thought. He followed Hopper to the door.

Townsend's voice suddenly filled the room.

Both men turned.

The minister stood on a chair, arms lifted shoulder height, palms up, as if he were blessing them all. "Gentlemen, we've come to toast each other, not to fight. Now isn't the time to curse the British, nor dwell on your tragic losses." He pointed to one man, then another. "Not time to think of the death of your son, your sister raising four babies alone. Your brother dead since the Battle of Saratoga. Our brother, Philip Parcell."

Daniel cocked his head. Why bring up Parcell here?

"Damn the British," the man next to Daniel muttered.

"It's not the time to consider those who have betrayed you." Townsend's smile was gentle, although his voice grew colder with each word. "There will be other times to curse the British, to seek vengeance on those who betray our cause."

"Damn them." Another man swayed as he cursed.

"Don't think of the spies among us. Not any of them." Townsend paused. "Not even of Mrs. Parcell reaping the benefits of British silver."

Within minutes "Damn the British" and "Damn Mrs. Parcell" echoed through the room, the curses weaving themselves into a single tight knot. The man who'd spit on Daniel's shoes was the first to leave. Others followed close behind.

Chapter Six

All three women started at a sudden pounding. The front door sprung open, the handle bouncing against the wall with a harsh thump.

Thomas Lockwood barreled into the house, his tawny hair flying loose from the tie that normally kept it bound. His chest rose and fell as if he were still running. "Half the men in town are on their way here. A few women, too. My carriage is outside. Come."

"Calm yourself, sir. Explain," Augusta commanded.

Thomas obeyed her. Most people did. He took a breath, swept his hair back and bowed to the elder Mrs. Parcell and then to Becca. "They're maddened by the rumor that your daughter-in-law is responsible for Mr. Parcell's death. That she told the British where to find him."

"Based on what information, Mr. Lockwood?" Augusta asked.

Thomas lowered his head. Two fingers fidgeted with a brass button on his brown wool waistcoat. "There was talk that Philip spent time with other women and that ...."

Augusta turned away.

"And what if he did? Is that anyone's business other than mine?" Becca's face flushed. "You may have been Philip's friend, Mr. Lockwood, but that's not your business either."

Thomas stared at the wall just beyond Becca's shoulder, as if he were too embarrassed to look at her.

Something hit the side of the house with a thud. The small glass panes shook.

Becca's heart jumped.

Thomas made a sweeping motion, a signal to the women to stay away from the door.

Ignoring him, Becca crept to the window.

The Parcell house sat about five yards up a rise from the road.

Minister Townsend and his wife stood like a pair of silent black crows a few feet from her front steps on the path that Becca and Annie had dug through the snow just yesterday. A crowd of townspeople milled about on the road. Men pushed one another. Others laughed as if they were attending a fair. Some held axes and clubs. A few men swayed to keep their balance.

Thomas placed a warm hand on her arm and gently pulled her away. "Stay back." He opened the front door, sweeping frigid air into the house.

"Lockwood, bring the little shrew out," someone yelled.

Becca felt weightless, as if none of this were real. She'd lived here for three years. She had never quite fit in, but still.

"Now gentlemen, wouldn't you be better off in front of a fire in your own homes?" Thomas' voice carried to the men at the edge of the Parcell yard.

Becca shivered.

"We've come for young Mrs. Parcell, Thomas. We all know what she did," Minister Townsend called.

His wife nodded vigorously. "She handed Philip to the British. She might as well a' plunged a knife in his back."

Becca grimaced. The minister's wife never thought she was good enough to marry Philip Parcell.

The mob's voices rose in counterpoint to the wind. Another rock hit the side of the house. Becca crept closer to the front door.

"If that were the truth, Minister, I'd be the first to hand her over," Thomas shouted. "Mr. Parcell was my friend. But I haven't seen any proof. Where's your proof?"

Townsend crossed thin arms across his broad belly. "Charity Adams heard Mrs. Parcell and Philip argue last spring. She'll tell you."

The mob pushed forward a fragile-looking woman in her mid-twenties. She was petite, no more than five feet tall, with a heart-shaped face and blonde hair peeking out from under a fashionable brown velvet hooded cape.

How dare he bring her here? How dare she come? Becca fought the humiliation that mixed with her anger.

"And you propose to arrest Mrs. Parcell on the word of Mistress Adams?" Thomas sounded amused, but his knuckles whitened as he gripped the entryway molding.

"Arrest?" one man shouted. "Who said we were here to arrest her?"

Raucous laughter crashed through the air. Becca stepped away from the door, truly scared for the first time.

Chapter Seven

Pine needles skittered across the road, leaving green gashes across the ice-encrusted snow.

Daniel leaned against a tree at the back of the crowd. The cold sliced through his greatcoat. It hung more like a cape now, with all the weight he'd lost aboard the prison hulk. So this was where Parcell's widow lived.

If the mob had its way, she might be gone by sundown, run out of town. Or worse.

Daniel had repeated Parcell's words to himself often enough: *"I hid something. Not on this ship. Find my wife. She has it."*

So, when the angry men left for her place, he followed. He was curious to meet the widow. And besides, maybe Parcell's list existed. Maybe he'd find it.

Daniel heard the minister call a woman's name, Charity Adams.

The mob pushed her forward. The Adams woman loped when she walked, as if one leg were slightly longer than the other. Her voice was surprisingly low and husky. "Philip told me about Becca. He told me a lot."

The mob laughed.

Her chin rose and she tossed her hair. "Mrs. Parcell knew Philip was a charitable man who helped me on occasion."

A few men whistled. A few women "tssk-ed" in disapproval.

What prize could be worth admitting to whoring and adultery before the entire town? Daniel wondered whether they would stone her.

"She threatened him at a dance last spring. I heard her." Charity Adams' voice was strong. "She said she'd make him pay."

Men thumped the ground with their clubs.

Another man yelled, "Bring out the Parcell woman."

The elfin blond woman retreated, pushing against the tide of drunk men and limping toward the street.

Rocks flew overhead. One crashed through a windowpane. From inside the house, Daniel heard a surprised cry.

A tall woman struggled to push past the man in the doorway. A hand covered the side of her pale forehead to staunch the blood oozing from a gash. Despite her injury, she looked, as Daniel's mother used to say, hopping mad. Strands of wavy black hair escaped from her white mobcap.

She lifted her arm to the mob, holding out her bloodstained hand. "Is this what you came for?"

The Parcell widow. Who else could it be? He shoved his way to the front of the crowd.

She was not the woman he would have expected that fop, Philip Parcell, to marry. She was no British beauty. Her hair was too dark and unruly, her bright eyes too far-set and her nose not quite thin and aquiline enough to grace the portraits painted by the best society artists. There was something vibrant about her, something quick and unsettling. Emotions travelled over her face like wind rippling on a summer lake. She looked nothing like the round-faced, blonde Dutch and English families that populated the town.

She looked nothing like his Amelia, god rest her gentle soul.

"You're an evil woman, Rebecca Parcell," Mrs. Townsend screeched. "We'll make you leave this town. You'll never come back."

The widow's fearlessness rattled Daniel. They'd already hurt her. It was going to get worse.

His weight shifted forward. He fought the urge to race forward and shield her from the mob. That would be daft, he thought, even as his chest tightened.

He was a stranger. He didn't know the widow. He didn't know why the minister had turned the town against her. Daniel was certain Townsend's words at the meeting house had been carefully chosen for that purpose.

He needed to do something. There was only one lifeline he could think to throw her. Parcell had said the list of traitors was hidden close by in the whiskey. "Where's the whiskey?" he yelled.

Becca's head shot up, her gaze searching the crowd.

The words meant something to her. That was promising. "Where's the whiskey?" he repeated, louder than before.

The man who stood next to him, with torn lace at his wrists and a greatcoat so thin it luffed in the wind, laughed and clapped Daniel on the back. Two or three others, then more, echoed the call for more drink. "Bring out the whiskey."

Becca's eyes widened, and her gaze pinned Daniel.

His breath caught. In this frozen, gray world, in the midst of this crowd, he was suddenly warm.

She took a step forward, and, with a swipe of her hand, wiped the blood and anger from her face. She folded her hands as if in prayer.

She suddenly appeared smaller, reduced.

He wondered how she managed that trick.

"Minister Townsend, good gentlemen. I apologize for my behavior in church." She looked skyward. "I pray you forgive me my failings, for I am only a woman alone in the world."

The crowd muttered, confused. This didn't sound like Philip Parcell's wife, a woman born and raised in the woods, at least until her father made his fortune and dragged her to Morristown. Daniel had already heard that bit of gossip in town.

"If my husband were here, he'd drink a toast to you all for your fellowship and your good will."

Her eyes flickered to his, then away. She *had* understood. He wished he could applaud her performance.

"But instead, good sirs, will you drink a toast to my husband? There are crates of his best whiskey left in the barn. They're all for you if you'll raise a toast in honor of Philip Parcell, a hero of the war."

Cheers erupted. Some, then most of the men, turned and struggled through the snow past the shagbark hickory and pine trees toward the faded gray barn farther up the hill.

To avoid standing out, Daniel followed the crowd. The image of Rebecca Parcell facing down the mob kept him company on the snowy path.

* * *

Who is he? Becca tracked the stranger's path, his greatcoat flapping behind him as he followed the crowd.

When he called out, he had looked at her with such intensity, as if he knew her. But she'd never seen him before. She'd remember a face like that.

She saw him just long enough to gather up an impression of hardness and grief. His features seemed to have been carved from stone, all hard angles and shadows. His head was bare, his dark hair unpowdered.

She thought he was middle-aged, perhaps thirty or more. Becca was a tall woman, but he seemed taller.

How does he know about Philip's whiskey?

Minister Townsend cleared his throat. "I didn't think you capable of showing humility."

Becca whirled to face him. She'd had enough. "What could I possibly have done that you would turn the town against me?" She forgot to lower her gaze or keep her voice low.

"Your question insults my intelligence." The parson's chest rose and fell like a fireplace bellows as he struggled to compose himself.

"I don't understand." She was shaken by his ferocity.

Thomas stepped out of the doorway, shouldering his way between Becca and the minister.

Townsend reached inside his coat and plucked out a parchment. It was rolled and tied with a delicate blue ribbon. "For you, madam."

Thomas attempted to grab the paper but Townsend snapped his arm back and thrust it toward Becca. He bowed mockingly and walked toward the road. His wife followed, silently for once, in his wake.

Becca inhaled, feeling the sharp cold of the day. Her head throbbed. She stepped back into the sitting room and rested the parchment carefully on a side table. When the stone hit her forehead, she'd seen sparks of light. The events of the afternoon were catching up to her. Becca crossed her arms to stop the trembling.

"I'll take some of that whiskey if there's any to be had." Thomas raked his hand through his hair. He pointed to the parchment. "Aren't you going to open it?"

"It can't be good news. The minister was too eager to hand it to me." Becca looked to her mother-in-law. "You read more quickly than I do."

Becca knew her numbers. But Augusta had only taught her to read last year. She didn't want to stumble over words in front of Thomas.

Augusta unrolled the parchment and began:

The Council of Safety
Ordered that the wife of Philip Parcell appear
Before the President of the Council on February 24, 1780
To show cause why she should not be removed unto the Enemies' lines
According to Law, and on default of her appearance that she should
Be removed accordingly.
Signed: William Livingston, Governor of New Jersey

No one spoke.

"Removed unto the Enemies' lines? What does it mean?" Becca asked.

Thomas rubbed both hands over his face. "It means that the government will take your home and everything you own unless you can prove you haven't helped the Loyalists.

"And if I don't appear?"

"They'll still take your property. And then you'll be banished."

"They can't do that." Her hands were so cold. She squeezed them together.

"They can. They will," Thomas answered. "The Council makes decisions like this when the Assembly isn't in session. And they banish Loyalists and take their property."

Thomas took the Order from Augusta. He smoothed the parchment on the table. "The government is short of money. They'll sell your farm by auction to fund the war."

"But I haven't helped the Loyalists. Doesn't the truth matter?" She turned from Augusta to Annie.

No one answered.

Thomas squinted at the small panes of wavy glass at the front of the house. "The men may return once the whiskey's gone. It's time to leave."

He was right. A drunken mob was dangerous.

"You will be my guests as long as you like." He spoke to Augusta, but his eyes followed Becca.

The heat rose from Becca's neck to her cheeks. She wasn't a maiden, but her reputation was already tarnished enough without giving the gossips any more reason to spread stories about her and Mr. Lockwood. At least Augusta's presence at the Lockwood house would limit the damage.

"And Carl will be glad to see you all," Thomas added.

Becca's father had insisted Carl be given a place in the Parcell house as a part of the dowry settlement. But after Philip's death, when there wasn't enough money to support two servants, Thomas Lockwood took him in.

Thomas escorted Augusta to the carriage. Annie followed. Becca stood just inside the kitchen door, feeling the life drain from the house. She lifted the last lit candle and exhaled slowly.

"Damn this war," she whispered, her voice as wispy as candle smoke. The room went dark.

Chapter Eight

The mob flung open the large double doors with a grating sound that drove away a cloud of blackbirds.

Daniel followed the half-drunk men into the darkened barn. Parcell's list probably didn't exist. But if this was where the whiskey was stored, it was a place to start looking.

Shadows. Men in closed spaces. Darkness. Just inside the barn doors, Daniel staggered as if a ship's deck still shifted beneath him. The smell of decay at the border of land and sea rose again to choke him—rotting sea grasses, putrid fish and the detritus of daily life. He heard the moans of the *Jersey's* prisoners. Again.

He wiped the sheen of sweat from his forehead with his good hand. This wasn't the British prison ship. It was just an old Dutch barn—the Parcell's barn—large and unpainted, the wood a dull gray against snowdrifts as tall as horses.

"Still want to talk to the widow Parcell after today?" Hopper stumbled toward Daniel, gripping a bottle of whiskey by its neck. He clapped his hand on Daniel's back. His blondish-gray eyebrows were perpetually raised as if the world was full of pleasant surprises. He held out a dark green bottle and offered it to Daniel.

Daniel gripped the neck of the bottle, wiped it with his sleeve and lifted it to his lips. But he couldn't erase the picture of Mrs. Parcell confronting these men. "What'll happen to the widow, do you think?"

Hopper snorted. He lifted his chin toward the back of the barn. "Her place'll be stripped bare by sunset. Everything taken or broken." His thick eyebrows rose even further as he grinned. "Tit for tat, right? British raids wipe us clean and we wipe clean the Tories, when we get the chance."

Three men passed bottles from makeshift pine shelves to a jostling crowd. The sound of splintering wood ripped across the barn from another dark corner.

"So she's a Tory?"

"That's what people say. And who's to disagree?" Hopper shrugged.

Some men, faces already flushed from drink, passed Daniel. Others carried away dark bottles.

"Why do they hate her so much?"

"Didn't used to hate her." Hopper scratched his side thoughtfully. "She were always pleasant enough. Never looked down on those of us with less. She just don't fit."

"Fit?"

"No. She never fit. My cousin Abel serves at the Widow Ford's mansion. He saw Mrs. Parcell at the balls the first year after she came. She'd stand in a corner tryin' her best to disappear, my cousin said. Quiet as a mouse, she was."

Daniel's mind conjured up the way Mrs. Parcell's lips had curled into a smile just before she invited the mob to drink her husband's whiskey. She was no mouse.

"If she's a quiet mouse," Daniel asked, "Why do they believe she wanted the British to kill her husband?"

"No one heard her say a peep against Mr. Parcell while he was alive. Then the rumors started. My wife–rest her soul–would'a dented my head with a pot if I strayed the way Parcell did."

Daniel felt a surge of sympathy for her. Marriage to Parcell must have been a humiliation. Daniel had looked at other women after he'd married. A fine woman's form was a sight to behold. But he'd belonged to Amelia and she to him. He hadn't strayed.

Hopper continued, "And Parcell didn't earn a shilling before he spent it."

Daniel nodded. So Parcell needed money. He had said as much on the ship. It seemed he'd been truthful about that, at least. So maybe about the list, too. The question was whether Mrs. Parcell was his partner in the endeavor.

Don't be going soft over Mrs. Parcell, he warned himself. He brought his attention back to Hopper. "But what about the rumors?"

Hopper swung the bottle to his lips, then swallowed. "They started right after General Washington came back to town. Maybe after Christmas."

Daniel nodded, looked past Hopper, then headed further into the dark. Glass shattered. Laughter rose on a tide of alcohol.

He walked the perimeter of the rough building. There were four animal pens but they were empty. He wondered whether Mrs. Parcell had sold her cows to the British for silver or settled for paper money from local farmers. He strained to see any space that could hide a paper list, but the pens had been cleaned out. He was wasting his time.

A long tool bench took up about ten feet of the back wall. The bench top was empty. For lack of a better idea, Daniel felt along the underside of the table.

No one seemed to be watching. Quickly, he poked his index finger into the first of three small cubbyholes at the back lip of the bench. Nothing. The second one was empty, too. Something in the third crumpled softly and he hooked his finger round the fragile object to retrieve it. In the dark, it was hard to make out the words and numbers on the torn piece of paper. Daniel shoved it into a coat pocket to study later.

Noise exploded inside the barn.

"That was my bottle, you goddam whore-son." The voice careened off the walls.

Daniel followed along the back wall, eyes scanning from floor to roof. There was an unexpected break in the pattern of vertical planks. He came to a halt and reached out with his good left hand, feeling the rough outline of a back door.

Someone howled. Other men hooted. A fight began near the large barrels.

Daniel pushed open the back door, keeping his eyes on the brawling men in the barn.

"I think you'd be better off back in the barn, friend." The words were amiable, but the large hand that clamped tight on his left shoulder was not.

Daniel leaned right. He swung. His left fist hit the blond man's belly. Daniel dropped, avoiding a counterpunch. Rising, he found a soldier in a blue and buff uniform on his hands and knees, heaving. Five more grim blue-and-buff soldiers tackled him to the ground.

* * *

"He surprised me is all. Anyone just off a prison ship would be jumpy." Daniel tried to look up, a fruitless effort, given that he was lying on his belly, a soldier's hand locked round the back of his neck.

The hand holding his neck loosened when Daniel mentioned the prison ship. "Go on," a voice growled.

"I'm off the *Jersey.*"

"You're lying." The hand tightened again.

Daniel felt an unaccustomed rush of anger. He wasn't lying. Not about this. "They fed us at six in the morning if they fed us at all. William Cunningham, Provost Cunningham, picked a few of us to march off the boat and hang when the spirit moved him."

He spoke loudly to drown out the voices of the *Jersey's* prisoners that only he seemed to hear. They weren't real. At least, he hoped they weren't.

Boots crunched on snow, then a new voice spoke: "Help the gentleman up."

Two soldiers grabbed his arms. Daniel slid, losing his balance when they let him go, like a puppet with cut strings. He could swear that the men who tackled him were all cousins. Each was the same height with the same broad-shouldered, patrician bearing.

"Shall we start over, then?" The blond-haired soldier Daniel had punched closed in. "I'm Major Caleb Gibbs. I command General Washington's personal guards, the Life Guards."

"The pleasure is mine." The note of sarcasm in his voice might be a little too obvious. "Daniel Alloway. Formerly of Elizabethtown. Formerly a printer."

37

They stood nose-to-nose.

The afternoon sun illuminated a smattering of pox marks along Gibbs's strong chin. His tight-lipped smile said he looked forward to beating Daniel to a pulp sometime in the near future. "You really escaped the *Jersey*?"

"I said so, didn't I?"

A scowling soldier reached for Daniel, but Gibbs made a chopping motion with one hand. The soldier stepped away.

"You knew Parcell before he was captured. No, that's not it." Gibbs searched Daniel's face. "You met him on the *Jersey*? Did he ask you to come here?"

Daniel was distracted by two of the buff-and-blue-clad soldiers standing behind Gibbs. One held lengths of tubing. He lifted them into the air and shook them as if expecting something to fall out. The other grunted as he pulled a cauldron off a stand. They were dismantling a still, Parcell's whiskey still.

Daniel hid his elation. By God, General Washington's men were looking for the list of turncoats. Why else would Washington send soldiers to search a farm? Why would they be interested in him now? Parcell hadn't lied.

It was always best to stick with as much of the truth as possible. "Parcell asked me to find his wife," Daniel said. That was true. "He wanted to ensure her safety if he didn't survive." That was not true. "He didn't. Didn't survive."

How much will they pay for what I know? How much more if I find the list?

He'd head to New Spain, maybe to Santa Fe. He'd read about the southwestern territory once in a booklet he printed. It was a warm place, entirely different from the colonies. He'd teach, perhaps. His mother had taught him to read.

"And you escaped the *Jersey*? We haven't heard of many escapes." Gibbs tilted his head as if weighing the truth behind the words.

Daniel cleared his throat. He didn't talk about the prison ship. Ever. But there was money at stake now. "Twenty of us were captured that day. I was heading home from a tavern outside of Elizabethtown. The redcoats were scavenging for food, stealing cattle. Whatever they could find. They found me.

"They said there were two ways to leave the prison hulk. We could join the British army or wait to die." He ran out of breath. *It's behind you now*, he reminded himself.

"You refused to join the redcoats? That speaks well of your patriotism." Gibbs handed Daniel a flask. Its amber glass glowed in the late afternoon light.

"Hardly patriotism." Daniel wiped the lip of the flask with his cuff and knocked back a swig. "I'm no Patriot. Not a Loyalist, either. It isn't–wasn't–my fight."

"Then why not go for a soldier?" Gibbs' eyes narrowed. "The British would have released you."

"I thought I'd be jailed for a few months and then freed. If I went for a soldier, I thought I'd be stuck for years, the way the war was going. The overconfidence of a young man." Daniel shrugged, knowing he'd never again have that young man's confidence. "Only six of us made it to the end of the month. There was small pox, there was yellow fever, and there was Cunningham."

For a moment, Daniel was back on the ship, his hand still whole. Philip had just died. The voices of the soldiers who saved him, the dead ones, whispered just beyond reach. Sometimes he thought they meant to reclaim him.

"I waited for an opportunity. When it came, I escaped." He held up his bad hand to signal that the story was over.

* * *

Death had a distinctive scent, especially in the dank heat of July. Daniel had turned his head that morning to find Parcell staring at him, his eyes clouding over.

He remembered thinking that it wasn't worth the breath to call out. Men died every day aboard the prison ship. Someone would come eventually.

The click-click of a guard's boots grew louder. The footsteps slowed and then stopped.

The kick was unexpected when it came. It lifted him off the deck. His ribs were on fire.

"You. Get him up top." Just his luck. The prisoners called this guard the Ferret for his small aggressions, prominent nose and regrettable absence of a chin.

Daniel pulled himself to his feet. He locked his legs to fight the nausea that crashed through him and reached forward.

Parcell's skin felt fragile, like an overripe peach. Yesterday, he thought the man would never shut up. And now?

Each morning, guards and prisoners piled the dead at the boat's bow. Ten, sometimes twenty, died each day from starvation, yellow fever, or God knew what else. A hush fell over the prisoners when they heard the first splash, then another, then a waterfall of bodies hit the rank water off the shoals of Brooklyn.

Daniel cursed as he dragged Parcell's body to the ship's bow. He didn't have the strength or the heart to lift him onto the mountain of the dead. He arranged the man's arms over his chest, then wiped his own hands on his dirt-caked breeches.

He winced at the brightness and looked east to the Brooklyn shore, toward freedom. Seagulls dove into waves that glittered white and teal blue beneath a clear summer sky. The British flag luffed in a light breeze.

The guards stayed away from the bodies when they could. Two sailors mopped the deck, their backs to Daniel. No one else was near.

He'd be joining the bodies on the bow within weeks, he estimated. He was losing his appetite. He knew what that meant. He'd seen it in others. His body was shutting down.

Why not join them now? It wasn't a plan. It was hardly a thought. He swiveled and saw the two deck hands still swabbing the deck, facing away from him. He sank to his knees, then burrowed his head and his shoulders into the pile of flesh and waited.

* * *

40

"You'll need to come with us," Gibbs said, calling Daniel back to the present.

He stared at Daniel's misshapen hand. A puckered red-brown scar began near the wrist and cut deeply across the web of skin dividing thumb from index finger and through the deep bed of his palm.

"Can't feel much," Daniel said. "Hard to set type when your fingers are numb. It happened when I escaped the *Jersey*. It was hard swimming to shore with this bleeding in the water." He didn't mean to sound bitter. What was the point?

Gibbs didn't grimace or look away.

Daniel liked the officer the better for it.

"I wasn't planning on a long visit." Daniel kept his voice light, but the cold reached round his heart and squeezed. After the *Jersey*, he couldn't be locked away again. He estimated his chance of slipping through the wall of guards. It wasn't good.

"You'll be our guest, not our prisoner." The Major flashed a surprisingly broad smile. "It'll save you the fee at Colonel Arnold's tavern."

Daniel's heartbeat slowed. *Not prison.*

And, as if saving the best for last: "You may get to meet General Washington."

Meeting Washington meant he'd have a chance to offer what he knew of Parcell's list of turncoats. For a price, of course.

Daniel bowed. "Anything for the general."

Chapter Nine

B ecca could almost believe that the war didn't exist. Candles blazed in seashell-shaped sconces. A checkerboard of black-and-white marble tiles shone in the light. The comforting scent of tallow and of lavender furniture wax perfumed the air of the Lockwood mansion.

Thomas swept through the front hall and disappeared, still calling for Carl.

The three women were momentarily alone.

Becca reached for Augusta's hand. Annie reached for hers. None of them spoke.

Overhead, floorboards creaked, voices murmured. Becca relaxed into the warmth of their touch.

Seconds passed, perhaps as much as a minute, before the urge to slip out the front door overwhelmed her. Without thinking, she angled toward the gleaming black door.

"It's not fair," Becca whispered. "If I leave, you'll be safe. They are after me, not you."

Annie snorted. Augusta muttered "nonsense." Their hands held hers fast.

Slowly, almost begrudgingly, Becca's fingers curled into their palms. It was the worst winter of the century. Some in town swore they'd seen birds freeze on the wing and fall dead to the ground. What would Augusta and Annie do without her? For just a moment, she allowed herself to wonder whether she might need them even more.

If she could only discover who wanted her out of Morristown so badly and why Minister Townsend hated her. Then none of them would have to leave.

Thomas strode back into the room.

The women stepped apart.

"You'll rest before dinner, won't you, Lady Augusta?" he asked.

"It has been a challenging day, I confess." Weariness showed in the bruised hollows beneath her eyes.

"One of the servants will show you to your room and call you for dinner. She'll take Annie round to meet the others." He bowed to Becca. "Carl will be down when he's finished with preparations for your visit."

A young red-headed servant stepped out of the shadows. Within minutes, she had escorted Annie and Augusta up the shadow-filled stairs in the rear of the hall.

"Let me get you settled now." Thomas' knuckles grazed the sensitive skin between Becca's shoulder and neck as he removed her wool cape.

Becca shivered at his touch. She crossed her arms and stepped away. "Might I impose, Mr. Lockwood?"

His eyes softened. "I am always at your service."

"Yes, you are."

Thomas had taken in Carl as a servant after Philip's death, sent servants to help with her harvest, and stood up to the minister for her. His intentions were clear. Which is why she had avoided being alone with him for months.

Becca cleared her throat. "Did Philip have enemies?"

"Enemies?" Thomas cocked an eyebrow.

She couldn't tell whether he was surprised or amused by the question. No matter.

"I am trying to understand how the town has come to hate me so." She paced, stepping from black squares to white and back. "I attend few gatherings, even fewer parties. I cannot think whose enmity I have earned. And so I wonder whether there is someone who was slighted by Philip, someone who seeks revenge against me."

"By proxy, you mean? As if he's transferred his hatred to you," Thomas clarified.

She advanced from black tile to white and back. "There was a stranger in the crowd today." She called up his image, the hard-set jaw, and the surprised, amused line of his smile when she sent the mob off to the barn. "He yelled for whiskey. Do you know him? Did he hate my husband?"

Thomas' eyes widened.

Oh, bollocks. She had been too sharp, too direct. She had shocked him. Becca lowered her gaze, folded her hands, and dipped a curtsy. "Forgive my outburst, Mr. Lockwood. I am overcome by the events of the day."

He bowed. "Of course, you are. Any lady would be."

That was the problem when one lived sequestered from society and its demands, she reminded herself. With each passing day, she became less dexterous in translating her thoughts into acceptable, ladylike sentences.

She cleared her throat. "The stranger?"

"Just someone looking for work, I warrant. No, I didn't know him."

Becca ignored the disappointment that washed over her. "And my husband. Did he have enemies?"

Thomas' face tightened. "Mr. Parcell was slow to repay loans. That was what I heard."

"Loans? There were no loans," Becca protested. "I would have known." The ledger book where she recorded everything spent for the farm sat tucked into the bag Annie had packed for her.

"No loans he told you of," Thomas corrected.

She swallowed past the lump in her throat. Philip lied about his dalliances. It seemed he also lied about money.

"Your husband's debts were the talk of Morristown, at least before your marriage. I assume he paid all his lenders back, because I stopped hearing complaints in the taverns after you were wed."

Becca pressed her lips tightly together. That explained how quickly Philip depleted her dowry. It went to pay off his debts.

"At least the complaints stopped for a while," Thomas continued.

"A while? There were more debts?"

Thomas nodded. "He begged me for a loan about a year ago. I gave him ten pounds. I didn't want to see anything happen to you or Lady Augusta. Even good businessman struggle to repay loans in wartime, and Parcell was not a good businessman." There was distaste in his voice. "I allowed him to repay me in whiskey. The money was more of a gift than a loan."

She placed a finger on his forearm, touched by his kindness. "I didn't know."

He raised his head. She recognized the look now, his eyes half closed, his head cocked to the right. He was waiting for her to step toward him. The pressure between them had been building for months.

She stared at his mouth. Her breathing slowed. Would it be so bad to say 'yes'?

"Rebecca, you know I will take care of you. You'll want for nothing. You'll have no more worries. No decisions." His voice warmed.

No decisions. She quite enjoyed making her own decisions about what to plant, when to awake, how to spend her day. She would lose all that. "There is so much to be straightened out first, Mr. Lockwood." *But why delay the inevitable?*

Becca had seen his expression on a mountain lion's face once, blessedly, from a distance. Intent, still, focused on its prey.

"No one in town would dare to bother you if we were...."

"Sir. Mrs. Rebecca's room is ready."

Becca started. She hadn't heard Carl on the stairs.

"I will see you at dinner." She fled before Thomas could say another word.

As she followed Carl up the stairs, she wondered whether General Washington felt this slightly hollow feeling in his stomach when he retreated–strategically retreated, as Augusta would say— to avoid surrender?

* * *

"If I hadna' interrupted, you would have ruined your chances. I heard it in your voice," Carl muttered on the stairway. The candle in his hand created pools of light that ebbed and flowed like water across the paneled walls. "You should marry Mr. Lockwood. It's not right, you being alone."

"Of course, I should marry him. Even I know that."

"Just nerves then?"

"Just nerves," she lied.

Becca had used a precious sheet of her ledger book to list the reasons for and against marrying Thomas, using Benjamin Franklin's popular new way to make a decision. "Moral algebra," he called this weighing of "pros" and "cons." When she couldn't think of anything to add to the "con" column, she shredded the sheet, held it in her open palm and puffed it into the fireplace with an angry breath.

"The two of you get along well enough. You'd be safe." Carl pushed open the first door to the left of the silent landing.

Becca stepped into a jewelry box of a bedroom and lost her train of thought. Its walls were covered in pink and white toile wallpaper. Matching pink and green striped curtains draped the canopy bed. She stared at the featherbed and practically felt the cool pillow brush her cheek. She was that tired.

Carl stooped near the fireplace to nudge the logs, releasing the scent of spruce. The fire's red glow highlighted the ropy veins on the back of his hands.

He had a full head of rusty brown hair when he came to work for her father. Her mother was gone by then, dead of a wasting illness, with Becca barely old enough to remember her. Her father rarely spoke to Becca or anyone else. It had been a time of silences.

Then Carl arrived. She thought he invented addition and subtraction just to entertain her. Their laughter woke her father from his grief.

Carl stood and wiped his hands on the side of his pants.

She felt a warm trickle of blood on her eyebrow and swiped the back of her hand against the cut on her forehead.

"I'll get something for that." Carl tugged an off-white handkerchief from his pocket. He poured water from a pitcher into a painted bowl standing on a side table and dipped a corner of the cloth into it, handing it to Becca. "Mr. Lockwood told me you were hurt, you daft girl."

She dabbed it against her forehead.

"It's common sense you're lacking," Carl grumbled as he walked to the bedroom door. "You should marry Mr. Lockwood. I know the master. He won't wait long before asking for your hand."

46

She supposed they'd marry eventually, two next-door neighbors, a widow and a bachelor. What could be more natural, especially in these perilous times? She was fond of Thomas. Maybe more than fond. Plenty of women remarried just months after being widowed. She just needed a little more time. A little more freedom.

Chapter Ten

Annie woke Becca the next morning, briskly pulling back the embroidered damask curtains surrounding the bed. Becca cringed as she sat up too quickly and squinted into the cold, gray daylight visible through the room's large window.

Annie peered at Becca's forehead, wrinkling her nose. "Well, you'll have a scar for sure, m'lady. I don't think there's much hope for it."

"Why, yes, it does still hurt, Annie. But thank you for your sympathy."

Annie blinked large blue eyes. "Since I knew your head would still hurt this morning, why would I waste time asking?"

Becca sighed. Annie's logic was difficult to dispute.

"Now, up you come. Mr. Lockwood and Lady Augusta finished breakfast hours ago."

Becca changed into yesterday's wool petticoats and hoops and the one gown that Annie had packed for her. She dressed her hair with Annie's help to cover the two-inch long cut. Ready for the morning, Becca walked down the stairs wearing soft velvet slippers. The edges of her green day dress were almost wide enough to sweep both sides of the staircase.

"Damn it, he can't use her like that." Thomas's voice carried from the formal dining room.

"This war is in its fifth year, Lockwood, and there's bloody little to show for it. A win here, and a win there. Hardly enough to defeat the British. If General Washington thinks he needs her, would you deny him?"

"She doesn't have the skills," Thomas argued.

Becca hesitated at the base of the stairs, unsure whether to move forward or retreat. Thomas thought she had no skills?

She was eye-to-eye with the painting of Mr. Lockwood Senior, one of many family portraits that hung outside the dining room. The resemblance between father and son was striking, with their sandy-colored hair and wide-set brown eyes. The artist had captured the look of optimistic challenge that characterized both men, portrayed through the set of their broad shoulders, the straightforward gaze, the lifted chin that implied all troubles could be surmounted.

Becca found that confidence poignant, given the end of the story. Thomas' father, then a British officer, was killed in the war against the French and the Indians twenty-five years ago. Thomas had been five.

She decided to borrow a bit of the Lockwood family confidence. She stiffened her back and took the last few steps into the dining room.

The table had space for at least sixteen people. Only one sat there now, his back to the door. The man relaxed in the ornately carved chair with its animal claw armrests, his legs stretched out and crossed in front of him. His fine leather boots were wet almost to the knee with melted snow, and he still wore his dark brown overcoat.

Thomas stood over the stranger, his hands balled into fists.

"Good morning, gentlemen. Am I too late for breakfast?" Becca asked brightly.

Perhaps she misunderstood the overheard conversation. Perhaps Thomas and his guest were talking about someone else. It was absurd to think that General Washington knew who she was.

The stranger twisted in his chair and stood.

Thomas relaxed his hands slowly and bowed, avoiding Becca's eyes.

They *were* talking about her.

"I'll have Carl bring breakfast out. May I introduce you to an acquaintance newly arrived from Philadelphia?"

"*Enchanté*, Mrs. Parcell. I am charmed to meet you." The man bowed crisply. A luminous smile lit his thick-featured face. "Mr. Lockwood sings your praises to the heavens, you know."

Thomas winced, as if regretting his guest's dramatic manners. "Mrs.

Parcell, may I introduce Count Casimir Gorzenski? He serves General Washington in an..." Thomas hesitated, as if searching for the right words. "...unofficial capacity."

"I serve the cause of freedom," the count corrected, "as we are all called to do. First, I fight in Poland and now, here."

If the count expected applause, he was disappointed.

"Well, I wish you well, of course." Becca's smile was frosty. "Thomas, is the water still hot?"

The count frowned. "Nature and reason dictate that all men are born free and must remain free. A woman such as yourself must agree with such a principle, *n'est-ce pas?*"

"I don't know about nature and reason, sir. But I do support freedom for all men and all *women*." She emphasized the final word.

He blinked and was silent. Thomas pulled the chair out for her.

She swept her skirts forward and sat. "For example, I support the freedom to go about my business without having to sell the Continental Army my corn for worthless paper money just because the government says I must."

Count Gorzenski pursed his lips in surprise. General Washington had just issued a martial order a week before that required all New Jersey farmers to sell food to his starving troops.

Was he shocked that a woman paid attention to news of the world? If so, then she'd made her point. "I also support freedom from fear that the Council of Safety will take away my farm for no reason except a suspicion they can't prove. I would like to be free of this war, as a matter of fact."

Her outburst raised the color in Thomas' cheeks.

I've embarrassed him. What on earth is wrong with me? The cut on her forehead throbbed again.

"That was unspeakably rude. I apologize. It has been a trying week. Can you forgive me, Count Gorzenski?" After that outburst, she wondered if the count would testify against her at the Council of Safety hearing next month.

The count crossed his arms over the wide lapels of his jacket. His eyes brightened. "Thomas, she is perfect. General Washington was right."

* * *

The full moon bathed the hills of snow in a bluish white glow. Becca told herself it was only the icy air that made her shiver. She pulled herself up to her full height and rapped on the door of the servant's entrance, twice for good measure.

The most important man on the North American continent should not know her name. He should not have invited a woman of her questionable social standing for a *tête-à-tête* on a cold January evening during the worst winter of this endless war.

A young soldier with cold, chapped fingers had delivered the vellum invitation that afternoon. His Excellency General George Washington requested the pleasure of her company at Mrs. Ford's home, his winter headquarters, at seven. The general apologized for requesting that she arrive via the servant's entrance. Given the recent unpleasantness, he thought Mrs. Parcell would be more comfortable if her arrival went unmarked by any observers.

She had already been stopped twice by faceless guards—their features shadowed by hats. They had demanded her name and her business, then accompanied her to the door.

It swung open.

"I'm Rebecca Parcell. I was told to…."

"This way, ma'am." The grim soldier at the door looked as pleased to see her as she was to be here.

She followed him into the back hall, past a pantry with shelves lined with clay pots holding herbs and oils and summer jams and vinegars. She heard a buzz of voices, the staccato bray of a high-pitched laugh and the dull thud of metal pans hitting wooden tables.

The chatter trickled into silence as they strode through a dark, low-ceilinged kitchen. The soldier led her past a fireplace in which at least five of the seven cooks Becca counted could have danced a jig. Finally, they entered the mansion's long, wide front hall.

Becca didn't know what she expected. But it certainly wasn't stacks of bedrolls lined on the floor, which, she guessed, was where the servants sleep.

"Wait ma'am." The soldier tiptoed to the doorway of a room off the main hall and knocked, his head lowered as if listening for a response. A chair scraped against the wooden floor. A single set of heavy footsteps grew louder.

The man framed in the doorway was as tall as the top of the paintings in the hall. His faded reddish-brown hair was unpowdered and pulled back simply at the nape of his neck. Light blue breeches framed his muscular legs, and he wore a well-tailored dark blue velvet jacket edged with dark brass buttons.

He bowed. "George Washington. Thank you for attending me." His voice was pitched slightly higher than she would have thought for a man of his size, and it reminded her of her husband's, as if the general had been raised in England. "I am honored."

She wobbled halfway into her curtsy. "Honored?"

"Indeed." He raised an amused eyebrow.

She stood. "Then you don't believe I support the Crown?"

"I understand that that you have cursed both the British and the Americans. Your sentiments were heartfelt, I hear. No, I do not believe you support the Crown."

She was relieved and horrified. "Then why am I here?"

"Will you dine with me, Mrs. Parcell?" It was another command.

His request left her queasy. Men did not dine alone with women other than their wives. She followed him reluctantly into the front parlor.

The room's plain, military furnishings took her aback. Where a grand mahogany table should stand, there was a Spartan worktable laid with a meal of corncakes, gravy and tea. She'd imagined the general would require elegance.

Later, the meal over, Washington leaned back in his chair, waiting as a young male servant silently cleared the table. Balancing the tray of china, the servant closed the door behind him.

"Well, to begin," he said, smoothing an invisible wrinkle on the sleeve of his jacket.

Finally.

"Your husband died on a British prison ship."

"Yes, he died serving you." Polite society took so long to get to the point.

"Quite the contrary." The melodic notes in his voice faded. "Your husband was a British spy."

"He was one of *your* spies," she corrected.

"No, madam. He spied for the King's men, not for me. He carried information about my troops to the British. His support for independence was a ruse. His reputation as a smuggler made his trips to the city seem harmless."

Becca tapped her fingers on the mahogany table, faster and faster. "That is not true."

He ignored her protest. "Early last spring, your husband decided that he deserved more than the British paid him for information. They turned down his demands for more money. Bad policy to concede to that sort of request." General Washington watched Becca over the rim of his teacup.

"And that's when your husband made a grievous error, a deadly one. He offered to sell me the names of men like himself who live here and work for the British. Mr. Parcell said he hid the list and would provide it to me upon payment. I did not share his correspondence. I did not speak of it to anyone."

She stood, scraping the chair against the floor. "I am not a traitor, but my husband is—was? That is what you wish me to believe?" Her voice rose in anger. He was toying with her.

"I could be lying about your husband, Mrs. Parcell, but I'm not." A flash of sadness crossed his face. He removed a stained piece of parchment from a pocket in the light blue silk lining of his waistcoat. He unfolded it and slid it across the table.

Becca stared at her husband's handwriting, with its large looping "g's" and high thrusting "t's." She sank back into the chair. Reaching out with one tentative finger, she slid the paper closer and read slowly, struggling at times with the words:

Your Excellency, In this Conflict, when Friend and Foe trade places with unfortunate fluidity, I grow weary of this Double Part I play, minor as it is. I write to make Amends by offering you the names of men I know who work against you while hidden in your midst.

I would provide this information gratis if I could. However, the World is a harsh place. I have need of Capital, sir, as do we all. I have safeguarded the list I offer you and will provide it to you upon your confirmation that my Family and I will be safe and will be Compensated for the Dangers I have endured.

The letter was dated May 1, 1779. Less than ten days later, the British captured Philip on the cliffs overlooking the Hudson River, where the British and Americans fought almost constantly.

She lifted her gaze. General Washington's expression was soft, almost sympathetic. "This must be a shock." He poured a tawny liquid from a carafe into two cut crystal glasses. He handed her one.

"You didn't bring me here to tell me that my husband was a traitor," Becca sputtered as her throat closed around the alcohol's warmth.

"No, I did not. Somehow the British knew your husband was ready to betray them," Washington said. "They killed him to ensure that I'd never learn the names of the turncoats."

Becca held the goblet up to her eyes and allowed the Madeira to blur into a warm, amber curtain. She'd been married to a stranger for three years. She hadn't known Philip at all.

To quench her sadness, she focused on the problem General Washington set out. She would treat it as she would a mathematical problem. She would eliminate extraneous facts until only pertinent information remained.

There was a dull thump and then the wail of one of the Ford children. Two servant girls giggled as they walked through the main hall outside the door. The sound of Becca's breathing seemed to fill the room.

Becca set the goblet on the table. "There's a turncoat on your staff."

"I never mentioned my staff." He studied her with such intensity that she shivered.

"You said that no one but you saw Philip's letter. But someone else must have, and only people welcome here, in your headquarters, could have found Philip's offer. It's obvious."

Her voice was clipped, low, as if they'd disagreed about the solution to a difficult equation. But they were not speaking of mathematics; they were talking of her husband and treason. She took another large sip of Madeira.

Washington changed the subject. At least, he seemed to. "This war has taught me many lessons. I've learned that enterprises which appear chimerical–that are the most farfetched–often succeed because they are unexpected. When I heard that you cursed the cause of liberty in church, you presented me with an unexpected opportunity."

Most people slightly bob or nod their head as they speak. Not the general. He remained still when he said: "Who would guess that a wife accused of turning her patriotic husband over to the Crown would assist General Washington? That would be quite far-fetched. Entirely unbelievable."

It took her a moment to understand. "You want me to spy? For you?"

He leaned forward as if to draw her toward him. "Help me find the Judas on my staff. Help me find the man responsible for your husband's death."

"I have no skills." She shook her head.

"You stood down a mob and faced unjust accusations," the general said. "You show formidable courage and you just deduced that it is someone on my staff who is betraying our cause."

"In other words, you have no one else for the task."

He didn't argue the point. "I can't stop you from leaving. But I can guarantee that you will keep the farm. In fact, I'm the only one who can. On my honor, you will have your home back in exchange for one favor."

"A favor involving spying."

"Flee to New York City for sanctuary. Stay with your husband's cousin."

"You know about Samuel?"

He lifted a palm as if to say: *Of course. We've been watching you.* "I have friends in New York who will ensure that society hears that your love of King and country led you to warn the British army of Mr. Parcell's treason.

You'll be celebrated throughout New York City."

"The rumors," she murmured.

"We will use them to our advantage."

"You said that Philip carried messages from Morristown to New York." She worked it out slowly. "The person who received them will know he was no Patriot. He'll know that everything I do or say is a lie."

"I am counting on it." He crossed to her and took hold of her cold hands. His were warm. "Whoever received your husband's messages will believe that you have Mr. Parcell's list of turncoats, that you want to sell it or that you know where it is. I need to know who received your husband's messages. Once you find him, my men will follow the new courier back to Morristown, back to the traitor on my staff."

"You would place me in grave danger." But Becca had made her decision. Augusta and Annie would be safe, and she would learn her husband's secrets. She wondered how soon she could leave for New York.

"You won't be alone. I have chosen someone to accompany you."

She lifted her chin. "And I did not hear you mention the Council of Safety."

The General's smile lit his blue eyes. "Help me find your husband's contact in the City, and, on my honor, you will be granted the Parcell farm outright. I will ensure that Governor Livingston ends the Council's inquiry."

She lifted the wide edges of her green gown and curtsied. "I am your humble servant."

Chapter Eleven

A stocky officer played the penny whistle in a corner. Others sat drinking ale, their legs stretched toward the fireplace in Major Caleb Gibbs' hut.

Daniel flung the dice onto the makeshift table which was no more than planks supported by two sawhorses. At his toss, the room erupted in cheers.

Gibbs looked up from his cards and lifted his tankard of ale in salute.

Daniel shrugged as if to say that luck was a mystery. At least his was. He'd spent a portion of yesterday afternoon on the cold, hard ground with a soldier's hand round his neck. Tonight, he held a goblet of French Bordeaux. Daniel focused on the cool, heavy feel of the glass in his hand, the sharp tang of the wine and the warmth of the room.

If life had taught him anything, it was that bad luck didn't last forever, but, then, neither did good. He'd enjoy the evening while it lasted.

"The general's not ready to see you," Gibbs said late last night.

Irritated, Daniel answered, "If what I know isn't worth his time, I'll be on my way."

Gibbs had grinned. "Stay another night. It's warmer here than in a hayloft somewhere else."

Gibbs was right.

A wall of cold air slammed Daniel's back.

"Well met, sir. I am heartily glad to see you," Gibbs called.

The penny whistle music slowed. All eyes turned toward the open door.

A slender man in his mid-twenties approached. His features were a quick pen and ink drawing, all sharp edges and fine lines. The gold epaulets on the shoulders of his blue and buff uniform gleamed. He had a thin, straight nose, a razor-sharp chin. The shape of his skull was visible through closely cropped auburn hair. He crossed the room and pounded Gibbs on the shoulder.

The penny whistle took up its high, cheerful tune again.

Caleb's smile matched the newcomer's. "May I introduce you to Mr. Alloway, the visitor we spoke of?"

"Mr. Hamilton is a fine friend," Caleb said to Daniel, "and a fearsome enemy."

Daniel masked his surprise. This stripling was the hero of the great battles in Trenton and Princeton? This youngster was the man Washington chose to become his personal aide?

"But I'm sure you and Mr. Hamilton will be great colleagues."

Colleagues?

"Your servant, sir." Hamilton's smile was a beam of light.

Daniel's eyes narrowed.

* * *

"I am not deserving of the honor." How many times had Daniel repeated that phrase? How was it that Hamilton never stopped talking?

The other officers had long departed. Gibbs was asleep, leaving Hamilton and Daniel before the banked fire with its sullen red flames.

Hamilton leaned forward. "We will win, you know." His violet-blue eyes pinned Daniel to his chair. "The British fight against the tides of history, which call all mankind to freedom. But we require your help."

Daniel felt the pull of the man's passionate intensity. "I have no love for the British," he said slowly, "not after the *Jersey*. You ask too much."

Hamilton lifted one thin, skeptical eyebrow.

Daniel wondered if the man practiced the expression in a mirror. "I can't help you," he repeated, rapping the back of his maimed hand against the arm of the pine chair. "Can't feel much. Can't set type when your fingers are numb."

"Most of the *Jersey's* prisoners die from malnutrition or yellow fever or torture," Hamilton said. "They've lost more than you. That hand isn't why you won't help us."

In the moan of the wind, Daniel heard whispers of the dead, the prisoners whose bodies had hidden and saved him. "As you like, then. I *won't* help. If the British capture me again in New York City, at best, I'll find myself back on the *Jersey*. And at worst...." He shrugged, his meaning obvious.

Hamilton's voice softened, carrying the heat of a warmer climate, an older place. "Ships sink in a storm when they are anchored too tightly, Mr. Alloway. We are living through our own storm now. Don't let your past tie you too tightly, lest you forfeit your future." Then he grinned. "We shall work well together."

"But I'm not...."

"I know. You're not worthy of the honor." Hamilton laughed.

The whispers of the dead prisoners grew louder. Why had Daniel thought it was a good idea to spend another night here? He couldn't recall. He was too busy watching his good luck disappear like wood smoke up a chimney.

The information he had hoped to sell–that Mrs. Parcell knew where to find her husband's list of turncoats–wasn't worth a ha'penny. Hamilton swore the widow knew nothing of her husband's treachery.

Daniel pictured her at the door of her home yesterday, chin raised, vibrant as a lightning storm in August. To his surprise, the whispers of the dead faded. But he had one last bit of business.

"How convenient for you that Mrs. Parcell has such a powerful reason to leave Morristown now, just when you need her," Daniel said. "Her neighbors are ready to hang her. Or do they still tar and feather in these parts?"

"Mrs. Parcell has agreed to assist our cause this evening. She'll leave for the city tomorrow," Hamilton said stiffly.

"She won't survive," Daniel said.

"She might, if you travel with her. But the widow's life is of no matter, not to you. She is not your responsibility. Isn't that so?"

"That's right." Daniel wanted to smash Hamilton's elegant face. "And I'm not fit to guard anyone." His gaze dropped to his right hand.

Hamilton's glance followed. "Think of yourself as a guide, not a guard. You were the last person to speak to her husband about his list. The widow may hear or see things in New York that trigger your own memories of that conversation. And you are familiar with the streets of the city. She is not."

Bells jingled as a sleigh passed by the cabin. The flirtatious sound of a woman's laughter trailed on the frigid night air followed by the lower notes of a man's response.

"You will be rewarded," Hamilton leaned forward, hands clasped, elbows on his thighs. "I understand you have made inquiries about ships to Cuba."

"That's a nice piece of intelligence." Daniel pushed forward in his seat, mirroring Hamilton's pose. *Finally.* Two weeks ago, passing through Elizabethtown, he had idly asked the port master the cost of a ticket to Cuba. The man must have sold the information to the general's spies just in the last few days. But Daniel had no real interest in the Caribbean.

"I suppose you'd like to get as far from New York City and the Loyalists as you can," Hamilton said casually.

"A fresh start and a warm climate have much to recommend them," Daniel answered.

Hamilton examined his fingernails as if they were enormously interesting. "It's unfortunate that the British blockade makes that sort of travel difficult."

"And it is rather expensive." Daniel surveyed a corner of the log cabin ceiling.

"We could provide assistance. Out of gratitude for services rendered, of course. We could get you to Georgia and pay for your passage to Cuba."

Daniel paused as if considering the offer. "I would prefer hard currency, enough for two passages to Cuba."

He'd buy himself a fresh start somewhere far from here. He wondered whether he would like Santa Fe.

Chapter Twelve

L ying in a messy cocoon of quilts, Becca's mind raced. If Philip had left behind a list of turncoats, wasn't there a chance he'd hidden it at home? Or had Washington's men searched her house on the few occasions it had been empty?

Becca kicked off the blankets. What if they had missed something? A square of moonlight fell on her bare legs. What if she found the list there? General Washington would keep his promise. Her life would continue in a straight, narrow line without upheaval. She wouldn't need to travel to New York. She and Annie and Augusta would be safe.

Minutes later, she was dressed and silently slipping on her boots at the back door.

She walked in the moon shadow of the tall pines that separated Thomas's house from her own. The homes were less than a mile apart, but she labored through snowdrifts that seemed to triple the distance.

Ice-encrusted tree branches creaked and glittered in the light of the three-quarter moon. Her woolen skirt was already wet to her knees and her feet burned with the cold, despite her boots.

Approaching the stand of trees behind her home, she searched the snow for footprints, animal or human. It was a habit from the days when she hunted, before her father came into wealth.

The snow was as smooth as parchment.

Then why was the hair on the back of her neck bristling? *Daft girl.*

She sprinted across the yard to the back door and slipped inside.

It was colder here than outside. Becca removed her gloves, cupped her hands over her mouth and blew warm breath onto her fingers, waiting for the trembling to stop.

She lifted what she needed from the small table next to the back door. Her fingers fumbled as she hammered the flint against a small piece of steel. The wick caught a spark and flared to life, dimly at first, with a blue tip.

Her father used to say that if the candle burns blue, the Devil's in the room. She chided herself for the superstitious thought.

Where first? Philip never invited her into his study and she rarely entered, even after his death.

She placed the candle on the top of his desk. Behind it on the wall was a framed copy of the Parcell family tree and a map of the streets of New York City.

She swept her hand through the first of three drawers. In a corner, there was a soft jumble of velvet cloth covering something hard-edged.

She upended the bag. Miniature metal soldiers tumbled into her palm. She gripped the toys until the cool metal warmed in her hand and their metal edges dug into her flesh.

She'd prayed for a child, but none came. Had Philip saved the soldiers for the son she hadn't given him? It was better this way, she repeated to herself. If she said it often enough, she might come to believe it.

She replaced the toys and moved on to the next drawer. The nubby cloth-covered ledger was identical to the ones she used daily to keep track of the household accounts. She strained to see the pages in the semi-darkness. They were blank. A few had been torn out.

Becca wasn't surprised. Philip never had the patience for details. He was always looking forward, rarely keeping track of what he had or what he owed.

She surveyed the last drawer, shook out the few books Philip kept, and ran her fingers around and behind the framed maps and paintings on the wall, nothing.

* * *

Daniel wove through a row of tall pines on the far side of the road. Hamilton said to stay away from Mrs. Parcell for now. But he didn't say to stay away from her house.

It wasn't likely that the list of turncoats was here. Even Philip couldn't have been arrogant enough to hide it at home and put his wife in danger. But he couldn't sleep. It was worth the time to take a look.

He studied the front of the house. At first, he thought he saw moonlight reflecting off one of the windows. No. The glow came from inside. A deeper shadow crossed the window, and then the light disappeared.

As he circled round to the back of the house, he heard muffled voices nearby.

Daniel shot a quick glance around the corner and pulled his head back. The short one in the middle held a large lantern. There were three of them. He couldn't hear what they were saying. But Daniel didn't need to hear the words to know they brought trouble.

He patted the flintlock pistol cinched in his belt. He was a terrible shot now that he couldn't hold a gun in his right hand. But he was still glad he had borrowed Caleb Gibbs' weapon. Major Gibbs was asleep at the time, but that was a detail he'd work out in the morning.

* * *

There were voices. Just men returning late from Mr. Dickerson's tavern, Becca told herself.

But the sounds of drunken laughter would have grown fainter if the men moved on. They sounded closer.

She blew out the candle.

The voices went silent.

Whoever they were, they knew she was here. She didn't care if they were Washington's men or Minister Townsend's. She rose and sprinted.

The front door crashed open as her hand grabbed the backdoor latch. Whoever stood at the front of the house had a lantern.

A high-pitched giggle sliced the air.

"Shut up, Flanagan," a deep voice growled.

Becca flung open the back door. A rectangle of light stretched across the snow, framing her shadow. She launched herself outside.

A large hand trapped her upper arm and yanked her sideways. The world tilted. She was whipped around and pulled in hard. Her cheek scraped metal buttons and wool. Another hand slapped itself across her mouth.

Becca made her body go limp. Then she brought one foot up and slammed it down on the man's instep. Her fingers gouged the hand trapping her mouth.

Her captor grunted, then shoved her to the ground away from the door.

Becca toppled onto her side. Her wrist went numb as snow wedged into her glove.

The stranger stepped into the doorway.

He pulled a pistol from his belt, aimed into the house, and fired.

Her ears rang from the blast. Wood shattered. Smoke and the acrid smell of gunpowder filled the air.

She scrambled to her feet as the snow slid away beneath her.

"They're out front. Get them," the shooter yelled.

Becca saw only snow pockmarked by the tracks of deer and rabbits. Was he trying to make the men in front think they'd be fighting an entire squadron?

There was a high-pitched squeal and footsteps clap-clapping on a wood floor. The light in the doorway wavered, then disappeared.

The shooter turned, glowering at her. "You're certainly a lot of trouble, Mrs. Parcell."

Chapter Thirteen

Becca lifted her skirt to run. She would lose him in the woods.

"I won't stop you. But they didn't go far. I didn't hear their horses." The stranger's voice was low with a broad burr that would have invited trust if her arm didn't still ache where he'd grabbed it.

That voice.

"You." She pirouetted back. "You yelled 'where's the whiskey.' I never would have thought to send the mob off for more spirits."

"You were resourceful enough without my help." He flung a half smile in her direction.

"There. We'll be able to see if they come back." She pointed to a small rise covered with spruce behind them.

Safe behind the wall of green, she whispered, "You've saved me twice now. I don't know who you are, and I don't know how to thank you, Mister...." She waited for the stranger to introduce himself.

He leaned toward her. Deep lines grooved the sides of his mouth. Lighter lines radiated from his eyes, which drooped slightly, as if they'd soaked up all the sadness he'd ever seen.

She was suddenly lightheaded. It was just the aftermath of fear. That was what she told herself.

"Thank me? You can tell me where Parcell hid his list of spies. Did you find it?"

"A pox on you." She felt as if she'd been slapped. He had tricked her into gratitude. She lifted her skirt again to run, kicking snow at him.

"I expected better manners from your husband's description," he drawled.

"Liar. My husband's dead." Her throat closed with the shock.

"I know. I was with him at the end."

"You were with him on the *Jersey*? Is this another trick?"

"He said to tell you he was sorry."

The wind was coming up just enough to bend the smallest branches of the trees. The cracking ice sounded like her heart. ·

"I would like to believe you." Memory hurtled her back to a late August afternoon, the first year of her marriage. In the woods beyond the field, Philip pulled her to him and tickled the hollow of her neck with a fern frond until she laughed. He kissed her, swearing he would dedicate his life to her happiness. That memory was as true as the sunlight that day, she would swear it, despite all the lies that followed.

His chin rose. "Dammit."

Becca followed his gaze.

The three men were close to the house now. Two carried rifles that gleamed in the moonlight. The third still held a lantern.

"You were going to run before. Go. Now," the stranger hissed.

"And you?" she prodded.

"Go, blast you."

Her eyes narrowed. "And leave you and your friends to search my house? I think not." Washington said no one else knew of Philip's list. Then how did the stranger know of it? Where did his loyalties lie?

He sighed, then jerked his chin toward the strangers. "Do you know them?"

She shook her head.

"Did they speak to you in the house? Did you hear anything?"

"Flanagan, one of them called the other. That was all." She shivered, recalling the high, unhinged giggle. "His laugh was strange."

"I thought never to see him again." There was broken glass in his voice. "Can you shoot?" he asked suddenly.

"Yes, I shoot well." She was hardly taller than a rifle when she'd learned.

He pulled the pistol from his waistband and presented it to her handle first. He fumbled, pulling three paper cones of gunpowder and a paper-wrapped lead ball from a pouch in one of his pockets.

Becca half-cocked the hammer, poured a measure of gunpowder down the barrel, and followed with the bullet.

* * *

The three moving shadows grew larger and more distinct. The smallest of the three held the now darkened lantern.

Daniel got a clear view of the small man and cursed under his breath.

"Don't." Becca thrust her arm out to protest as if she already knew his intent. The pistol wobbled in her other hand.

The short intruder had sunken cheeks, a snub nose, and a sadly receding chin that barely supported large front teeth visible beneath his short upper lip.

"Sod you." Daniel stepped out into the open with his hands raised to show that he carried no weapon. He prayed that Becca was as good a shot as she claimed.

"I thought you was dead." A nervous, high-pitched giggle escaped from the short man's mouth.

The two larger shadows stepped back. One turned his head. In profile, Daniel saw the outline of a large hooked nose.

"Naw," Daniel said, echoing the short man's accent. "I just went for a swim in the harbor and kept going." He controlled the urge to grab the redcoat's throat. *Go easy. This isn't the Jersey. You got away.* "But what about you, Ferret? Did you skip out on Cunningham, too?"

Ferret was one of the most timid of Bill Cunningham's guards on board the prison ship. He stepped on the prisoners' hands while the men lay in tight rows below deck or kicked over the one foul tin cup of water allotted each day. He never had the nerve to do worse. Ferret Flanagan was afraid of his own shadow, afraid even of prisoners in chains who were more dead than alive.

Ferret's meager cheeks puffed out in response to Daniel's question. "Provost Cunningham's giving me more important work to do now. I...."

The lantern jumped as one of the other two men slapped Ferret across the back of his head. "Shut up, Flanagan."

"Awww. You oughtn't do that." Ferret rubbed his skull. "I was just...."

The sound was deafening. Ferret looked down, swiped a finger to his chest and pulled it away covered with something shiny. His body shivered like a leaf on a branch bending in the wind. His small close-set eyes looked into Daniel's in surprise.

The blast came from the trees where the widow hid.

The Ferret crumpled into the snow, his eyes turned to the winter constellation Orion. Blood bubbled out from between his buckteeth. The Ferret's companions ran.

Daniel rushed to the man. For a moment, his foot hovered over the Ferret. But he couldn't bring himself to crush the man's hand. He fell to his knees and placed his hand over the guard's nose. No breath.

Mrs. Parcell stepped out from the curtain of trees. She held the pistol limply, her eyes wide and staring.

He rose. "You didn't have to shoot to kill."

"I didn't shoot at all." Her voice was faint.

Branches crackled and Becca whirled, lifting the pistol in both hands.

"My apologies for the fright, madam." From the shadow of the trees, a soldier stepped forward. He wore the blue and buff uniform of General Washington's personal guards.

The smell of gunpowder drifted from the musket that rested in the crook of his arm. "Sergeant Eli Bartlett, ma'am."

Four more men in dark coats, each holding a long thin musket, stepped into the clearing.

Sergeant Bartlett passed Becca and approached the Ferret, examining the body without expression.

"Why did you kill him?" Daniel struggled to tamp down his anger. He should have been pleased. He hated Flanagan. "We could have learned something. We could have heard why they came."

"I been with the army five years. I only shoot to kill." Bartlett had a round face and a small, well-formed chin. His eyes were two deep holes filled with the night's darkness.

"How'd you know which of us to kill?" Daniel asked.

"I wasn't certain."

Daniel believed him. His stomach clenched.

"But I see Mrs. Parcell in the woods," Bartlett said. "I see she has a pistol. She could have shot you, but she didn't. She only took aim when the others showed up. I figured the others was the ones Major Gibbs wanted taken care of."

"Gibbs said to kill him?"

"Well, in a manner. Mr. Lockwood came roaring into the commander's hut about an hour ago. He says Mrs. Parcell is gone and if anything happens to her, there'll be hell to pay. Mr. Lockwood and General Washington are friends."

"Mr. Lockwood told you to shoot to kill?" Becca sounded outraged.

"No. Captain Gibbs said to make sure nothing happened to Mrs. Parcell or General Washington would hear of it." Bartlett shrugged. "I made sure nothing happened. And now, Mrs. Parcell is to come back with us to Mr. Lockwood's house. I am commanded." His cold eyes examined Daniel, as if assessing another target. "I don't have orders about you."

Becca's voice was loud. "I, sir, am *not* commanded. I'm staying here. You can go to hell."

I couldn't have said it better, Daniel thought.

Four of the men who stood behind Sergeant Bartlett materialized in a line behind Becca, blocking her retreat.

Daniel didn't blame her for wanting to protect her house from the likes of him after what just happened.

"Sergeant," Daniel began in his most benign voice, "if Mrs. Parcell agrees to return to Mr. Lockwood's house with you, can you leave a few of the men to guard the house for the night?"

Bartlett's expression didn't change. Then he nodded once. "If the lady accompanies us, I'll leave men behind."

* * *

Becca focused on each step, raising one foot high and then the other to avoid the snow cascading into her boots.

Could she have killed Flanagan? She had thought so. But she wasn't certain when she stared at the dead man with the absurd nickname, the man with the high wild laugh.

Now she was trapped between Sergeant Bartlett and the stranger as if they feared she would slip away. Maybe she would.

Their pace was too fast, but she refused to ask them to slow down.

The gunshots had terrified her. She'd thought they were aimed at the stranger. *Oh, bullocks.* Becca still didn't know his name.

She borrowed Augusta's most commanding manner. "You seem to know me, but we are not introduced." Without a formal introduction, they would never speak to each other in society.

"Your most obedient servant, madam. Daniel Alloway." His greatcoat fluttered open as he bowed, revealing worn pants and a loose top.

She had been wrong about his eyes. They held humor as well as sadness.

"Indeed, I am at your service for the foreseeable future. I am to accompany you to New York."

She stiffened. "Are you? Then you are better informed than I." Shouldn't he have told her that when they first met? She slowed her steps to fall behind Mr. Alloway.

She only half listened to his conversation with Sergeant Bartlett until the soldier scooped up a fistful of snow and hurled it against a tree. An owl in one of its branches hooted in protest and took flight.

"And the officers are spending their money on parties while the men have nothing. I eat meat twice a week," Bartlett said. "But there are ten thousand men sleeping cold and hungry in Jockey Hollow. They're eating bark this winter. The Congress can't stop arguing long enough to pay for food."

How would the soldiers' families feel about General Washington's war if they knew his soldiers were starving? Becca asked, "Do you have family waiting for you at home?"

"No. No family. Don't know what most of us soldiers will do when the war ends. Guess I'll go back to Rhode Island. We missed our chance to learn a trade. We'll be too old to apprentice."

They walked the rest of the way in silence, their footsteps sounding in time to their breath.

Lights blazed in the tall windows of the Lockwood house. Thomas stood in the doorway with his legs planted wide.

Becca stumbled.

"You had to know you weren't safe. What were you thinking?" Thomas ignored Daniel and Sergeant Bartlett. He stepped aside to let her enter.

The candles in sconces along the wall flared brightly. The black and white checkerboard tiles gleamed, and a nearby clock announced the time with a high, sweet chime. Three a.m.

She understood worry that disguised itself as anger and tried to keep the offense she felt out of her voice. He was not her husband, not yet. "I thought if I went home, I might be able to find...."

"Well met, Major Gibbs," Daniel stood with one foot over the entryway, shaking hands with an officer in blue and buff. Sergeant Bartlett had disappeared.

In the light, Becca saw that the fingers of Mr. Alloway's right hand were cupped into a clawlike curve.

"Who the hell are you?" Thomas asked.

Major Gibbs' posture was rigid. "May I present Mr. Alloway. He will be taking Mrs. Parcell into New York."

Daniel bent a laconic bow to Thomas. "Your servant, sir."

Thomas stared at Daniel's maimed hand, and his eyebrows rose. "This is who General Washington expects to protect my, to protect Mrs. Parcell? You are certain, Gibbs?"

"Feel free to address me directly, Mr. Lockwood," Daniel said mildly.

"All right, then. Come in and shut the door."

"Not tonight."

"By God, Alloway. I insist." Thomas's face reddened.

Becca watched, exasperated. Their instant dislike was obvious.

"If you'd like to invite me for breakfast, after I have gotten some sleep, I would be happy to talk then. Not for long, of course. We leave for New

York in a few hours. Till then, Mrs. Parcell." Ignoring Thomas, he stepped back into the cold and shut the door.

Chapter Fourteen

Daniel dreamed of the Ferret, of Philip Parcell and of Cunningham in the few hours of broken sleep he managed.

Now, in the predawn gloom, he watched two of Mr. Lockwood's servants totter past him, holding opposite ends of a large trunk.

Reading from a sheaf of papers, Alexander Hamilton stepped out of the servant's way without looking up. He raised his head and grinned at Daniel. "I half expected to find you on the road to the Ohio Territory."

"The thought crossed my mind," Daniel said.

"But you decided to help the new nation." Hamilton clapped him on the back.

"I'll leave the new nation to you and General Washington."

"You're one of us, sir. You just haven't recognized the fact yet."

Daniel shook his head. "I beg to differ, Mr. Hamilton."

The servants wrestled the large trunk atop the green and black coach. They added a second smaller trunk, strapping both to the roof.

"One last thing, Mrs. Parcell," Hamilton called to Becca.

Her dark hair was tucked severely beneath another white mobcap. Her gown was a muddy brown calico with a square neckline and narrow white lace border filled with a handkerchief that was pinned so high that only her long, pale neck was bared.

She looked pale and brittle, her eyes not quite focusing.

Good. She was right to be frightened. In her place, he would have moved on. He always moved on.

"I have your passports for the trip," Hamilton said. He handed them to

Becca.

"Passports?"

"You can't travel to New York without them," Hamilton said. "If any of our soldiers stop you close to the Hudson River, you'll need them."

"Best to get on the road now." Hamilton offered his arm to Augusta.

"Another moment." Thomas Lockwood strode across the front porch of his whitewashed mansion. He wore a grey suit jacket with gold basketweave buttons, a crimson cloth waistcoat, and a fine Holland shirt with ruffle lace cuffs.

The outfit surely cost Lockwood more than Daniel's rent payments over the past three years, maybe four.

Thomas didn't bother to lower his voice. "If Alloway makes you uncomfortable, if you think there's any danger at all, send for me. If it were up to me, I would not let anyone like that near you."

"Feel free to go in my stead," Daniel called back. At least there was entertainment in goading Lockwood. It helped Daniel avoid thinking about the choice he'd made. If the British recaptured him in New York, he doubted he'd escape again. But the prize money Mr. Hamilton offered was worth the risk. At least, it had seemed worthwhile when he agreed.

There had to be easier ways to earn money, ways that didn't include risking his own life. But there weren't. He'd almost starved more than once in the seven months since escaping the *Jersey*. Alexander Hamilton was the only person he knew who had any use for a former printer with only one good hand, no property, and no other skills.

Lockwood drew Mrs. Parcell closer.

Daniel grinned when she stepped away, although he couldn't explain his reaction. Who was Rebecca Parcell to him, after all?

Chapter Fifteen

Thin curlicues of smoke rose from the occasional small home they passed.

With any luck, they'd make the ferry to New York City this afternoon, Daniel thought as they passed the endless snow banks lining each side of the road.

But he didn't expect luck today. At least, not the good kind. Lockwood's black carriage was too well-appointed. They were a target for every British soldier and brigand in this lawless territory.

Hamilton had arranged their stay at a discreet friend's home in Turkey Hill last night. Their host had sent them off with breakfast and fresh hot coals for their foot warmers. Thomas Lockwood's fur blankets added to their comfort.

Augusta and Annie slept as the carriage rumbled over the icy, rutted road. Becca tugged at the soft blanket on her lap as if she were kneading dough. Sitting across from Daniel, she seemed as preoccupied with her thoughts as he was with his.

Was she thinking of her husband? When he told her of Parcell's apology last night, she had stared up at him with an expression that was so haunted and open, it stole his breath. He'd had the sense to push her away by asking whether she had found her husband's list of spies. She'd spun away from him as if he were poison.

Confound her. She was nothing to him. That's what he had told Mr. Hamilton.

Fabrications slid from his tongue as easily as the truth, but he never lied to himself: He was drawn to this woman. But attachments were dangerous. They led to loss, to tragedy. He pushed aside thoughts of his wife's gentle smile and of his son's fingernails, each as small as the tiniest seashell. God rest their souls.

His gaze slid to the two other women to ensure that they were still asleep. He leaned toward Becca. "Your husband must have other relatives further up the Hudson. In Nova Scotia, perhaps?" he whispered.

Becca bent forward across the narrow empty space, her face inches from his. "You mean to keep me away from New York?"

She smelled of lavender and honey. His stomach tightened. "I do. You don't know what it is like there. You can't imagine."

His mind drifted, and he was back on the *Jersey*, burrowing beneath the jumble of dead prisoners and surrounded by the stench of death. A wheel struck another rock. The carriage skid, bringing him back to the present. "You need to find a safer path than this. There's still time to stop the driver."

She studied him. "You have no future if we fail. You have no other options. That is what you claimed yesterday. Then why...?" Her smile widened. "I see. You are worried for my safety."

If she was of a mind to trust him, this would put an end to it.

From a pocket in his greatcoat, he retrieved the crumbled scrap of paper he'd grabbed from Parcell's barn while the mob helped itself to the whiskey.

He rested the torn note on one thigh. With his good hand, he stroked the butterscotch-colored sheet until its creases relaxed.

He didn't know why he'd kept the torn paper. It was part of an invoice, a bill of lading, he thought, as he read partial words— *une 7, 1779* and *le of whiskey* and *7 bottles* and *latbush, Brooklyn, New Yor*. Then seven lines of numbers followed by a sum.

All it proved was that Philip smuggled whiskey into New York and sold it illegally to the British, a fact Daniel already knew.

He reached across the carriage and handed the invoice to Mrs. Parcell. "Here. I stole this from you."

She gave him a quizzical look and took the scrap. "Where did you...this is my husband's writing." Her eyes narrowed. "You stole this?"

In this light, her eyes were the color of twilight, he decided.

"I did. If I could have found your husband's list of turncoats and left without involving you, this trip—all of this—would have been unnecessary," Daniel said. "The barn was a place to start looking, that was all. So was your house last night."

And if his motives weren't clear enough, he added, "I would have left with my reward, and you would have been left with the mob."

Becca's dark blue eyes lit with approval. "You could have kept this to yourself, but you didn't. You returned what you took."

* * *

What a strange, haunted man, she thought. Mr. Alloway was working so hard to make her think ill of him. She was certain he would list all his faults and failures before they reached New York.

Annie uncurled and stretched.

Augusta placed a shaking hand on Becca's wrist. "Why don't you read Philip's note?"

Becca hadn't noticed her wake. She hesitated.

"Go on. I am not made of porcelain." The older woman pulled her hand away and hid it beneath the brown fur blanket laid across her lap.

It would have been impossible to keep from Augusta what General Washington had told her last night. Becca had gone straight to her mother-in-law's room when she returned from the Widow Ford's mansion.

Augusta had sat in a pale pink robe, her still-thick silver hair in a braid that reached her rib cage. "You are certain?" Her posture grew more rigid, as if she had replayed her son's past and turned to salt.

"It was Philip's handwriting."

The bluish cords on the side of Augusta's neck had stood in relief against her pale skin.

Becca caught the cut crystal water goblet as it slipped from Augusta's grip.

"If he were here, I would strangle him," Augusta whispered. Then her eyes widened and she covered her mouth with both hands. Tears filled her eyes.

Becca knew that jumble of rage and grief and the way it tore one into a thousand pieces. She placed the goblet on a nearby table.

The carriage slid on a rock, and Becca regained her focus on the paper. "I wish it was a note. It's only numbers." For a moment, the numerals blurred on the page.

"How odd." She examined the sheet more closely. Her lips moved and one finger followed the figures on the bill of lading back and forth, and again more quickly. "The sums are all wrong and the charges make no sense." Her index finger traveled up and down the columns.

Philip had been careless of numbers, but this was more than carelessness.

Daniel and Augusta bent forward to survey the torn paper. "What do you mean?" Daniel asked.

"Don't you see it? She pointed to one figure. "Here are bottles sold for seven Spanish dollars, nine shillings, four pence." Her finger moved down the page. "And another bottle sold for three pounds, two shillings, eight pence. Each bottle of whiskey should cost the same. These are all different."

"It could be in code. Not many people would stop to look so closely at someone else's bill," Daniel said.

She lifted her head to find his inches away, focused on the sheet of paper. His green eyes met hers. She lost track of the numbers.

"Code?" Augusta asked sharply.

Daniel cleared his throat. "I could be wrong. But I've seen ciphers before. All printers publish advertisements that appear to make little sense. Some really don't. Others are coded messages." With a grin, the severity that marked his face fell away.

Suddenly warm, Becca loosened the ribbon at the neck of her cape. She struggled to focus on the code. "You printed messages in code for General Washington's friends?"

He shrugged. "A customer's political beliefs were none of my business so long as they paid in sterling. I don't see a great difference between the two sides, m'lady. On one, there's the tyranny of a single man who lives three thousand miles away. On the other, the tyranny of three thousand men closer to home."

Augusta frowned in disapproval. "We may all have to choose before this war is over."

"I would prefer to be out of this country entirely and saved the trouble of choosing," Daniel said.

Becca changed the subject. She did not like the way her own opinion sounded coming out of Mr. Alloway's mouth. "If you know so much about codes, what does this one say?"

"Can't tell without the key. The key is a type of dictionary, really. It would allow anyone with a copy to translate words into numbers and back. There's always a key to unlock a code."

Becca stroked the torn sheet of paper again. "And how do we locate this key?"

"Do any of you know who bought Parcell's whiskey?" He turned from Becca and Annie to Augusta.

Becca smiled slowly. "The spies wrote messages to each other on the bills and receipts for Philip's whiskey. That's what you're saying."

She felt a lightness that was almost hope. "All I need to do is find the men who purchased my husband's whiskey. One of them is the man we are searching for."

Daniel grimaced. "That's right. Should be simple."

Chapter Sixteen

"You sloppy, addlepated incompetents," William Cunningham roared. "You let Alloway escape?"

The two men stood at attention, their brown capes rimmed with a dark border of melted snow, wet hair plastered to their skulls. Their faces were as grim as the weather.

It had taken them three days to return from Morristown.

"No, sir. Yes, sir. I'm sorry, sir." A bead of melted ice—or was it sweat—trickled from the taller guard's sideburn to his jaw.

Cunningham sat in the only chair in the small, cold room. A battered pine table held a tankard of ale. A single lantern fought the late afternoon shadows. He struggled to remember the guard's name. Jack? No, Jackson. Hadn't there been a third guard who traveled to Morristown? No matter.

The provost of New York's prisons pushed down on the armrests of his chair and lifted his heavy body.

Jackson's close-set gaze hovered somewhere over Cunningham's head. "No one was supposed to be at the Parcell house." His prominent nose cast a bird-like shadow on the far wall.

"We didn't let Alloway escape. We never had him. Not really, sir," the shorter, rotund guard added.

Cunningham circled the two men. "You're Humphrey, aren't you?"

The shorter guard nodded, then, at Cunningham's glare, spoke up. "I mean, yes, sir."

Cunningham rammed his boot into the side of Humphrey's knee without warning. The guard collapsed on to the stone floor. He didn't cry out. He knew better. They all knew better.

Jackson stood so still that it was hard to tell if he was breathing. One eyelid twitched.

"And the other task?" Cunningham asked. He'd given the guards a second job, one more important than Alloway.

At least it was more important to Cunningham, which was all that mattered.

"If you've failed at that, too, you can join the gentlemen upstairs." Cunningham's voice was soft.

Humphrey turned a gasp into a cough.

The hundreds of "gentlemen upstairs" were captured Continental soldiers, imprisoned in a former sugar warehouse. The six-story building had no roof. The men were left to warm themselves as best they could.

Cunningham exaggerated the scowl on his face, hiding his excitement.

Philip Parcell had been little more than a courier, ferrying notes from Morristown to New York City. The mayor was the delivery point, although Cunningham couldn't for the life of him believe anyone would trust Matthews with the job.

Jackson reached into the scarred leather pouch strapped across his chest and pulled out a creased parchment sealed with red wax. He extended the folded sheet of paper.

Cunningham clasped his hands behind his back and returned to his desk, leaving Jackson with an outstretched arm. He wanted to savor the details. "Go on."

"We watched Mayor Matthews' house, like you said to, for anyone delivering bottles." Jackson slowly lowered his arm, still holding the correspondence. "There was one in particular. We couldn't tell if it was whiskey. You said to watch for whiskey. But he came out of the mayor's place with a package, flat-like, not too big. That's how we knew he was the one you wanted. We sent you a note. We followed the new messenger back to Morristown."

Cunningham cut him off. "Who was the package delivered to?"

Jackson hesitated. "We didn't see."

81

"You didn't see." Cunningham reached back and flung the tankard at Jackson so quickly that the guard barely had time to flinch. "You damn whoreson."

The ceramic mug nicked the guard's ear and hit the back wall near the floor. A chunk of dull gray plaster spun across the stone floor.

Jackson spoke quickly. "We delivered your message. And there was an answer, sir. Whoever he is, he answered." His wounded ear was turning a dull purple.

Cunningham lowered his fist, breathless with the effort. It was difficult to pull back one's temper. Were he not a man with exquisite control, it would be impossible. "Continue."

"The new courier left his package in one of the meeting houses. It was late. After midnight," Jackson continued. "Took us hours to find it. Dark as Hades in that place. The man with the package slipped it into a prayer book on one of the benches." Jackson's lips curled, then straightened. "So we tucked your letter away there, too."

Cunningham's temper rose in earnest. "And yet you didn't see the man who came to claim the package?"

"It could'a been anyone or no one. The sun rose and it was Sunday. The meeting house was filled all day."

Humphrey crawled to his feet. "They don't like strangers there. We couldn't stay any place too long."

Jackson and Cunningham glowered at him, and Humphrey clamped his lips together.

"We went into the church on Monday before light. And we found this in the prayer book." Jackson held out the folded paper again.

The provost inhaled deeply, his stomach pressing against his tight vest. He forced himself not to grab the parchment. "Is there anything else?"

Jackson licked his lips. "No, sir."

"Then leave it there." Cunningham jerked his chin toward the table. "And go."

A half hour later, one hand tapping the opened letter, Cunningham stared blindly out the frost-trimmed window.

82

The mayor's "Correspondent" in Morristown had accepted his offer.

Shouldn't The Correspondent work directly with someone who knew how to get things done, a man such as himself? The thought had haunted Cunningham for days after he met with Mayor Matthews on the Brooklyn dock.

He recalled the way the mayor's nostrils flared each time they met, as if Cunningham had soiled himself. *Let the mayor dance to my tune*, he'd thought.

That was when he followed one of the kitchen maids to church two Sundays ago.

He chose her because of the turquoise ribbon she'd tied into a bow around her neck after the heavy kitchen door closed behind her. Whatever pittance she was paid, she spent on frivolous, gaudy objects like her ribbon. She strove to better herself.

Some are satisfied with their lot in life, he thought. She was not among that lot. Neither was he. She was the one he needed.

Fear and avarice were a heady perfume. He offered her fear first, wrapped his fingers tightly round her plump upper arm as she passed him on the street. He dragged her into the alleyway. She smelled of stale clothes and sharp, cheap perfume. Her breath came in violent huffs of white smoke in the winter cold.

Then, giving avarice its due, he offered the servant money for information about the unusual packages the mayor regularly received.

With the back of her hand, she wiped spittle from her chin. "A man brings crates of spirits. Two, three times a month. Used to be a different one. A different man." Her words came in a rush. "Whatever time it is, we have to tell the mayor when the bottles arrive or there's hell to pay. We can't touch them 'til he's been down to the kitchen to see them."

"Is that odd?" Cunningham asked.

She snorted. "The mayor in the kitchen?"

He slapped her face for her cheeky tone, then slid the thin edge of a silver coin along her beribboned neck. He handed her the coin while telling her what he would do to her if she mentioned their conversation.

She scrunched her eyes shut as if to erase the image, pivoted and fled the alleyway.

The next day and the days after that, Cunningham set his men to watch the mayor's kitchen door. They'd followed the man who delivered spirits back to Morristown with the letter Cunningham penned.

Cunningham had merely asked whether a sensible man would prefer to do business with someone like himself, someone with a record of efficiency and accomplishment, or someone like the mayor who was afraid of his own shadow.

He reread the letter his men had brought back from Morristown.

"Your correspondence was most welcome. Your reputation precedes you." Cunningham nodded with satisfaction.

"Have you not found, Mr. Cunningham," he read, "that those who define themselves as having refined tastes leave tasks too unsavory for their delicate constitutions to the likes of us?

"Many in the British High Command would prefer not to know the means I use to help them end the war. We will allow those refined men to fight in their staid military rows with their 'honor' intact.

"Yes, I said 'we.' Join me, Mr. Cunningham. You and I shall bring the unfortunate American insurrection to an end in our own way. I have a plan."

Cunningham's mouth pursed as he finished the letter. He still didn't know The Correspondent's identity. But he had a promise of greater compensation than even he could have imagined.

He had little time to find the item that The Correspondent needed delivered to Morristown and even less time to kill Alloway.

Alloway would be here soon, The Correspondent wrote, and Cunningham would make sure he never left.

Chapter Seventeen

A loud crack blasted the carriage. The horses' panicked whinnying frightened Becca more than the rifle shot. The wheels shuddered, and the coach careened into a ditch, thundering to a stop.

Becca tumbled forward onto Daniel. She grabbed his shoulders to steady herself. He gripped her waist. She wondered if she looked as stunned as he did, then shimmied back into her seat.

The carriage door flew open.

Annie shrieked as a grinning death mask of a face appeared through the window.

Half the man's bald head was scarred and puckered as if part of his face had melted in some conflagration. He laughed at Annie's shock, showing tea-colored teeth. Footsteps thudded on the carriage roof.

The driver howled in pain. Then there was silence.

Becca's heart raced. She fished for her drawstring bag.

The bald man flew back with a yowl. Becca heard laughter. Through the window, a group of white and black men jeered at the bald man on the ground. Some wore British red coats; others, American blue jackets. There were brown breeches on some, full length pants on others.

These were no soldiers, despite the piecemeal uniforms. Had they killed the men who'd originally owned the clothes? Becca felt for the weapon inside her bag.

"Step out of the carriage, ladies and gentlemen," a deep, cheerful voice boomed.

Becca gripped the black horn handle of her knife, its blade folded in for safety.

Daniel blocked her path to the carriage door, then stepped out.

She heard a leather whip crack, and he disappeared. She lightly held her thumb over the cold metal latch that would release the blade.

Augusta tapped Becca's wrist and mouthed the words "Don't move."

Moments later, a massive hand gripped the shiny white edge of the carriage door. The man attached to the hand grunted as he pulled himself through the entrance. Everything about him was oversized, from his large, fleshy nose to his ears, shaped like pitcher handles. His free hand clasped the worn thick handle of a black leather whip, its tail wrapped and doubled within his fist.

"I asked you to leave the carriage. My invitations are so rarely declined that my curiosity was piqued." He wore the worn jacket of a redcoat uniform with frayed black trim. One shiny button hung loose. But instead of the black breeches she knew were part of the British uniform, he wore long brown leather pants.

His voice was gravel scraped over rock, but his cultured accent would have made him welcome in the best British homes, the same homes that would have welcomed Augusta and her family.

Augusta blinked in apparent surprise as he spoke.

She interrupted the intruder who appeared to be in his fifties. "I'm afraid that this weather and my old bones don't mix well. Will you forgive us our rudeness?" Her free hand rose and fluttered just below her collarbone, where the hollow of her throat showed above white lace.

The bear of a man exposed strong white teeth in a broad grin that turned to laughter. "Madam, in four years of traveling these roads, I've never been so prettily lied to." A narrow band of grizzled gray hair was just visible beneath the man's powdered white wig.

Augusta echoed his laugh.

The ruffian took the seat directly across from her next to Annie. The servant pushed herself as far back into the shadowed corner of the carriage as possible.

"My business with passengers is conducted quickly, and then I send them on their way. But in this case, it may take more time."

"And what is your business, sir?" Augusta peered up at him through lowered lashes.

Becca's eyes widened in astonishment.

He spread his hands, the whip handle balanced loosely on one palm. "Freedom and liberty, madam." Another rumble of laughter escaped from his impressive belly and threatened to loosen several more buttons from his red jacket.

Annie shrank even further into the corner.

Becca examined his redcoat jacket. "*You* are a Patriot?"

"We fight for our liberty and freedom, m'lady. Ours." He thumped the whip handle against the carriage wall. It left a black mark on the blue satin lining.

"Here. This spot. This Neutral Ground. That's what they call it. It's free from all oversight, though the Americans and Tories tear each other apart trying to win it over."

He pointed toward the men who stood watch outside. "They're refugees, my men are. We welcome former slaves. We welcome men whose farms were taken when they wouldn't pledge allegiance to the new government."

He aimed the whip handle out the window at the bald man, who was busy wiping dirt from his pants. "The redcoats burned down Amos's house near here. Amos was in it at the time. So was his wife. His wife is gone. Such men find their way to me."

He opened both arms as if welcoming them to his new country. "And we are free of them all, British and Patriots alike. Some call us the Highland Gang. I say we're merely taking back a bit of what we've lost from everyone who passes through."

"You're a bandit." Becca didn't like the way he looked at Augusta.

"You'll have to excuse my daughter-in-law. She's very young." The pointy heel of Augusta's yellow silk shoe gouged Rebecca's ankle.

Becca turned a yowl into a hiccup.

"Shouldn't you be home with your family?" He scowled at her.

"My husband is dead. I have no children, not that it's your business."

The Englishman nodded, a quick dismissal. He spoke to Augusta. "Your name, Madam?"

Becca turned from one to the other. Their accents were almost identical.

"Augusta Parcell. My daughter-in-law is Mrs. Rebecca Parcell. This is our Annie. Annie McDonald." Her spine straightened even further. "My son was Philip Parcell."

The Englishman extended his hand to Augusta more gracefully than Becca would have expected, then gently supported and lifted the older woman's thin hand to his lips. "John Mason, ma'am. Honored to make your acquaintance. I knew your son."

Chapter Eighteen

"You were flirting," Becca hissed. She knew her anger was uncalled for, but it was positively disconcerting. And besides, Augusta was so...so...well, not young.

"I distracted him," Augusta said. "Mr. Mason was of the gentry. I know the accent. I knew men like him when I was young. They were third or fourth sons in a good family with nothing to inherit and no interest in the church or army." She seemed lost in her own thoughts. "I wonder if my parents knew his?"

The carriage bounced forward again over rocks and chunks of ice. Mr. Mason had invited them for tea. They were not free to reject the invitation. He rode along behind them with his men.

"You couldn't have seen how he looked at you. He would have devoured you if he could."

"Annie was screaming and you were ready to launch yourself at anyone who came through the door," Augusta answered. "I made Mr. Mason recall that, at some point in his life, he was a gentleman."

"I was *not* screaming, Mrs. P." Annie raised her chin. "I was giving warning."

Augusta nodded. "Loudly giving warning."

Annie "tssked" and turned to the window.

"I fear for you," Becca whispered to Augusta.

"He won't harm us...not now. We've interested him...all of us, and he likes to be entertained, I think." She paused. "And how are Mr. Alloway and the driver?"

Becca smiled. "You are changing the subject. They are both well."

"If you call a few conks on the head 'doing well,'" Annie said.

Becca had sworn that she'd leap from the carriage window if Mason didn't permit her to see that Daniel and the carriage driver were safe. Mason had glowered at her, his heavy eyebrows almost obscuring his eyes. "I am not a monster, madam. Go. Quickly." Mason hadn't permitted Daniel back into the carriage. He sat next to the carriage driver now.

Augusta's voice softened. "Mr. Mason reminds me of Philip's father. No, don't protest."

Becca had begun to do just that.

"He was reckless. He gambled, and he lost everything. He lost my dowry. Philip was just old enough to remember what we'd had. But that's an old story." She picked a small piece of lint from her forest green velvet cape and held it between her fingers before flicking it away.

The carriage stopped before a red sandstone brick home with a fairytale curved roof built in the old Dutch fashion. It was the type of house a well-to-do merchant might own, solid, conservative and built to last.

A half hour later, John Mason poured tea from a bell-shaped silver teapot into white porcelain cups. The house belonged to Mason's friend, he explained, a tradesperson who sold his wares to British and Americans alike. The merchant's sales to the Tories in New York were illegal. But that just increased the profit to be made, Mason said.

He placed Daniel and Becca in parlor chairs that caught the glare of the cold afternoon sun and made them squint. He sat next to Augusta on an upholstered couch facing them. One of Mason's bandits escorted Annie to the kitchen for tea.

Daniel examined the teacup and cleaned the edge of it with his shirttail before taking a tentative sip. His hair was wildly tangled from his tumble in the snow. His swollen cheek was an angry red.

A tug of anger left Becca shaky. She rested the thin porcelain cup on a nearby table. Mr. Alloway wasn't complaining of the blow. But there'd been no need to land it in the first place.

"Your son thought it was a grand game, that he could skate on the ice and never fall through," Mason said to Augusta. "I don't think he ever looked over his shoulder." Another rumble of laughter. "Now, me. I'm always looking over my shoulder. I look over both shoulders."

Augusta leaned toward Mason as if he'd offered her a treasure. And he had, Becca thought. He was sharing memories of her son.

"If my husband was so careless, how did he survive for so long?" Becca challenged. "He was travelling into New York City for at least a year before the British took him." She wished Mr. Mason wouldn't sit so close to Augusta.

With his sharp-bladed knife, Mason stabbed a piece of cheese from the long wooden platter set in the middle of the pine table and transferred it to his other hand. He chewed thoughtfully and swallowed. "He survived that long because I let him. I was paid to protect him and his whiskey."

The teacup wobbled in Becca's hand.

"If you were paid to protect him, then you failed, didn't you?" Daniel asked.

Mason's knife winged through the air. The blade caught the wall behind Daniel's seat, less than six inches from his left ear.

Daniel exploded out of his chair. The scarred bandit, Amos, and another one of Mason's men burst from theirs. They clamped their hands on Daniel's shoulders to force him back into his seat.

"The payments stopped," Mason said calmly. He reached for a second knife resting on the platter as if he hadn't just thrown the first. "And so my protection stopped. The British took your son as he made his next trip to New York."

Becca's arms and legs suddenly felt heavy, as if her sadness had weight. The body remembers grief, even when the mind has tucked it away, she knew. Her father's death, and then Philip's, taught her that.

Augusta no longer leaned toward Mason. Her head was bowed, her thin hands clasped in her lap.

Mason studied her. He withdrew his hand from the knife. "I am sorry, Mrs. Parcell. I don't think your son would have recognized a trap if it came with a sign."

"Philip would still be alive if you had done something." Becca's voice was rough.

"No." Mason slapped his thigh. "Untrue."

"You let them take my husband."

Mason roared. "Let them?"

Daniel struggled to rise with Amos' hand still clamped to his shoulder.

"I couldn't know what would happen," Mason said.

Augusta's breath fluttered like a bird's wing.

His voice gentled. "Your son had made that trip often enough. There were four redcoats. Parcell went willingly, as always. My men saw it all."

"You're certain?" Daniel's voice was sharp.

Mason nodded. "Parcell rode through the Neutral Ground with the lobsterbacks in as cheerful a mood as you please, my men said. He hauled a cart to carry his crates of whiskey."

"Lobsterbacks?" Becca asked.

"Sorry, m'lady. The redcoats, you might say."

One of Mason's men guffawed.

"Who paid you to protect Parcell?" Daniel asked.

Mason's eyes went cold. "I'm not in the habit of giving away anything of value, not even information. Do you have something to trade? Something I might want?" His eyes slipped to Augusta.

Becca raised her voice, fearing again for her mother-in-law. "Your answer isn't worth a shilling. It won't guarantee we arrive safely in New York City. I might pay for information and safe passage. That might be worth something."

Mason's attention turned from Augusta to Becca.

She allowed herself a moment of relief.

"You *might* pay? And what do you have that I *might* want?" Mason cocked his head as if amused to be negotiating with a young woman.

His changeable moods left her dizzy. "Two pounds sterling silver." She actually had sewn five pounds, the few remaining pieces of her dowry silver, into her petticoat before they left Morristown.

"On what terms?" Mason was all business now.

"Half now and half when we reach the city." Becca crossed her arms. She had sat like this at her father's forge, arguing with his customers about the price of horseshoes.

Mason threw his hands up in mock surrender. "Perhaps this country is birthing something new in the world if it produces such women as you. I accept."

His ready agreement surprised her. She leaned down and slid one hand beneath the hem of her brown gown to the rough red linsey-woolsey petticoat. She ripped a seam and removed one silver coin, then laid it on the table as the afternoon sky faded to pearl gray.

Mason flipped the coin in his palm, then placed it on a side table as if to ensure that his men would see he had extracted payment.

"Amos," Mason called. "You and Tom, go have a nice cup of ale and visit with Miss Annie 'til I call. Go on now, and show her your best behavior."

A minute later, Mason leaned toward Becca, his elbows propped on beefy legs. "My apologies for all that. My reputation would suffer were I to let anyone through here without some payment." Becca was becoming accustomed to the low rumble that passed for his laugh. He scooped the coin off the table and dropped it into her palm.

"And the man who ordered protection for my husband?" She held her breath, waiting for the bandit to explode in anger again.

"The mayor of New York. That's who paid me to keep Mr. Parcell safe. Self-important bastard. Mayor Matthews, I mean, not your son." He bowed his head to Augusta. "Excuse my language, m'lady. Told me once that Philip was just a messenger boy."

"The mayor of New York City?" Disbelief was stamped on Daniel's face. "But why did he pay you for protection?"

Mason shrugged. "I took his money. I didn't ask questions."

"Did you ask why he stopped paying?" Becca asked.

"No. He told me once that Mr. Parcell carried messages that could end the war. I think he regretted sharing that information. He never spoke of it again," Mason said. "Anything else, you'll need to learn for yourself."

Chapter Nineteen

Becca felt Daniel approach before he reached the end of the dock. His footsteps vibrated through the old wood. She glanced at him, then turned back to the harbor, studying the glowing white ice floes that raced the tide back to the sea.

He didn't speak, and she was glad of it. His presence was comfort enough. The thought surprised her.

They had made the last ferry of the day, thanks to Mr. Mason. "I guaranteed your safety," he'd rumbled. "I keep my promises." Amos had traveled with them across the half-frozen harbor, although Becca wasn't certain whether he was there to protect them or report their conversation to Mr. Mason.

The bandit leaped from the boat as it thumped into the dock, then dashed up Broadway to bring word of their arrival to Cousin Samuel. Augusta and Annie waited inside the ferryman's rough hut.

"Is this as foolhardy a venture as I think?" Becca stared over the dark bay.

"Go home, Mrs. Parcell. Go back to Morristown. It's not too late," Daniel said.

She laughed. "I suppose that's an answer. But I can't go home, not with Minister Townsend and his friends waiting." At least the cut on her forehead had stopped throbbing. "And I have nowhere else to go."

"You could marry Mr. Lockwood." He studied her.

"I won't have to if we find my husband's list." Daniel's scrutiny was making her uncomfortable.

"Not a love match?"

"Mr. Lockwood is a fine man, a gentleman," she said stiffly. "Any woman would be honored to be his wife."

"Any woman but you?" His sympathetic voice removed the sting from the words.

"That is not your concern." How had he managed to pull the truth from her heart?

He bowed. "I meant no offense, madam."

"What about you? Can't you go home?" she asked.

"I don't have one." His tone was brusque. He might as well have shut the door in her face. He didn't want to talk of his past. But she was curious.

"You must have had a home, once."

He stared across the harbor.

In the distance, she heard the dull sound of hoofs on packed snow.

Finally, Daniel cleared his throat. "My wife and son died. I left."

They were your home." She couldn't imagine the pain of losing a child nor a well-loved wife. At least she had Augusta and Annie and the hope of keeping her land.

"They were."

A single word of condolence would turn him to stone. Becca was certain of it. So she fisted one hand on her hip and mimicked Annie's speech: "Well, if either of us had a lick of sense, we'd leave and join the Highland Gang. Mr. Mason would welcome us, I warrant."

Daniel flashed the smile that made her stomach flutter, and they both laughed, even if only to push away the darkness.

The clip-clop of horseshoes grew louder.

Annie burst from the small hut, her arms crossed, lips tight with irritation. "I thought I'd get old waiting for you."

"You could never be old, luv," Amos cooed, hopping down from the carriage.

"Hogwash, you brute." She swiped at his hand.

Becca's eyebrows rose. Annie had made a conquest.

* * *

Blackened buildings stretched for blocks to the west of Broadway. Ruined lumber rose from the wreckage like a stack of discarded bones.

How could England treat its subjects like this? Daniel wondered. *Who wouldn't struggle for a different future?*

He pointed to the destruction. "The fire started just after the redcoats ran the Patriots out of here in '76. The British say General Washington ordered the City torched when the Army abandoned it." He spoke over the dull thump of the horses' hooves on snow.

"We all heard about the Great Fire. But this. It's terrible," Becca said.

"Four hundred buildings gone," he added. "And the British haven't lifted a finger to rebuild any of them."

They passed a young Black boy, who giggled as he slid forward on the ice, trailing his mother. "Keep up now," she called to him.

Daniel had heard that former slaves were streaming in to New York City from New Jersey now that the British had promised them freedom.

The smell of spoiled meat assaulted the carriage. Augusta and Annie lifted handkerchiefs to their nose.

"They're burning animal fat for warmth. Wood's too expensive."

Augusta "tssked."

Dotting the side streets, campfires illuminated the canvas tents pitched by the ruins.

Daniel pointed to one of them. "Canvas Town, they call it. The people who lived here before the fire didn't have much. Now? They're in tents, along with most of the bandits and gangs and whores in town."

"Where do they get the tents?" Annie asked.

"From old ship spars and sails," Daniel said.

He swiveled to watch Becca and lost his train of thought. He never spoke of his wife or son. Never. But something about her pulled the truth from him. She had understood. His wife and son had been his home.

Anger flared. He didn't want to be understood, dammit. He was here to find Parcell's list – or, at least, the man who received Parcell's messages – and leave.

What had Washington been thinking sending her here? She wouldn't know whom to trust. He leaned toward her. "Don't wander into Canvas Town while you're here. It's not safe for the likes of you."

"I'm not planning to tour Canvas Town." Her back straightened.

"And don't go knocking on the mayor's door to ask why he killed your husband."

Augusta gasped.

"That was not necessary." Becca leaned forward to meet him. "Don't you think I'm frightened enough?"

"You need to understand the risks." His voice rose. She was offended. Good. He hoped it would make her more careful.

Her voice rose, too. "General Washington thinks I am capable enough."

"As capable as can be, Mrs. Rebecca." He recalled the way she held the pistol the other night. "But these are dangerous times and this is a dangerous place." Then he rapped on the side of the carriage. "Stop here," he called to the driver.

Her fingers tightened on the skirt of her gown. Then she lengthened her neck and nodded. "Thank you for taking us this far, sir. We wish you godspeed."

"I'm afraid you're not done with me." Daniel silently cursed in all the languages he'd learned in the waterfront taverns of Elizabethtown. What if something happened to her while he was gone? "But I need a safe place to hide, and Mr. Hamilton has made arrangements."

She smoothed the folds in her gown. "How will we find you?" She sounded unconcerned. "That is, if we needed to."

"There's a print shop at the foot of Wall Street. The owner sells books, too. Leave a message there. Just ask to procure a book. I'll know you want to see me. The owner's name is Rivington."

The carriage slowed and Daniel leaped out before the horses stopped moving. He strode a few steps, then turned, watching the carriage gallop up Broadway until it disappeared in the dark.

Chapter Twenty

Daniel's right palm ached as he swept the knotted pine floor of James Rivington's print shop. He'd tried not to wonder whether feeling was returning to his injured hand. He'd trained himself not to hope.

The masthead of the newspaper resting on the pine counter at the front of shop read: "Printer to the King's Most Excellent Majesty." Rivington had put Daniel to work cleaning the shop. The printer called it hiding in plain sight.

Daniel didn't care what the printer called it. He kept his back to the broad window that fronted Wall Street.

He couldn't escape the feeling that he was being watched and would wake to find himself back on the prison ship.

His thoughts returned to Becca. That's what Lady Augusta called her. He'd been here days and hadn't learned anything about her husband's list of spies. Worse, he hadn't heard from her. He had half a mind to stroll over to the cousin's house and stand watch until he caught sight of her.

The bell at the front door rang. A blast of air snaked around Daniel as a soldier entered.

Daniel caught a glimpse of the man before pivoting away. He hunched his shoulders and continued sweeping to an easy rhythm.

The soldier whispered something to Rivington.

Daniel tensed. He balanced on the balls of his feet, ready to fight or run.

"Just my cousin's son," Rivington responded. "He's a bit teched. Harmless, so long as you don't speak to him. Have some of this to warm yourself."

Daniel exhaled. He stared at the broom as if he'd forgotten he was holding it, then pulled it back and forth again in short, even strokes.

"I don't know why they're sending us to meet with that Washington fellow in the dead of winter." The snub-nosed officer cupped both hands around the hot drink that Rivington handed to him.

Daniel smelled the sweet aroma of hot chocolate laced with the rich bite of rum. His mouth watered.

"As if anything will come of a prisoner exchange mission." The officer lifted the cup again to his mouth. Then he placed it on the battered counter that separated him from Rivington. "Well, they'll be missing me if I don't get back."

He reached into his brown leather pouch, flicking a piece of folded parchment onto the counter. "Here's news for the next paper, straight from the Governor." The officer winked and strode to the door.

"There's always a drink waiting for you. You're always welcome, sir." Rivington's warm voice followed the man.

The soldier smiled, his hand on the doorknob. "Thanks, Rivington. I'll see you next week, then. We won't be leaving for Morristown 'til after that." The heavy wooden door slammed shut as the Redcoat stepped back into the flow of bustling Wall Street.

Rivington flung the letter he was handed onto a shelf below counter level. "Alloway," he grumbled, "stop eavesdropping."

Daniel grunted and continued sweeping.

Rivington swung back to his cases of lead type. His fingers flew as he placed the lead plugs, one letter at a time, into a composing stick.

Transforming small lumps of metal into books that enraged or entertained or made readers cry was a kind of alchemy, Daniel thought, like turning lead into gold. It was the only job he'd ever wanted. Ignoring the dull ache in his hand, he tightened his grip on the broom as much as the injured fingers allowed and swept away his envy.

Alexander Hamilton's instructions were clear. Daniel was to find his way to Rivington's press. He would be safe here, Hamilton said. After all, what better cover for an American spy than printing the most notorious Loyalist newspaper in all the colonies?

Patriots had hung Rivington in effigy, destroyed his printing press and driven him back to England as the war began, Daniel recalled. Rivington returned to New York City in '77 once the English were firmly in control with a new press and appointment as the King's printer.

After the shop closed for the day, the two men trudged upstairs to the printer's apartment. After they ate, Rivington sat in a down-filled chair near the fire. He closed his eyes and rested his feet on a small wooden stool. His liver-spotted hand lay on a pile of books perched on his side table.

Daniel sat across from him, still finishing his evening meal. He swept a third biscuit through the remains of the beef stew. The tender crumb soaked up the rich brown gravy, redolent of carrots, potatoes and beef. The biscuit melted in his mouth.

Rivington's head remained erect, despite the closed eyes, suggesting that he was just resting and not sleeping.

Daniel liked a man who knew how to be quiet. So many people felt the need to fill silence, even when they had nothing to say. Becca knew how to be still.

"Mr. Hamilton didn't give me much notice you'd be arriving, just a note directing me to help you as I could. He said you would explain." Rivington opened one eye to confirm that Daniel was listening, then closed it again.

Daniel swept biscuit crumbs from the table into his hand and deposited them onto the empty white stoneware plate. Alexander Hamilton trusted Rivington with his life. At least that's what Hamilton told Daniel. But that didn't mean Daniel had reason to trust the man. He didn't answer.

Rivington dropped his feet from the stool and sat up, focusing intelligent brown eyes on Daniel. "All right, Mr. Alloway," he said, the day's exhaustion clear in his voice. "I'll go first, though you know enough already to guarantee my hanging. Soldiers brag to the man who prints the news. And as you've already guessed, I pass along any information I hear to my friends in Morristown."

"But you're the King's printer," Daniel prodded.

Rivington's eyebrows dropped into a straight, gray line. Then his good humor returned. "General Washington and I thought it would make my loyalty to the Crown as clear as New York Harbor. Quite the ruse, eh?"

Rivington tamped tobacco into a red ware bowl and began to smoke the reed stem pipe. "Now, you, sir. What do you fight for?"

Daniel hesitated only a moment. "I fight for myself, Mr. Rivington. Just myself." He kept his eyes trained on his empty plate. He didn't want to encourage the old man to lecture.

Rivington nodded as if this was the answer he expected. "Let me tell you something about yourself, Mr. Alloway."

Daniel pushed his chair back from the table. Listening politely was the price he'd have to pay, he supposed, for a good meal and a bed.

"You came here with nothing or almost nothing, and someone gave you a chance. Maybe you apprenticed. Mayhap someone handed you food when you were hungry." Rivington examined Daniel's empty plate and smiled. "And you held tight and worked to build the life you wanted."

Daniel's stomach tightened as he recalled his first days in America. He had staggered off the ship in Philadelphia after eight weeks at sea. It had felt like an eternity to the twenty-three-year-old. And he had grown so accustomed to the pitch of the ocean that it took hours before the Earth stop tilting beneath his feet. All he carried was the handful of shillings his father had pressed into his hand and a piece of wrinkled, grubby paper with the name and address of his mother's third cousin, a printer.

Daniel brought his attention back to Rivington.

"My point precisely, Mr. Alloway. You're part of a new country, perhaps a new world. You have the freedom to decide what you will do and who you will be here." Rivington slapped the book under his hand, then smoothed the cover as if petting a kitten.

"You sound like Alexander Hamilton," Daniel mumbled.

"Or he sounds like me," Rivington corrected. "We met a few times when he was a student at King's College. I'm fond of the boy."

Rivington leaned back and closed his eyes again. "You belong here, Daniel. This country is making you over into a new type of man, one that has never existed before, a self-made man. And whether you acknowledge it or not, you are creating a type of country that hasn't ever existed. Acknowledge what you see and you'll know what you stand for."

Daniel surveyed the book-lined wall behind Rivington's head.

The index finger on his good left hand traced the cool edge of the now-empty white dinner plate. How many times would he need to reinvent himself?

There was something about Rivington's calm, steady thoughts that reminded Daniel of his father. "Mr. Hamilton sent me here to find a list of spies," Daniel began. He recounted what he knew of Philip Parcell.

The printer blew a lazy rivulet of smoke from his pipe toward the ceiling. "So Parcell was the courier?"

"And the mayor is surely passing those messages along to the British Command. Smuggling whiskey gave Parcell the excuse to come and go. Ever hear of him?"

The rich scent of tobacco perfumed the air.

"No. Never met the man. But I wonder." Another silence. "Just after the summer ended, a few of the young officers came in to deliver an article for my news sheet."

Rivington's tone was frosty, letting Daniel know what he really thought of printing the so-called news sanctioned by the British government.

"One of them mentioned that the Lord God might have more of an interest in watching over the 'new courier' than the old one, and his friends laughed. It was such an odd thing to say that it stuck with me. Probably has nothing to do with your Philip Parcell."

"A new courier," Daniel repeated. "Makes sense. They had to replace Mr. Parcell." He shook his head. "I don't know about the rest of what you heard."

Rivington rose slowly. "I'm off to bed. Printers wake up early, you'll recall."

Daniel was silent. He remembered.

Much later, he stared out the window of Rivington's spare bedroom. Moonlight illuminated the narrow wooden buildings across the street. He couldn't sleep. "What do you fight for?" Rivington asked. He wondered whether a one-handed printer could fight for anything. He wondered who replaced Philip in delivering messages to Mayor Matthews.

And finally, he wondered whether Becca was sleeping soundly or if she, too, was looking out at the same moon, bedeviled by worry.

Chapter Twenty-One

The two men were still there, hunched in the cold, unmoving and grim as crows.

Daniel risked a single glance, then retreated back into the alleyway. He lifted a finger to scratch the itch beneath the borrowed wig, then turned his attention to the pantomime playing out across the snow-covered street.

The spindly boy dressed in tea-colored rags rushed the steps. He pounded the gleaming black door with one hand. In the other, he clutched a rectangular package.

Daniel had wrapped it in twine an hour ago. He'd handed the boy a coin with the promise of another after the delivery.

The door opened, and a bow-legged butler peered left, right, then down at the small boy. His mouth scowled in displeasure. He jabbed a finger toward the side of the building, to the servant's entrance no doubt, then pulled his arm back to swing the door shut.

The child was quicker. He flung the package at the butler's shins and ran.

"You get back here, boy." The servant stood rigid with affront, his gaze following the boy until he disappeared around a corner. Then he stooped to retrieve the package.

Daniel smiled with satisfaction.

* * *

The front hall of Cousin Samuel's house shed its tentative air of prosperity in the twilight. Bits of ceiling plaster powdered the wooden floors, twinkling dully by the light of the sconces. The floral wallpaper faded to a lifeless brown.

Becca sank to her knees, squeezing her fingers into the narrow space between the hall table and the wall. Her fingers spider-walked along the back of the table searching for parchment or a pouch that might hold paper. Nothing. It was the result she expected. She felt the sting of disappointment, nonetheless.

Each evening, she added to the list in her account book of places her husband had *not* hidden his list of spies. She had searched the basement, the library, even the kitchen during the rare hours of the day when Samuel was absent.

He had dogged her steps all week. It had been nearly impossible to search the house for anything her husband might have left behind.

In her mind, she conjured Philip's face and demanded his help. But his image was indistinct, as if he refused to show his true self to her even now, and he refused to answer. She wondered what Daniel would think of her search.

He had said she should request a book from Rivington's print shop if she wanted to speak to him. But she was too proud to send a note when she had learned nothing.

Rising, Becca glared at the stack of tasteful ivory and white visiting cards and invitations that rested on the table. Her arrival had made quite the splash with the cream of New York British society. Becca hated that General Washington was right.

The finest ladies of the city awaited her response to their calling cards. If she copied her mother-in-law's manners and spoke as little as possible, Becca might actually carry off this masquerade, convincing them that she was loyal to the King.

Except she'd rather muck out a stable than sit in the fine drawing rooms overlooking Great Queen Street. Becca scooped several of the invitations up and idly fanned them out. She imagined sweeping them all into the fireplace.

But that wasn't an option. She was one week closer to the hearing that could brand her a traitor, and she'd learned nothing about her husband's movements here.

She'd been imprisoned—it felt like imprisonment—in Cousin Samuel's house for more than a week, the dressmaker her only visitor. Her wardrobe was barbaric, entirely unsuitable, Samuel had said, wincing with disapproval.

She and Augusta gasped at the price the dressmaker quoted to make three ball gowns and two day dresses. If *monsieur* wants dresses so quickly, the French dressmaker will need to work day and night, she explained. Samuel accepted the price before Becca could protest.

That was another mystery. His table was meager. He retained a single servant. His home needed repair. And yet, he had told the dressmaker that money was no object.

The back of Becca's neck tightened.

"Cousin?"

She turned, still holding the small white cards.

Samuel Parcell stood at the far end of the entryway. He was a tall man in his mid-forties with a tight peevish mouth, a thin nose and thinning brown hair. His jacket was yellow-striped and his breeches were a contrasting—perhaps too contrasting—shade of maroon. Wrinkles prematurely crisscrossed his cheeks. He carried himself with an air of permanent grievance.

He held a small paper-wrapped package before him as if it was a lantern lighting his way. He stared disapprovingly at her day dress.

Becca's gaze followed his. Two circles of white dust, like twin mouths open in surprise, were stamped on the skirt of her navy wool gown, where she had kneeled on the floor. She flushed, then straightened her spine. Wiping the dust away would make her appear guilty of doing exactly what she had been, searching his house.

Annie stood behind Samuel, her expression grim.

"You were expecting a package?" Samuel asked.

Annie nodded violently.

"Yes." Becca's nod was more subdued.

"I told you, sir. It's a book the missus ordered. It was delivered to the wrong house. Nice of the neighbor's butler to send a girl over with the package. Very neighborly." Annie spoke slowly, as if every word mattered.

A book. Daniel. Relief and alarm washed over her. He was still here. But what was wrong?

"I'm so pleased it has arrived." Becca tried to sound slightly bored, as if the delivery hardly mattered. She reached for the book.

"I don't recall you sending a messenger." His eyes narrowed. "What book did you request?"

Her mind went blank. "A book that would be of interest to...to a lady." She fanned the invitations she held before her.

Samuel's gaze settled on the white cards in her hand. He lurched for them, plucking the invitations from Becca's fist. He tossed the package onto the hallway table behind her.

"An invitation from Mrs. Lathrop." He lifted a second invitation. "And the mayor's wife has invited us all to a ball next week. All of society wants to meet you," he crowed. "I am back in everyone's good graces."

"Had you fallen from their good graces?" Becca was curious despite herself.

"These are the first invitations I've received in months. Me. My family. A family of our quality." He covered his thin chest with one fluttering hand. "I've been an outcast ever since your husband, ever since Cousin Philip..." Samuel spit the name, "...betrayed the King. And society is willing to receive me now because I'm hosting you and Aunt Augusta."

Samuel doesn't know Philip was a spy, Becca thought with surprise. *And he hated my husband.* She wondered what Daniel would make of that.

Daniel. Becca shifted until her wide skirt blocked Samuel's view of the hall table where the package lay. Facing Samuel, she groped for the paper-wrapped book. There. She wrapped her hand around it, then slid the package low behind the wide skirt of her gown.

She felt a spark of pity for this superficial man. The world was at war and all Samuel could think about was which parties he could attend. The world was at war and all *she* cared about was her farm. *It's not the same,* she told herself, pushing away the uncomfortable thought.

"Will you excuse us, Cousin?" She curtsied, backing her way toward the stairs. "The dressmaker will be arriving for a fitting. Annie, help me prepare."

The two women swept up the stairs and burst into their small dressing room.

Painted cupids danced on the dressing room ceiling. One lacked an eye, another a finger and a third a nose where the old paint had peeled away. A dark water stain nearly obliterated a coy shepherdess. The room was as cold as all the others in Cousin Samuel's house.

Becca pulled one end of the twine, which fell away at once from the brown paper wrapping.

"I thought I heard footsteps." Augusta stood at the doorway wearing a bright green robe and a lumpy, warm yellow shawl. "Oh, lovely." She exhaled. "I can't wait to read it."

Volume One of Fanny Burney's novel *Evelina* emerged from the wrapping.

Becca opened the cover, careful not to crack the spine. Books were expensive. Inside was a folded piece of almost transparent parchment. She shook out the paper, her eyes trailing to the bottom of the page.

The impatient scrawl trailed off to a signature that read Your humble and undeserving servant. But there was no name attached to the missive.

Becca's lips moved as she read each word.

Can anything, my good madam, be more painful to a friendly Mind than a necessity of communicating Disagreeable Intelligence? That is how Mrs. Burney begins the Novel you hold and it is how I must begin this Letter.

Her index finger traced Daniel's handwriting. She imagined his long fingers curved around the quill pen, pressed against the paper.

You of all people know my true Heart, dearest Friend. The thought of your virtuous Mind and cultivated Understanding bring ease to my troubled Soul, which yearns for the Day that we can be reunited.

She was suddenly uncertain that he had penned the correspondence. Dearest friend? Why would he claim that she knew his heart? She shook her head to focus.

Yet that Day is not yet at hand. I pray that the Fates will soon increase the allotment of Joy they reserve for us both and that we may then be reunited, perhaps by May Or ...

May or June? July? He had lost the word in the rush to finish the sentence, she guessed.

The Greeks envisioned the Fates as three Goddesses draped in white. But in these reduced Times, I imagine them to be two darkly-dressed Men who watch us from the Street. A fantastical Conceit, I know. But do not doubt my Constancy. You are not rid of me.

She smiled. You are not rid of me. That was what Daniel had told her in the carriage.

Becca reread the paragraph. The Fates. Greeks. By May or? She read it a third time, gasped and ran to the window. The mayor. Two darkly-dressed Men watching. Pressing herself against the wall, she peeked through the glass.

Two men stood hunched in front of the house across the street. One had his arms crossed as if trying to stay warm.

Becca threw her head back and laughed.

"Ma'am?" Annie asked with concern.

Becca whirled back to the two women. "It's from Mr. Alloway. He is well. At least, I think he is. He's warning us that we're being watched. He thinks the mayor has sent them." She stepped further away from the window.

"Watched? And you are pleased?" Augusta's elegant chin rose in indignation.

"Yes." Becca passed the parchment to Augusta. "And no."

Augusta held the letter at arm's length to read it. "But why is his note so obscure? Why didn't Mr. Alloway sign it?"

Becca recalled how the twine had practically unknotted itself as she opened the package. "Because there was a chance that someone else might see it. And he was right. Someone opened the package before it reached us." Becca was certain of it. "He had the book delivered to the wrong house on purpose, I wager."

Annie rose, peeking out the window. "A butler wouldn't mind sending the scullery maid over with the book, so long as it didn't take too long. And a servant would know to go to the back door, not the front."

"So those two men across the street would be none the wiser," Becca completed Annie's sentence.

The three women fell silent. Becca wondered when she would see Daniel again and why Samuel had opened her package.

Chapter Twenty-Two

"You have accomplished the impossible, Mrs. Parcell." Mrs. Lathrop linked her arm with Becca's as they led the guests into the music room. She was a short, plump woman whose frothy pink gown matched her cheerful temperament. She had been in constant motion since greeting her twenty-four guests.

Becca had counted the number of guests to calm her nerves.

"And what would that be?" Becca tilted her head down to listen, curious despite herself.

"So many newcomers try to fit in, and by trying, fail," her hostess said. "You vanquished the heart of society this evening."

"I hardly said a word," Becca protested.

"It was brilliant of you to remain a mystery. Simply brilliant," Mrs. Lathrop gushed.

A mystery? Becca had been petrified into silence when she'd stepped into the front hall which was lit with more candles than any five homes in Morristown.

But as the conversation swirled around her, she reached two surprising conclusions. First, New Yorkers spoke quickly and endlessly, which gave her a slight headache and led to her second discovery. They were all so busy waiting to express their own opinions that they hardly noticed she merely nodded or answered "you are too kind" to each inquiry.

Finally, she took as deep a breath as her stays allowed and realized her fright had evaporated. Then she turned her attention to each of the guests.

Which of them knew her husband?

"One of our guests is calling you *'la bella silenziosa.'*" Mrs. Lathrop gave her an appraising gaze. "I think it becomes you."

"*La bell?*"

"It means the beautiful silent one. It's Italian." Mrs. Lathrop pulled on Becca's arm. "One day, when we become friends, you must tell me what you were really thinking during dinner."

Becca stumbled in surprise. Had others noticed that her scrutiny at dinner was far from casual?

Mrs. Lathrop caught Becca's elbow, and she teased, "It wouldn't do to take a fall with all the men watching." The metal rings on her hostess' plump bejeweled fingers gouged her forearm.

"We're not all as fearsome as you might...." A sudden smile lit Mrs. Lathrop's face. She dropped Becca's arm.

Becca followed her hostess' gaze to the front hallway which led into the room. Several new guests were joining the party for the concert that was about to begin. She turned a gasp into a cough.

"Lockwood. We weren't expecting you," Mr. Lathrop crowed. Much older than his wife, he limped to the front hallway entrance, his gold-tipped cane striking the parquet floor with each step.

Thomas's tawny hair was covered by a simple white wig. His breeches emphasized muscular thighs. He wore a forest green velvet waistcoat with ivory buttons and an ivory vest.

"I hope I'm not putting you out. I didn't realize you had guests or I wouldn't have stopped in." Thomas's eyes swept past Becca as if they were strangers.

At the sight of him, she felt a swirl of homesickness. But why was he here? Why didn't he acknowledge her?

Several of the men surrounded Thomas, thumping him on the back or laughing as if they were old friends.

The musicians sensed that they'd lost the audience's attention and softened the music until it was hardly audible.

Mrs. Lathrop swept forward. "And have you met our guest of honor, Mr. Lockwood?"

"No," he said before Becca could answer.

"But you must meet. I would have thought…from the same colony, and all that." Mrs. Lathrop's attention swiveled from Thomas to Becca and back, as if she sensed an undercurrent that she didn't understand. "Mrs. Parcell, let me introduce Mr. Thomas Lockwood."

She dropped into a curtsey to avoid letting Mrs. Lathrop see her redden. She rose, trying to hide her confusion behind her fan. "What brings you to New York City, Mr. Lockwood?" Why did everyone here seem to know him?

His tone was light. "I had expected a communication that failed to arrive. Success in my business requires diligence. I came to ensure that nothing was amiss."

"Oh." He had been worried about her. "But with the war going on …."

"Insurrection," Mr. Lathrop corrected her.

Of course, Becca thought. The British considered the American uprising a treasonous insurrection, not a war for independence.

"With the insurrection, communications can be delayed," Becca said. "Isn't that so?" Thomas had told her to write to him and she hadn't. Should she feel guilty? Instead, she felt irritated. If she'd wanted his help, she would have asked for it. "There's no call to put oneself in danger."

Mr. Lathrop slapped Thomas on the back and laughed. "Danger? Not Mr. Lockwood. He and I don't have political opinions. We have opinions about commerce, about the price of tea and the quality of West Indies sugar. Merchants are welcome everywhere."

Mr. Lathrop turned away from the women. "What do you hear about the ports in South Carolina? The armies will all be moving south come spring, won't they? Excuse us, ladies."

Becca and Mrs. Lathrop watched the two men drift away, heads close in conversation.

Mrs. Lathrop's eyes narrowed. "Mrs. Parcell, are you certain you've never met Mr. Lockwood?"

"The musicians are sheer perfection, Mrs. Lathrop." Augusta raised her voice. "What will we be hearing this evening?"

Becca hadn't heard her mother-in-law approach.

The hostess blinked, seeming to notice the absence of music. She swept her hand high above her head. The cello and viola answered her call. The chamber music soared, and the guests took seats in small groupings of chairs placed around the large room.

Becca waited until the music cast its spell, and the quiet whispers of the audience fell away. Pleading a small headache, she set off for the drawing room.

She didn't have long to wait. "How did you find me?" She stood in the middle of the long blue and yellow room, her hands clutching the back of a delicate mahogany chair.

A King Charles spaniel stared at them from its perch on an overstuffed yellow couch.

Thomas rested the small glass of sherry he carried on a side table. He lifted his hands, palms open. "I didn't know that you would be here. Not specifically. This is the third party I've visited without an invitation." His smile was boyish.

"You shouldn't have come," she scolded. "There was no reason to put yourself in danger."

"I am suitably chastised." His broad face reflected satisfaction. "You're worried about me."

"Of course, I am," she said. "I should have let you know that I was fine. I should have written. I apologize. But it's not safe for you here. And what would General Washington think if he knew you were here surrounded by the English?"

Thomas shoved away the chair that stood between them. "The general sent me." He drew close. "We both wanted to assure ourselves that you were well."

She blinked away sudden emotion. She might be frightened, but she wasn't alone. She had overreacted.

"Have you learned anything more about your husband's list?" Thomas asked. "The general is impatient. He expected to hear from you by now, as well."

"Samuel insisted on having dresses made for us before he'd allow me to accept any invitations. This is the first dinner I've attended." It sounded like an excuse, even to her own ears.

"Nothing to report?" Thomas cocked his head.

"Not yet. No." Then she recalled Mr. Mason. "I heard something about the mayor of New York City."

"Stay away from the mayor." His voice was sharp.

"But if he knows something about Philip, I should learn as much as I can. That's why I'm here."

He lifted his hand to her upper arm and shook it gently. "Promise you'll stay away from him."

She stared at the hand that circled her silk-clad arm until he released it.

"I'll do what I need to do, Thomas. I won't lose the farm because you're afraid for me." She didn't tell him that the idea of facing the mayor scared her to death. She didn't tell him that Daniel Alloway had given her the same advice.

"And where is Mr. Alloway? Is he here protecting you? Is he disguised as a servant?"

Becca flushed. "I don't know."

Thomas' face darkened. "I told General Washington it was a mistake to send him. I have to leave in the morning. I actually do have a ship that requires my attention."

For the first time, she wondered how Thomas' ships, at least some of them, managed to evade the British blockade that kept European goods from the colonies.

"If something goes wrong," he said, "if you fear anything, send a message to Carl. He'll find me wherever I am. Hang Mr. Alloway. I'll come for you right away."

"There you are, Thomas," Mrs. Lathrop trilled. The door had opened silently.

Thomas nodded toward the small glass of sherry he'd left on the table. "Lady Augusta asked me to bring her daughter-in-law a cordial for her headache."

"Everyone is asking for the wonderful Mr. Lockwood." Perhaps Mrs.

Lathrop's expression dimmed slightly when she turned to Becca. "They're asking for you, too, Mrs. Parcell."

Chapter Twenty-Three

North of Beekman and Bayard Streets, north of Mulberry and Mott, north of the tanneries with their noxious scent of decaying animals, William Cunningham kept a room on the third floor of a boarding house for occasions such as this.

He planted his broad palms on the straw-filled mattress and grunted, lifting himself off her.

Her eyes were clenched shut. If he had taken the trouble to notice, he would have felt her heart beat like the wings of a frantic moth. A turquoise ribbon lay on the mattress near her head.

He sat at the edge of the bed, buttoning his breeches. He hadn't bothered removing them.

His gaze traveled to the narrow box, about ten inches long, which sat next to a small dark bottle on the unpainted pine table beneath the room's single window.

Damn The Correspondent, Cunningham thought as his breathing slowed to normal.

He wasn't a servant to be ordered about. He was the man's partner. He deserved more information. But the last letter had arrived from Morristown with enough silver to ensure that Cunningham would obey. For now.

And so he'd claimed the brief moment of oblivion the girl provided, a respite from the anger that clawed at him daily. Who could blame him?

"What did you tell the mayor?" he asked, then repeated the question when she didn't answer.

"The cook. I told the cook." Her voice was an empty husk.

He felt the mattress shift. She rolled away from him.

"All right, then. The cook. What did you tell her?"

Men's laughter rose through the stairwell. A door below slammed shut. The boarding house grew quiet again.

She grabbed a bedpost and lifted herself, hunching as if some deep pain prevented her from standing straight. "I asked for the morning off, like you told me to. I said my sister was sick. I said she needed me to find the apothecary. That she needed belladonna for her stomach or she wouldn't be able to work, and she'd lose her position."

Everyone knew that servant girls who got sick or pregnant would end up on the streets.

"The cook believed you?" He examined her more closely. Her head was bowed, her back turned to him.

"*She's* got a heart," the servant mumbled, turning the sentence into an accusation.

His voice held amusement. "You didn't complain about my heart when I offered you money."

Cunningham waited for her to leave for church again this past Sunday. She wore the ribbon then, too, just as she did the first time he stopped her outside the Mayor's home. This past Sunday, they huddled in the alley and he told her what he needed.

"All you asked then was how much you'd be paid," he added.

"I said I'd go to the apothecary for you. That was all."

Cunningham had a new thought. He stood. His fingers bunched into a fist.

"You didn't tell the apothecary who I was, did you?"

She clenched the sides of her gown. "No. You said not to."

He examined her expression, her stance, and the blonde hair that was loose and curled around her neck. He believed her. His fists relaxed. "One can't be too careful."

He was a careful man, a man who measured risks by the centimeter. The Correspondent, curse him, hadn't told him how the belladonna was to be used. It was such an odd request that it raised Cunningham's hackles.

He didn't want anyone being able to trace the purchase back to him, not until he understood why the medication was so urgently required.

Cunningham stepped to the table and lifted the bottle to the light. The wavy glass was marked with a label that read *TR Bellad*, tincture of belladonna. But the liquid could just as easily be muddy water and not the compound the Correspondent sought.

"You watched the man fill the box?"

"Yes, that, too," she said.

He had no experience of medicines and herbs. That was why he paid twice, once for the tincture and, again, for the leaves from which it was made. He hoped that demanding the leaves made it less likely that the apothecary would cheat him.

"I did what you said. I watched Apothecary Carey fill the pouch with the leaves," she said.

"Good. You can go." He swept up the pouch he'd left hanging from the bedpost and fished for coins. He held them out to her in his square, fleshy palm. "Here. What I promised."

She raised her gaze to his. "I am not a whore."

He didn't think she was. In fact, he didn't think about her at all. "Oh for… take the money," he said with annoyance. He grabbed her hand and pressed the coins into it, squeezing her fingers around them.

After she fled, Cunningham sat on the stool near the grime-clouded window, his head resting against the wall. He rolled the turquoise ribbon between his thumb and index finger, thinking about the Correspondent's last letter.

Damn him.

"Don't harm Rebecca Parcell," it read.

How was Cunningham to find Parcell's list if he couldn't threaten the widow?

"Kill Alloway when you find him."

Cunningham would be happy to oblige. But his men had watched Samuel Parcell's house for weeks. Alloway hadn't presented himself.

"Purchase the tincture."

The blue ribbon spun faster and faster between his fingers.

Cunningham stared at the small bottle.

Why did the Correspondent need the plant extract?

What was his plan? Who was he?

Finally, the spinning slowed. The ribbon slipped from his fingers.

He stood, stretching his neck left then right. Those with diligence and intelligence could find a solution to every problem. His own efforts today were proof of that.

First, he would kill Alloway. Then he would deliver the tincture to Morristown himself. He would find the Correspondent and demand answers.

He was no man's servant.

Chapter Twenty-Four

The women stood in the front hall ready to leave Mrs. Lathrop's house after a late-day tea.

"You must tell us," Miss De Lancey laughed. "Did you really shoot a wildcat?"

"I heard it was a bear," Miss Ludlow's eyes widened with excitement.

Becca forced herself to smile as she tied the collar of her dark cloak beneath her chin.

"Who started these rumors?" She was horrified and amused at the version of herself society had created. Had she been as silly as these girls when she was fifteen?

"I will see you in the carriage," Augusta said in a tone that conveyed she'd had enough of the conversation. Then she nodded and slipped out the door.

"You answered our question with a question," Miss De Lancey teased. "It must be true then."

"Which? The bear or the cat?" Becca asked.

"Tell us," Miss Ludlow begged.

Becca suddenly felt smothered by all the falsehoods she'd told since her arrival in New York. She was not the woman who betrayed her husband for love of King and country. She was not the silly country girl who only wished society to embrace her. What harm could there be in feeding society the tiniest teaspoon of truth?

"Only one black bear, and only because he was ready to maul my father." She recalled the flies that circled the bear's carcass almost immediately after, the regret she'd felt at the need to take down the magnificent beast. "I was terrified."

The girls shrieked. They were playacting. She already regretted her words. Finally, with a promise to see Miss Ludlow and Miss De Lancey again soon, she stepped out of the house and into the cold.

At the curb, Cousin Samuel's driver adjusted the harness on one of the two horses.

Becca called to him as she tiptoed onto one of the mounting blocks that dotted the street and opened the carriage door.

On the seat, a red plaid blanket was folded neatly into thirds and then again into a square.

The carriage was empty. Becca leaped down from the carriage, slipping on the snow. The street was empty. She rounded the carriage and grabbed the driver's arm. "Where is Lady Augusta?"

"She went with the gentleman, meek as a lamb she was." He pulled away, offended.

"What gentleman. When?" Her breath came in sharp gasps.

One of the horses whinnied as if to hurry them along.

"A few minutes ago." He jerked his chin to Mrs. Lathrop's front door. "A coach comes 'round the corner. It stops here." He pointed next to the carriage. "The man steps out. He bows a 'how'dya'do' and greets Lady Augusta like they was old friends."

The coachman scratched his ear. "Funny, though. Her voice was all cold like it gets with a stranger who don't have a right to talk to you. I didn't hear it all. But he said as how it would be good for everyone if she went back to the house."

"Back to my cousin's house?"

"Well, he didn't say, now you mention it. And madam had a message for you." His lips tightened in reproach. "I would a' told you right away if you hadn't grabbed my arm. Lady Augusta says to me, 'I know my daughter-in-law will worry. Tell her she would have done the same. She would have accepted the kind offer.'"

"Accepted what offer? From whom?" She wanted to shake his arm again to make him hurry.

The coachman's chest puffed out in pride. "Why the mayor's offer. The mayor of New York City himself took your mother-in-law."

"Hurry, then." The wind wrapped itself around her throat. Mayor Matthews had paid to keep Philip safe until last summer. And when he stopped paying protection money, Philip died. What did the mayor want with Augusta?

The coachman wouldn't meet her gaze as he helped her down to the granite step at the curb in front of Cousin Samuel's house. She felt a pang of remorse. She would apologize to him later for her behavior.

Becca heard men's voices rise from the drawing room as she slipped through the front door. She tiptoed closer.

"She's had no visitors, you say?"

"Only the dressmaker," Samuel said. "She comes almost every day lately. But no one else. I told that to your men, both of them, each time they came."

Both of them. The men who'd been watching her. *Each time they came.* No wonder Samuel had been listening to her from the shadows since they'd arrived. How much was the mayor paying him to eavesdrop?

The grandfather clock chimed five o'clock. Becca stepped into the drawing room.

The stranger sat facing the door in the room's best wing chair, the one whose pink satin upholstery was not shredded along the arm rails.

A tray of golden scones, a pot of jam and one of clotted cream were arrayed along a half-moon table beside him.

Samuel hovered nearby.

Augusta sat in a smaller chair on the far side of the fireplace.

Becca swayed with relief.

The stranger stood. He was as tall as General Washington and as fastidious in his clothing, but the overall effect was more of dissipation than strength. He wore a velvet maroon waist coat with gold embroidery and brass buttons, which failed to hide a growing paunch. A gold lace jabot framed the jowls along his jaw line.

Becca sprinted to Augusta and crouched by her chair. "Are you well?"

The older woman patted her hand but didn't speak.

123

Augusta was *not* well. Her palm was icy. Becca rose, anger replacing fear. "Cousin. Would you introduce us?"

The mayor didn't wait for Samuel to speak. "It's a pleasure, Mrs. Parcell. The beautiful silent one. Isn't that what they call you? Your praises are sung everywhere." His forehead furrowed. "But it seems I have upset you."

Her hands curved into fists. "You took Lady Augusta. Why?"

"Take?" Matthews' eyebrows rose in surprise.

"Pay her no mind, Your Honor. Her disposition is unsociable, despite what people say. It is unnatural, in fact." Samuel's glare threatened to burn her alive.

The cords along the sides of Augusta's neck were taut. "The mayor told me that he hated the thought of anything happening to me or to you. He told me that this could be a dangerous city, and that it was within his purview to keep the two of us safe."

That was why Augusta left the coachman with that message: "Tell her she would have done the same. She would have accepted the kind offer."

Becca caught a moment of irritation in the mayor's face before it disappeared. "Quite right, madam. It was my privilege to ensure your safety."

"Safety? You threatened her," Becca said. The mayor had made his point. Neither she nor Augusta were safe from him so long as they remained here.

"What a refreshing directness of expression. Would you mind leaving us, Lady Augusta?" The mayor's voice cooled, "And you too, Samuel."

A moment later, Matthews strolled to the window and stared out at the stone-fronted two- and three-story homes across the way. The border between buildings and sky had been erased as evening darkened to charcoal gray.

His movements were stiff, exaggerated, as if he watched himself from a distance and, with each movement, asked himself how an important man should stand or walk.

He was a small man in a large man's body, she thought.

He turned. "Sit. Please."

She remained standing.

"I suppose I've earned your suspicion. But I mean you no harm. Truly. And if I had my way, we would meet only at parties and speak only of the weather or the evening's meal."

He threatened at one moment and was kind the next. "Your Honor, I have no talent for subtlety. If there's something you wish to say, could you get to it?"

His smile was sad. "The problem is that your husband was not one of General Washington's spies. Which means that you did not turn him over to the British Army. You, madam, are here under false pretenses."

She was aware suddenly of everything in the room, the cold creeping in through the windows, the threadbare navy rug, a chip in the dish that held pastries. This feeling was familiar. It was the moment when hunter and prey recognized each other but hadn't yet decided whether to attack or retreat.

Admit nothing. "The mob in Morristown left me with this." She lifted a sweep of hair from her forehead and exposed the new scar. "I came here for protection. I had nowhere else to go."

He continued as if she hadn't spoken. "Your husband made his own fate, madam, as do we all."

There was something regretful in his expression. "I know you take no side in this battle. Yet you'll lose your home if you fail to satisfy your General Washington. Is this the freedom the American traitors offer you?" he scoffed. "Threatening to steal your land? Placing you here in danger?"

How does he know?

Matthews' hand rose and swung wide appearing to take in the entire city, the forest paths native people had walked for centuries, the mansions with their gilded moldings, the harbors that brought goods from as far as China. "Isn't this what we all want? To be left alone to live a peaceful life?"

Becca started to nod, then stopped herself. That was exactly what she wanted. But not from the man who threatened Lady Augusta and who had a hand in her husband's death. "I have already asked you twice. What do you want?"

He leaned toward her. "I can give you that life, Mrs. Parcell. That is what I came to tell you. I am authorized to grant you land, a farm in your name.

You'll own it outright with the servants to run it. It's a fertile spot just off the Bloomingdale Road north of here. All yours: not your cousin's, not your mother-in-law's. The road's name means 'flower valley' in Dutch. I hear it's a lovely place."

Land that no one could take from her. Ever. A safe place with no dark shadows. A farm in a valley of flowers. She would take care of Augusta and Annie. She wondered whether honeysuckle grew there each June.

"There's only one thing." Matthews' eyes drew her with a warmth she'd missed since her father died.

Perhaps she'd misjudged him. Becca leaned forward.

"I need to speak to Mr. Alloway."

"Ah." The mayor thought to lure her with the promise of land. He'd almost succeeded. She flushed with shame. "I don't know where he is."

The kind expression faded. "You don't—"

"Know where he is." She closed her eyes to hide her thoughts. She had killed a bear to save her father, but this was different. She couldn't sacrifice Daniel to keep Augusta safe. And she wouldn't sacrifice either for land.

"And yet Mr. Alloway is here to protect you."

"I cannot help you." She lifted her gaze. There really was a traitor in Morristown. How else would Matthews know that General Washington sent Daniel to accompany her?

Matthews' shrug was eloquent, as if he'd expected the answer. "I will guarantee Lady Augusta's safety until my ball tomorrow evening. You have until then to tell me where your Mr. Alloway can be found. After that, her safety is in your hands. Think about that as you consider your options."

Chapter Twenty-Five

Pools of candlelight lit the snow-coated sidewalk outside Mayor Matthews' residence on Water Street, just steps from the East River. Its endless windows and honey-colored bricks seemed to glow in the winter darkness.

Becca craned her neck to watch the mayor's guests arrive.

"It's not too late," Augusta said. "We need not attend."

"Rubbish," Samuel sputtered. "This is the party of the season, and you're the guest of honor."

Carriage after carriage deposited couples dressed in velvets, brocades and silk. The women dipped their heads in greeting, their hair glittering with pearls, feathers and jewels. Men called to one another, their posture declaring that their presence honored their host. Then they disappeared into the house, past servants waiting at attention by the twin columns that bordered the entrance.

Augusta grasped Becca's hand as their carriage slowed.

"The plan is sound. You said so last evening," Becca whispered.

"Plan?" Samuel's eyes narrowed with suspicion. "Are you searching for a new husband? What plan?"

Becca ignored him. The thought of standing next to the mayor, of having to speak to him tonight, scared her. But the idea of returning to Morristown without more information for General Washington scared her even more. Thomas had said that the general was growing impatient. She swallowed the lump in her throat. She'd learned nothing of her husband's list of spies and found nothing of Philip's hidden in Samuel's house. She needed this plan to work.

The carriage slowed to a stop, and a bald servant opened the carriage door.

On the sidewalk, Becca paused. Her eyes strained west, skimming the shores of the river as if the prison hulk where Philip spent his last days could materialize in the dark. She pulled the edges of her silver cloak round her throat.

Augusta touched her elbow and the two women swept into the mansion with Samuel trailing behind.

* * *

On any other night, Becca would have admired the soaring height of the ceiling, the four large marble fireplaces and five crystal chandeliers. The candlelight was doubled as it reflected off gold-leafed mirrors hung on each double-height wall.

Tonight, pinned in place between her host and hostess, she hardly noticed. The reception line was endless.

Becca's navy gown shimmered with crystals that spilled diagonally from its low bodice across her hips to the gown's edge. "Like shooting stars," the dressmaker had said. She was right. The dress was a masterpiece. But Becca's shoulder muscles ached with the effort of balancing the weight of her hair, which threatened to topple her each time she nodded to a new guest. Teased into a gem-encrusted, powdered spectacle, it extended a foot above the top of her head.

"How brave you are, my dear," one woman murmured to Becca. The next lady in line used almost the same phrase. Then the next, all while examining her from head to toe.

What could she possibly say? How kind of you to believe that I led my husband to his death? Becca swallowed her outrage until it was a lump just below her heart.

The chilly front hall grew warmer as new guests arrived. Voices mingled with the sound of musicians playing a minuet in the ballroom.

CHAPTER TWENTY-FIVE

The final guest in the reception line was a frail gentleman wearing a faded black velvet coat. He looked like he had been ancient back when the war against the French and Native Americans began twenty years ago. He completed his unsteady bow to the mayor's wife and stopped abruptly before her.

"Mr. Riker, madam. At your service." He winked at Becca and smiled. "We met at the Lathrops."

"Of course," she murmured. The shoes pinched her feet. Her head was beginning to ache.

"I knew your husband."

She was halfway through her nod when she heard what he said. "You knew my husband?"

His sparse eyebrows rose so high that they creased his forehead into dunes. "Should have known he was a rum cove after I bought his whiskey. It was despicable." The smile widened.

A rum cove. Yes, Philip was a rogue. She grinned in response. She couldn't help it. "Where did you meet him?"

"Why, here of course." He blinked cloudy blue eyes. His powdered wig was slightly fuzzy, as if it had been packed and unpacked too many times over the years. Mr. Riker was taller than she. But she didn't feel as if he were looking down at her.

"You met Mr. Parcell here? At the mayor's house?" She must stop repeating his every word.

"Of course." He beamed. "The politicians and merchants accomplish most of their work at parties such as this."

She hoped he wasn't serious. But Cousin Samuel had told her that this was the heart of the merchant community. Old merchant families like the de Peysters, the Schermerhorns and the Waltons had built their fortunes here.

She suddenly wondered how the mayor had made enough money to build a home in the wealthiest quarter of town.

"Did you know my husband well, Mr. Riker?"

"No, not well. I saw him at the occasional ball. A pity about his–ahhh–po-

129

litical affiliation. It was a surprise to me, I admit."

"Why?"

"Because in all our conversations, he never mentioned the politics of the day. He seemed to have no interest." Mr. Riker shook his head.

Her husband had no interest in politics until he developed a pretend passion for independence to disguise his spycraft.

From the corner of her eyes, Becca watched two lines form between the mayor's eyes. *He doesn't like my questions.*

"What did you speak of then?"

"Why, he was intrigued by my collection of maps of North America. Or perhaps he was humoring me."

Her mouth opened then closed. Philip had no interest in maps, either. There was one framed map in Philip's study, but it was a common decoration.

"No need to upset Mrs. Parcell with memories of her husband, Riker," the mayor interrupted. "You go on now. I wouldn't want you to miss a free meal."

Mrs. Matthews gasped at her husband's rudeness.

Was that a look of revulsion on her face, Becca wondered, or was it just that the unfortunate shade of olive green she wore that made the mayor's wife look slightly nauseated?

The old man frowned at Matthews before returning his attention to Becca. "Thank you for making an old man's evening. I enjoyed our conversation." He bowed over her hand, nodded to Mrs. Matthews, and walked past the mayor with the thump of his brass-headed cane.

Matthews lifted his arm, inviting Becca to take it.

It took all the discipline she could muster to place her hand lightly on his forearm. His coat sleeve was a soft velvet. Her palm barely brushed the fabric.

"Excuse us, Mrs. Matthews," he said to his wife with the old formality between spouses. But he'd already turned his back on her as he led Becca away.

A river of velvet-, brocade-, and silk-clad men and women split around them like water flowing round two rocks in the long hall.

Finally, in a quiet alcove across from the ballroom, he leaned toward her, his false sympathetic smile locked firmly in place. "If you answer my question about Mr. Alloway quickly, we can spend the rest of the evening as I promised. We will speak only of the weather or the evening's meal."

"Do you have need of a new courier? I didn't mention it yesterday. I meant to, but you surprised me." Becca blurted the words she and Augusta practiced last night.

A dark flush bloomed along Matthews' jawline. "No, I don't need a new messenger. We have one. I need Mr. Alloway."

She felt a surge of triumph. *We* have a new messenger. The network of spies still existed. Someone had replaced Philip as its messenger.

Becca crossed her arms. Would he tell her more? "But I live in Morristown. I could be there, where you needed me." She widened her eyes. "And it would be safer to use me as a messenger than a man. The soldiers don't suspect women of smuggling."

A pulse quivered beneath his right eye. He brought his face close to hers. "This is my city, Mrs. Parcell. I know everything that happens here. Everything. And you are safe here only as long as I say you are safe." His voice was soft. "Your husband was safe only so long as I said he was safe."

Becca locked her knees so they wouldn't shake. The bandit, Mr. Mason, had told her the truth. The mayor had paid, then stopped paying, for Philip's safety. If she had her knife, she might have stabbed Matthews right then.

"Now where is Mr. Alloway?"

She pushed her jaw out. "You can go to...."

"I have been looking simply everywhere for you, Mrs. Parcell." Phoebe Lathrop rushed toward Becca, her plump arms wide in greeting.

The mayor pulled his chin back to avoid being hit by the petite model of a British ship of the line, a war ship, that decorated Mrs. Lathrop's foot-tall coiffure.

Becca blew her breath out through pursed lips and counted backward to calm herself. *100. 89. 78. 67.* Better.

"Such a lovely party, Your Honor." Mrs. Lathrop lifted one hand to the bodice of her dress.

Matthews' eyes followed the motion of her hand as it landed on her ample breasts. "My honor entirely, Mrs. Lathrop."

"I didn't realize that you and Mrs. Parcell were such–close–friends." Her gaze turned from one to the other with bright pleasure, as if she were watching a play at the Theatre Royal on John Street.

"Excusing the interruption, sir." A young footman slid toward Matthews, whispering into his ear. The mayor's mouth flattened into a grimace. Then he swerved away down the long hall without taking his leave.

Mrs. Lathrop flicked open her blue and white chinoiserie fan as if flinging a knife. "And what are we women to do while the men speak of business? Your husband was the same, you know. He would stop mid-sentence if the mayor called. They would hide themselves in the mayor's library, even at a party such as this."

"Did you ever overhear them?" Becca asked.

"No. I hear enough about the war from my husband. Such dull talk."

"The mayor's library? Is it...?"

"Down the hall and to the right." Mrs. Lathrop bobbed her head. The miniature ship floating on her wig listed as a real boat would in heavy weather.

What was so important, Becca wondered, that Matthews would desert his guests? "Would you excuse me, Mrs. Lathrop?"

The woman gripped Becca's arm. "I do have a question, first. It's rather personal."

Mrs. Lathrop lifted the fan to her mouth to hide her conversation. "I intend to engage in a flirtation with your Mr. Lockwood. Because we are friends, I wanted you to know." She watched Becca carefully.

"Excuse me?" Becca couldn't possibly have heard right.

"No? You disapprove." Mrs. Lathrop's laughter was warm and throaty. She tapped Becca on the arm with her fan. "I saw the way you looked at Mr. Lockwood. Or to be precise, the way you did *not* look at Mr. Lockwood. You are not lovers."

"Of course not," she sputtered. "But I don't. I haven't." What type of city was this where women spoke of lovers with mere acquaintances?

And then Becca realized that she wasn't angry. She was not jealous. She felt–nothing. "Mr. Lockwood is not mine," Becca said and discovered that it was true. "Please. Do not worry on my account."

The fan snapped shut. "Why, thank you. That is quite a relief. I knew we should be friends."

Becca shook her head to clear it. "I hope you will forgive me." She curtsied, then followed the mayor's trail past the ballroom and down the long hallway.

* * *

William Cunningham lounged against the open doorway to the library, admiring the broad marble hallway of the mayor's mansion.

He winked at several of the youngest ladies as they passed. He could tell the moment they recognized him. Their expressions froze, and they rushed by, fans snapping shut. The men nodded curtly, then altered course.

All the years of waiting, of toadying up to men like Matthews, were over. Or they would be over tonight. Cunningham stroked the yellow silk wallpaper on which he leaned. Perhaps he would purchase a similar wall covering for the mansion he would buy after the war was won.

The mayor barely stopped to greet the men of the city as he zigzagged down the long gleaming hallway.

His smile tightened when he saw Cunningham. "Pleased you could make it." Matthews' voice carried. He grasped Cunningham's upper arm, his thumb jamming into his skin.

"Pleased to finally be invited." Cunningham's tone was ironic. He wasn't invited. He'd never been invited.

He covered Matthews' hand, in turn, with an iron grip. From a distance, they would look like close friends.

"In here. Now," Matthews gestured toward the library.

Cunningham shook off Matthews' hand and sauntered into the room.

The mayor kicked the door shut behind him. It reopened an inch with the absence of force behind the blow.

Can't even do that right, Cunningham thought, leaning against the large mahogany desk at the far end of the study.

"What were you thinking, coming here?" Matthews asked.

Cunningham scooped up a lead crystal paperweight from the desk. He felt its weight, its sharp edges. It would be so simple to bash in the mayor's head. "Sir Henry Clinton is sending a delegation of three men to Morristown."

Matthews' eyebrows lifted. "How did you learn that?"

"They leave in two days," Cunningham continued. "You will invite them to dinner tomorrow, and I will speak to them."

"I don't take orders from you," Matthews spit.

"In fact, you do." He savored the look on the mayor's face. More puzzlement than shock. The shock would come. "You haven't heard from the man in Morristown lately, the one you call The Correspondent." It was a statement. Not a question. "And you won't be hearing from him again."

The parchment rustled as Cunningham pulled it from his pocket. He held it out.

Matthews took it. He chewed on his bottom lip as he read the brief note, then lifted his head. There was a reddish rim around his mouth, as if he'd bitten the flesh around it. "How did you find him?"

This was almost too satisfying. "My men followed your new messenger back to Morristown. I sent them with a letter for your Correspondent. I pointed out your prior failures in spycraft.

"I told him you'd already bungled an attempt to kill Washington with, of all things, a bowl of poisoned peas. I said you were still a laughingstock among those who knew." It was back in '76. "Why give the mayor another chance to fail? I asked him." Cunningham leaned against the desk.

Matthews flinched. "That wasn't my fault. I'm not the one who picked Hickey for the job."

"And then I offered my services. Of course, you'll be paid for any services you render going forward," Cunningham said.

He waited for the mayor to fully understand that their roles had changed. "I have a package for the British officers leaving for Morristown. I'll hand it to them at the dinner you'll arrange."

"What's this dinner about?"

134

CHAPTER TWENTY-FIVE

He'd save the best for last. "That isn't your concern."

Matthews stared at the red and blue Turkish rug beneath his feet.

Footsteps echoed in the hallway, the sounds of a man's heavy boots and a quicker, lighter set of steps.

Cunningham watched the mayor's chest rise and fall. He'd wasted his wife's dowry on his gambling debts, the gossips said. He collected new ones as quickly as old ones were retired. He would take what he could get, even if it meant taking orders from Cunningham.

Matthews rubbed his hand along his forehead as if to wipe away his thoughts. "What about Alloway? What did you say about my compensation?"

It's over. I've won. "If you can manage to find him, we'll discuss compensation." Cunningham released the heavy paperweight. One sharp corner gashed the desk's dark wood.

Whatever plan The Correspondent's cabal had put in place was drawing close to success. But that wasn't anything that Matthews needed to know.

"Should I kill Alloway?" the mayor asked.

"No. You'd bungle it. I'll take care of it."

* * *

Becca zigzagged through the crowd. A few women trilled her name, but she turned her head away, pretending not to hear.

Turning a corner, she strode as quickly as her heels allowed down a long hallway papered in a nubby yellow silk. The floor gleamed with black-and-white tiles.

She heard Matthews before she saw him. His voice boomed, "So pleased you could make it."

There. Down the hall, the mayor gripped the upper arm of a stocky stranger whose light blue waistcoat was trimmed in thick gold braid. The man's smile displayed small, widely spaced teeth.

Even from a distance, Becca caught the barely disguised contempt in the shorter man's grin.

The mayor released the stranger's arm and the two men disappeared into the study.

She glided toward the door, stopping when she heard their voices. The door was open a crack.

"What were you thinking coming here?" the mayor asked.

What if they walked out now? She slipped into an adjacent room to listen undetected. In the dark, her shoulder hit something heavy. She reached out and found her hands tangled in hard wire strings. A harp. A music room. She kept hold of the strings so they wouldn't twang.

A few minutes later, Matthews asked, "Should I kill Alloway?"

"No. I'll take care of it," the stranger answered as calmly as if he were offering to pour cream for tea.

The conversation ended. The first man left. His footsteps were light and faded fast. The second man had a heavier tread. She waited.

A queasy mix of exhilaration and nausea roiled her stomach. Daniel was still alive. But the stranger spoke of his death as if it was of no matter. A life should matter, she thought. Daniel's life mattered.

Seconds passed. Minutes, perhaps.

Becca uncurled her stiff fingers from the harp strings. Days ago, she sent a note to Mr. Rivington's print shop requesting a book, *The Castle of Otranto*. She wanted to speak to Daniel, and her message was intended to bring him.

Cousin Samuel had snatched the response from the small boy who delivered it. He read the terse note out loud: *"Sadly, Madam, the Book is not currently available."*

She sent a second note to Mr. Rivington's shop after Mrs. Lathrop's party. This time, Becca found the opened, discarded response on the front hall table: *The Proprietor understands the distress the Reader must feel when a Book is unavailable. Be assured that the Shop will deliver the Title that Madam seeks as soon as it is found.*

Found? She felt the same irritation now that she had felt when she read that note. She would find Daniel whether or not he wished to be "found." He needed to leave New York, tonight if possible.

Over the sound of her breath, Becca listened for footsteps. The hall was silent. She slipped out to retrace her steps, then hesitated, peeking into the mayor's study. A framed map of New York City above the desk was flanked by portraits of Mr. and Mrs. Matthews. The artist had captured a feeling of dread in the mayor's eyes.

Becca wondered how he could stand to see that image of himself each day.

In the distance, a high-pitched bell trilled. The guests were gathering for dinner.

Chapter Twenty-Six

"I don't care if you faint. You are staying," Samuel said through teeth clenched into a smile. He nodded at the endless de Peyster and de Lancey relatives who stopped to bow and curtsey to them in the wide hall.

The crowd flowed toward the dining room, their voices loud with drink and good spirits.

Becca pulled against his hand, which held her forearm tight. He had flung himself at her as she fought her way against the throng toward the cloakroom to retrieve her cloak.

He hadn't let go of her since.

The mayor and his wife stood to the right of the dining room entrance as their guests flowed into the room.

"Steady. Just another minute now," Augusta whispered.

Becca prayed her mother-in-law was right.

She saw the moment Matthews noticed her. His head rose as if she'd called to him. He strode toward her.

Becca tugged at Samuel's arm again. She caught a flash of movement out of the corner of her eye. A man in a gold and white brocade waistcoat and gold breeches headed toward the mayor, blocking Matthews. Mr. Gold-and-white brocade gestured broadly as he spoke. The white lace at his cuffs sparkled as brightly as whitecaps on a summer day.

There was something familiar about him, Becca thought.

Augusta's expression brightened.

"Now you can go," Samuel purred, dropping her arm. "Everyone important has seen me." A glow of satisfaction lit his face as he ambled toward the dining room.

Becca whirled to Augusta. "Tell the mayor I've taken ill but that I agree to his terms."

"I will not." Augusta's chin lifted in affront.

"I must leave. I'll explain later. But I can't leave worrying about you. I need to know that you're safe," Becca said. Matthews had used Augusta's safety to threaten Becca. "Tell the mayor I agree to his terms."

Augusta's attention was frozen on the mayor and the stranger. She nodded, a half smile on her lips.

Becca lifted the edges of her navy gown and ran toward the front door, not stopping for her cape.

Samuel's coachman was walking two horses in slow circles in the street to keep them warm in the winter chill. At the sight of her, he hurried the animals back to the carriage.

Within minutes, the mayor's mansion was behind her.

* * *

In the dressing room of Samuel's house, Becca placed her fingers at the back of her wig and began to remove each of the small pins that kept it in place. "I don't know what I would do without your friendship. You do know that?"

"Oh, stop your nonsense," Annie mumbled, though she flushed pink at the praise.

Becca lifted the wig and held it out to Annie, raising it over her head.

A short time later, Becca blew out the candles in the room. She peered out the window, her gaze following the woman in the elegant powdered wig standing on the front stoop. The driver assisted her into the carriage.

Annie and Becca looked nothing alike. But she hoped that the men who'd followed her back to Cousin Samuel's house would only notice the fine wig sitting atop Annie's head and the green cape that belonged to Augusta.

She hoped that, in the dark, they would assume Becca had merely stopped here briefly in between parties.

Becca held her breath as Annie and the driver pulled away. They would return to the mayor's house. Annie would wait in the carriage until Samuel and Augusta were ready to leave the party.

Becca had counted to thirty when she saw the cart with two drivers, cloaked in shadows, pull away from the curb down the street and follow after Annie.

She retraced her steps to study the finely etched map of New York City that hung on the wall of Samuel's library. She would find her way to Mr. Rivington's shop to warn Daniel.

A walk straight down Queen Street to Rivington's place would leave her exposed. The safest path was down Maiden Lane to the docks and then back to Wall Street. She could hide in any number of small alleys if necessary.

Eventually, she pulled the hood of Annie's black wool cape low over her face and disappeared into the dark alley behind the house. At each corner, she stopped to listen, waiting to ensure she was alone. It took longer but made her feel safe.

At the edge of the river, a cheerful blurry voice barreled through the frigid night air in front of her. *"T'was Summer and softly the breezes were blowing. And sweetly the nightingale sang from the tree-e-e-e-e."*

Becca held still. He looked like an abandoned heap of old clothes. Just a drunk singing off the evening's ale, she told herself.

Go forward or turn back? She broke away from the wall and slid forward on ice into the shadow of a pile of barrels near the East River. That was when she heard more footsteps.

"Oy, Humphrey," an exasperated voice called.

I know that voice. Becca peeked around the side of the rough wooden barrel.

A tall shadow of a man stood over the drunk. In profile, she saw an outsized, hooked nose.

The memory rose so quickly it might have been waiting for her call. A man with a nose like this, a man with this voice, had stood behind the Ferret in the shadows. He and another man ran when Sergeant Bartlett took his shot.

"You were supposed to follow her, you sod, not getting cock'd." She heard the slick sound of skin slapping skin. "I had to get the others to watch her because of you."

Becca squatted behind the barrel. She placed one hand on the icy ground for balance. Her hand burned with the cold. She ignored it.

Humphrey moaned. "I watched her good. I watched her in that carriage all the way to the mayor's," Humphrey whined. "She won't be going nowhere 'til after midnight. It's cold. There was a tavern. You'd a gone in, too."

"Cunningham said not to leave her and what do you do?" Another slap.

"Ahh, she ain't goin' nowhere. Not for a while. Want to head back to the tavern?" Humphrey asked hopefully.

The metallic taste of blood filled Becca's mouth. She'd bitten the inside of her lip. There should be an alley behind her that traversed straight through to the print shop. She swiveled and found the dark passage she expected between two warehouse walls. If she could cross the few feet of open space while the barrels blocked her from the men's view, she might reach the alley undetected.

"If I didn't have to take over your shift in an hour, I'd go back and tell Cunningham to cut your damn ears off." The second man kicked a barrel near his drunken colleague.

Becca pushed against the balls of her feet, aiming for the alley. Something pulled her back. She heard her cape begin to rip. The barrel that hid her bobbled, scraping the frozen ground. She froze.

"Aww, thanks Jackson."

"Get up. You're going to be sober, like it or not."

Humphrey squealed. "My ear. Let go."

Another slap. "Get up. Now."

A pair of steady footsteps and a second unsteady set shuffled across ice heading toward her.

Becca's hand groped along the taut edge of the cape. A piece of wool was impaled on a sharp edge of the metal barrel hoop. She tugged, and the barrel began to tip again. It froze at an unnatural angle, half upright, half fallen.

"I wish to God they'd give your job to the boss' new messenger. I'm tired of carrying you," Jackson muttered.

Becca's gaze climbed from one dark barrel hoop to the next, past the rivets, to a hand holding the barrel steady.

She craned her neck further. Daniel stood glowering down at her. Gently righting the barrel, he stooped and grabbed a handful of ice, flinging it low and far down the street.

The ice pellets landed beneath the overhang of the building where Humphrey was singing.

Becca shrugged off her cape.

"The hell?" Jackson said, more a question than a curse. Footsteps headed toward the ice pellets.

"Just ice off the roof, I warrant." Humphrey hummed under his breath.

Daniel jerked his chin toward the dark passageway as Jackson went to investigate. Becca held her skirts up to her knees and sprinted, following Daniel into the alley.

Chapter Twenty-Seven

Daniel and Becca sprinted through the alley and onto Queen Street. Dark window fronts seemed to follow their progress as they ran down the snow-swept street. Daniel led Becca toward a dimly lit window.

Within, Daniel watched Mr. Rivington stoop over his long gray printing press, oiling its sides. The light of a single lantern cast a warm glow round him. A stained brown apron covered his dressing gown. A white cap covered grizzled gray hair.

Daniel tapped softly on the glass window. Rivington's head jerked up. He disappeared from view. The room went dark.

A moment later, the door swung out, and Daniel and Becca tumbled into the shop. Rivington searched the street behind them, then closed the wooden door. A lock clicked into place. The sweet smell of printer's ink permeated the air.

Rivington hardly seemed surprised to find them on his doorstep in the last hours of the night. He nodded curtly to Daniel, then said, "You must be Rebecca Parcell. I expected to meet you, madam, but not at this hour. Step away from the window, please."

Becca followed Rivington past the counter and toward stairs along the back wall of the shop.

Daniel trailed behind, feeling pressure build in his chest. She could have been killed. *My fault.* At the foot of the stairs, he exploded, "Do you know what could have happened to you wandering the streets like that?"

"Wandering?" Becca poked his chest with one long finger. "I came for you.

You didn't answer my note."

"I should have stopped you when you left your cousin's bloody house."

Her chin lifted as Daniel knew it would. "You were following me?" Her eyes narrowed. He knew that expression, too.

"Yes, I followed you. Every day." He'd memorized the way her wide skirts swung when she walked, the curve of her waist, how she lifted her face to the sky just before entering a home as if she craved the extra moment of fresh air. When he closed his eyes, her image visited him unbidden.

"Ever since I saw you were watched," he continued, "I sent you a note to warn you. I thought you had enough sense to know danger." He stopped at the expression on her face. Perhaps he'd gone too far.

"Why, you bloody, pig-headed…." she sputtered, seeming to search for the right insult. " …Man. I bloody well can take care of myself. And that is a good thing, because you did not answer my note." Her face inches from his, she poked him again and again to punctuate each word.

"You were being watched. I couldn't come to you and you couldn't come to me." He grabbed her hand.

They both went still. The tip of her tongue flicked to the side of her lips. Her eyes were violet in the low light.

"If you're finished now," Rivington said drily.

She swallowed and slowly slipped her hand from his.

The printer directed them up the stairs in the dark. "That's right, madam. Six steps to go. Now just three. There's a landing. Just through that door."

Daniel exhaled a shuddering breath. He felt the imprint of her finger on his chest. Its warmth radiated throughout his body. *Damnation.*

* * *

She was a widow, after all, not a girl. She recognized the sensations washing over her, through her, really. The throbbing sensation low in her stomach, the way her skin warmed when he took her hand.

She sensed Daniel close behind her on the stairs. What would happen if she stopped suddenly, she wondered, if he didn't notice in time? How would his chest feel pressed against her back, his thighs curved into the back of her legs?

She flushed. There was something clearly wrong with her. Philip had been right. "You act like a whore in bed, not a lady," he'd said once as he rolled away from her. She hadn't known that there were rules for how ladies behaved in the marriage bed. The last thing she needed now was the distraction of her body's reaction to Mr. Alloway. *Damnation.*

"We'll get you warm and see you back safe to your cousin's." Mr. Rivington was surprisingly nimble. He slipped past her, then closed the curtains in the room to which he'd directed her.

She listened to the hiss of a match, then watched the candle flare to life. The comfortable sitting room was sepia-toned in the gentle light. It held a round dining table and several chairs, most of which were covered in books. Daniel prowled the room, positioning himself behind the dining table, close to the wall and as far as possible from Becca.

"Tell us why you came," Rivington said.

Becca came to rest behind a chair as far from Daniel as possible. "I had to come." She rearranged the events of the evening until they lined up as neatly as a column of numbers. "I attended the mayor's ball tonight. I heard Mr. Matthews talking to someone. They said they mean to kill Daniel."

She stopped for a breath. "Not 'they,' not the mayor. The other man said he would kill you." Becca lifted her gaze to him just long enough to make certain she had his attention, then lowered her chin to her chest.

"Did you see him, the other man?" Rivington asked.

"He was shorter than the mayor. Portly. And his smile." She shuddered. "Those teeth."

"Small teeth like a child's?" Daniel's voice was distant, as if the answer didn't matter.

She nodded.

"Cunningham." Rivington turned to Daniel. "Cunningham is looking for you. You need to go."

"I recognized one of the men in the alley," she said. "You knew his friend, the Ferret." Her stomach dipped at the memory of the short man who'd

145

been killed in her yard.

"Cunningham's men." Daniel looked past her.

"They mentioned his name." Becca almost turned around, half expecting to see the two men who'd been searching for her.

"And have you led them to me?" Rivington's voice was sharp.

"No, she's not foolhardy. Not that foolhardy," Daniel corrected himself.

"How do you know they didn't follow you?" Rivington asked.

"I heard one of them. They said they were looking for a tavern," Becca said. The wild energy of the night was draining, leaving her cold and aching.

"I heard them, too," Daniel added. "And there were no footsteps behind us. We were careful."

"We have a bit of time then. The only tavern open all night is on the Bowery," Rivington said. "We'll get you warm and make plans to see you back safe to Morristown."

Chapter Twenty-Eight

D aniel trailed Becca down the printer's narrow stairs.

In his mind, he watched her rush forward, growing smaller and smaller with distance. She would return to Morristown, to her farm. He would move on. He always did. His memory of her would grow distant with time. The thought unsettled him.

One of Rivington's servants waited outside to escort Becca back to Samuel's house. The printer had promised to send a carriage for Becca, Daniel, Augusta and Annie by late tomorrow. They would leave for home.

Daniel placed the stump of a candle he held on a rough wooden table near the printer's back wall. It was a display of his wares, papered with the broadsides, maps, and fliers he printed along with his newspaper, the *Royal Gazette*.

"Your cousin won't be happy you're leaving." He sounded stiff, even to himself. "You were his entrée to this season's social events."

"I won't miss Samuel, although I should be grateful for his hospitality." Becca tightened the tie on the thin, dark cape she'd borrowed from one of the printer's servants, since Annie's had been left behind near the docks. The collar caught her hair, and she swept her hand behind her neck to free it.

Her dark hair cascaded down her back. Daniel had the urge to run his hands through it, then sweep it away to bare her neck and…. He tried to stretch his bad hand to force himself to focus on anything but her neck.

"Is it important that a delegation of redcoats will be visiting Morristown?" Becca asked.

Upstairs, she had told Rivington and Daniel about Cunningham's direction to Mayor Matthews: make sure that the delegation heading to Morristown meets here for dinner before they leave.

"If Cunningham and the mayor thought it was important, it must mean something," Daniel said. "Warning General Washington should be enough to earn your farm back."

"Thank you, sir." She dropped a playful curtsy. "And he shall reward you with silver." A sliver of bare skin glowed at the base of her neck.

He stared, then stepped out from behind the printer's counter.

The front window, with its multiple panes, reflected back into the room a wavy, broken image of the two of them facing each other.

Daniel bowed, pointing one foot forward as the gentry would. *What are you doing?* He lifted her hand to his lips. *Proving I'm alive.*

His mouth hovered over the tender center of her palm. He turned her wrist and pressed his lips to the back of her hand.

She didn't pull away. Then her hand went rigid.

He released it in surprise.

She stared over his shoulder, eyes wide.

He swiveled but saw only the printer's back wall display of broadsides, fliers and maps.

"It's the map," she said with wonder.

Daniel shook his head. His thoughts still focused on the feel of her skin on his lips.

"Mr. Riker said that my husband was interested in maps."

"Mr. Riker?"

"An old gentleman at the mayor's party." Becca pointed at the back wall, ignoring him. "Philip has that map in his study. The mayor has the same one in his. I saw it."

"I see the map but not your point," Daniel said.

"You found an invoice in my barn. The numbers made no sense. You said it could be in code." She smiled with excitement. "You said the way to figure out a code is to find the key, something Philip and the person who received his messages both own. What if that map is the key?"

The map consisted of a drawing of the island of Manhattan, framed by a border of cockleshells and leaves that appeared to bend in the wind. The lower portion of New York City included drawings of buildings, each marked by a letter.

He studied it, wishing he had printed something as fine as this map.

She swept past him. "Look. Here." Becca's fingers slid to a box on the top left portion of the map. "Here's the map's legend."

Daniel examined the box with its symbols that made sense of the map. The legend was simple. 'A' stood for the Military Hospital, 'B' for Trinity Church, 'C' for King's College and so on through 'Z.' Building names were matched to letters on the map.

Her fingers pointed to elegantly penned letters scattered over the map of the city. "And what do you see?"

Daniel shrugged. "If I want to know where to find St. Paul's Church, I'll look for an 'A' on the map." His finger came to rest just above hers. He inhaled her signature lavender scent.

Then he saw it. Building 'A'–St. Paul's—was located on the map at the intersection of a vertical and horizontal line. Numbers from one to ten traveled across the bottom of the map. Numbers from one to eight were set vertically along the left-hand margin.

"If I needed to write a word with the letter 'A,'" Daniel said, "I'd write 2-4, because the A is located along the horizontal line labeled '2' and along the vertical line labeled '4.'"

"You could write every letter of the alphabet by using two numbers that way." There was bright triumph in her eyes. "The traitors were writing their messages on receipts for Philip's whiskey. It might just be a jumble of numbers, but no one looks too closely."

"Except you. It's brilliant." They stood in a cocoon of wavering candlelight. Her face was inches from his.

Daniel memorized this moment, knowing that he would end it with his next breath. "Even if this is the code your husband used, that piece of paper I found in your barn must be almost a year old. It can't have anything to do with what's happening now."

149

"Oh." The light in her eyes dimmed.

He stepped away until his back bumped into the printer's counter. "The British must have changed the code by now."

"The British probably tore up this code when Philip died." She sighed, pushing away a strand of her hair.

He wanted to see her face light up again. "I'll make a copy of the map, and I'll bring the invoice tomorrow. We can look at them together."

She rewarded him with another luminous smile. "I'll see you in the afternoon." She slipped through the door to meet the waiting servant.

Chapter Twenty-Nine

The voices cursed, howled, and crooned. The sound battered his chest until he feared his heart would fracture. Daniel jolted awake, gulping air, kicking off the rough wool blanket in the small, dark room.

He swung his legs to the cold plank floor, not noticing the chill, and waited for his breath to calm as the voices faded to silence.

The voices belonged to the men who'd saved his life, the dead prisoners on the deck of the *Jersey*. He'd burrowed beneath them, almost suffocating under their weight in the heat of that summer day, until Cunningham's men shoveled them into the harbor.

He squeezed his eyes shut, as if that could block the memory: the shock of the water, bloated faces, arms, the weight of bodies, then kicking upward, and the searing pain when the sharp edge of an anchor chain sliced his hand.

Not real. The voices aren't real, he repeated to himself.

He'd find it easier to be grateful to the prisoners if he knew why they bothered to haunt him. On nights like this, with the echo of Cunningham's name fresh in his mind, he thought they were extending an invitation to join them.

There'd be no more sleep for him tonight. Restless, he rose and paced the small, dark room. He strode three steps from the bed to the window, back to the bed, then the window again. A slight glow lit the darkness, although daybreak was still a while off. Becca had left about two hours ago, he guessed.

He needed a distraction. Daniel wedged his hand between the feather bed and the straw mattress. He groped for Philip Parcell's invoice.

He slipped from his room and hovered at the top of the stairs. He listened. One snort; a second, then a mumble. Mr. Rivington was still asleep. Daniel carried a small taper downstairs and rested it in a saucer on a desk behind the shop's counter. The light wouldn't be visible from the street.

He removed the New York City map from its spot of honor on the wall and placed it gingerly on the counter. He borrowed a fresh piece of paper, and a pen and ink from the print shop desk, laid the fake invoice next to it and set to work.

Becca had called it a map code. Here would be the proof. Her hair had smelled of lavender. He shook his head to clear it and got to work.

It didn't take long. The portion of the message in his hand read *crate to back door. Thursday only. Watch for chalk mark.*

Daniel's index finger tapped the desk. Deliveries to whose back door?

The mayor's door. Daniel answered his own question. Mayor Matthews received messages from the "Correspondent" who lived in Morristown. That was what Becca heard at the ball last night.

Daniel dipped his pen into the inkwell and filled one more sheet, the goose quill scraping gently against the paper.

He blew out the sputtering candle. Then he returned everything to its place, crept upstairs, and dressed in silence. He shrugged on his greatcoat and walked uptown as a weak winter sun rose over the city.

"Deliveries Thursday only," the torn invoice read. Today was Thursday.

* * *

The frozen streets were filled with merchants loading goods onto wagons and horses. Servants rushed to market holding baskets with mittened hands and stopped to examine the day's goods. Wood houses gave way to mansions of granite and marble.

It wasn't fear of being discovered that slowed his step as he approached an ornate wrought-iron gate in front of the mayor's mansion. It was the slash of chalk on the otherwise shining gate that led to the kitchen building next to the house.

Crate to back door. Thursdays only the encoded note had said and *watch for the chalk*. There was the chalk mark.

What a brilliant signal, he thought. Just place a chalk mark in public when it's safe to deliver a message. Have the messenger erase it with the sleeve of his coat when he comes.

Daniel stood in an alley across the street and watched the dawn food deliveries to the mayor's mansion. Men hunched against the weather in their dark wool coats. They pushed wheelbarrows of oysters, cod, peacocks, duck, lamb and cured pork to the door, then waited for servants to unload the parade of food. Daniel guessed that there would be another party this evening.

Would a new messenger deliver a crate of whiskey or something else? And who would notice one extra delivery on a day with so many headed to the kitchen?

He strained to remember. Someone had talked about a new messenger. Rivington said he'd overheard something odd a Redcoat soldier had said: "The Lord might take better care of the new courier than the old."

Daniel's hair was stiff with the cold. He cupped his hands over his mouth and exhaled slowly for the paltry warmth his breath provided.

The rush of deliverymen fell to a trickle. The rich smell of roasting pork escaped from the kitchen across the street.

Daniel's stomach grumbled. He must have been addlepated to come out, he thought. He should get back to Rivington's shop.

He knew why he risked walking the streets this morning. He lied to others; never to himself. Becca had made all their discoveries. About the code. About the mayor and Cunningham. He'd done little more than follow her in the shadows. Daniel wanted to do something to earn her respect and his own.

So he crossed the icy street. He passed through the gate with the chalk mark. He knocked on the kitchen door.

A woman with frazzled gray hair and an equally frazzled expression yanked the door open. She wiped a beefy hand across her forehead, which was red with the heat of the kitchen. "Just leave yer delivery for my girl to bring in. Is that too hard to do?" She began to close the door.

Daniel tried on his most charming smile. "It looks like the master's hosting a big party tonight. Might you need extra help in the kitchen?"

"Who says I need help? Don't I always manage?" Her eyes narrowed with suspicion.

"Who has enough good help these days, with people coming and going with the insurrection? Everything's topsy-turvy ain't it?" Daniel added a hint of her accent to his speech.

"Well, that's true. Two girls left last week. Just up and went, they did." She wiped her hands on her apron. "Can't blame them, the way the master treats us." The cook blew her cheeks out. "And now I've got sixty dishes to make for tonight. Sixty."

"I can keep the fires going and carry the heavy things. You won't have to answer the door. I'll do that, too. It'll give you and the girls more time to cook."

Her look of suspicion returned.

"All I'm asking for my time is a meal or two." Playing on the cook's sympathy might be more productive than flirting. "I'll be no trouble."

She blinked, caught by a thought Daniel couldn't read. "Come in then. Be quick." She cuffed him on the side of his arm. "My boy's your age. Forced into the Navy, he was. They pressed him, damn the British. I pray someone'd take him in if he were a bag o' bones like you."

Daniel almost felt guilty as he walked behind her into the mayor's house.

* * *

The cook stabbed Daniel's chest with a still-warm baguette from the marble-topped pastry table. "You won't have the strength to carry a pigeon breast if you don't put some meat on those bones."

He grinned and bit into the firm, warm crust.

That was hours ago. The cook's curses multiplied as the kitchen heated up.

He wrestled a side of beef into the kitchen for her attention and dropped it on the massive oak table in the center of the room. His numb right hand was no problem so long as he balanced the larger cuts of meat or bags on his forearms.

The servant girls feverishly cut potatoes, carrots, apples and dark green herbs. The kitchen smelled of butter and fruit from the apple pies in the oven, of pork and beef tenderloin roasting in the main fireplace, and of savory spices.

He brought in turtles for soup, turnips and French champagne, doing his best to examine each delivery for something that didn't belong there, a sign that it held some secret.

As if it would be that easy, he thought with distaste. What a wasted effort. Of course the British changed the code and the day of the week that any new messengers made deliveries. Any fool would know better than to maintain the same code, the same routine.

It was time to collect his backpack from Rivington's place and wait for the carriage. The heat from the kitchen was suffocating. Daniel moved to the kitchen door, prepared to leave. He wiped sweat from his brow with the back of his numb hand and felt a slight prickling in his thumb. The new sensation made him pause, wondering if he had imagined it.

There was a demanding knock, as if someone was kicked the kitchen door, and it rattled. The sound put Daniel's teeth on edge. Let the merchant stand in the cold and learn some manners. He waited for the next kick and then slowly turned the handle. The cold air sliced through the heat of the kitchen.

"Sorry, I didn't hear you," he drawled.

"Damn it. I can't stand here all day."

Daniel grabbed for the open crate as it was shoved at his chest.

Crate to back door.

A streak of chalk ran from the man's cuff to the elbow of his wool coat sleeve.

Watch for chalk mark. Thursday.

A surge of energy clambered up his spine.

155

The delivery man's aggrieved voice came from the middle of his black broad-rimmed felt hat. He swiveled away from the door, calling, "I'll be back in an hour."

Glass clinked as Daniel balanced the crate.

Daniel set the crate down on the honey-colored wood floor. Was the message in the crate? Beneath one of the bottles? Was it Parcell's whiskey or someone else's?

Daniel could examine the bottles or catch the messenger. He couldn't do both. His gaze flickered from the messenger to the crate and back.

"Are ye bird-witted? Close the door," the cook yelled.

There was only one choice. Daniel scooped up a single bottle and sprinted out the door. This would do as a weapon.

The man in the wide-brimmed hat sauntered as he crossed the street. He was near the alley where Daniel had stood earlier to watch the mayor's house. He followed the new messenger, slamming the bottle against the mayor's gate as he passed it. Glass and whiskey exploded in a waterfall of glittering shards.

The new messenger turned at the sound, his eyes widening as Daniel slid toward him. "Help. I am attacked."

The man had a rare talent for stating the obvious. Daniel used his momentum, pushing the messenger into the alley. He pinned the man to the rough brick wall with his right forearm, holding the jagged edges of the broken bottle near his face.

Daniel's hold on the neck of the bottle loosened with surprise then tightened. He recognized the petulant, self-satisfied face of the man who had led the mob to Becca's house. Minister Townsend.

Rivington had overheard one of the redcoats joke that the Lord might take better care of the new courier than the old. Now it made sense. The minister was the new courier.

"There's nothing to steal. I have no money." Townsend's breath was ragged.

"Not money. That's not what I'm after, Minister."

Townsend recoiled at the use of his title.

"You delivered a box to the mayor's house. Who gave it to you?" Daniel raised the broken bottle to Townsend's eye level. Daniel's hand shook with the effort of holding the jagged edges of the bottle away from the parson's throat. Townsend had accused Becca of treason when, instead, he was the traitor.

The minister's eyes widened like a spooked horse. "A friend. Just a friend."

"What friend?"

Townsend slapped ineffectively against Daniel's arm. He blustered, "How dare you treat a minister this way?"

Daniel didn't bother rolling his eyes. "We'll let General Washington decide if I've mistreated you. He'll want to know why a Morristown pastor is delivering whiskey to the British. Is its Parcell's whiskey?"

A vein below Townsend's left eye throbbed. "I'm loyal to the general."

"Yet here you are delivering messages to the British in New York." Daniel maintained the pressure on Townsend's chest. He should walk away now. He and Becca had earned their rewards. They knew that Parcell, and now Townsend, delivered messages to the mayor. That's what General Washington wanted to know.

But it wasn't enough. Not now. Who wrote the notes that Townsend delivered to New York? Would he threaten Becca next?

During his weeks on the prison ship, Daniel learned that people needed to tell their secrets. They needed to know that their lives mattered, and they only mattered if they could shape those secrets into a story that they could relate.

He saw the moment that Townsend decided to tell his tale. The minister's cheeks sagged until his face resembled a drawing of a Greek drama mask that Daniel had printed once.

"I didn't mean for it to happen." Townsend looked into Daniel's eyes to make sure he was listening. "A man's got to live. Continental paper is worth nothing now. I believed Parcell when he said he'd repay me with interest. He was a gentleman."

"You loaned money to Parcell?"

"I lent him all I had for his damn whiskey still. He lost it all. I lost it all."

"And then?" Daniel asked.

"And then Parcell died a hero." The whites of Townsend's eyes were pink from the cold or self-pity. "And how would it look if the minister went after the local hero's widow to repay a debt? I couldn't. And besides, I had nothing in writing."

"So the widow inherited a farm and her freedom, and you were locked into poverty." Daniel released some of the pressure. He knew enough not to hurry the man. "You were desperate." *And you hated her for her good fortune.*

"And that's why you took Parcell's place."

Townsend looked confused. "His place?"

Daniel searched the minister's face. Townsend didn't know that Parcell had also been a messenger. "Go on." Whoever was in charge of the ring of spies in Morristown kept himself hidden from the minister.

"I was desperate. My salary wouldn't keep the missus and me, not with what the war has done to money. The minister's eyes shifted to the mud-stained snow. Townsend muttered something that Daniel couldn't hear.

"What?"

"At the end of the summer, I was ready to take my life, though it's a mortal sin. I said so at one of the taverns. I was drinking. Some of Washington's officers were passing through. I told them I was finished."

Daniel's brow wrinkled. "You told Washington's men?"

"They bought me rum." The minister grimaced.

"Who did you drink with? Which of Washington's men?"

"There was a man called Gibbs. I've seen him and a few others in Morristown. I was drunk. It was last summer. I don't know."

Not Gibbs. Daniel liked Caleb Gibbs, the commander of General Washington's personal guards. "And yet here you are." Daniel pressed down again on his chest.

Townsend looked down at the frozen ground and licked his colorless lips. "There was an envelope on my doorstep the next morning. After I drank with the soldiers last summer. After Parcell died without paying me back my money.

"It said I'd be paid three pounds sterling to deliver whiskey to the City. It said if I didn't do it, someone else would. So why shouldn't I be the one to make the money?"

Daniel kept the disgust from his voice. "And sometimes you bring something back to Morristown."

"Yes." Townsend was starting to regret his loose tongue. Daniel could tell. His answers were getting shorter.

"Ever open the pouches?"

"No. Why should I?"

"And when you travel back to Morristown, where do you leave the packages?"

Townsend couldn't meet Daniel's eyes. "In my church. In one of the Bibles."

"Do you find your payments in the Bible, too?"

"Yes." Townsend began to cry and snot fell from his pointy nose. "The next morning."

Before the war, Daniel took it for granted that evil was larger than life, the giant monster in a child's dream. Now he knew better. Evil was the Ferret's booted foot on a weak man's hand. It was Minister Townsend spreading rumors about Becca for spite to leave her adrift in the world. Adrift like Daniel.

He took a different tack. "And do you deliver messages to Bill Cunningham?"

Townsend's thin eyebrows drew together. "Who?"

The minister didn't know Cunningham. "Do you deliver crates of whiskey to anyone other than the mayor?"

Townsend shook his head.

Daniel slid his forearm up to Townsend's throat and pushed. "How do you know when there are messages to take back to Morristown?"

"The chalk."

Daniel lifted the cut whiskey bottle.

"When I see the chalk, I have to erase it," he rasped. "Then I come back in an hour and pick up an envelope."

"Who hands you the message?" Daniel asked.

"No one important. A footman."

"I saw the chalk. The footman will be waiting for you in an hour, won't he?"

"You *want* me to pick up the message?" Townsend asked.

"I insist." Daniel smiled. "And if you do, I'll make sure to tell General Washington of your assistance."

Daniel released the gasping parson and watched him dash down Water Street. He waited until Townsend was a block away, then changed his grip on the broken bottle and flung it against the nearby wall.

He retrieved the only portion of the bottle he cared about and plunged it into the pocket of his cape for safekeeping.

Chapter Thirty

"Don't pack? None of it?" Annie's glance swept the dressing room. Creamy dark velvets, gleaming brocades and gowns of silk embroidered with olive and purple blooms were draped from pegs forming an exotic cocoon of fabric.

"Not any of it," Becca said with satisfaction. She couldn't wait to shed "the silent beautiful one"—what an absurd name society had given her–and the hip pads, petticoats and gowns that went with the masquerade.

"Whoever is watching us will think we are making just another social call," she continued. That was part of the plan Mr. Rivington had suggested a few hours ago, just before she and Daniel found the map.

"No need to repeat yourself," Annie grumbled. "I know what's what. Mr. Rivington's carriage will meet us in front of Mrs. Lathrop's house later on. He'll take us to the ferry." Annie stroked a white silk stocking draped over a dressing room chair. Silver threads, carefully cross-stitched along the edges of the heel, glistened in the morning light.

Becca laughed at the look of regret on Annie's face. "Oh, go ahead. The stockings will fit in your pocket. Take them."

"They're too good for the likes of me." Annie said regretfully.

"This isn't England, Annie. You are as equal here as anyone else."

"Equality is a fancy word, Miss Rebecca. It's for the gentry, not me."

"If that is so, then we will need more insurrections, won't we?" Exhaustion had nudged Becca's mind onto an unexpected path. She recalled the way Daniel had pointed toward the city of canvas tents —Canvas Town–when they first arrived. The British had left the residents to freeze this winter.

"I think we've had enough insurrections for now, missus." Annie folded the stockings and tucked them into the pocket tied round her waist.

Samuel's voice rose from the dining room. Augusta would be keeping him busy downstairs discussing notable Parcell ancestors until it was almost time to go. That was part of the plan, too.

Becca turned to the window. The two men she'd seen last night on the docks were back. They lounged on the front stoop across the street. The stouter one sat on a snow-covered step. She watched his chin sink to his chest, then jerk up, once, twice. He was the one who'd had too much to drink, she thought, and he was paying for it. His hook-nosed friend stared motionless at Samuel's front door.

A man wearing black breeches, a black jacket with tails and white stockings sprinted around the corner. She could just make out the decorative 'M's on the coat tails. He was one of Mayor Matthews' servants. Above his dark servant's uniform, too thin for such a cold morning, a pale face swung left then right, as if he were looking for someone.

Becca had a clear view of his face. He was the nervous footman who had whispered into the mayor's ear at the ball. He hesitated, spotted the two men standing across from Cousin Samuel's house, then raced toward them. His hands gestured broadly as he spoke, his back to Becca. He twisted, pointed back down the street.

The two men who'd stood guard all morning came to attention. They dashed after the servant.

"Why would the mayor and Cunningham call off their watchmen?" She watched them turn east toward the river. The realization came quickly. "They found Daniel."

"You can't know that," Annie said.

"They've watched this house for weeks hoping Daniel would come for me. The only reason they'd leave is if they caught him." Becca covered her mouth with the palm that Daniel had kissed just hours ago.

She took two deep breaths and struggled to speak slowly. "They were heading for the river. There's a ferry to Brooklyn at one of the wharfs. That's where the prison ships are docked." Becca felt her pulse beat in the hollow of her throat.

"If that's true, you can't help him." Annie was as blunt as ever.

The part of Becca's mind that added, subtracted, and tallied accounts agreed with Annie.

"I have to try." Becca swept up the servant's cape she had borrowed from Mr. Rivington.

"What will you do?" Annie blocked the door.

"I won't know until I'm doing it."

"Lady Augusta will be very upset if something happens to you." Annie's round face crumpled. "*I* will be very upset."

"Oh, Annie. I'll try to be careful, I promise." Becca gripped Annie's solid upper arms, shaking them gently.

When the servant stepped away, Becca raced down the stairs.

The speed of her footsteps brought Samuel to the hallway. "Cousin, where? What?" he scowled his questions as she sped out the door.

She turned left outside the house and right at the corner. The wind lifted snowflakes, which swirled like a white paisley print come to life.

The men she followed were fading shapes in a white world now. She squinted to keep them in sight. At the wharf up ahead, they stopped before two more men.

Becca flattened herself behind an empty wagon parked on the opposite side of the street. She hadn't stopped to change from slippers to boots. Her feet were numb. If the men returned the way they'd come, they'd see her. There had to be a more secure hiding place than this.

She scanned the buildings, counted down from five, and rushed across the street, clutching her dress high to avoid tripping on its fabric. She reached the alley across the way, holding her breath in case the men on the dock had spotted her.

"Don't you have the sense to keep yourself safe?" The whispered growl tore through her.

All the curses she'd ever heard at her father's forge exploded from her lips in a whispered frenzy of anxiety and relief. She whirled to face Daniel. "Are you still following me?"

"I believe *you* are following *me*." His gaze softened.

"I thought the mayor had you."

He shrugged away her concern, then jerked his chin toward the men on the dock. "As long as you are here, you can meet the new messenger."

Becca craned to see, then gasped and pulled her head back quickly into the shadows. What she saw made no sense.

"I caught Minister Townsend at the mayor's house," Daniel said. "He was dropping off whiskey, just the way your husband must have."

"He accused me of treason. And he knew it was a lie." Her breath rose like smoke in the frozen air. "Why?"

"Revenge, I suppose. He thought your husband ruined his life. He wanted you to lose everything, too."

"And I still might." Her fingers itched for a weapon. "Who gives him the messages to deliver? Who is the turncoat in Morristown?"

"He says he doesn't know," Daniel murmured.

"And you believe the minister?"

"He would have told me if he knew." Daniel's smile was grim. "I was choking him at the time. But he might have lied. He could have been more afraid of the mayor than of me."

"What do you mean?"

"After Townsend and I spoke, he agreed to go back to the mayor's house to pick up the return message meant for Morristown."

"After you tried to choke him? You let him go?" She peeked out of the alley. Minister Townsend's shoulders were hunched. She'd never seen him in as humble a pose.

Daniel nodded. "I told him to continue as if he hadn't met me. I would have taken the new message from him. I wanted to bring it to General Washington. That would have been worth a reward, eh? But I knew there was trouble when he didn't come out again quickly. He must have told the mayor that he saw me."

"He knows who you are?" Becca asked.

"I met him in Morristown. We were introduced."

Her hands curled into fists. "I could kill him."

"You won't have the chance," Daniel whispered. "Townsend's not of much use to them, now that we know why he travels to New York."

She shivered. Philip had been of no use to them, either, not after he offered General Washington the list of spies.

Cunningham's man, Jackson, the tall, hook-nosed one, jerked back his arm and put his weight behind a punch that doubled Townsend over. Jackson whispered into his ear, and the minister violently shook his head.

Townsend pointed in the direction of the mayor's house.

"He's asking the minister where he saw me, I warrant," Daniel whispered.

Jackson's head tilted as he listened to Townsend's response. He patted the parson on the back and drew him in for an embrace.

The other guards stepped away. Jackson's other hand swung around the minister's back as if the two were dancing.

Townsend jerked and fell face first. His palms pushed down against the dock as he tried to lift himself up. His upper body shook, stiffened, then collapsed.

Jackson barked at the guards and pointed toward Mayor Matthews' house. They split up. One rushed down the street away from Murray's Wharf. Others headed toward Wall Street.

Becca took short gulping breaths. She had wished him dead.

"Get ready to move." Daniel's tone was urgent.

"But the minister...."

"He's dead or soon will be. Leave him."

She was already sprinting toward the dock. Daniel followed.

Becca dropped to her knees. The knife handle planted in Townsend's back trembled with each breath he took. His left hand twitched in the snow. His face was turned to the harbor.

She reached for the knife, then pulled her hand away. Removing it would kill the man.

So much blood. Her father had died of the bloody flux. He hadn't wanted Becca to know of his illness. Carl had fetched her on what would be the last day of his life. She'd held his hand for hours. He'd squeezed her hand once. She was certain of it.

Her shoulders sagged. No one should die alone, not even Townsend.

"I'm here. I won't leave." Kneeling on the slippery snow-covered dock, it was all the comfort she had to give.

At the sound of her voice, the parson's eyes fluttered open. "Go to Hell, you and your husband." Blood seeped from the side of his mouth.

She pushed away in surprise and toppled back, kicking up a plume of snow.

Daniel kneeled. "Unlike Mrs. Parcell, I don't particularly care whether you live or die. But Mrs. Parcell didn't stab you. I can make the people who did this pay. I swear I will."

"Make them pay," Townsend coughed. "Just wanted..." his eyes closed "... my money back."

Becca stared at her blood-covered hands. She wiped them on the snow, leaving streaks of red.

Daniel placed his face close to the dying man. "But you have to tell me who. Who wrote the messages?"

"If I knew, I would tell." A rattling breath. "An educated man. Good handwriting." A pause. "Hated Washington, must've."

"Who?" Daniel demanded.

But there would be no answer. The parson stared open-eyed at the gray, icy water.

The wind whistled off the river. Becca wondered whether it carried off the preacher's soul. She stood.

"An educated man with a good hand. That narrows things down." Daniel raked his hand through his dark hair. "It could be any of Washington's officers. They're all from good families. They all have educated handwriting."

"But they don't all hate General Washington, surely," she said.

Daniel's chin rose. He tensed. "My apologies, Mrs. Parcell."

He launched himself at her and catapulted the two of them off the edge of the dock. The sky and frozen river were identical shades of gray as she tumbled. She didn't even have time to lose her breath.

Her wrist hit the ice. The pain forced the breath from her lungs. His hand tugged at her ankle, and he yanked her hard beneath the dock.

Daniel's icy hand covered Becca's mouth. His other arm circled her waist holding her tightly against his chest in the darkness.

How dare he? She elbowed him in the stomach and heard a satisfying "whuff" of breath, but he didn't loosen his grip.

"It's a wild goose chase, I tell you," a gravelly voice shouted from the dock.

Becca jammed herself against Daniel and pushed them even further into the shadows.

"Alloway's on a sled bound for Jersey now. Maybe for Brooklyn. That's where I'd be."

"Who asked you?" a bored voice called back.

"Something moved. I saw it," a deeper voice argued.

At least three of them, Becca thought.

"Well, this one's dead," the bored voice said.

Daniel's large hand still covered her mouth. Her back was pressed against his chest. Each breath he took seemed to vibrate through her body. Her face warmed beneath the palm of his hand.

"No sign of 'em near the mayor's. Nothing here. Can't say I blame the parson for lying. Should we check the ferry slips?"

"As good a place as any."

"I saw something I tell you."

"Stuff it, Mike. Move on."

The voices faded.

Chapter Thirty-One

Buoys were locked into ice on the frozen East River. During a long-ago summer, Daniel and the lads hid from work under the docks back in Cornwall. It still wasn't a bad place to hide.

He removed his good hand from Becca's mouth. The heat of her breath set his skin humming. His other arm still held her tight, her back curved against his chest. He felt her shiver, then, slowly, regretfully, he swept his arm away, pushed himself up and offered her his hand for balance.

Hidden beneath the dock, Daniel reached into the inside pocket of his coat and pulled out the single cork he'd stolen from the minister's delivery. He raised it. "This is from one of the whiskey bottles the minister left at the mayor's door. All the other bottles in the crate had unmarked corks. So I took this one."

Becca's forehead creased. "It can't be Philip's whiskey. The mob drank whatever was left of it."

"At least one of the bottles belonged to your husband." He held up the cork until she put out her hand for it. A scrolling letter "P" was burned into its circular top. "There aren't many places to hide a message in a whiskey bottle, not if you want to keep the ink dry."

She rolled the cork in her open palm. A dimple formed in one of her cheeks as she smiled. Her index finger delicately touched a dent in the bottom round end of the cork.

A small indentation was sealed with a piece of wax, as if it contained something that needed to be kept dry.

The cork jumped in Becca's hand as a shiver swept through her. Her skirt was soaked from the ice. Her slippers, too.

The cold could be a dangerous adversary. "I know a place," he said, taking the cork back from her. "We'll get warm and read the message."

* * *

Becca lost track of their location as Daniel led her through snow-filled streets and alleys.

Her thoughts dissolved like snowflakes as quickly as they formed. She felt the now-familiar fluttering in her stomach, thinking of his lips on her palm at the print shop. Philip was right. She was no lady. But still. Her husband never made her feel.... She squeezed her eyes shut to quiet her mind.

Daniel stopped. She smashed into him.

He bent to listen at the door of a gray shed, little more than a weathered lean-to behind a substantial brick house, then pulled open the rope handle.

Inside the room, a copper vat of steaming water was set over a banked fire. It added a layer of dampness to whitewashed walls and tables. The warmth was so welcome that Becca sighed.

She tiptoed over a cobblestone floor to a second tub on the far side of the fireplace and found just what she expected, clothes soaking in the cauldron. She wrinkled her nose at the acrid scent of lye. A small mountain of dirty clothes smothered a table with too-skinny legs in the corner.

There were kitchen noises on the other side of the wall, whispers of the safer world they'd left behind, clinking dishes, pots and pans, and young servants giggling when they should be working.

"This is your safe place? A wash house?" She stopped to stroke a silk skirt that was draped over a rickety drying rack. She rubbed the gold-threaded hem between her fingers and lifted her eyebrows. "Quite a well-to-do family."

Daniel leaned against the far wall with his arms crossed. "You could say that."

She didn't like the look on his face, an expression hovering between despair and wild humor. A horrifying thought crossed her mind. She focused on the sounds of the kitchen through the wall. No. Only a madman would come here.

"And this house belongs to someone who entertains quite a bit, doesn't it?" Her stomach flip-flopped.

He lifted a shoulder.

She winced. "We're not behind the mayor's house, are we?"

"It will be fine. Really." He sounded more hopeful than certain.

The dolly stick used to whisk clothes clean leaned against the blackened fireplace bricks. Becca grabbed it and advanced toward Daniel. "How could you bring me here?" she hissed. "I'd be better off on my own. I always am." Did he want to die? Did he want them both to be captured?

His hands came up in surrender. "This is the last place the mayor's men will look for us. They're off at the ferry slip now."

She lowered the stick but didn't loosen her grip. The heat of the room teased a trickle of sweat down her back. "They'll kill you if they find you here. Do you care so little?"

"The cook took me under her wing," Daniel said. He pointed to the second door in the room, the one connecting the washroom to the kitchen. "She said she and the laundress are the only people who use this space." His mouth curved into a half smile. "And you were too cold. It's safe, Becca, a safe place to read the message."

Becca's long fingers combed through strands of black hair, damp now with the laundry room's humidity. "Besides, we don't have the map. How will we read the new message, if there is one?" She thought she sounded like a tired child.

Daniel removed his great coat. He shook off the rough brown vest he wore. Paper crinkled.

Tacked to the vest's lining with a few clumsy stitches was a piece of parchment with a shaky inked drawing.

"But that's wonderful. What made you think to copy Rivington's map?"

He shrugged. "Easier than stealing it."

Becca reached her hand out. "The cork. May I?"

He dropped it into her open palm.

She pried loose the tiny slip of wax and used a thumbnail to expand the indentation. A hollowness nestled inside the cork, and she gently broke it open. She lifted a rolled paper, no bigger than the length of her fingertip to first knuckle from its hiding place, and held it up for Daniel's examination.

Holding the side of her skirt out, she sank to the floor and held her other hand out. "The map?"

Daniel lowered himself to the ground and smoothed the drawing on the floor between them.

She squinted. Three short rows of miniature numbers marched across the slip of paper. Becca moved the index finger of her free hand from one section of the map to the next. She hummed with the pleasure of working with the numbers, then slowly read out loud as she translated:

Delegatn arrive M'town by Feb 21. Instrctns to cm.

She grinned at Daniel. They had done it. But her sense of triumph dimmed. They were out of time. "There are just days until the twenty-first. And we still don't know what it all means."

Daniel nodded, stretching his neck. "Who's leaving for Morristown?" he asked. "Why would British soldiers ever be welcome in Morristown? And who's the man...," he grinned, "...or woman in Morristown waiting to give the officers their instructions?"

Her head rose. Something had changed. There was a sudden absence of sound. No pans clanked. No servants giggled. Then she heard a man's voice.

"The crate, you stupid cow. Who moved it?"

Then a dull thud and a woman crying out.

Becca pointed to the mountain of laundry spilling over the table in the corner and dipped her head in pantomime as if she were about to hide there. She pointed at Daniel, then back to the table.

He shook his head.

Becca rolled her eyes. "Trust me," she mouthed without sound. "Please."

Chapter Thirty-Two

Becca pulled a wet chemise and two petticoats from the cauldron and thrust them back into the water once, then twice. She kept her back to the door and tried to remember to breathe. She was bedraggled enough to pass for a washwoman.

The laundry room door slammed open. She snatched a brick-sized bar of tawny soap from the mantel. She lifted one arm over her eyes to shield them from the glare of light from the kitchen.

The large, broad-shouldered intruder spent a moment too long looking her up and down. "Who are you?" he demanded.

Becca lowered her arm. She thought of Annie and answered as she might. "Who do you think I am?" she asked with a grace note of acid in her voice. "I'm the Queen of England." Becca turned away and plunged the soap into the hot water, scrubbing away at a petticoat.

He crossed the room and cuffed the back of her skull before she could react.

She staggered to keep her footing.

"It's no time for servants to do laundry. The master's dinner starts in two hours. I asked who you are."

A floorboard creaked near the table where Daniel hid. She raised her voice to mask the noise he made and let him know she was all right. "Aoww, there ain't any call for that." Becca pressed a hand to her head. She wasn't playacting. The top of her head was exploding.

Hitting her seemed to have relaxed the man. He wore long pants like a workman, not breeches, and his red hair was tied back, exposing a receding hairline and freckled forehead. His jaw was as wide as his neck. She wondered how many women he'd beaten.

He didn't like women, not really, she thought. He wasn't comfortable with them. *Not comfortable.* It might work, and, besides, she couldn't think of anything else.

"Mistress is having her courses," Becca whined. "She needs her clean pads whether or not there's a party tonight."

The thug's broad face went blank.

"Her courses," Becca said with emphasis. "Her monthlies? M'lady's time of the month? With or without a dinner party, m'lady needs me to clean the blood off her pads." She scooped a sodden linen cloth out of the washing vat and took a step toward him as if she wanted him to examine the rag. It was a plain handkerchief. She prayed he wouldn't get close enough to notice.

His eyes went wide. He stepped back, hands splayed in front of him to ward off the offering. "Has anyone been through here?"

There was no sarcasm in her voice this time. "No." She held the dripping sponge in one hand and the square of linen in her other.

"Get back to work, then." He backed away, his eyes averted from the sodden cloth as if it might attack him. Then he slammed the kitchen door and was gone.

Becca dropped the sponge and linen on the floor.

Daniel crossed to her in three steps. His hand gently probed the back of her head.

She winced at the pain.

An odd buzzing in her ears made her strain to hear him.

"I shouldn't have brought you here. I should have…. Dammit, just breathe. Slowly."

* * *

He grabbed her waist to support her. "You need to sit." Of course she was in shock.

Her eyes were round, almost empty. She shook her head as her knees buckled.

She had risked her life to hide him. His throat tightened. Was this guilt? He didn't care for the unfamiliar feeling.

He couldn't say what changed. Her breathing, perhaps his. Her expression grave, she lifted her face. Her palm flattened on his chest, and his world shrank to her lips and the warm hand on his ribcage.

The part of his mind that still functioned knew he should step away. He didn't. Then he stopped thinking altogether. He captured her mouth and lost his breath in her. Her lips relaxed and opened as if her body recognized his.

He caressed the line of her jaw, her neck, and her collarbone. The calluses he'd earned as a printer had worn away, leaving his fingertips sensitive to the warmth of her skin.

This wasn't the time or place. And she wasn't the right woman. Not for what he wanted from her at this moment. He had no prospects and nothing to offer. He'd be moving on as soon as Hamilton's reward money was in his pocket.

He ripped himself away from her.

Becca fumbled with the wrinkled neckerchief peeking above her dress, looking everywhere but at him.

"That was inexcusable. I beg your pardon, Mrs. Parcell." He still felt the heat of her fingers on his back.

Becca's voice was shaky. "And now?"

Now? Now he wanted to dive into her. "I'll accompany you to your cousin's house. You'll find your way to Mrs. Lathrop's and the carriage to Morristown."

"And you'll join us?" She stared out the laundry room's one small, dirty window at the gray midafternoon light.

He nodded. "I'll join you."

"I'll be fine. I can walk from here." Her voice was clipped. She scooped up her cape from the stool and shrugged it over her shoulders.

A soft click shot through the quiet room. The mayor's cook squeezed through the kitchen door and then closed it. She favored her left leg as she walked. An angry red scrape extended from her cheek to her mouth.

Daniel strode across the room to support the older woman. He led her to the three-legged stool, the only chair in the room. He had thought her a large woman when he saw her bullying the scullery maid and young servant girls this morning. But she was smaller than Becca.

She shrugged off his arm and lowered herself by inches to the stool. Her face tightened with pain. "Just came in for a moment a' peace and quiet." She grimaced. "Thought you'd have enough sense to stay gone."

Becca shook out the wet linen handkerchief that scared away the mayor's thug. She knelt before the cook and dabbed tears from her face.

"Thanks, missus. I can do it myself." The cook took the square of cloth and squinted up at Daniel.

"How did the mayor know that a bottle was missing?" he asked.

"He sent for the whiskey after you bolted. We took it up, and he comes storming into the kitchen, pitching a fit." She examined the stained handkerchief matter-of-factly. "I tell him the whiskey bottles must'a been delivered that way. And then the master sent that animal to rough me up. I told them I hadn't seen you or the whiskey."

"You shouldn't have put yourself in harm's way for me." Daniel sounded angrier than he intended. Guilt again?

"I won't lift a finger to help them, the bastards."

Becca crouched next to the cook. "Why don't you leave the city? You could find work anywhere."

"Leave my home for that lot?" She pushed out her chin like a bulldog. "I'll be here long after they're gone."

Daniel grinned. He was surprised the mayor wasn't afraid of the cook. "Can you rest here?"

She closed her eyes. "No. The master is wanting a small dinner at seven before the ball. I need to get back." She strained to rise.

He clasped her elbow and helped her up, then leaned over and kissed her soft cheek. "I'm in your debt."

The cook straightened his collar and, on tiptoes, whispered, "Just help someone else's son one day."

He swore he would. This promise was different from most he'd made since he reached America. This one he meant to keep.

The cook walked toward the kitchen with more of a swagger than a limp.

"You mentioned the mayor's dinner. Who are his guests?" Becca asked as the cook reached for the door.

"There'll be three of the young men tonight. Officers. The mayor said they are leaving for the Jersies in the morning before light. That's why he wanted an early dinner." She shut the door behind her.

"The delegation must arrive in Morristown by February 21." Daniel repeated the message from the whiskey bottle. He bowed to Becca. "It would be a shame to miss the mayor's dinner. Think what we might learn from the delegation bound for Morristown."

She grabbed Daniel's coat sleeve and pulled. "Cunningham will be at the dinner. That's what he told the mayor at the ball last night. You have to leave."

"I'll stay awhile."

He heard a short, unladylike snort. "You're daft."

The sharp edge of her voice reassured and disappointed him. Becca was fine. More than fine. The kiss had meant nothing to her.

"We don't know what they're planning," he said. "We only know that the officers arriving tonight are in the middle of it. I'll find a way to listen."

"We know enough. We know that Philip delivered his messages to Mayor Matthews. That's all General Washington wanted from us." Her voice softened. "They'll find you."

She was right. But in his mind, he saw the image of the mayor's thug lifting his hand to Becca, heard the cook cry out. He would stay.

"I'll have a better chance if I leave after dark," he said. "Pull your hood up and carry the laundry basket. They won't look twice at a washwoman."

She grabbed the basket that leaned against the wall and collected the skirts, petticoats and shirts scattered around the room.

Two vertical worry lines materialized between her eyebrows. "I'll hold the carriage for you 'til eleven. We won't leave for Morristown until then." She pushed the door open with her back and was gone.

Chapter Thirty-Three

Men, their hats pulled low to fight the wind, rushed wagons along Queen Street toward ships nearly landlocked in the harbor.

Becca hadn't meant to reach for Daniel like that. She had been scared and hurt. That was all. He didn't want her. Fine. But he had kissed her, hadn't he, before he pulled away?

"Wake up, ya' slag."

She jumped. The wheelbarrow missed her by inches.

The farm was what mattered, she thought, the farm and getting word to General Washington as quickly as possible, certainly before the redcoats arrived in Morristown.

Just a few blocks further and up the granite steps, Becca lowered the laundry basket onto the floor of Samuel's front hall. She balanced on one foot and then the other to pull her boots off. Snow fell from her shoes in clumps on the worn parquet tiles. She stood and listened.

The familiar sounds of home unsettled her in her cousin's empty house. The tinny knock of the grandfather clock came from the wrong corner. The rattling of wind was ominously loud without voices to muffle the sound.

She just needed a good night's sleep. She would go home to Morristown and lock the door behind her. Daniel Alloway could go hang himself.

Then she heard voices. Unfamiliar male laughter rose from the servant's quarters. Becca tiptoed toward the stairs.

"Good afternoon, Mrs. Parcell."

The deep, unmistakable rumble froze Becca in place.

In the tea-colored light of her cousin's sitting room, John Mason and

Augusta sat in pale matching wing chairs facing Becca. Augusta wore the light blue gown that made her silver hair shimmer.

Is she wearing her good day dress for Mr. Mason?

Mason extended the pinky of his massive hand and brought a seashell-thin teacup to his lips. A small crescent of dirt was lodged beneath the nail. The diamonds on his shoe buckles glistened.

Sitting on opposite sides of the small, round table, Mr. Mason and Augusta looked like matching bookends. Not that they looked alike. But there was an ease, as if they understood each other, as if they'd grown up with the same type of governesses and attended the same type of garden parties in England, as if they were already comfortable enough to sit together in silence.

Becca ignored Mason. "Where is Cousin Samuel?" she asked Augusta.

"Your cousin is visiting a friend," Mason said.

"At your suggestion?" Becca was sure it was an order, not a suggestion.

"Perhaps." Mason shrugged.

"You'll have to leave now. We have a prior engagement." Becca knew she was rude and didn't care.

Augusta's eyes narrowed. "It was kind of Mr. Mason to see me home from the mayor's ball last night, and I asked him in to visit."

"Lady Augusta was worried about you." Mason stared balefully at her.

"I couldn't let you know that I was all right." Becca conjured up the image of Minister Townsend on the dock, the knife in his back. She sank into a worn velvet arm chair. "I am sorry, Augusta. Truly."

She turned back to Mr. Mason "I mean no offense," she lied. "But you knew Philip was a British spy. You took money from Mayor Matthews. And you conveniently arrive at his ball last night and here today. It's difficult to see how you manage to appear at just the right time with just the right assistance." She paused. "Is the mayor paying you to follow us?"

Mason half rose from his seat. "You impertinent young..."

"John," Augusta said softly.

"*John?*" Becca stared aghast at Augusta, who blushed. First names were reserved for one's closest friends and family.

Mason sat again, pulling at his cuffs to straighten them. "I had business in the city this week, business with Matthews, in fact."

"What business?" Becca asked.

"A cow. A side of beef for the mayor's table. When the price is right, I do many things. And the mayor's price was generous."

She shook her head. "That doesn't explain why you are here."

"Then the mayor offered to pay me for information about you, Mrs. Parcell. And he asked after your Mr. Alloway," Mason continued. "None of us are who we thought we were when the war began. The lines have blurred. But there are lines one can't cross and ever come back. I told the mayor I didn't know Alloway or the widow Parcell, and then I came here to help."

He glanced at Augusta and his expression softened. "This war has caused you and your mother-in-law enough distress. I will not be the cause of more."

She heard something different in his voice. It might have been honesty.

"I thought the mayor's interest in you and Lady Augusta was unhealthy. Unhealthy for the two of you. I decided to stay in the city for another day or two." His rumbling laughter was unexpected.

"I don't think Matthews even recognized me last night," he continued. "I don't usually dress for him."

"You weren't invited?" Becca shouldn't have been surprised.

Mason flicked a bit of dust from his well-cut green jacket.

Mason was a thief. Most likely worse. She'd bet her life that he wouldn't hurt Augusta. But trusting him felt like jumping off a cliff. "I want to leave, Mr. Mason. If you can help us, I would be grateful. There should be a carriage from Mr. Riv...from a friend."

He slapped his knees with both hands and stood. "No need to wait. We will leave now."

"Not yet," Becca stuttered.

His large blunt face grew grave. "Is it Mr. Alloway?"

Whatever he saw in Becca's face confirmed his theory. "Oh, my dear, I'm afraid he won't be joining us."

* * *

179

Daniel inched down along the laundry room wall until he squatted on his haunches. He leaned his head back and shut his eyes. It wasn't the most restful position, but he didn't mean to sleep.

There were two things he knew for certain. He should have left this burned wreck of a city days ago, and, if Cunningham caught him, he wouldn't survive. Make that three things he knew. He should have nothing more to do with Rebecca Parcell. He lost his focus around her and that was dangerous.

His eyes ached with exhaustion. He closed them as late afternoon shadows darkened the room.

His memories chased him when he was this weary. He heard them whisper just beyond reach, the voices of the prisoners who saved him, the dead ones. Sometimes he thought they still meant to reclaim him.

He rose slowly, his legs deadened, his injured hand clutched to his chest. He examined it for reassurance. There was no blood on his palm, no sting of seawater doubling the searing pain. His heartbeat slowly returned to normal.

The dream never changed. In it, he relived his escape from the *Jersey*.

Daniel scrubbed his hands over his face. Cook had promised to take him to the game room before serving dinner. She said he'd be able to eavesdrop on the mayor's guests from there.

He walked to the bucket near the fireplace, spooned clean water into his cupped hand with a dented ladle, and sipped.

"Sir." The cook's wavery voice called from behind the kitchen door and pulled him back to the present.

"Of course. Come."

The door crashed open.

Tears marked her face. Cunningham's man, Jackson, gripped the back of her neck with one hand.

"My son," she wheezed. "They said they would kill him if I didn't say where you were."

Jackson pushed the cook back into the kitchen.

A shorter man took his place in the doorway. The gleaming brass buttons of his vest emphasized the curve of his belly. His hands were clasped behind his back.

"That someone so forgettable should cause such agitation." Provost Marshall William Cunningham gently shook his head as he made a show of studying Daniel.

Cunningham removed kidskin gloves from soft white hands and folded them carefully, placing them in an inner coat pocket. "I can't say I recall your face, Mr. Alloway."

"I remember yours." Daniel's heartbeat slowed. It was as if the eight months since he'd escaped the *Jersey* were a dream. Cunningham's small eyes, his stare, hot and bright, were real.

"But I'm baffled. You brought Mrs. Parcell safely to New York." He circled Daniel. "You should have left then and collected your fee from Alexander Hamilton. Why didn't you?"

Daniel didn't answer. *How did he know?*

"Is Parcell's list of colleagues here? In the mayor's own house?" Cunningham scanned the laundry room.

Daniel didn't answer.

"It hardly matters." Cunningham laughed, a breathy, strangled sound. "It's too late to do Mr. Washington any good."

"The traitors will move on him soon?"

"The real patriots, you mean. British patriots. Oh, quite soon. No harm in telling you now, I suppose." Cunningham's smile exposed his small, widely spaced teeth.

Daniel hid a shudder. He recalled that smile, a child's teeth in a monster's face. Cunningham intended to kill him. The *Jersey's* prisoners crooned a whispered invitation to join them.

"And the person paying you to find the list...is a friend of General Washington's?" Daniel asked.

"Friend?" Cunningham barked a laugh. "I don't think so."

"Really?" Every man had a story, Daniel thought. Even the provost might need to tell his tale.

"He wrote that the debts Mr. Washington has incurred are finally coming due," Cunningham said.

Daniel's thoughts raced. Mr. Hamilton? Not likely. Who else was close enough to the general? Caleb Gibbs, the commander of General Washington's Life Guards? He was in and out of the general's quarters constantly. He'd served Washington for a long time. What about the soldier who shot the Ferret?

Jackson stepped through the doorway again. "'Scusing the interruption. But the mayor says it's time. He's giving them officers orders for Morris-town."

The provost turned to Daniel, all business now. "The list. Where is it?"

After all the nightmares, Daniel thought, Cunningham had found him. His own story would end soon, but not without this.

He spit in the man's face.

The provost wiped his cheek with the back of his hand. His faced tightened into a rictus of elation.

Daniel felt the ghost of Becca's kiss. He waited for the knife or the bullet.

Cunningham stabbed a finger at Jackson. "Get him on the *Jersey* at first light. For now, leave him at the Sugar House."

Chapter Thirty-Four

"**M**y carriage passed the mayor's house earlier this afternoon," Mr. Mason began. "The man who commands the prisons was at his door."

He raised his hand. "Don't ask me whether I know Cunningham. A man in my position knows the people he needs to know. Cunningham entered the house with two of his men." His voice was dry. "I don't think it was a social visit."

"When was that?" Goosebumps rose on Becca's arms.

"Perhaps two hours ago."

"I was there." Her voice was faint.

Mr. Mason's thick eyebrows rose. "That was foolhardy, Mrs. Parcell. There's no point waiting for your friend. If you left Mr. Alloway behind, then Cunningham has him."

She stared at the teacup. She wanted to sweep it across the room, to hear it smash.

"The mayor is entertaining tonight. He'll want Alloway gone and on his way to the Sugar House before his guests arrive. He's there already, I warrant."

"Sugar house?" Becca was confused.

"The prisons are filled past the brim with American soldiers. The British are jamming them into the old warehouses. They're all going to the one used to store sugar for now."

"Can't your men stop them?" She wrapped her arms around herself.

"I admit it would be–amusing–to steal Mr. Alloway from Mr. Cunningham."

ham. I don't much care for the man. I won't steal food out of a dying man's mouth. Cunningham does, and he enjoys it."

A burning branch collapsed in the fireplace and Becca jumped. Sparks lifted like fireflies up the chimney.

"You despise him." Augusta glided toward the fireplace. She removed a slip of wood from the tinderbox, touched its edge to the fire, and then circled the room to light candles on tables and in wall sconces.

"Despise?" Mason tested the word. "Perhaps. I've lost some of my men to his prisons."

"Then take Daniel from Cunningham," Becca urged. "There will be satisfaction in that, won't there?"

"I won't put my men at risk for your 'satisfaction,' madam." He leaned toward her. "The guards don't look twice at women there to see their men. But the redcoats would shoot my men from forty paces."

Becca felt a slow smile spread across her face.

* * *

"I didn't join up to hide behind no lady's petticoats," one of the bandits muttered, then spit.

"You're not hiding behind them. You're hiding in them," said Amos, the bald bandit who had so scared Annie.

The other bandits sniggered.

"Walk off now and I'm done with you." Mason's voice was calm.

They all fell silent.

Mason had said that the guards wouldn't look twice at members of the gentler sex. And so that was the disguise his men wore. They "borrowed" everything they could from Cousin Samuel's servants and then purchased additional capes and skirts—as many as they could without calling too much attention to themselves—from servants in the surrounding houses.

Becca thought she caught a look of admiration from Mr. Mason when she made her proposal. That was after he roared with laughter.

But she felt the bandits' animosity now, like the tip of a knife tickling her spine, even as they followed her down the empty street.

She pulled her shoulders back. She didn't look back at any of the costumed men surrounding her. Would they disappear into the night and leave her alone at the gate? Even if they stayed, would they fight for her?

The tall outline of the Sugar House was just visible through the snowfall. With its deep, narrow windows and nine-foot wooden fence, it looked more like a medieval dungeon than a warehouse. Two guards paced behind the front gate.

Mason touched her elbow, and they all stepped around the corner from the prison where they wouldn't be seen.

His eyes locked on hers. "If you are not very sure you can execute this plan, then walk away now. There's no shame in that."

She was certain of only one thing: If they failed to find Daniel, he'd be killed. "If we manage to get into the prison and don't find Mr. Alloway quickly, we'll leave. I'll get your men out."

They would beg to bring their men food in the prison. If she was successful, three women—Becca and two costumed bandits—would enter the prison. Three would leave, but one of those three would be Daniel.

Becca wore two capes, one over the other, and two skirts. She'd pass the additional skirt and cape to Daniel. She would stay behind, then claim that she had merely been searching for her husband. So much depended on the guards and on Mr. Mason's bandits.

She had never been so glad for bad weather. The curtain of white and the darkness should blur the not-so-female contours of the costumed men. Mason had paid the servants at Samuel's house generously for the use of skirts and petticoats. But the men were all wearing their own boots. None of the women's shoes fit the bandits' feet.

Her plan seemed sound when she explained it in Cousin Samuel's kitchen. Now, it felt as insubstantial as the snowflakes rimming her eyelashes.

"Alloway's not a bad sort." Amos' scarred face stretched into a death's head grin. "Might as well give it a try. Don't mind poking Cunningham where it hurts, either."

"We should begin," she whispered to Mason.

He nodded then seized her wrist, pulling her to him slowly. "If any of my boys die here, I will hold you accountable."

Becca brought her face close to Mason's. He smelled of citrus and bayberry, expensive scents that surprised her. "Tell your men to run if things go badly. Tell them that." She shook off his hand.

"My men don't run, Mrs. Parcell. If the soldiers attack them, they'll stand and fight."

Her forehead creased. "That's not sensible."

"They'll see it as a matter of honor. Honor is all some of them have."

She nodded, then pushed through the bandits in their ridiculous navy, green and red capes, one with overskirts that hardly covered his shins.

Amos and another bandit followed her through the gates of the Sugar House. All the others waited on the street just outside.

Two redcoat guards watched Becca approach. One held his musket like a shepherd's crook, the butt resting on the snow and bayonet pointing skyward. He was tall, but he hunched his shoulders as if hoping to go unnoticed.

The second guard's uniform was so clean it practically glowed red in the dark. She made herself look into his eyes and not at the large dark mole just to the right side of his nose. He sneered as she approached.

Becca needed to distract the guards as she begged for entry to the prison to see her husband. She needed to make such a scene that they wouldn't look too closely at the ungainly, masculine-looking women who—she hoped—would be standing behind her.

Her mouth opened, but no words escaped. She hadn't cried for Philip since the night Minister Townsend informed her of his death. But on this frigid night, when she needed to imitate grief, she began to shed real tears for a man she hardly knew—for Daniel—that left her mute.

The taller soldier looked nervously to his colleague.

She had been silent too long.

The shorter guard changed his grip on his gun and swept it back and up. Feet shuffled behind her, as if Mason's two men were preparing to fight.

Say something. "My husband. You took him." Her voice cracked. "Please. I need to see him. Please."

Becca felt a weight in her hand and recalled the plan. With a jerky motion, she lifted the knotted handkerchief she held. "See, I have bread for him. Please."

The handkerchief swung in the air.

The shorter soldier, the one with the mole, didn't ask her husband's name. "Who are they?" He pointed with his bayonet at Amos and the other disguised bandit behind her.

"My aunts."

The two bandits curtsied awkwardly, their faces dark shapes beneath the hoods of their capes.

The soldier swung his bayonet back to Becca. Without warning, he slashed the white handkerchief she held, missing her hand by inches.

The biscuits she had packed at Cousin Samuel's house flew across the ice. Becca gasped and her hand opened. The handkerchief fluttered to the ground.

"You don't have anything for him now. Go home." His smile was spiteful.

"I can't go home," she screamed. *Because I will never stop blaming myself for your death.* She spoke directly to Daniel as if he could hear. "I have to see my husband."

"And I need to see my Jim," Amos called in a falsetto voice.

She stepped over to the taller, nervous redcoat and shook her fist in his face. "Is this how the Crown treats the ladies of New York?"

The two bandits drew closer.

"Go home. All of you." The shorter soldier leaned in toward Becca, sweeping the butt of his musket above her head. The muscles in his neck tensed.

She sensed the two men behind her go still, and her stomach clenched. She needed to stop the guards from looking at them too closely.

She shoved one arm out to the side, her palm facing back, a signal intended to stop them from attacking. She needed to get them back safely to Mr. Mason.

"Mike," the tall guard called, and the shorter redcoat lowered his gun.

The gritty sound of wheels grew louder. She thought she heard a horse neigh.

She steadied herself. "Get ready to leave," she whispered.

Was Daniel at a window watching her? Was he slumped against a wall waiting to be taken at daybreak to the *Jersey*? *I failed you. I am so, so sorry.*

She took a step toward the gate. Her legs felt heavy, as if the air was pressing down on her. This was grief, she knew.

"Rather stay and fight," Amos whispered.

Becca shook her head. What was the point?

The carriage slowed at the prison's front gate, where the other bandits dressed as women waited. They shuffled forward to join Becca's two "aunties" at the prison's front gate.

Becca wondered whether Mr. Mason was watching from the corner or waiting for them at the meeting place he designated.

The taller soldier pushed through the disguised men to meet the carriage. "You're late," he called to the driver.

"Not my damned fault," he grumbled. "Line of damn carriages at the mayor's place. A party. Cunningham didn't want the gents and ladies to see us go by, damn them all."

The tall soldier shrugged, dismissing him, then squinted at Mason's men. "Who's all this, then?"

"More of my aunties." Becca's heartbeat thumped in her throat.

Amos had complained the loudest about wearing petticoats. He took her elbow and cursed the redcoats under his breath. Mason's men didn't scare her now; they made her feel safe.

The tall soldier stepped toward Amos. "What kind of auntie is this?"

The carriage door swung open and a body was flung onto the ground. Icy grit spit from the wheels of the carriage as it pulled away.

The body hit the ice and rolled onto its back. The man's breath escaped in cold white puffs, his face turned to the sky. He scrambled to a low crouch as if ready to bolt, then froze, his gaze on Becca's.

Elation washed over her. "Now," she roared.

A flurry of skirts jumped the taller guard. One bandit slammed his head into the soldier's stomach, driving him to the ground. Another grabbed the guard's musket and jabbed its butt into his back. Others picked Daniel up by his arms and began dragging him away from the Sugar House.

"Mike, get the others." The tall soldier's voice rose in panic. He curled himself into a ball to protect himself from the blows.

The shorter guard ran to help, yelling for reinforcements. He stopped halfway to the gate, turned and raised his musket.

"Watch out," Becca bellowed.

One of Mason's men whirled around. His white teeth flashed in an exuberant grin. He lifted a pistol and shot. The shorter guard reared back and dropped his gun. Blood blossomed from Mike's forearm.

Other guards exploded out of the prison's front door.

Mason's bandits formed a line before the gate, their skirts flapping in the wind. Almost in unison, they lifted pistols from beneath their capes and shot.

Three British guards staggered. The others drew back to load their weapons.

Two bandits had their arms locked around Daniel's back and half carried, half-dragged him away from the prison.

Howls of laughter rose from the prison's narrow open windows. Pale faces peeked out. Arms waved or were raised in salute.

Becca couldn't help herself. Daniel was alive. They'd saved him. She curtsied to the audience of prisoners and blew a kiss. Their roar of approval rang in her ears as she followed the bandits up Crown Street away from the prison. In her entire life, she had never felt so afraid and so free. If she had the breath for it, she would laugh. She tried and it sounded like a sob.

She watched the two bandits in front of her half-carry Daniel. Within two blocks, he had found his stride and they released him. He stumbled, caught himself, and ran. Becca and Amos sped to catch up. He wasn't hurt, at least, not badly hurt.

A cannon blast shattered the night. A flock of frightened mourning doves lifted into the dark with an eerie whistling sound, then veered toward the river.

"We're in for it now," Amos wheezed. "They know there's been an escape. That's what the cannon's for." He lost his breath but kept running. "The guards on the street will stop every man they see."

Becca cursed, and Amos laughed at her unladylike language.

"Damn skirts," he groused. "Don't know how you run in 'em."

Chapter Thirty-Five

One by one, the bandits disappeared into alleys and side streets until Becca heard only the rasp of her own breath and Daniel's. She listened for footsteps at each corner they passed. When she heard only the low moan of the wind, they plunged forward across the next dark, open street.

Ahead she saw the burned border of the ruined city with its ghostly white tents and charred buildings. Canvas Town. A curtain of icicles lined the shuttered windows of the only intact building on this block. The red glow of a lantern lit a small window.

"There." Becca breathed. "That must be Mrs. Amity's home."

"This is where Mason said to meet? Here?" Daniel sounded stunned.

"Why, yes. I'm certain," Becca said. "Mrs. Amity's house in Canvas Town."

They crept along the side of the house. At the back door, she turned a fierce smile in his direction. "I'll never forget this night." She expected the triumph she felt to be stamped on his face. Instead, there was a bleak, quizzical look in his brown eyes that emphasized their slight downward slant.

"What's wrong?" Becca asked as the door opened.

A pair of hands enclosed her waist and pulled her into the warm room. Amos lifted her into the air. "Huzzah for Mrs. Parcell, boys."

Becca placed her hands on the bandit's shoulders for balance and laughed as he twirled her, Daniel's puzzling reaction forgotten. "Huzzah for us all," she called.

Some of the bandits stood and applauded. Others held up mugs of ale to

together.

toast her. They all talked at once.

"She's one of us, now."

"Did you see her?"

"She didn't blink when that lobsterback almost hit her."

Becca wanted to stay here, twirling in the air, safe in a warm room where she was welcomed among the colony's most infamous bandits. Where she belonged.

"Put her down now, Amos," Mason said with good humor.

He lowered her to the ground with care.

She took a quick count of the ruffians. Not one of the men was missing. Their discarded petticoats and skirts were puddled in heaps of cloth on rosewood chairs and tables.

"And Lady Augusta and Annie? They are well?"

"As I promised. Safe and away from the city," Mr. Mason called. The mayor had kidnapped Augusta once, which was more than enough. Mr. Mason had promised them the safety of his home in Bergen County surrounded by bandits.

Mason sat at a table in the midst of his men, vest unbuttoned, a slash of dirt marking one sleeve. His grizzled gray hair had escaped the confines of the pomade and powder. He looked more like the bandit Becca first met in the Neutral Ground than the fine gentleman at the mayor's ball.

"And congratulations on your freedom, Mr. Alloway." Mason lifted a small glass of port to Daniel. Its crystal facets reflected soft candlelight in sharp, dark angles. A large mirror hung on the wall behind Mason. It appeared to double the number of men sitting on the fine carved chairs and French-style couches in Canvas Town.

Daniel leaned against the wall. His arms were crossed and gaze shuttered.

Was he hurt? Becca wondered. He'd been able to run, but something was wrong.

"I expected a greater show of appreciation for those who saved you tonight." Mason took a delicate sip of port. "Not many women would have put themselves in harm's way for the likes of you."

Daniel's eyes shifted to Becca. "I'm aware of my obligation to Mrs. Parcell.

I'm grateful to your men as well." He nodded to them, once to the left, then to the right.

"You sound like a dinner guest praising food you don't care for," Becca snapped. He didn't appear to be injured. *Why isn't he celebrating?*

The bandits fell silent.

A howl of feminine laughter sounded from the next room, followed by a chorus of male chuckles. Some of the bandits smirked.

A woman bustled into the room holding a pewter tray heaped with gingerbread cakes and roasted meats. "Men are starved for nothing at Mrs. Amity's," she said with a voice that lifted and fell like music. Her wig was styled in powdered curls, her complexion as pale as any noble lady's. She wore a cotton chintz gown in off white with alternating thick and thin red stripes. The hem of the dress exposed her ankles and a bit more.

"To our hostess, Mrs. Amity." Mason raised his cup again.

"To Mrs. Amity," the men responded with gusto.

She dropped a graceful curtsy, then rose and winked at Mason. "You know you are always welcome here, Mr. Mason."

Mason stood and bowed. "I rarely find rest here, madam. But I am grateful for your hospitality."

The red light at the door. The shrieks on the other side of the wall. Becca suddenly realized what type of business establishment Mrs. Amity ran.

A few of Mason's men guffawed. Most were already jostling for access to the supper tray. They grabbed plates, utensils and poured from pitchers of ale lined along a drop-leaf table that was set in front of a painted green wall.

The smell of butter, cloves and sugar made Becca's mouth water. She hadn't eaten since breakfast.

"I can still depend on your protection, Mr. Mason?" The music was gone from Mrs. Amity's voice. "The war's been good for my business and yours. But it won't last forever. The next government may be less tolerant of my establishment."

"You've heard something?"

"Most of my gentlemen think we don't have the intelligence to understand them. They sometimes say more than they should in our presence." Mrs.

Amity's lip curled before she ironed her expression into pleasant neutrality.

"Everyone is talking," she continued. "Less than two weeks ago, before dawn, more than two hundred dragoons left New York for Morristown."

"I know. They rode past us," Mason answered.

"No one battles during the winter. They wait for spring to take up arms," Becca said.

Mason and Mrs. Amity turned to Becca with matching looks of surprise, as if a pet spaniel had just spoken.

"Most men think we women don't have the intelligence to understand them." Becca copied the woman's singsong tone and curled lip precisely, then tucked her chin into chest. Lady Augusta would be horrified at her manners.

Mrs. Amity threw her head back and laughed, then patted her wig to ensure it hadn't shifted with her sudden movement. "I like her, Mr. Mason."

She raised a glass to Becca, then turned back to Mason. "Some of my gentlemen say the dragoons were sent to capture General Washington. They brag that there wasn't a Rebel soldier in sight, that they could have captured him without a battle if not for the snow. The roads were impassable. They were forced back to New York."

Mrs. Amity's gaze flickered left to right to confirm that no one would overhear. She lowered her voice. "My gentlemen whisper that they expect a new attempt on General Washington's life. Soon." Then she trilled: "Oh, my goodness. We women are such gossips. Pay no attention. I hardly pay myself any mind."

Becca took a moment to admire her hostess, a woman who managed to hide and demonstrate her intelligence at the same time.

Mrs. Amity lifted an elegant finger to Becca's chin and frowned, examining her face from one angle, then the other. "A bit tall, but just what some of the gentlemen fancy. If you decide to stay, you'll be welcome to make your home here."

Becca's face flushed. Should she be shamed or flattered by the offer? She bowed her head the way Augusta would, with gracious civility. "I appreciate your offer, ma'am. But I'll be returning to Morristown soon." After all, Mrs.

Amity was hiding them from the British soldiers. That took courage. And without a home, how many choices were available to women? She wouldn't judge.

"Ah, well. My door is open to you, dear." Then Mrs. Amity pursed her lips into a seductive pout that made the bandits catch their breath. She curtsied, displaying ample cleavage, and closed the door behind her.

"I intended no disrespect when I asked you to meet us here," Mason said.

Becca's eyes widened. He *was* a minder reader.

"We'll be safe for the night. The redcoats rarely dare to send troops into Canvas Town." He waved his hand toward the window and the ruins outside that were draped in darkness. "They haven't lifted a finger to rebuild from the Great Fire." He shook his head in disgust. "The soldiers have few friends here. Mrs. Amity makes sure that the poorest families have food. They watch out for her."

"A word, Mrs. Parcell?" Daniel said.

The cup wobbled in her hand. "Certainly, Mr. Alloway."

Mr. Mason jerked his chin toward the closed door at the far end of the room. "Mrs. Amity's study will give you a bit of quiet. But be quick if you want any sleep. The redcoats will be out looking for you at first light, and we'll have you gone by then."

* * *

Daniel was grateful to Becca. Of course he was. But the thanks he owed her stuck in his throat. He was disconcerted, unbalanced. He was ready to face death. He wasn't as certain about facing life.

He'd expected to die, in fact, almost every day since he'd left the *Jersey*, as if his escape had been in error. If he'd had the words for it, he would have explained that.

The last thing he'd thought to see was Rebecca Parcell leaning over him at the Sugar House, her face as fierce as an avenging angel. Looking into her eyes, he was surprised to find that he preferred to live. It was a revelation, and he wondered whether newborns felt like this. Was their skin raw with the ache of sensation? He welcomed it all: the scrape of gravel at the entrance to the prison, the clotted snow, the icy air, even the aches after being tossed to the ground.

Becca rose and stalked toward Mrs. Amity's study.

Daniel followed, plucking a candle from one of the sconces just before he passed through the door.

He slid the light into an unglazed clay candle holder on Mrs. Amity's desk, bathing the small, cold room in a wavering yellow light. The few pieces of furniture were rough pine, serviceable but lacking decoration. Two uncomfortable looking chairs flanked the fireplace. An empty teacup sat on one, as if daring any guests to sit there.

When he turned, Becca poked his chest. "Should I have left you at the Sugar House?" Another poke. "Would that have made you happier?" Poke.

Her lips were slightly chapped. Without thinking, he lifted his index finger to her bottom lip to smooth the skin there.

She went still.

"I was a bit surprised, I admit, to still be among the living." Slowly, watching for any change in her expression, he swept his finger along her jawline, then her neck, the dip at her collarbone. It was the sensation of her skin that called to him. "I am in your debt."

How strength and softness could coexist in her so perfectly was miraculous. He didn't mean to kiss her. But she closed her eyes just then, and her breath shuddered.

In the next room, the bandits sang *"derry down, down. Hey, derry down."* Daniel pulled himself away two verses later.

Her eyes were heavy-lidded. A small smile hovered on her lips.

I am in your debt, he had said to her. He owed her whatever honor a jobless, cantankerous ruffian like himself could muster. He owed her more than he could pay. He would make it right.

"Mrs. Parcell. Becca." He cleared his throat. "I won't be returning to Morristown."

Her smile evaporated.

"The reward. You take it. Yours and mine."

CHAPTER THIRTY-FIVE

"Why would I do that?"

"I need to know that you'll be cared for. After," Daniel said. After he left her, he meant, but couldn't make himself say. "The money I'm promised will take care of that."

"You've earned that reward. You'll need money. After." She didn't mention his leave-taking, either.

"I will manage," he said. She was right. He needed money to travel west. But that didn't change anything.

"No." She crossed her arms.

Any moment she would begin to pace, he thought, as if only repetitive motion could calm her. He knew her that well now.

There. She stepped toward the cold fireplace with its blue and white Dutch tiles, then turned, repeating her steps.

She was stubborn; so was he. If she wouldn't let him secure her future this way, he would find another way.

"Then you'll need to marry me." The proposal tumbled out unbidden, as if it had been waiting for the right moment to make itself known.

"And why will I need to marry you?" She froze, mid-stride. Her winged eyebrows rose.

"It is the honorable thing to do." He was as surprised as Becca by his proposal.

"Honorable." Her voice went flat.

"Because you were willing to give your life for me," he said. "It is the honorable thing to do." His thoughts strayed from honor. He would slip his arm around her each night as they fell asleep. In the morning, she would wake slowly, reach for him, and then....

"*Your* honor?" she asked.

"Why yes." The proposal had been unexpected, but it felt exactly right.

"So you will sacrifice the rest of your life to repay me?" Anger crackled round her.

"I don't know how else to repay you." He had cared so little about the truth since Amelia's death. But he found that he cared very much for it now. This was the truth. "I have nothing to give, nothing but myself."

Becca's face emptied of expression. "I am an independent woman, Mr. Alloway. I will not wed again, certainly not to a man who considers marrying me a sacrifice."

"Sacrifice? I didn't mention sacrifice."

"The estate of marriage and I are not well-matched." Regret washed over her face, and he wondered whether she was thinking of Philip Parcell.

"And yet I owe you my life," he said.

She stepped out of the circle of candlelight that enveloped them and into the shadows. "We have been suitable business partners, have we not? Let us continue as we were. That will be sufficient repayment."

Her reasonable tone of voice set his teeth on edge. He wished she would scream. "As we were? Entirely as we were?"

"Indeed. A temporary arrangement is what we have. A business arrangement." She straightened her skirt.

"A business arrangement?" He was offended but felt a whiff of relief at her refusal.

"And since we have already accomplished what General Washington asked of us—we know that the mayor of New York City received my husband's and the minister's messages—we should not require each other's company for too much longer." She swept by him and out of the room as if he were a ghost she no longer saw.

Chapter Thirty-Six

The wind raced across the bay early the next morning and whipped strands of hair across Becca's face. She scanned the gray ice for other travelers heading to New Jersey over the hard-frozen surface of New York Harbor. The only sign of life was a raccoon scuttling along the shore and back into the wheat-colored beach grass.

Mason's hand rested on the window of the black carriage. It was half hidden behind a copse of thickets at water's edge.

The carriage was on loan from Mrs. Amity. Two of her ladies had escorted their gentlemen callers to the door in the middle of the night and practically bumped into redcoat soldiers searching the street. They heard the soldiers question their clients. Had either of them seen a gaunt man and a tall woman with messy black hair traveling together? "Of course not," they'd said.

Daniel and the driver stood near the two lead horses. The short, bow-legged driver with blonde hair crooned to the gentle animals and patted their long noses.

Becca kept her gaze pinned on Mr. Mason. Daniel had thought he was doing the right thing last night, the honorable thing. She could tell by the way he held himself, his back rigid, chin thrust forward. She imagined a brave man would stand just so as the noose was placed round his neck. She would not be Daniel's noose. She rubbed her gloved hands together in the carriage. She couldn't seem to warm them.

This was a fine time to discover that she was in love with him. *I have nothing to give you, nothing but myself*, he had said, as if that wasn't the greatest gift of all. The greatest gift for the worst of all reasons: obligation. Why couldn't people be as straightforward and easy to decipher as numbers? Why couldn't *she*?

"You have your passport?" Mason asked.

"Yes." Becca blushed at the thoughts Mr. Mason had interrupted. Then she touched the thick paper in her pocket that Mr. Hamilton had given her. It let her pass freely to and from New York City.

Mason scowled. "And your blasted account book? I don't see why you insist upon bringing it."

Becca placed her hand on Mason's to stop his questions. "I won't forget what you've done for us."

"No call to get sentimental, Mrs. Rebecca. You're not safe yet." Mason looked past the carriage. Her gratitude seemed to embarrass him. "Best to leave now. It's already late."

The first low rays of the sun painted the frozen palisades with a pale iridescence. In some places, the snow-covered ice resembled curdled cream; in others, scattered shards of glass.

"But why?" she asked Mason. "Why do all this for us?" She opened her free hand and swung it around, pointing to the closed carriage and the harbor beyond. "I know you have a *tendresse* for Lady Augusta. But you're risking yourself and your men for me. Why?"

"I promised your mother-in-law I'd keep you safe. I'll keep her safe as well," he said. "Isn't that enough?"

She shook her head. "I don't believe you."

"You don't believe I care for your mother-in-law?" He glowered.

"I don't believe it's just about Lady Augusta." Becca examined him more closely. "Why, Mr. Mason, I believe you have principles."

He stuck out his lower lip. "Nonsense, madam. None of that talk. I do what's best for me." He pounded his chest with one hand to emphasize the point. "The British won't win, and I prefer to be on the winning side. Simple as that."

"You are fighting for liberty, aren't you?"

His thunderous eyebrows drew together. "I am the much-feared head of the Highland Gang, madam. Do not spread rumors that I side with freedom over tyranny. It's bad for business."

"As you wish." She smiled and leaned back in the carriage. Who would have thought Mr. Mason had principles?

Mason nodded to the driver, who lifted one leg onto the step and vaulted into the front seat. Daniel swung the far door of the carriage open and entered more tentatively, his bad hand held close to his chest.

A whip cracked. The horses hurtled forward, their hooves sounding with a solid thump on the uneven ice as the driver sang to his darlings. The wheels lurched and creaked forward. Becca faced the carriage window, erasing Daniel from her sight.

She measured time from the death of those she loved: There was before; There was after. Carl taught her mathematics *after* her mother died. She killed a bear *before* her father's passing. Philip died *after* she discovered he never loved her.

She could not tolerate the thought of Daniel becoming another way she measured her life: before Daniel left; after. Because Daniel was going to leave.

She would keep her distance.

The carriage slid and her knees bumped his. She pulled away, flinging the scratchy lap blanket over her legs.

Keep your distance. Short of flinging herself or Daniel from the coach, there was only one thing to do. She leaned forward.

His lips lifted into a slow smile.

Then she stretched her hand below her seat, slid out the small wooden box she had insisted that Mason's men leave there, and lifted it on to her lap. She plucked the account book and her traveling ink set from their resting place. She slid two fingers along the thick cover, then tried to focus on the snowy, expensive paper. Philip had given it to her last spring. "Now, Mr. Alloway. Shall we begin?"

"Begin?"

The ink would splatter as the carriage wheels slid on the ice, but there was no help for that. She held the pen above the page as if waiting for Daniel to speak. "Let us record what we have learned and the questions that remain."

For example, she wanted to ask, how long will I miss when you when you leave?

Daniel sighed. "Let's begin then. We know that Mr. Parcell's list of spies exists. Or at least the British believe it exists. Otherwise, they wouldn't have threatened you, and they wouldn't be looking for me."

Becca's shoulders relaxed. If he could act as if last night's conversation never happened, so could she. "We know Minister Townsend was a turncoat," she said. "He was the new messenger."

She began a list, and the familiar activity slowed her heartbeat. How ironic, she thought, that writing a list of possible spies and murderers was as comforting as listing the tasks one wished to complete that day.

"We know that Philip and others in Morristown wedged messages to the British into the whiskey bottle corks." Daniel rubbed his hands together to warm them.

Becca felt the cold, too. She lifted her ledger to tuck a fur blanket more tightly around her. "You stayed with some of the general's guards in Morristown, didn't you? Did any strike you as particularly unhappy or angry?"

"None of the soldiers are happy, not with the food shortages, but I haven't heard any angry enough to betray their country. I'll talk to Major Gibbs when we get back. He's in charge of Washington's personal guards."

"What?"

"Gibbs has access to General Washington and the Widow Ford's mansion." Daniel grimaced. "I hate thinking he might be involved in this. I like the man." He paused. "We still haven't found your husband's list of spies."

"You're not certain we've earned General Washington's reward?" Becca asked.

Daniel was silent, which was a kind of answer. Finally, he asked, "Where would Mr. Parcell hide that list? Where did he go when he wanted to be alone? Who were his friends?"

"I'm not the person to ask." Becca twisted the pen in her hands until pockmarks of ink bespattered the page. "It seems I hardly knew him." She tried not to sound bitter. Her husband had kept so many secrets from her.

"Who knew him, then?" Daniel's voice softened.

"Charity Adams." Becca slapped the account book shut on her lap. She flushed thinking of Philip's mistress, the woman who'd accused her of threatening Philip in front of half the town. She tucked away the traveling writing kit.

"Who else?" Daniel asked.

"Thomas loaned Philip money. Thomas Lockwood." Becca had barely dodged his proposal of marriage before leaving for New York.

Daniel grunted, his immediate antipathy to Lockwood not calling for any additional response.

"We should speak to Carl, too," Becca said. "He might have heard something from other servants."

"I wonder whether Hopper would know anything helpful?" Daniel asked.

"Hopper?" Becca felt her forehead crease in confusion.

Daniel grinned. "I don't know why they call him Hopper, either. He's an old man who took me in when I first came to Morristown."

She didn't notice the increase in the horses' pace until one of them whinnied, then screamed in distress.

"Redcoats," the driver called. "To our rear."

Becca stretched to the left, looking back toward the city. Other carriages were crossing the frozen harbor. But three men on horseback barreled toward them, their red coats the only splash of color on the gray ice.

She jerked her head to the right. The ferry dock at the Jersey shore was in clear view. She lurched sideways and hit the upholstered carriage wall.

She felt the blast of an explosion.

The ice popped with an eerie keening sound. The carriage rolled up and down as if it were a boat on the waves. The motion thrummed through her body.

The blanket fell from Becca's lap and she grasped the edge of the seat. The horses pulled to the right. The driver yelled and brought the animals back under control.

Becca leaned out the window to track the sound, ignoring the frigid air clawing at her bare neck. The few other carriages on the frozen harbor scattered. Shouts from their passengers carried on the wind.

She turned to the Jersey side.

On the dock, smoke spewed from the mouth of a short, squat cannon. She squinted but could only make out a mass of men in blue and buff uniforms, their bayonets pointing toward the sky like silver exclamation points.

Another explosion. The frozen bay groaned in protest.

The cannon ball's landing spot was marked by a black hole in the ice. The three redcoats veered left to avoid it, urging their horses to close the gap between themselves and the carriage. They were close now. One of the soldiers had hair so bright it was almost orange.

"They're turning back." Daniel reached for her hand. She squeezed it.

A splintering sound beneath them made the hair on her arms rise.

The driver cursed at his horses and cracked his whip. His horses broke into a gallop.

The blue coats on the near shore roared with approval.

Becca left her hand in Daniel's for one beat, then two, before sliding her fingers away.

The carriage came to a rest on the shore next to the ferry slip. A wall of Washington's guards, all about the same height, grinned in triumph, waiting for her to alight.

She hesitated before opening the door. These pleased-looking men almost killed her. Was there a mathematical equation to determine how grateful she should be? "Rescues us from capture" minus "causes near death by drowning" equaled...what precisely?

Chapter Thirty-Seven

Becca absently noticed that her hands were shaking as she opened the carriage door.

"You canting gypsy. Scum of the earth. Who authorized that shot?" An officer roared into the faces of three soldiers. They stood at grim-faced attention near a short cannon that was mounted on a field carriage aimed into the harbor.

The one with empty, dark eyes looked familiar. Something about him made her stomach twist.

As if sensing her stare, the bellowing young officer stopped mid-curse, clamped his jaw shut and strode up to her.

"Major Gibbs?" Daniel said.

Gibbs swept off his hat, with its white plume tipped in blue, and bowed. His eyes had an open surprised look, although his face was frozen with fury. "Major Gibbs, madam, of His Excellency's guards, at your service."

She curtseyed. "As I am at yours. You and your men have my gratitude."

"Gratitude?" Gibbs spit. "My men practically killed you. I'll keep every last one of them here until I find out who fired that howitzer. It wasn't me." His chin jutted forward, daring anyone to argue.

Her gaze flickered to Gibbs' men standing near the small cannon, which she thought was called a howitzer. "They intended to hit us?" There was a moment when she thought that might be the case, but she hadn't really believed it.

"No. Just carelessness, which is no less excusable," Gibbs said.

Becca wondered whether he was as upset as he seemed. Did he give the command to shoot and then deny it when they came ashore?

Two of the three soldiers began to disassemble the weapon. The third, the one wearing the Life Guard's uniform, vanished.

She shivered. His face was familiar. Why couldn't she remember?

"They swear they heard someone pass along an order from me to shoot," Gibbs said. "But none of them can say who gave the order."

Daniel's green eyes darkened. "How did you know to be here today? Why here? Why now?"

"We *didn't* know. General Washington received a warning two nights ago, a message that you might be crossing back to New Jersey in haste. He ordered us to leave for the closest ferry point this morning. He was afraid you might be intercepted. And he was right."

It must have taken at least two days for the note to reach General Washington, Becca calculated, and another two days for Major Gibbs and his men to reach the ferry slip.

Four days ago, she and Daniel had just left Mr. Rivington's print shop. Mr. Rivington must have sent the note, she surmised.

Becca studied the soldiers forced on a two-day march on the chance she and Daniel might land here.

"It could have been worse, Mrs. Parcell." Gibbs followed her gaze. "If you'd stayed in New York City another week or if your driver chose another route, we might have been waiting for you here until spring."

"It would have been worse if that cannon strike killed us." Daniel's voice was dry.

Gibbs' cheeks flushed an angry red. "On my honor, I will have you back in Morristown in two days. After you." He bowed stiffly and swept his arm out, pointing to the road where a soldier harnessed two horses to a dull brown coach.

At the carriage entrance, Becca turned back, wincing into the icy wind and searching for the guard who seemed so familiar.

She remembered now. She had met Daniel that night. She'd met the man they called the Ferret, and she'd met Sergeant Bartlett, the man with the dark, empty eyes who killed him.

Chapter Thirty-Eight

"This entire charade would be unnecessary if we had talked to General Washington yesterday or the day before. Who is Mr. Hamilton to tell me when I can speak to him?" Becca pulled her dark blue cloak more tightly around her neck.

Alexander Hamilton had shooed them away from Washington's winter headquarters with no explanation two days ago, the morning after they reached Morristown. But he sent a note this morning commanding her to attend Thomas Lockwood's party. Daniel's invitation was delivered to Major Gibbs' hut, where he was staying for now.

Becca missed a step on the lantern-lit walkway that led to Lockwood's front door and gasped when snow filled her slipper.

"This charade couldn't be more necessary." Daniel caught her arm. He was clean-shaven now, his shoulder-length hair pulled into an austere queue. Mr. Hamilton had convinced some of the taller officers to lend Daniel a silk waistcoat of ivory with gold trim, as well as a matching coat, pale breeches and a fine white linen shirt.

Becca steadied herself, and he slowly released her.

"We can't be seen talking to General Washington at his headquarters. Here, he can disappear for a few minutes and we'll be led to meet him. No one will notice."

"Not notice? Minister Townsend's friends will be here, won't they?" Becca kicked her foot to dislodge the snow from her slipper. She recalled dances like tonight's with Philip, Mary Ford whispering behind her back, condescending smirks from women who had French dance masters to teach them the steps. This was the last place she wanted to be.

In a small voice, she said, "If I have to dance a minuet, I shall make a fool of myself."

"Becca." Daniel repeated her name twice before she looked up. "Standing still, you outshine them all."

His words hung in the frigid air between them.

"Ridiculous," she said but leaned toward him for comfort.

The door squeaked as it swung open. She spun toward it.

"Welcome home, Mrs. Parcell." Thomas Lockwood filled the doorway. His knuckles shown white on the door latch he held.

Becca stepped away from Daniel.

Carl stood behind his master. He lifted his hand to his chest and, in a small tight gesture not visible to Lockwood, pointed to a window near the front door, then shook his head.

Becca flushed. Thomas had watched her through that window.

"Welcome to you, too, Mr. Alloway." Lockwood made room for them to enter.

Becca inched past him, then surveyed the room.

Brightly dressed young officers and their wives sailed past the entryway. The women were dressed in wide hooped gowns and ruffled sleeves. The men had powdered their hair whiter than the snow that blanketed the town. She heard the usual clinking of glasses and the ripple of laughter as toasts were offered.

After the balls of New York, the evening's entertainment seemed almost quaint. No, that wasn't it. The music here was more straightforward. The guests laughed more easily. The voices were louder.

We're not British, she thought with surprise. In all the flowery language about independence, she hadn't heard anyone state what was obvious to her now. They were not English. They were American.

"Sweet lady," Thomas's voice boomed. "Your virtues have taken up my thoughts in your absence, and I am much pleased to see you here."

The buzz of laughter dwindled. A nearby knot of people turned to listen.

"What are you doing?" she hissed.

"It is obvious, isn't it?" Daniel's voice was dry.

It *was* obvious. A proposal in public. She couldn't catch her breath.

"Mr. Alloway is correct. You know my feelings. I am tired of hiding them from our friends and neighbors."

"You are making me uncomfortable." Becca enunciated each word.

"A toast," Thomas called. He grabbed a glass of wine from a nearby sideboard. His eyes dropped to Daniel's maimed hand. "Will you require assistance lifting a cup?" he added more loudly than necessary.

"Not from you." Daniel held Thomas' gaze.

"How fortuitous." Thomas' grin didn't reach his eyes.

"There you are, Mr. Lockwood," a guest called. "His Excellency is asking for you."

Thomas' face darkened but even he wouldn't keep General Washington waiting. He bowed, then strode away.

Chapter Thirty-Nine

Voices softened as she and Daniel passed. One person, then another, turned, then quickly looked away. Mary Ford dipped her chin in greeting. Eliza Codington followed suit. Joshua Harrington nodded just enough to avoid rudeness.

"Steady now," Daniel whispered as they headed toward the refreshment table at the back of the hallway. Becca felt his warm breath on her neck. "The Sugar House was worse."

He was right, and at least no one would be throwing rocks at her tonight. She tamped down memories of the mob at her front door and forced her shoulders to relax.

A burst of laughter punctuated the end of a story at the far end of the hall.

Washington stood beneath the portrait of Thomas Lockwood's father. Becca studied the general and his retinue. He wore a black velvet suit and towered over most of the men surrounding him. They looked satisfied, as if they were absorbing some of his glory through proximity.

Washington raised his arm, pointing to the portrait. "That wasn't the only time Mr. Lockwood and I got into a scrape." His face grew somber.

Becca wove her way through the crowd to listen. Daniel followed.

"I'd already had two horses shot out from under me." Washington spoke over the group to Thomas, who stood at the edge of the circle. "Your father stood by me, in front of me, right in front of me, when the bullet hit him. He saved my life. I always say that."

"Yes. You always say that." Thomas lifted the goblet he still held as if to toast the general.

Washington shook his head. "Hard to believe it's been twenty-five years since we lost him at Fort Duquesne. It was a sad day." His voice faded and Becca was reminded of his age. General Washington was old to have so much to bear. She'd heard he was forty-eight.

"He knew Thomas's father?" Daniel asked in a low tone.

"They were friends back in the fifties, both in the Virginia Militia," Becca answered. "General Washington took the family under his wing after Mr. Lockwood senior died." Few people talked about the war against the French any more. It was as if the new war had erased the old.

"A toast to one of the finest officers I have known," Washington called. The men surrounding him lifted their glasses. "A toast."

Thomas' glass rose more slowly.

Becca stared at the large portrait of Mr. Lockwood senior hanging on the wall above Washington and felt a pang of sadness for Thomas. She and Thomas had both lost their parents. But he was so much younger than she when his father died. Thomas still idolized him, she knew.

The quartet's music rose and, in three-quarter time, swept the rest of the party onto the dance floor. Daniel pushed against the crowd, protecting Becca, who followed behind him, until they popped out of the room like a cork bobbing to the surface of the water.

"There now. As promised." He flicked his hand into the air and bowed. "I've saved you from the minuet, Mrs. Parcell." A web of rare smile lines formed around Daniel's eyes.

Becca smiled in return, curtsying deeply in her velvet burgundy gown. "Kind, sir. Your virtues increase and multiply in abundant felicity." Daniel had managed to turn her old fear of dancing into a game.

"Nicely executed, both of you." Alexander Hamilton leaned against the doorway.

Becca wobbled as she rose, feeling heat rise from her chest to her cheeks.

Hamilton pushed off from the wall in a lithe motion and approached. "General Washington requests that you wait for him below. This way, please."

* * *

211

Green bottles. Amber jugs. Stout and squat. Tall and thin. Rows of bottles lay in notched grooves along dark wood shelves lining the plastered walls. Becca paced the small wine cellar. She hugged herself for warmth, swerving and turning just short of the corks and shelves.

"Sighing won't make the time pass more quickly." Daniel's eyes were closed. He sat in an uncomfortable straight-backed wood chair, one of three in the center of the room that circled an upended wooden crate. He leaned back, his long legs stretched forward and crossed at the ankle. His hands were clasped across his vest. They'd been left here alone for at least an hour.

Becca exhaled briskly, then paced again.

"My apologies for keeping you waiting." The slightly high voice was gracious yet businesslike.

Daniel scrambled to his feet and bowed.

Becca curtsied.

"Mr. Lockwood was gracious to arrange this party for me—for us—on a day's notice and…" General Washington's gaze circled the cellar. His face brightened. "…to stock my favorite Madeira."

Hamilton slipped through the door behind Washington and closed it.

Washington took two steps toward a dark bottle on a nearby shelf. He lifted and examined it with satisfaction, then gently replaced it. He seemed too large for the space. The ceiling barely cleared his powdered hair.

Becca wondered whether he was making a show of the Madeira to put them at ease. It would take more than a discussion of wine for her heart to stop galloping.

"Now tell me what you've learned." Washington swept his hand to the chairs, inviting Becca and Daniel to sit. He joined them in the third chair.

"But didn't Mr. Hamilton report—?" Daniel's forehead creased.

"What you told him. Yes," Washington interrupted. "In your own words, please. And from the beginning."

Becca and Daniel described how they discovered and decoded the messages that were delivered to Mayor Matthews.

"And one of the messages ordered something to be delivered to redcoat officers arriving here by February twenty-first," Becca added. "Does that make any sense?"

Washington and Hamilton exchanged glances.

"They are here at my invitation," Washington said.

"Your invitation?" Becca didn't meant to sound shocked.

"They're here to negotiate a prisoner exchange," Washington said. "Failure is more likely than success. But if there's a chance to save some of our good men, then it is worth having them here."

"Can't you question the English officers? They're right here," Becca protested.

Washington's thin eyebrows might have risen a jot in surprise.

She tucked her chin into her chest. She shouldn't have spoken.

"It has taken considerable diplomacy to have the British senior command accept our request for this delegation." Hamilton paused to ensure he had her attention. "We will be treating them with all due courtesies. They are our honored guests."

Must he lecture, she thought with irritation born of her disappointment. There was no plot. The delegation had arrived at Washington's invitation.

"You've learned nothing else about the traitors? And you haven't found Mr. Parcell's list?" Hamilton asked.

Daniel hesitated. "No."

Washington slapped the top of the barrel standing next to his chair.

Becca flinched. "We've done what you asked. We discovered who received the Turncoats' messages in New York."

Washington rose and motioned to Hamilton to come closer. The gold metal buttons on his cuff caught the candlelight as he whispered into his aide's ear.

Hamilton's mouth tightened. He nodded.

"You said you didn't expect us to find the list of spies. You said it would be enough if we could discover who received their messages." Becca didn't need either man to speak. The information they'd brought back wasn't enough.

"You never meant to reward us." Daniel's voice was cold.

"I'm sorry, Alloway," Hamilton began.

213

"Madam, you recall our conversation one way. I remember it differently." Washington said. "I promised to safeguard your farm if you untangled your husband's treason. You haven't. I can't help you–either of you—unless you have more to share."

He seemed so certain. Becca teetered on the edge of doubt for just a moment. Had she twisted her memory to fit her desire? No. "You said my home would be safe if I learned who received my husband's messages. I did." Her voice roughened. "Now you keep your promise."

"How hard have you fought for your own freedom and your land?" Washington asked. "Do you expect me to do less for our nation's independence?" His eyes were almost gray in this light. "Very few of us are who we thought we were when the war began. The lines have blurred."

"You've changed the terms of our agreement. There are lines one can't cross and ever come back," Becca echoed Mr. Mason's warning. "Have you crossed those lines, General?"

Hamilton stepped toward her. Daniel cleared his throat as if to drown out her rudeness.

She didn't care. What was the worst they could do? Accuse her of treason? Morristown already had.

"If my soul is forfeit, it is for the most worthy of causes." Washington's face momentarily filled with grief. Perhaps Becca had imagined it. Then he bowed, lifted a taper from one of the sconces and was gone.

To calm herself, Becca counted the bottles shelved along the far wall. Eight across. Four down. Thirty-two in total. She thought she recognized two bottles of Philip's whiskey. But not even numbers calmed her tonight. She smacked open the cellar door and burst into the dark, empty hallway. General Washington was gone. She needed fresh air.

Behind her, Daniel murmured to Hamilton, "Let her go."

Chapter Forty

B ecca moved forward, scraping the palm of her hand against the rough granite wall. In her haste, she had forgotten to take a candle.

She could just imagine the look on Mr. Hamilton's face if she tiptoed back for a light. He'd be the soul of gentility and offer to guide her upstairs himself, but it would seal his judgment of her. "She can't even find her way out of the cellar," he'd tell General Washington later. "How did we expect her to find the traitors?"

When Hamilton led them down the kitchen stairs, they traveled down a long hall to a "T," then made a right turn. She would reverse her steps to find the stairs. She would stop in the kitchen to say goodbye to Carl, then slip away. She'd had enough of Thomas' party.

Her thoughts bounced and crashed, picking up speed like a rockslide. She would lose her home. What would happen to Augusta and Annie? Should she start for Mr. Mason's place in the morning? No one would dare call her a traitor if she married Thomas. At the thought, the memory of Daniel's lips on hers flooded her mind.

A wisp of hair tickled her forehead. She swiped it away with her hand, then froze. There shouldn't be a breeze. Not here in the cellar hallway.

"You came." The voice was a harsh whisper.

There must be a door that led outside. One of Thomas' servants must be helping another slip back into the house when he should have been here all along. She'd wait to move forward until they were gone to avoid embarrassing either one of them.

"Don't ask me to do anything else," the second man begged. "I shouldn't be meeting you here. You shouldn't have made me." He sounded frightened.

"I'm happy to call on you at the officers' huts. Is that what you want?" the whispering man jeered.

"No. No. This is better."

Not servants. Becca shrank against the wall, straining to hear. Why was a soldier–an officer—sneaking into Thomas Lockwood's cellar? What was frightening him? *This isn't your war*, she reminded herself. Not after her talk with General Washington.

"This pouch needs to be delivered tonight. You know who to see."

"I told you. I can't."

The whispering man's voice softened. "It's only a pouch. There's no danger in it. He needs it tonight."

"I'll be hanged for treason."

"The widow Parcell is looking for you, I've heard. I hope she doesn't find you." The whispering voice taunted.

The cellar's chill seeped into her bones. How did the man with the harsh voice know she was searching for turncoats? What was in the pouch that threatened treason?

"You told me she wouldn't come back. You promised." The frightened voice teetered on the edge of panic.

Not come back. Becca shivered, recalling the mayor's veiled threats and the race across New York Harbor. She almost hadn't returned to Morristown.

"A pouch is such a small thing. This one fits in your coat, yes?"

"Can't I give it to him at the ball? We'll all be going."

"No. Not then." The whisperer changed the subject. "How many sentries are assigned to the redcoats?"

"There are four."

"Make sure you're one of them in the morning."

She heard the rhythmic *shush* of footsteps climbing stairs. A thin dagger of light struck the far wall as the kitchen door opened above, then disappeared.

Another click. It carried a hint of fresh, icy air. Then nothing. No voices. No cold air. No movement.

Becca crept forward. She turned the corner. One step. Another.

Along the skin of her neck, she felt the imaginary, delicate scrape of animal teeth. She slowed, stopped. Hunting with her father, she'd come to respect her body's warnings, even if she didn't understand them.

She couldn't say how she knew that someone was watching, not until she saw a shadow move near the cellar door.

Her thoughts beat to the rhythm of her heart: She had no knife, no bow, no weapon.

One of the two men had closed the door but remained inside, as if he knew she was there, as if he was waiting for her. The whispering man, she guessed. The other had been too jittery.

Hamilton's confident laughter and Daniel's low-pitched voice fractured the silence.

She pivoted toward them. They were leaving the wine cellar.

When she turned back, the whispering man was gone.

Becca raced up the stairs, not thinking, hardly noticing the crunch beneath one heel. The evening's betrayal crashed over her.

She turned left at the landing and fled through the front hallway in search of her cloak. She found it in a small sitting room off the main hallway. She fumbled with the cape, which fell in a shining pool of dark blue velvet. She scooped it up and noticed something impaled on the heel of her shoe.

It was a dried leaf, broad at its base and ending in a sharp, thin tip. She tore it away, shoving the leaf in an inside pocket of her cape.

She swung open the front door.

"Are you leaving?" Thomas stood behind her, his face filled with concern.

Not now. Not now. Becca stepped away from the door and curtsied. "My manners are abysmal. I meant to thank you for your hospitality before I left."

"I didn't have a chance to make the toast I intended. I thought you were avoiding me." He stepped closer.

"No, of course not." Of course she was.

"But you are upset. I can see that. Has Mr. Alloway offended you?"

"No, of course not." She resisted the pull of his concern.

"What then?"

I don't want to marry you, she thought. But this wasn't the time or place for that conversation. Instead, other words, equally true, tumbled out. "The Council of Safety meets next week. They'll decide whether I'm a traitor. I am a poor guest until then, I'm afraid."

His face relaxed into its familiar lion-like smile. "The governor and General Washington will both attend the ball. I'll have a word with them about your dilemma."

She threw open the door and ran, calling behind her, "That would be wonderful."

Thomas' smile grew. He stepped outside, his voice rising. "And I have another idea. Why don't you...?"

Becca stepped into the carriage, holding a servant's arm for balance.

"...and I attend the..."

She swept her gown round her as the door snapped shut. The driver cracked a whip into the air. The wheels rumbled over the ice as the carriage pulled away.

"...ball together," Thomas Lockwood called into the wind.

Becca rested her head against the cushion and replayed the conversation she overheard in the cellar hallway. If she'd had her account book with her, she would have written down her questions.

Who were the two men in the cellar?

What was in the pouch?

Who was to receive it?

Why must it be delivered before General Washington's ball?

And which of the four American soldiers assigned to shadow the British delegation was a traitor?

It was none of her affair, she reminded herself. Not anymore. *Curse your war and your independence.* That's what she'd cried in Minister Townsend's church.

She squeezed her eyes shut to erase the image of General Washington's grief-filled face when he spoke of honor.

The carriage slowed as it reached the front door of the Parcell house.

Becca shifted uncomfortably in her seat. She'd been wrong to leave the party. She would speak to Daniel and find Hamilton first thing in the morning. She would tell them both about the pouch and the package that was to be delivered before the ball. She inhaled a deep breath of frigid night air. There was still time.

* * *

The music soared. Couples formed lines, then circled each other. Hands touched and released. Eyes met. Partners were twirled then exchanged. On the dance floor, men and women challenged one another as equals. The air was charged with energy, and the ballroom windows fogged as the room grew warm. Daniel felt the vibrations of stomping feet through the floorboards.

Lockwood only shrugged when Daniel asked where Becca was. Carl finally told him that she'd left half an hour ago. He couldn't blame her, not after their meeting with Washington.

Hamilton was in constant motion now, pulling aside guests for quiet conversations. Daniel found then lost track of him countless times.

Daniel wasn't done with him.

His gaze tracked General Washington as he followed the steps of each dance. The commander's normally somber face was washed pink with exertion and laughter.

He swung away from the dancers, listening to the sound of his own footsteps as he walked through the now-empty front hall. He stopped to consider the shadowy portrait of Mr. Lockwood senior that hung there.

"Alloway. Still here I see."

Daniel didn't turn. "Do you make it a habit to sneak up on people?"

"I wasn't certain you would speak to me after that scene with the General," Hamilton said.

They stood alone in the semidarkness of the front hall. The candles in the sconces along the wall were burned to short stubs.

"Do the ends always justify the means, Mr. Hamilton? Did you have to be so hard on her?" Daniel kept his tone mild when all he wanted was to push

219

Hamilton into the wall.

"We did." Hamilton ignored the first part of the question.

"Why?"

"Why what?"

"You did everything you could to goad her. Did you mean to drive her to recklessness? She'll do anything to keep that farm. You know that."

"I didn't favor taking advantage of her predicament," Hamilton answered quietly.

"You disagree with the General?"

"I didn't say that." Hamilton answered.

"How much can he expect from her? What is it he wants?"

"As much as she's capable of. More than she's done."

Daniel shoved his good hand into Hamilton's chest, creasing his pristine, starched cravat. "This is how you build loyalty to your new country?"

Hamilton caught himself, lifting both hands palm out. "The soldiers are starving. Money is worthless. Less than half the colony supports our cause. We've pursued freedom for five years without an end in sight. The British are as tired of this war as we are. They're planning something and we need every weapon we have, including you and Mrs. Parcell."

"They're planning something." Daniel stepped away to stop himself from shoving Hamilton again. "Do you intend me to be satisfied with that?"

Hamilton hesitated, surveying the empty hall. "The British expect us to surrender. Soon." His voice was hardly a whisper. "And yet how can that be? Armies do not fight in the winter."

"Your information is reliable?" Daniel asked.

"Unfortunately, it is. Your hunt for the turncoats' list is critical. We need to know what the British are planning."

"But if we fail to find your spies, will you leave Mrs. Parcell homeless? How long will she be able to live?" Daniel could manage to find his way west with or without Hamilton's damn reward. But what options did Becca have?

Hamilton's eyes slid to the left. "Whatever I think, it will be up to the general. But it would be best if you could learn something more."

Daniel was adept at reading half-truths, untruths and the rare honesty in men's eyes. Hamilton didn't believe they could succeed.

Chapter Forty-One

He was trapped in a jungle of flesh and punched away the bodies of the dead. Blood trailed behind him like a curled red ribbon. He fought to the surface of the murky bay. His right hand was on fire.

Daniel kicked his way into consciousness the next morning and slammed a fist into something solid. He heard a grunt and opened his eyes.

Caleb Gibbs stood over him, holding his jaw. "That's a fine thank you for a night's lodging."

"Sorry. You surprised me." Daniel swung his legs to the floor and scrubbed his face with his hands.

It was barely dawn.

Would the dreams stop if he walked out the door, headed to the Great Wagon Road and just kept going? What would it be like to live in the desert near the town he'd read of, Santa Fe? There would be nothing familiar there. Nothing to trigger his nightmares.

Gibbs jerked his head toward the door. "Mrs. Parcell sent a boy for you. He says to come."

Daniel stepped to a wobbly table near the cot holding a water bowl. He broke the thin skin of ice on the surface and pressed the cold water into his face. He shook droplets off his hands, retrieved his rucksack from the bench, and dressed quickly.

He should have left Lockwood's party to find her last night.

Major Gibbs grabbed his uniform from a hook on the wall, pulled on a red vest, then slipped into his woolen blue and buff jacket and white breeches. He gave Daniel a curious look. "Is there something between you and the widow?"

Daniel wasn't certain what was between them. "No. I owe her a debt, that's all. I owe you a debt, as well. I would have slept in a barn last night if you hadn't invited me in."

Daniel wondered whether Gibbs still believed in independence as fiercely as he must have in 1776. Did he resent how much time the war had stolen from his life? Did he hate Washington?

"By the way, did you know Parcell, the widow's husband?" Daniel asked casually.

"No, never did." Gibbs didn't hesitate as he straightened his jacket. He didn't even sound interested.

Daniel persisted. "Were any of your men near Morristown last summer when he disappeared? Did any of them know Parcell?"

Gibbs shrugged. "No reason they would. Most of them hadn't even joined the Army in '77, the last time we were here." He stared up to the corner of the ceiling.

"You've thought of something," Daniel said.

"Do you remember Sergeant Bartlett?" Gibbs asked. "He brought you and the widow back to Lockwood's the night before you both left for New York. Ask him about Parcell."

"Why?"

"He delivered posts up and down the coast for General Washington, from Maryland and up the Hudson River to Albany. Maybe he met Mrs. Parcell's husband."

* * *

Daniel followed the scent of sweet cornmeal and molasses through Becca's door.

"Don't leave yet," Becca called to the boy who fetched Daniel. She placed three warm cakes wrapped in a red handkerchief in his hand before sending him on his way.

Daniel studied the plaster overhead. Chunks were missing, and there was

Chunks were missing and here was [handwritten note in top margin]

a fresh gash in the wood above the door. The sound of splintering wood echoed in his memory. He made those scars, after his shot missed the Ferret and his friends. It seemed like years, not weeks, ago.

Becca's hair was scraped back, almost entirely hidden beneath a white mobcap. The angry red gash on her forehead, a souvenir from the mob's visit to her home, was fading. Over and over, she wiped the back, then the front, of her hands on the plain linen apron that covered her dark day dress.

He recognized the nervous gesture for what it was. "You better start from the beginning," he said. "I knew you were angry last night. Is that why you left?"

"No." Over a breakfast of corn cakes and cider, Becca told him of the two men in the shadows, of the pouch and the Americans who were to guard the Redcoat delegation.

She dipped a piece of the corncake into a pool of molasses and lifted it to her mouth, flicking her tongue to wipe a dab of the syrup from the side of her lips.

Daniel watched, momentarily mesmerized. He cleared his throat. "You're sure the whispering man said the envelope was to be passed along before the Assembly ball?"

She nodded.

"Have you told Hamilton?"

"I sent my neighbor's boy, the one you met, to find him." Becca frowned. "But Mr. Hamilton was gone to inspect troops. Jockey Hollow, I suppose. He is to return this afternoon."

"He told me something else last night after you left," Daniel said, recounting his conversation with Hamilton.

"They're certain?" Becca asked.

"They're not certain of anything. They don't know what the British are planning. They only know that whatever they're planning is expected to end the war before the snow melts. That is why the general is pressing us so." He hesitated. "I understand why you want nothing more to do with them."

"I have changed my mind." Becca drew her fork through the molasses

224

over and over again in a figure eight.

"But you were so angry." Daniel rocked back in his chair. He hadn't expected this.

"I was. I am."

They sat quietly with that.

She sighed. "The English in New York are holding so tightly to how things have always been. Did you notice that?" She tilted her head. "And I think I have done the same. It is exhausting." She swept her hand up and around the tidy room. "I haven't moved a single thing in this house since my husband died. Not even a candlestick."

Daniel raised his eyebrows in sympathy. He wasn't certain what she meant, but he didn't interrupt her.

She leaned toward him. "I know I'm not being clear. So much destruction has come from fighting to keep things as they are, from ignoring that it's all changing."

Daniel felt a stab of sorrow and of clarity as bright as the sunlight licking the ledger on the table near Becca. He hadn't escaped his past, either, neither the ghosts that tied him to the prison ship nor grief over the deaths of his wife and son.

"That's what their freedom is, I think, General Washington's and Mr. Hamilton's," Becca said. "Freedom to change."

Freedom to step away from the past, or at least part of it. "It takes courage," he said quietly.

They sat with that for a moment, too.

"So you trust them?" Daniel asked.

"No, not entirely. I don't forgive them for last night. But I would like to help them." She grew serious "And I would like to undo some of the damage Philip caused."

"Then we'll keep looking for your husband's list," Daniel said.

She rewarded him with a broad smile.

"Did the men in the cellar say anything else? Was there anything else you noticed? Even if it seems unimportant."

She cocked her head in thought. Her straight-backed chair rocked as she

Her straight-backed chair rocked as she

stood in one jerky motion, and then she rushed to the back of the house. She returned carrying a book and the blue cloak she wore last night. She gently laid the book on the table, then fumbled with the cape.

"I stepped on this on the cellar stairs just after the scared soldier climbed back to the kitchen." Becca removed a long thin torn leaf from an internal pocket and placed it on the table where they could both examine it.

"A leaf?" Daniel tried to keep amusement out of his voice.

She flushed. "You said to tell you everything." She swiped the partial leaf to the edge of the table "Never mind."

She brought an inkwell and quill to the table, then sat again and reached for her ledger book. "I will make a list of people to interview about Philip." She opened the book. "We could start this morning."

Daniel regretfully eyed the last two corn cakes. It seemed the morning meal was over.

Becca lifted a pen and began to write with small, even letters. "One of us will have to follow the redcoat delegation." She hesitated, gauging his response.

Daniel stretched his long legs out under the table. "Each of the officers could head in different directions. We might not learn anything."

"Can you think of a better idea?" Two furrows etched her forehead. "Do you know where they're staying?"

"At Colonel Arnold's tavern. Someone mentioned it at Lockwood's last night."

Becca watched him with expectant eyes, fringed with those long, dark lashes.

She couldn't sit at a tavern all day. He could. Men did. "I'll start my day at the tavern. I'll watch the redcoats."

"Thank you." She lifted a hand to the hollow at the base of her throat.

Daniel remembered the feel of the skin on her neck when he kissed her at the mayor's house. He had stroked his hand along her collarbone and rested the base of his thumb at just that spot. He shifted his gaze to the tabletop and ran a finger along the smooth wood.

"And what will you do while I'm making new friends at the tavern?"

"I'll speak to people who knew my husband. Mrs. Townsend and…" Becca took a breath. "And Philip's mistress. They might know where he would hide something valuable. It's clear that I don't."

"You couldn't have known. Your husband didn't want you to. Isn't it time you let Philip take responsibility for his own mistakes?" Daniel snapped. "Parcell wanted more than he had, and he hid what he was doing from you."

She was silent for one beat, two, then a small smile bloomed on her face. "No one has ever put it quite like that."

"It's past time someone did." If Parcell were alive, Daniel would have throttled him. He turned back to his plate, making short work of the last two corn cakes.

"Then we'll begin," Becca said. "I'll start with the minister's wife. Then I'll find Charity Adams." Becca pulled a thick wool cape from a peg at the back of the room.

She sounded as if she were girding for battle. Daniel almost felt sorry for Parcell's mistress.

Chapter Forty-Two

Becca watched Major General Nathanael Greene bellow at one soldier, then another, as they carted chairs into the seventy-foot-long army storehouse on the Morristown Green. Ready or not, the building would host General Washington's Assembly ball tonight.

Standing on Mrs. Townsend's doorstep, she wondered whether each of Washington's officers really paid $400 to attend the party. That's what she had heard. It was an outrageous sum. But it was hard to tell what a dollar was worth these days.

The front door squeaked open.

"Why, Mrs. Parcell. How unexpected." Polly Cooper blocked the entrance. Her expression radiated indecision and disapproval. "Did you leave a card for Mrs. Townsend? No? I don't suppose you would think to."

Becca craned her neck to see past her. Inside the room, dishes in winter shades of brown, yellow and tan, crisps filled with preserved fruits, corn bread, and a chicken stew with potatoes, carrots and onions were laid out on a table. At least ten women surrounded the minister's wife like ladies-in-waiting circling their queen.

"She's leaving tomorrow for Nova Scotia, you know. The new minister is due." Polly shrugged. No further explanation was needed. The house was meant for the minister and his family. The new minister would live here.

Becca softened in unexpected sympathy. She and Mrs. Townsend were both widows. Becca feared losing her home; the minister's wife already had.

"Let her in," Mrs. Townsend called in her deep voice. In the back of the crowded sitting room, she sat between two thin women who each held one of her hands.

The two women stood as Becca approached, as if a signal had passed between them.

"I am pleased you came." Mrs. Townsend's eyes were puffy and red-rimmed, cheeks slack. Grief was stamped on her face.

"I am sorry for your loss. Truly." Becca stooped and covered Mrs. Townsend's hand with her own.

Mrs. Townsend nodded, then lifted her face, and Becca stooped to listen. She was close enough to see a spot of decay on the top of a front tooth.

"I've lost everything because of you and your husband." Mrs. Townsend clamped her hand round Becca's. "And you will lose everything, too. I wanted you to know." Her eyes shone with malice.

With the last low, rumbling sound, Becca's shoulders tightened.

That whisper.

The guttural low voice was unmistakable. No wonder the whispering man's voice sounded familiar. Mrs. Townsend was at the cellar door last night. She was tall and broad enough to be mistaken in the dark for a man.

Becca forced herself to lean closer. "What was in the package, Mrs. Townsend? I saw you last night. In the cellar. I think you saw me, too."

Mrs. Townsend's hand stiffened on hers. Then it lifted. She slapped Becca's cheek. "Stupid girl. You should have stayed away."

Becca reeled back, ignoring the pain. She clenched her nails into her palms to stop herself from punching the older woman. "I was a stupid girl," she said when she caught her breath. "I didn't see what my husband was doing." She paused. "Did you?"

She meant her words to be cryptic, unless the minister's wife knew exactly what she meant, that both of their husbands had betrayed the cause of independence.

Mrs. Townsend's eyes narrowed as she inspected all the women in the room, so obviously watching and holding their breath. "I'm sick of the pack of you." She waved one arm as if to sweep away flies, placed her hands with their reddened knuckles on her knees and rose slowly. "In the kitchen. Now."

Becca followed the minister's wife into a dark, meager room perfumed with rancid meat.

Mrs. Townsend slammed the door behind her so violently that Becca was surprised it didn't splinter. "Do you think Mr. Townsend could have done it without me?"

"No, I suppose not." Becca worked it out as she spoke. She had thought Mrs. Townsend merely followed in the minister's wake. She was wrong. "You pushed your husband to work for the British, didn't you?"

The minister's wife didn't disagree. "It was good money when we had none, thanks to your husband and his whiskey." She grabbed a pale ceramic pitcher on the table and flung it across the room. The pottery shattered, and a stain of yellow ale exploded across the wall.

The loan. The minister loaned Philip money for his whiskey business. The loan was never repaid. That's what Townsend told Daniel.

"Everything was fine until you went to New York. Did you want to be the new messenger?" The minister's wife laid her hand on the other side of the table near a carving knife, its dark handle still greasy with the remnant of an animal carcass.

"Why not?" Could she goad Mrs. Townsend into saying more? "Why shouldn't I deliver messages to New York?" Becca watched Mrs. Townsend's hand, sitting so close to the knife.

"Because after tonight, it won't matter. The list you seek won't matter."

"The list? Do you have it?"

The minister's wife blanched.

"Who else knows about the list?" Becca pressed.

"Curse you," Mrs. Townsend whispered in her odd rumble. She stretched across the table for the knife. Becca got there first.

"Help me. I am attacked." Mrs. Townsend yelled in a high, plaintive voice.

The door between the kitchen and sitting room sprung open instantly, as if the ladies had all been pressed up against it.

Becca dropped the knife and fled through the door that led to the back garden.

Chapter Forty-Three

With horrified fascination, Daniel watched the tavern owner's beefy hand, wrapped like a shroud in a soiled bar towel, squeeze into another glass and methodically twist back and forth. It was anyone's guess whether the glasses were cleaner or dirtier for the effort.

Colonel Jacob Arnold, as everyone called him, placed the cloudy glass onto a shelf and picked up another. Without lifting his head, he asked, "What can I get for you?"

Daniel scanned the room before answering. The morning light cast a soft glow onto its whitewashed walls. Mugs of ale thunked on wooden tables. Laughter punctuated quiet morning conversations. Sergeant Bartlett sat with three other members of Washington's guards, playing Goose, a board game Daniel remembered from his childhood.

The whispering man Becca heard last night told the soldier to make sure he was one of the four sent to guard the redcoat delegation. Daniel hadn't noticed the young sergeant at Lockwood's party last night. He studied the other three American soldiers playing Goose, wondering which of the three was plotting treason. He recognized two but didn't know any of them.

From the other side of the room, Hopper caught Daniel's eye and discretely lifted his glass. Daniel smiled back, recalling how the old man befriended him on his first day in Morristown.

Above his head, on the second floor where the Redcoat delegation was housed, Daniel heard the scraping sound of chairs and footsteps. He was here to learn what he could about the British plot, whatever it might be. But it couldn't hurt to know more about Becca's husband while he was at it.

He leaned over the small bar, widened his eyes and wondered if he were trying too hard to appear trustworthy. "I'm looking for friends of Philip Parcell."

Arnold lowered the glass. "Don't know that he had many friends, God rest his soul. We weren't good enough for the likes of him." Arnold's features were an island crammed into the center of his face, with close-set eyes and a prominent nose that stretched too close to his upper lip. What saved his face from ugliness was the bright look of interest he wore. "Why do you want to know?"

"Parcell smuggled his whiskey into New York City." Daniel watched Arnold carefully but didn't see surprise there.

The barkeep shrugged. "If I arrested everyone who sold goods to the British, I'd be stacking them four-bodies high to the jail's ceiling."

Daniel remembered hearing that Colonel Arnold was also Morristown's sheriff.

"People have to live." Another shrug. "It's a hard winter and a long war. The soldiers are stealing food from the townspeople. That doesn't help." He slapped the dirty towel on the bar's surface. "You'd best not be accusing me of smuggling."

"Then it's a good thing I'm not accusing you." Daniel planted his elbows on the bar, leaning forward to emphasize his point. Behind the bar, he saw the flash of green glass in the sunlight. It was a bottle, one he recognized. He pointed. "Is that Parcell's whiskey?"

Arnold frowned. He filled one of his mugs with ale from a pitcher beneath the counter and placed it before Daniel. He poured a second glass, slurped softly and asked: "What's your interest, friend?"

Arnold's reactions were too slow, too studied. Daniel came to attention. "Nothing in particular. I enjoyed his spirits once or twice. Did Philip sell you his whiskey?"

"It was swill."

"That's a 'yes,' then?"

The tavern owner scratched the side of his nose. "Yes, I bought it. But not often. He sold it cheap. I took what he offered."

"But something bothered you about the whiskey besides the taste." Daniel smiled to make the question appear less pointed.

Arnold stiffened, as if he were deciding whether or not to answer. "Two or three times, I had customers come in and buy the entire bottle. People passing through. No one I knew."

"The entire bottle?" Daniel repeated.

Arnold's head canted to the left. "Funny that. Maybe that's why I remember."

"What do you mean?"

"I'd find bottles of Parcell's whiskey sitting out front in the morning, still full. I supposed that the men who purchased it couldn't stand the drink, either."

"But without the cork?" Daniel asked.

Arnold's eyebrows rose. "Yes. Without the cork."

They were silent.

"The thing is," Arnold said more slowly, "It's started happening again."

"But Parcell's dead," Daniel said.

Colonel Arnold's finger slowly traced drops of ale on the bar top. "Mr. Lockwood brings it now." He looked up quickly. In response to something he saw in Daniel's expression, he said defensively, "Lockwood's a good man. He's friends with General Washington."

"Who buys bottles of Lockwood's whiskey now?" Daniel kept his voice neutral.

"A soldier now and then passing through. I can't rightly say." Arnold frowned, the tip of his nose almost covering his top lip. "I don't take notice of who pays for what." He sounded embarrassed by the admission.

Daniel took another sip of ale, breathing in the sharp yeasty smell of hops. "Has Lockwood sold you any bottles recently, say in the last day or two?"

"The one you saw." Arnold pointed to a low shelf behind the bar.

"Hard for customers to see the whiskey down there," Daniel commented.

"I know. But Lockwood's important enough to grant small favors. He wanted the bottles just so." The Colonel's face darkened. The tavern owner might not understand everything yet, but he seemed to be getting the sense that he'd been used.

"You don't like him, do you?" Daniel asked.

"I don't pay too much attention to what men say when they're arsy varsey with drink, or I wouldn't have any friends left. And I never heard Lockwood say another negative thing about General Washington, mind you."

"Another thing?" Daniel took a slow sip of the ale. "What did he say the one time?"

Arnold shrugged. "It was a few years ago, back in '77. The general's first winter here." His voice softened in memory. "The whole town celebrated the army's arrival then. Not like now. We never thought the war would go on so long."

He shook his head as if to focus. "Lockwood took more ale than he should have. Cursed General Washington for a coward. Said Washington was cowering behind his Da' and that's when his father took the bullet."

"When did all this happen?" Daniel asked, although he knew.

"About twenty years ago. Back in the war against the French. I'm guessing Lockwood was a lad then, not even ten. General Washington felt some responsibility, I heard. Rumor is, he lent Mr. Lockwood the capital to start as a merchant, and look how well he's done."

Plenty of men had reason to curse Washington, Daniel thought. But if Lockwood really was one of the British spies, what would be simpler than hiding messages in plain sight, in bottles of whiskey at a bar, with Colonel Arnold none the wiser?

Floor planks creaked at the weight of booted footsteps on the stairs. The tavern quieted.

Arnold's mouth twisted into a stiff smile. "A good morning to you, gentlemen."

Daniel turned.

Three of the four redcoat officers stared at Arnold before choosing a table as far as possible from the other customers.

The fourth officer nodded curtly and asked: "Is breakfast too much to hope for?" He sniffed, as if he'd already found the meal unsatisfactory.

Arnold's face went still. Then he wiped his hands on the dirty towel and stepped out from behind the bar to take the breakfast orders.

Everyone in the tavern, including Daniel, seemed to follow Arnold's progress. Bartlett and the three American soldiers came to attention, staring across the room at the British.

This wouldn't be the time or place for the turncoats to pass along the packet Becca heard discussed. Too many eyes were watching.

Daniel half listened to news about the weather and whispers about what the British were paying to smuggle Jersey cattle into the city. He stared idly at his injured hand, trying to shift his thumb toward his index finger. It was becoming a daily habit. Today, it felt like a thousand tiny needles pricking his palm. He repeated the motion, toying with the new sensation. He hardly noticed when Arnold moved back behind the bar.

"A word, barkeep," a voice called. It was one of the British officers. Daniel turned his head away as the man approached.

"Is there whiskey I can purchase? Something you keep behind the bar, perhaps?"

Out of the corner of his eye, Daniel watched a hand framed in crisp white lace point to a low shelf. "What about that one?"

He looked up in time to see Arnold blink in surprise.

Well, I'll be damned, Daniel thought. Lockwood laid in the whiskey at the tavern and the British picked it up.

Men passed through Morristown heading in all directions. Messages for other turncoats or the British could be tucked away in the whiskey corks, picked up at Colonel Arnold's tavern and delivered throughout the colonies.

A short time later, the British officers returned to their rooms on the second floor.

Becca was fine, he told himself. Lockwood wouldn't hurt her. But Daniel felt a fierce urge to see her. He needed to know she was safe.

Daniel pushed away from the bar. He wondered whether Becca would believe that Lockwood was the turncoat they sought. Or would she think Daniel was jealous?

Jealous? Daniel didn't like Lockwood, or, to be precise, he didn't like the man's assumption that Becca was his, as if she were property. But he hadn't been jealous a day in his life, he told himself. He stepped toward the tavern door.

A hand gripped his shoulder. "Have a drink with me?" Sergeant Bartlett's heavy-lidded eyes were trained on Daniel as if nothing were more important than sharing the mug he held out.

Daniel smiled to soften the rejection. "Another time, perhaps."

"Please."

Daniel remembered the crack of the rifle that killed Ferret. Bartlett might have saved his life that night. He shrugged his acceptance. He would be quick about it.

A quarter mug later, Daniel regretted his good intentions. Bartlett hadn't stopped talking.

"And then my mother died," Bartlett continued.

"She never told you where your father went?" Daniel grew curious despite himself.

"My father drank himself out of every teaching job he ever held. He headed out from Rhode Island and never returned. That's what my mother said."

After Amelia and Silas died, Daniel's father had patiently pulled him back from the far shore of grief. Daniel downed more ale to hide the pity he felt for Bartlett. What did it do to a man to know his father chose to leave him behind?

Bartlett's eyes tracked Daniel's hand as it lifted the mug to his lips.

"Your father was educated?"

"He taught mathematics," Bartlett said.

A weight barreled into Daniel's back so suddenly that his chest jammed into the bar.

"Sorry, mate." Hopper staggered back. His coarse shirt was emblazoned on the breast with the motto "liberty or death." His eyes were unfocused.

Colonel Arnold grabbed the drunken man by the ruff of his neck. "You crump-footed boozer." He shook Hopper gently.

Hopper flapped his hands vaguely in Daniel's direction. "I don't mean no trouble, sirs. I'm going now. Just watch me." He managed to avoid patrons and tables as he reeled toward the tavern door.

Daniel shook droplets of ale from his sleeve, wondering why Hopper was acting as if they'd never met. Drink was a funny thing. "I need to be on my way in any case."

Bartlett didn't protest.

* * *

The road to the Parcell farm grew quiet past the bustle of the Green. Daniel listened to the loud-mouthed blue jays and to the rhythmic beating of galloping hooves, soft, then loud, then roaring.

The galloping sound grew inside his chest, trampling his heart to bursting. Suddenly doubled over with cramps, he fell to his knees and vomited until his throat was raw. His right hand burned, and when he lifted it, it burst into flame. He rolled in the snow to extinguish the fire and screamed.

"Steady now. You're all right." A pair of strong hands lifted Daniel and placed him gently on something soft. He tried to focus on the smiling, skeletal face of Philip Parcell. Water and seaweed streamed from his collar.

"But you're dead," Daniel said as the world went dark.

Chapter Forty-Four

Becca wore a shroud of anxiety as she trudged to Charity Adams' house. Some women might relish the chance to confront their husband's mistress; she wasn't one of them.

By the time she heard the clip-clop of hooves on the snow-covered road, the horsemen were upon her. She tensed until she saw Carl. He rode behind Major Caleb Gibbs.

Washington's guard pulled back hard on the reins as he neared. "I've searched half the town for you." He leaped off his horse in one practiced motion, holding the horse's reins and patting his flank.

"It's about Mr. Alloway. Mr. Hamilton and I were riding back to Morristown. We came upon a local man driving a wagon. Mr. Alloway was in back. He said Alloway drank something that didn't agree with him. Mr. Hamilton sent them off to your house, then he told me to find you." The guard's gaze slipped from Becca to the horizon behind her.

"I was passing by and asked to help," Carl called.

"Mr. Hamilton sent you to find me because Mr. Alloway has a stomach ache?" That was hardly an emergency.

Gibbs' lips tightened. The change in expression was slight, hardly noticeable, yet she understood.

"But Mr. Alloway is well?" Her throat closed round the words.

"It might be poison," Gibbs said stiffly. "That's what the local man said. Hard to tell."

"Well, didn't you ask Mr. Alloway?" Becca's asked.

Gibbs cleared his throat. "Couldn't ask him. He was not...awake."

Becca heard a mourning dove's coo, noticed a spot on Major Gibbs's cheek that his razor missed. It was an odd feeling, to see everything so clearly and yet feel so distant. "Is he dead?"

"Not when I saw him."

She locked her knees to stop them from buckling.

Gibbs turned to Carl, using the easy tone of someone accustomed to being obeyed. "You take Mrs. Parcell home."

Carl slid off his horse. Pale freckles peeked through his wispy white hair, which floated in the wind.

She rejected his offer of help and pulled herself onto the horse, arranging her skirts to ride sidesaddle. The old servant grabbed the reins and began to walk toward home.

"Alloway's a good man," Carl said gruffly.

"He is." It was the kind of thing people said about the dead at funerals.

"But he can't take care of you, poppet, even if he lives. It's time you said 'yes' to Mr. Lockwood. Do it soon."

Becca resisted the urge to quicken the horse's pace and leave Carl behind.

* * *

Hopper burst through the front door of her home.

"Where?" Becca jumped off the horse.

"In your room, m'lady, beggin' your pardon. I carried him up as if he were a babe. I hope you don't mind." He twisted his hat between his two hands as if he were kneading bread.

Becca flung herself up the stairs and halted outside the bedroom door. She splayed her hand on it, closing her eyes, taking one breath, then another. Then she pushed the door open. When she saw Daniel's chest rise and fall beneath her heavy wool blanket, she stood stone still.

His face was the color of the bleached linen pillowcase beneath his head. He wore one of Philip's old nightshirts. Hopper must have removed his clothes, which hung from a peg on the rear wall.

From the doorway, Carl spoke. "You ought not be alone with him. T'ain't right."

"I don't need a chaperone. I'm not a maiden." She twisted to frown.

When Carl didn't move, she added, "And I'll leave the door open."

He nodded.

"And thank you for bringing me. Will you stay for tea? Ask Hopper to stay, as well."

Carl slipped down the stairs.

She pulled the small chair close to the bed and sat. Her hand reached for Daniel's. With her thumb, she traced the curved axis of the scar along his palm, then lowered her lips to his forehead, tasting the salty tang of his skin.

His skin was warm, not hot. She left her lips on his forehead.

When she was little more than a baby, someone had kissed her forehead like this. It was a faint memory, one of the few Becca had of her mother. But she didn't feel motherly about the tall, still man in the bed.

His eyes fluttered open. His pupils were dilated, more black than green. He held her gaze. "Testing for fever?"

Her throat closed, and she nodded.

"You should check again." He closed his eyes.

Her lips grazed his forehead. She trailed slow kisses along the side of his face.

"I'm fine, Becca, or I soon will be."

"You don't look fine."

"No. I suppose I don't. I'm feeling better, though. I had waking dreams. I thought the men I knew on the *Jersey* took me with them. I saw your husband."

"You've dreamed of them before." Somehow, she knew.

"Them, but not your husband. Hopper pushed the drink out of my hand. He followed me out of Arnold's tavern. I think he saved me."

"Drink?"

"Poison, Hopper says." Daniel pushed himself to a sitting position, leaning against the pillows propped on the bed.

"How?"

"Sergeant Bartlett added a powder to my glass of ale. Hopper saw it."

Becca leaned back. Her shoulder blades pressed into the wood cross rails. "The cannon fire. The sergeant was there. He meant to kill us when we crossed New York Harbor."

"That would have saved him the trouble of buying me a drink today." Daniel stared at her with his strange dark eyes.

"Sergeant Bartlett was at the tavern?"

"He was one of the sentries watching the redcoats." He paused. "Some water, please."

"I should let you rest."

He shook his head.

She poured a half-cup from the pitcher on the night table and sank onto the bed, her hip touching his. She lowered the lip of the cup to his mouth. "I talked to Mrs. Townsend this morning. She was the person I heard in Thomas' cellar last night."

"But there was a man in the cellar," he said. "That's what you said."

"That's what I thought. But when she whispers..." Becca shivered, recalling the minister's angry widow. "It was her. I'm positive. Mrs. Townsend gave Sergeant Bartlett the package on the stairs last night. She said he needed to be one of the guards assigned to the delegation."

Daniel sipped the drink. "Lockwood plays a part, too." In fits and starts, he told her what he heard and saw at Arnold's tavern before drinking with Bartlett.

"Not Thomas. That's not possible." Becca felt as if she was suffocating. She didn't care that most people believed fresh air was dangerous. She rose and shoved open the nearby window.

When her cheeks hurt with the cold, she closed the window and returned to Daniel's side, placing her cold palm on the back of his neck.

He rumbled with pleasure. "You certainly have a touch, Mrs. Parcell."

"Perhaps you do have a fever after all." The compliment pleased her. "What worries me is why the package is to be delivered before General Washington's ball tonight."

"Most of the Continental Army's senior officers will be there." Daniel's voice slurred as he fought sleep.

"I'll find Mr. Hamilton," she said, feeling the urgency. "I'll ask Carl to stay with you."

"No. Have Carl go with you. And don't stop to talk to Lockwood." Daniel's eyes fluttered and closed.

Becca went alone, asking Carl and Hopper to watch Daniel. Now, she stared up at Mrs. Theodosia Ford's large home, taking in its two chimneys and Palladian windows.

One of the general's guards stood at attention, his cheeks ruddy with cold. He nodded to her without expression.

Becca's mimicked her mother-in-law's demeanor. "Mrs. Parcell for Alexander Hamilton."

"'E's expecting you?" The guard's cold-paled lips barely moved.

The window next to the front door clattered.

She turned at the sound.

Hamilton's sharp face was framed within the panes. He pointed at Becca, then tapped his finger to his own chest.

"Well, 'e's expecting you now." The guard grinned. "Oy," he called to a soldier at the corner of the house.

Moments later, Becca found herself in the wide front hall accompanied by one of the guards. Officers crossed from one room to the next. Two bantered about the girls they'd meet at tonight's party.

From behind a half-closed door on the right, an angry voice complained: "How do they expect me to march my soldiers when they don't have enough food to eat."

The soldier rapped on the door to the left.

Becca was halfway through the door when Hamilton called, "Come."

He stood near a large map resting on a table. Several older officers surrounded him, slouching or leaning back in chairs. They stared at her without surprise, as if neither her sudden entrance nor anything else could shock them after years of battle.

She bobbed a curtsy. They came to their feet, some more slowly than others, and bowed. She ignored them. "Mr. Hamilton. I have news."

Out of the corner of her eye, she caught General Knox winking at another officer, as if she were merely one of the many young women in town scheming to capture Hamilton's heart. Becca felt her cheeks flush.

She was surprised when Hamilton dismissed the officers without hesitation. "Thank you for your time, gentlemen," he said. "I'll see you at the Assembly this evening."

"How is Mr. Alloway? Is he...has he?" Hamilton seemed at a loss about how to phrase the question.

"He's alive," she said. "It was kind of you to send Major Gibbs to find me." Why did she find it so difficult to thank the man?

Hamilton gestured to a chair.

"Mr. Alloway was poisoned." She remained standing. "One of General Washington's guards tried to kill him."

Hamilton's finely etched eyebrows rose as he listened to her story.

"But Mr. Lockwood can't be involved," Becca concluded.

"Leaving Mr. Lockwood aside, I'll send for Bartlett. And it's evident that the ball tonight presents a risk. But what risk?" He began to pace. "How much harm can four British officers do? They can't be planning a direct attack."

"Then it won't be a direct attack." Becca paced in an opposite direction. She couldn't seem to stand still, either.

He swung toward her. "I can arrest the British delegation before the ball. I'll send them to our prisoner of war camp in Princeton." Hamilton raked his hand through his hair. "No. General Washington won't approve. He can cancel the ball. That's the answer."

"If the ball goes on, you might catch the Americans who are helping the British," Becca said. "You'll lose that chance if you cancel the party."

He cocked his head, studying her. "That's sound thinking, Mrs. Parcell." He seemed surprised.

"Most women exercise sound thinking, Mr. Hamilton. But it's a rare man willing to admit it." Becca managed to nod while looking down her nose at him.

"I am suitably chastised." He smiled for the first time since she entered the room.

He was almost too handsome when he grinned like that, she thought with disapproval.

Then he grew serious. "I'll speak to General Washington. We can arrange for additional guards to attend this evening." Hamilton turned to usher her from the room. "Assume the Assembly will proceed unless you hear from me."

"And my farm, sir?" This was happening too quickly. "Yesterday, the general thought our warnings were not clear enough to warrant a reward. You agreed. Is this enough?"

His shoulders tensed. "I can make no promises. You have not found what General Washington seeks."

"The list of spies," she snapped. "But what we have learned—"

"Has great value. I can only promise that I will argue for you and your farm."

"And Mr. Alloway?" she prodded. *If he lives,* she did not add.

"I will fight for him, too." Hamilton's face grew tight as a statue. "And now for Sergeant Bartlett."

The conversation with Bartlett would not be pleasant. This was a side of Mr. Hamilton she hadn't seen.

"We'll proceed more slowly with Mr. Lockwood. And you are free to resume your life as if we had never disrupted it. We are grateful to you." He bowed her out of the mansion.

Outside, Becca watched Mrs. Ford's servants cut wood. Others brushed the officers' horses. She'd been dismissed. Well, good riddance. They can fight the rest of the war without me. I'll go home. I'll take out my ledger and start planning spring crops. She could practically feel the smooth paper beneath her fingers.

Then why did she feel so unsettled? It was as if Mr. Hamilton had asked her to add a row of numbers, then taken away the problem before she could sum it all up. She needed to know the total.

She'd make one more stop before returning home.

Chapter Forty-Five

Surrounding the small house on the road to Bottle Hill was a copse of apple trees, their branches clawing the sky. Flecks of red paint clung to the door, which was worn to gray wood. Someone had carefully swept the snow from the smooth granite step that led to the house.

The shadow of a woman passed across the window on the right as the curtain fluttered. Becca squinted to see more, fighting the glare of sunlight reflected off a nearby scythe leaning against the house.

She rapped the door harder than necessary.

It inched open to reveal a sliver of a face. One delicate eyebrow, a deep blue eye, a corner of a rosebud mouth, and a slice of translucent, creamy skin.

The one eye scanned up to Becca's face and the eyebrow lifted. "I expected you sooner. Months ago, in fact."

The door swung open. Charity's strawberry blond hair and pale skin glowed, despite the dim light. Her eyes lifted at the outer corners, as if she knew a secret that amused her.

After the midday glare of sun on snow, Becca squinted to make sense of the shadowy interior. The dirt-packed floor absorbed most of the light that the small windows allowed into the house. Smoke-stained beams floated above wood plank walls in the one-room house.

"You *expected* me?" Becca laughed with astonishment. "I've kept away from you for more than a year." She knew of Philip's affair with Charity Adams months before he died. She had avoided the woman ever since.

"And you were almost too late. Were you too ashamed to come earlier?"

Dimples marked Charity's flawless cheeks as she smiled, proving, Becca thought, that some women save their sweetest expression for their most cutting remarks.

"Why should I be ashamed? I wasn't the one dancing with another woman's husband." A year ago, even months ago, Charity's question would have flattened her. Becca stretched her mouth into a smile that, she hoped, mirrored Charity's.

"Don't put on airs with me, Mrs. Parcell. It doesn't matter what fine clothes you wear. The good families of Morristown look at you and see me." She stroked her hand over the bodice of her gown from breast to waist. "Someone just slightly better than a whore. We're not so different. Neither of us will ever be welcome here."

Charity might be right; she might not. "I suppose I'll live. I suppose you will, too." That it mattered so little to Becca was a revelation. She shrugged, feeling suddenly, inexplicably lighter.

Charity's eyes narrowed, then, abruptly, she threw her head back and laughed. "I suppose I will." Her hand fluttered, inviting Becca to sit.

Becca sank into one of the rough wooden chairs at the table, feeling much less awkward than she'd expected. "You said you expected me. Why?" She heard a faint thump from the outside of the house.

Charity stood on the other side of the table. "I thought it was a cruel trick, you know."

Becca did not know. "What was?"

"Leaving a message for his wife with his...with me."

"He was more careless than cruel." Becca clasped her shaking hands.

"You're right. But carelessness can be cruel, too." Charity laughed again.

Was Charity more than careless? Was she lying? "How do I know you're telling the truth?" Becca asked. "You told the whole town I turned Philip over to the British because I was jealous of you. You lied about me then. You could be lying now."

"You might have turned Philip over." Charity cocked her head. "It could have been true."

"You knew it wasn't. What you said almost got me killed."

"I was sorry about that." Charity's nose wrinkled. "I don't like crowds."

"Why were you with Minister Townsend's mob if you don't like crowds?"

"For money," she said matter-of-factly. "It wasn't my idea, you know, blaming you for Philip's capture. Blame the minister's wife. She's the one who paid me. I suppose she hates you."

"I'm quite certain she does." Becca felt the sting of Mrs. Townsend's slap again.

"She hates me, too." Charity paused. "I was making hot chocolate. Will you join me?" Without waiting for an answer, she pulled two white porcelain cups from a shelf against the wall and placed them on the scratched wood table in the middle of the room. Grabbing a towel, she draped it over her hands and lifted a dented pot from a hanging pole near the fireplace. She poured the boiling liquid into a small ceramic pitcher and lowered the pot to its resting place. The ginger and cinnamon in the melted chocolate scented the air. Steam rose as Charity poured the hot chocolate into two chipped mugs.

The two women lifted their mugs and sipped at the same time.

"The chocolate was a gift from one of my friends," Charity said. "I save almost everything my friends give me." She smiled gently. "Your husband was quite generous."

With my dowry money, Becca thought.

"But I have enough now to buy a tavern," Charity continued. "I'll be leaving for the Ohio Territory after the ball tonight."

She looked up slyly at Becca. "That's why you should believe I'm telling the truth about Philip's message. There's nothing I need from you. There's nothing I need from anyone here. Not now."

Charity was right. She had little reason to lie. "All right, then." She couldn't wait any longer. "Can I have my husband's message?" Becca swallowed. "Please."

Two steps brought Charity to the bricks on the side of the wide fireplace. She lifted her hand to feel along the grout lines. Her fingers moved, then stopped, and she pulled at one particular brick. It came loose with a low grating scrape.

Goosebumps rose on Becca's arms. Philip was suddenly present in this room, neither alive nor dead. Her husband had told Daniel that she had the list of spies. He had trusted that she would search for it. Or, more likely, he'd known that trouble would follow her once he died and that she'd need to find the list.

"When did he ask you to hide this note?" Becca asked.

"Last summer. Just before his last trip to New York," Charity said.

"What did my husband say when he gave you the paper to hide?" It could be the list of spies, Becca thought. It was possible, just possible. The timing was right. Philip had offered to sell the list to General Washington by then.

"He said that if something happened to him, this might keep you alive."

Or it might get me killed. Becca's heart thundered in her chest.

Charity drew a thin roll of paper from its hiding place and turned. She held it with two fingers. "I'm glad to be rid of your husband's note, you know. Someone has been through my things twice now when I've been out. I think they were looking for this."

"Do you know who?"

"Who cares?" Charity shrugged. "They didn't find it."

"Why keep it for me?" Becca's eyes stayed focused on the note.

"I may be a whore, but I keep my promises. I promised Philip I would give this to you if you came." Charity pursed her lips to blow dust off the document. She placed it on the table near the hot chocolate. Then she lounged back in her chair.

Becca studied Philip's mistress. "You read it, didn't you?" Becca cupped her hand over the note as if to protect it.

One of Charity's fingers circled the edge of her cup of chocolate. "I thought I might be able to sell the information. But it made no sense."

Don't get angry. Becca corrected herself. *Don't get angrier.* She flattened the paper. It was a sheet of lined account paper, with a row of numbers in her own handwriting and three words in Philip's scrawl: *Here it is.*

Becca flipped the paper. Nothing. She raised her head. "Is this a jest?"

"No. We didn't laugh. We hardly discussed it." Charity licked the froth from the hot chocolate off her upper lip. Her face held neither guilt nor triumph.

Becca rose slowly. She understood less now than she had when she knocked on Charity's door. She swept the note into the pocket tied to her gown and stood.

She wasn't certain what rules of deportment applied upon leaving a husband's mistress. "Thank you for keeping Philip's note for me," she said. "I hope your journey west is an easy one."

* * *

Becca tightened her wool cape. There was a dampness to the cold that promised more snow.

Philip's note must mean something, but what? She idly followed the progress of a gray squirrel leaping across the yard.

As she did, her eyes locked onto a line of dark red pockmarks, each no bigger than a nail head. They led in a jagged line from the walkway to a twisted apple tree and a circle of gouged snow. The snow was powdery where it had been kicked up at the edge of the saucer-shaped depression.

Then she saw him, a soldier leaning against the side of the tree as if he were resting. He wore the black polished boots, buff breeches and blue jacket of Washington's personal guards. He faced away from the road.

Hesitating, Becca took one step toward him, then another. Something was wrong.

A knife flashed in his hand. He drew it back and forth, sharpening the long curved blade of a scythe. He'd planted its handle in the snow and didn't seem to notice the blood circled his wrist.

Sergeant Bartlett. "Your wrist. You nicked it with the knife," she said, as if he required the explanation.

He inspected the cut, then pushed away from the tree, slipping the knife into a leather holder at his belt with the injured hand. It took two tries.

"I'm surprised to see you." She took one step, then another back toward Charity Adams' front door. She glanced to the house. A curtain fluttered, then fell closed. The door did not open. There was no help there.

"I followed you." Bartlett swayed, then leaned on the scythe's handle for balance.

He was tangle-footed with drink, she realized. How long had he stayed at the tavern once Daniel left? But she wasn't about to turn her back on a man—not even a drunk man—with a sharp weapon in his hand.

"You have your husband's list."

"That's not true. I don't." She calculated the risks and benefits of running. They stood about ten strides apart. Sergeant Bartlett was probably faster than she, but Becca knew the woods better than he did, and she had the advantage of sobriety. She took another step back.

"Even if you don't have it, I have my orders." Bartlett lifted the curved blade to his face. He narrowed one eye and closed the other, as if to better assess its sharpness.

Becca brushed her hand along the side of her cape, feeling the hard outline of the small knife she kept sheathed in an inside pocket.

"I don't like killing for money. There's no honor in it." Bartlett swayed as he carefully enunciated each word. His uninjured hand held the scythe loosely. "I wish we'd never started."

We. "You and the minister's wife? Did she give you orders?"

Becca planted her legs, holding still, when all she wanted to do was barrel into him and snatch the farm tool with the sharp blade.

He widened his eyes as if to force them to focus. "Didn't start this way," he said mournfully. "'Twas only to put money away for after the war. Whoever wins, we'll go home without a trade, without property." His speech was slowing.

The sergeant had lost his future—at least he thought it had—and now he had lost himself. She would not feel sorry for him, Becca told herself. No, she would not.

"You said you wished *we* never started. You and my husband? Did you know Mr. Parcell?"

"Mr. Parcell? I knew him at the end. His end. I wish we'd never started," he repeated. The bottom of his dark eyes grew red-rimmed.

How much time did she have before he lost consciousness or lunged at her? "You and Thomas Lockwood?"

"Mr. Lockwood? We all know him." Bartlett's face hardened, as if some part of him was withdrawing to avoid seeing what he was about to do. He flipped the scythe blade-down, swinging it gently side to side as if to harvest the snow.

She was out of time. Becca pushed off the balls of her feet to race toward the deep woods behind Charity's house.

"Stop." A new voice snapped through the air, a voice she recognized.

Carl jumped from the driver's seat of an unfamiliar dark blue carriage. The snow had muffled the sound of its approach.

Becca stumbled as she changed direction and sprinted to Carl, to safety, her boots crunching through the thin veneer of ice topping the snow. Then she whirled back to search for Bartlett.

Even from this distance, she saw the anguish on his face. He dropped the scythe and staggered into the woods.

Carl ran a few steps past her as if to follow Bartlett.

"Let him go. I'm not hurt," Becca called.

Carl's tri-corner hat fell into the snow as he staggered to a stop. Becca watched his back rise and fall as he caught his breath.

"How did you know where to find me?" she asked.

"I didn't. I started at the Widow Ford's Mansion and prayed for luck." He held out his hand for hers as she climbed into the carriage. "You're cold as ice," Carl clucked with disapproval.

His hands were even colder. "I'm thankful. More than thankful." She tensed for more bad news. "But Mr. Alloway? You were to stay with him. Is he worse?"

"I left him in good hands." Carl smiled for the first time. "You'll see when you get home."

Chapter Forty-Six

Carl slowed the carriage to a stop by Becca's front door. A bald, scarred face with a jack 'o lantern grin leered at her through its window.

"Amos." She leaped from the cab, laughing. "When did you arrive?"

"Hours ago."

For a moment, she felt as if she were flying, as free as the night she and Mr. Mason's men rescued Daniel from the Sugar House.

Becca flew into the house. Behind her, she heard the leather straps creak as the horses took up the weight of the carriage and pulled away.

Daniel leaned against the far wall. He was dressed in clothes Becca didn't recognize, but her attention was elsewhere.

Augusta sat in the wing chair by the window as if she'd never left. Her bright yellow gown was barely creased despite the long day's ride. Mr. Mason stood behind the chair, his hand resting on its back. In his brown wool vest and velvet-bordered overcoat, he might have been any merchant of the middling sort, not the bandit Becca knew him to be.

Augusta rose and extended her arms.

Becca stepped into them, hiccupped twice, then shocked herself by bursting into a brief, violent, storm of tears. She hadn't let herself feel how empty the house was without Augusta and Annie until this very moment.

"You can't be that surprised. I promised I'd return." Augusta pulled away to inspect Becca, then placed a warm hand on her cheek.

"I know. But it was easier to think you were gone forever."

"Easier?" Augusta huffed.

Becca swiped the back of one hand across her eyes. "That way, I couldn't be disappointed if you chose to stay away."

"None of that talk, Mrs. Rebecca." Mr. Mason beamed at Augusta. "Nothing stops your mother-in-law. Not even the British army will venture out here in this snow, but she insisted we come." His gaze methodically assessed the house.

Becca couldn't tell whether he was calculating the value of its contents or merely locating windows and doors in case a quick escape was required.

"John is teasing." Augusta's face sparkled. "He insisted we arrive today. I was happy to agree."

He's been good to her, Becca thought.

"Today? Why today?" Daniel asked.

Becca turned slowly toward him.

Shadows were still stamped beneath Daniel's eyes, but his color had improved. He grinned at her from a chair by the wooden table near the fireplace.

"Why today? Heard there might be a spot of trouble. Needed to see for myself. Never pays to ignore the drumbeat of information," Mason said.

"The Assembly ball tonight?" Becca asked, still watching Daniel.

"Possibly." His mouth clamped shut as if that was all he intended to say.

"Trouble? Do you know what type of trouble?" Daniel asked.

"Sadly, I do not." Mason studied him. "My clothes almost fit you, so long as the belt doesn't give way."

"I thank you for the shirt and the breeches," Daniel said. "But most assuredly, I thank you for the belt."

Mason roared with good humor at the not-so-veiled reference to his wider girth.

Daniel's lips curved into a lopsided smile, and Becca felt buoyed up, weightless with sudden joy. If she could lock the door and hold this one moment tight, keep these people close to her, she swore she would.

If she could lock the door. Keep them close. Here it is. She repeated the phrases silently over and over. *Keep them close. Here it is.* Not "keep them close. Keep it close. And that was when she knew where to find Philip's hidden list of spies.

She sprinted up the narrow stairs, ignoring the worried questions Augusta called up to her, and plucked the familiar leather-covered account book from the small bedside table. She flew with it down to the sitting room and lay the book on the dining table. To make room for it, she shoved aside an empty mug, a plate, and the leaf shard she had presented to Daniel in the morning.

The ledger held the small, daily decisions of her life: purchases and sales, calculations and plans. She kept it close. Always. Philip had known that. Her hand hovered over its pages. *Here it is*, he'd written on a sheet of her account paper, a sheet just like all the others in her ledger. She couldn't seem to make herself begin. Ripping it would be like shredding apart her life.

"Philip left me a message. He wanted to make sure that his list would reach General Washington, even if he...." Becca turned to Augusta.

"Yes. Even if he died. Go on." Augusta's tone teetered toward impatience. She wouldn't brook pity.

"He hid a message for me," Becca continued. "He trusted that I would find it. But it made no sense. He wrote 'here it is' on a piece of my ledger paper."

No one spoke. Sap trapped within a log popped, sending glowing ashes swirling.

She ran her hands over the book's edges, its binding, the front and back cover as if she were blind and identifying an object by touch.

Daniel eyed the ledger uncertainly.

Becca tapped the book. "He knew the ledger was never far from my side. What safer place could he find to hide the list of turncoats? He gave this latest ledger to me at the end of last spring." Her voice softened with memory. "I thought his gift was kind. He knew the numbers soothed me." She corrected herself. "I thought he knew. By that time, he had offered the list to General Washington."

Then she rushed to the wing chair where Augusta did her needlework and pulled out her mother-in-law's sewing basket from underneath the seat.

Back at the table with a pair of scissors, Becca sliced through the cloth cover. She slipped her hand between the leather and rigid board. She repeated the exercise on the back cover. Nothing.

She opened the front and back covers of the sliced book like wings, pulling one side forward and one back until they tore off the spine. Pages floated to the floor.

Philip was careless and his affections slight, but he wouldn't taunt her like this. His message must mean something.

Annie silently leaned over the table, reaching across it to clear the forks and knives and other items left from breakfast.

"Get something for Mr. Mason's men to eat first, please. The table can wait," Augusta murmured.

"I should serve you and Mrs. Rebecca first," Annie grumbled, but she bobbed a curtsy and retreated.

"I must be missing something." Becca rubbed her forehead. What had she seen? It was in the back of Mr. Rivington's print shop, the night that Daniel kissed her hand. What? Next to the printing press, Mr. Rivington kept his bookbinding tools.

The printer left pages pressed in a frame as if he were subjecting the book to torture. She'd never seen the spine of a book without its leather cover before that night. Linen tape and cords held the pages together.

She pushed back her chair, stooped and vanished.

"Perhaps the afternoon was too much for Mrs. Rebecca," Mason whispered.

"Give her a minute," Daniel said.

"Where is it?" She crawled through the carpet of paper, hemmed in by the three pairs of legs surrounding her.

There. She grabbed the spine of her book, inched backwards and rose. She tore out the remainder of the pages. But its spine, covered in calfskin, held up to the assault.

Becca slid her hand into her pocket, pulling out her knife. She inserted the blade between the spine's brown leather and the paper and cords beneath it and twisted as if shucking an oyster.

Something squeezed beneath the leather and the linen bands that held the now-ragged page edges. A quarter sheet of thin paper was folded over and over like a fan.

Funny that her heart should beat this hard when all she'd done was kill a book.

She wedged her index finger into the narrow space just as one of Mason's bandits slipped into the dining room. She covered the ragged book spine with a fold of her gown.

"Excusing the interruption, Mr. Mason. You said to watch outside. There's a carriage coming. Maybe dark green. Maybe black. Hard to tell with the snow coming down."

Becca hadn't noticed. It was snowing now.

His dark eyes brightened. "There's rich takings."

"I'm afraid we'll have to leave this carriage alone," Mason said with regret.

"That's Mr. Lockwood's carriage. I wonder why Carl is coming back." Becca hadn't given a thought to him since the moment he'd stopped the carriage. "I owe him a great debt, although I might have been fine."

"You were attacked?" Daniel and Mason spoke at the same time.

"Well. Not quite attacked." She should think before she spoke. "Sergeant Bartlett held a scythe, just barely. He was rather drunk, and I did have a knife. All in all, it was not precisely an attack, more of a threat, really."

A blue vein stood out in relief on the side of Daniel's forehead as he pushed away from the table.

"Oh, for goodness sake," she said. "There's no time for this now. Be angry later."

"I'm not angry," he roared.

She fanned the book spine containing Philip's list at him and hissed, "This first."

On the other side of the front door, Carl's boots stamped on the wooden porch to shake off snow.

"Good evening, to the lovely Mrs. Parcells," called Thomas Lockwood's cheerful voice.

Thomas, not Carl.

Becca jammed the spine of the book into the drawstring bag within her skirt. The ledger sheets on the floor tore as she stepped through them.

She imagined a sheet of account paper divided into vertical columns and horizontal. In her mind's eye, she placed the note and all the events of the past weeks into one of the imaginary columns, then reordered them until they made sense.

Thomas had been in and out of the Widow Ford's Mansion all winter. He was one of the few people who could have seen her husband's offer to sell the general a list of hidden spies working for the British. He and General Washington had visited back and forth over the five years of the war. Thomas would have been welcomed into the general's private rooms.

She blocked his way, feeling brittle as glass. "I thought you'd be at the ball, Mr. Lockwood."

His name would be on the list. She was certain of it.

"Not without you, Mrs. Rebecca." His eyes crinkled as he smiled.

"You cannot possibly attend a ball in those clothes." Augusta sounded aghast.

Becca tucked her chin, eyeing the now-limp lace fichu at the bodice of her bedraggled blue day dress. "I don't recall an invitation." She raised her chin, looking into Thomas' familiar, affectionate brown eyes. She only wanted to choke him.

"I called to you as you left last evening. I was certain you heard my invitation." His face fell.

"I heard your voice as the carriage pulled away last evening, but I couldn't make out the words." She stopped, frantic for an excuse that would get him to leave. "I twisted my ankle this afternoon in any case." She pressed all her weight onto one leg to create a limp as she walked toward him. "I can't attend the ball this evening." Not very imaginative, but she was still a terrible liar, and it was the best she could do.

"My dear, you're hurt. You shouldn't be standing." He took her elbow.

She made herself lean her weight on his arm as if her leg really were injured, as if she didn't want to pull away from his touch.

Thomas lowered her gently into a chair at the table and bent over her. His gaze slipped to the torn ledger sheets on the floor. Something snapped shut

THE TURNCOAT'S WIDOW

in the back of his eyes.

He can't know what I'm searching for. She widened her eyes, signaling to Augusta. *Help.*

"We'd hate to make you late, Mr. Lockwood," Augusta said. "Perhaps there will be more time for a visit another day?"

The clock chimed seven. General Washington's party was about to begin.

"No need to worry, madam. There's plenty of time." Lockwood whipped back the tails of his black velvet jacket to avoid crushing them, sat gracefully next to Becca, and stretched his legs beneath the table.

"Well." He smiled at them all, as if settling in for the evening. "I'd be grateful if you would introduce me to your guest." He nodded to Mason. "And for a cup of tea if it's not too much trouble."

Augusta hesitated. "Of course. Annie," she called. "Raspberry leaf tea for Mr. Lockwood, please. And I'd be delighted to introduce you to—"

"A friend from up north. Happy to make your acquaintance." Mr. Mason pushed his head forward, as if it was too heavy for his neck. He held his hands loosely in his lap, like an old man.

Thomas dismissed Mason and turned to Daniel. "And Mr. Alloway. I thought you had left our town."

"First the missus brings us home with no notice, and now guests." Annie trundled into the room with a tray holding a single teacup and small pieces of sugar chipped from the sugar cone in the kitchen.

"And with me not even cleaning the table since breakfast. I have standards for this house, you know." She swept invisible crumbs from the table into the palm of her hand. "You'd think we lived in a barn." She lifted a narrow, long leaf.

Becca had forgotten the leaf she'd found on the stairs at Thomas's house last night.

"Ahh," Mason straightened in his chair. "If I didn't know better, I'd think it was the beautiful lady. I haven't seen one of these since my mother attended the balls in London."

"It was all the rage, wasn't it?" Augusta's eyes lit with memory. "My mother applied eye drops made from it. She was careful with it, of course. All the

258

ladies thought it made their eyes shine."

The hair on the back of Becca's neck rose, but she didn't understand why. It was only a leaf.

Augusta saw the confusion on her face. "Belladonna, my dear. It means beautiful lady in Italian. You wouldn't think something like that could kill. It causes waking dreams and nausea. Then the heart seizes and stops." Augusta turned to Mason. "I didn't think it grew here."

"It doesn't." Mason sounded like himself again, not the old man he portrayed once Lockwood stepped into the room. "It's found throughout Europe, though."

Hallucinations. Nausea. Becca steadied herself. Daniel's symptoms.

Thomas pinched the delicate stem, twirling it between his thumb and index finger. "To me, it looks more like an ash tree leaf or perhaps one from a black willow." He smiled at Becca. "And your eyes are beautiful enough without its assistance."

Daniel stretched out his legs beneath the table, his pose a mirror image of Thomas's. "Mrs. Rebecca found that leaf at your party last night. Any idea what it was doing there?"

"You'd have a better idea than I would, Mr. Alloway. You spent more time in the cellar last night than I did." Thomas released the dried leaf and reached for the teacup.

"Yes, I do have a better idea. Daniel idly pulled the leaf closer. "Ever taste it?" He crushed it in one hand and sprinkled its dust next to Thomas Lockwood's teacup, then clapped his hands over it.

Lockwood stared at the cup without moving, then pulled back his hand. His expression was carefully neutral.

He knows it's poison, she thought.

"I'd best get to the ball, then. I'm so sorry you won't be accompanying me, Mrs. Parcell." Thomas bowed to Augusta, then lifted Becca's hand.

Shouldn't evil stamp itself on a man's face? Shouldn't there be a warning for those careful enough to notice? All Becca saw was the same Thomas she'd known for years. His light brown eyes, golden pale cheeks and slightly upturned lips were unchanged. How had she missed his resemblance to the stern, self-satisfied portrait of his father hanging in the front hallway of his home?

She tugged her hand away from his. "Goodbye, Mr. Lockwood."

He softly closed the door behind him.

"You didn't say that you'd found the leaf in the cellar. Neither did I." Daniel said.

"Yet he knew." Becca raised her gaze to his. "He said you'd spent more time in the cellar than he. He knew the belladonna was delivered there."

"How did the poison make its way here?" Mason asked.

"The British officers brought it," Daniel said. "The message Becca translated at the mayor's house. It said the redcoat delegation would be bringing a package. It could have been the belladonna."

"That's what the minister's wife handed to Sergeant Bartlett. That's what the sergeant used to poison you," Becca said.

"It's possible." Daniel sounded uncertain. "But Bartlett was ordered to hand off the package to someone else. Who and why?"

They all turned to Becca.

Tucked in the pocket against her body, the leather spine was warm in her hand. She pulled out the slice of paper from its slim hiding spot, unfolded it and angled the sheet to catch the light of the nearest sconce.

Mr. Mason and Daniel leaned over to watch. Augusta sat rigid.

"Philip's handwriting." Becca skimmed the short list. Thomas Lockwood was listed. So were the Townsends, Sergeant Bartlett, and two other American officers whose names weren't familiar.

But it wasn't the names that made her squeeze her eyes shut.

"What is it?" Augusta asked.

"It's going to happen tonight. They're going to poison someone. That's what the belladonna is for. The redcoats will be at the ball. General Washington. All his officers." Panic choked her. "We'll leave now."

Daniel blocked her way. "It's dangerous."

She remembered racing down the street with him and Mason's bandits, how it felt to do something that mattered. "I'm the one with the list." She smiled, patting her pocket. "I'm coming."

CHAPTER FORTY-SIX

He cursed under his breath in French, Italian and German and moved aside.

"Amos," Mason bellowed from the kitchen. "Bring the horses."

Chapter Forty-Seven

A few barrels of pork tack and gunpowder lined the walls of the Storehouse. The bottle of Madeira rested on top of one of the barrels. The men sat on two others.

Clad in a servant's navy jacket, William Cunningham sipped from his glass. The caramel-colored drink tasted of apricots and sunshine.

He sighed, appreciating the complex flavors, and crossed one thin leg over the other. Cunningham was careful not to dislodge the padding in his stockings that enhanced his calf muscles. This masquerade required the costume, but vanity alone required the padding.

"Everything went well?" The Correspondent asked, sitting in the shadows.

"Quite well. The delegation has the bottle you sent them, Washington's favorite," Cunningham said. "They understand the timing."

"And do they know what's in the bottle?"

"No. They're good soldiers. All they know is that they're to toast General Washington an hour from now with his favorite Madeira."

Cunningham didn't trust anyone else to ensure that all went well. That was why he had insisted on accompanying the delegation. Its four members didn't questioned the mayor when he said that Cunningham would travel with them to Morristown.

Gentlemen had their own code, Cunningham thought with contempt. Each member of the delegation wouldn't hesitate to kill Washington in battle. But they would never countenance the events planned for this evening.

"You were right. The mayor would not have managed this as well as you," the man in the shadows acknowledged.

"If he were capable, his first attempt would have succeeded. A bowl of peas. What a ridiculous way to poison someone." If Matthews had come up with something better, Washington would have died in '76.

"I hope you don't mind playing a servant," The Correspondent said.

Cunningham's hands curled into fists. "No. It's perfect. I'll be able to watch it all. No one heeds the servants, right?" He toasted his companion, who chuckled.

"And Sergeant Bartlett will arrive soon?"

"No, I'm afraid he won't attend the ball." Was that a note of pride in The Correspondent's voice? Cunningham wondered. Curious. "He's called too much attention to himself already, given his unfortunate involvement with Mr. Alloway and Mrs. Parcell."

Bartlett had become a liability. He knew enough to be dangerous and, worse, no longer cared whether he lived or died. Since he cared so little, Cunningham had obliged him.

"Wise of him," The Correspondent said. "Where did you speak to him?"

"At the powder mill, just as you suggested. It was empty. A good choice."

Empty, except for the recently deceased Sergeant Bartlett. Cunningham had left the young soldier draped over the rim of the rough, massive mill stone. He exhaled a shuddering breath of pleasure, took a last sip and placed his glass on the flat side of a barrel.

"The Sergeant won't have a chance to disappoint you again. I've removed him." By the time the body was found, the war might be over.

"Removed?" The Correspondent asked.

"Killed." Cunningham smiled. "I best take my place upstairs." He rose and started up the stairs. There would be surprises for Mr. Washington this evening. There would be surprises for everyone.

The quartet was rehearsing a gavotte, and the music grew louder as he neared the second-floor landing. The music almost drowned out the sound of keening below.

Chapter Forty-Eight

They stopped on the wind-sheltered side of the Presbyterian Church. Across the Morristown Green, lanterns lined the storehouse porch like sparkling beads on a necklace. One carriage pulled away as another stopped to unload its passengers. Becca heard a woman laugh with excitement and saw the back of her swirling pink satin gown. Then the door opened and the sound and gown were gone.

"I've taken you as far as I can, m'dear," Mason pulled his horse next to hers.

"You're not coming with us?" she asked.

"He can't." Daniel met Mason's gaze. "Washington's officers are all inside. To a man, each would be proud to capture the leader of the Highland Gang. Mr. Mason would hang there." He jerked his head toward the west side of the Green. Daniel couldn't see it in the dark, but he knew where the gallows stood.

"We'll pay our respects to the dead and wait for you there." Mr. Mason pointed to the cemetery at the back of the church. The cemetery wasn't visible from the party.

"We'll leave our horses with you, then." Daniel swung his leg over his stallion's flank and jumped to the ground.

Becca slipped from her borrowed horse and joined him.

Moments later, she pulled her shoulders back and looked down her nose at the soldier guarding the door to the party. Becca hoped the darkness and her well-born manner disguised the shortcomings of her dress. The mud-stained day gown was hardly fit for cleaning a stable, let alone for attending the social event of the season.

"There must be a mistake. Check again," Daniel said with his most ingratiating smile to the guard who blocked their path.

His crooked finger slid down the list and his mouth moved as he sounded out guests' names on the page.

"Mr. Hamilton promised to add us to the list," Daniel said. "Perhaps if you look again."

The guard looked up with a smile. "There you are. Here at the bottom. You must have just paid for your ticket."

It was considerate of Hamilton to add their names to the guest list, Becca thought, although it would have been even more considerate if he had bothered to mention it to her when she saw him earlier.

"There. Just as I said." Daniel took Becca's arm and stepped around the tall, broad-chested soldier.

The guard brought the attendee list up to his close-set eyes. "No. This way." He pointed to the stairs at the far side of the porch that led down and away from the party. "Mr. Hamilton wants to see you downstairs." The guard pointed to a hastily written scrawl at the bottom of the attendee list different from the neatly penned names of the party guests.

Good, Becca thought with satisfaction. She and Daniel would hand the list to Hamilton and go home. That would save her from making an appearance at the ball in her inappropriate day dress.

At the bottom of the staircase, Becca stepped toes first to avoid tripping on something she couldn't see. The room's single candle seemed to levitate in a fluted tin sconce that was nailed to the wall.

Even without much light, she felt the hopelessness of this place. A few barrels and shovels were strewn in no particular order in the long, dark space like giant chess pieces abandoned on a board. The barrels probably held gunpowder, Becca thought. She couldn't imagine there was any food left here. The soldiers were all going hungry. She heard a rustle.

"Stand behind me." Daniel whispered as he slipped in front of her.

"Mr. Hamilton?" Becca called. Why would he abandon the party to meet them here? "Let's go back."

She didn't move in time.

A barrel tipped with a crash. An arm shot out, grabbed her waist and clamped her limbs to her side in a one-armed hold.

Her breath rushed out as she was dragged into the deeper shadows. She knew this captor, knew his smell even though it was mixed now with sweat and alcohol. Knew the feel of his arms.

Knew what he had done.

She struggled to regain her footing. But then she felt the sharp edge of a knife at her neck.

"Why? Why set all of this in motion?" The cold metal burned her skin.

Carl yanked her closer. "You found your husband's list."

"I did. Your name wasn't on it."

"Spymaster—?" Philip had written. Thomas Lockwood's name was penned last, almost as an afterthought. "But I think I knew, anyway."

"How?"

She hadn't believed it. Not until this moment. *Keep him talking.* "General Washington thought that only someone on his staff could have seen my husband's letter, the one offering to sell the list of Turncoats. It didn't cross my mind, not at first, that you could have seen Philip's letter to the general. You lived with us then." *Where is Daniel?*

"Your husband left the letter on his desk. I read it over his shoulder one day when I brought him tea." Carl's voice was hollow, as if he were talking to her from a great distance.

Goosebumps rose on her arms. "You told the British about Philip. He died because of you."

"Why couldn't you leave it be? If it weren't for you, my son would be alive." He tightened his one-handed grip around her, his chest to her back.

"Your son?" The flat side of the knife seemed to burn her neck.

"Cut her and I'll kill you." Daniel's voice was cold.

She couldn't see him in the dark.

"As if I care, with him dead." Carl's voice broke. "My Eli. My son."

Eli. Eli Bartlett. The names clicked together in Becca's mind. *Dead.* Then Becca made another connection. "Sergeant Bartlett told Daniel that his father taught mathematics. That was you."

"You never told me you had a son." Her breath escaped in short puffs that left her dizzy. She was good and frightened now.

Daniel's footsteps approached then receded as if he were searching for the right angle, a way to attack Carl without harming her.

"I was dead to him," Carl's voice cracked. "He was four. I'd been drinking. Wasn't the first time I hit them." His voice trickled to a stop, then restarted "After I broke Eli's arm, I promised my Rosie, my wife, I'd never see either of them again. And I didn't mean to see him. I didn't." He yanked Becca tight again. "I heard Rosie took back her old name. Bartlett."

"I didn't have anything to do with Sergeant Bartlett's death." She strained to twist her neck away from the knife. Her heart was breaking. The man she'd known her entire life – –almost her entire life – –was a stranger.

"When did you find your son again?" Daniel asked from the darkness.

Becca heard him move to her left.

"He came three winters ago, the last time the army spent time here. I saw him at the tavern." Carl swayed, but the knife stayed at her neck. "He delivered a message to General Washington. I was outside waiting for Mr. Parcell. Eli came out the door. I would have known him anywhere." He tightened his grip on her. "He's the image of his mother."

Becca tried not to move against the blade. *Where's Daniel?*

"It was the war, you see."

She didn't see.

"He didn't own land. He didn't have a future. I gave him one. Me. I gave him a future until, until...." Carl's knife flashed before her face. "Get back."

Daniel's footsteps receded.

Keep him talking. "Gave him a future how?"

The blade shivered in his hand. "Money. The British pay for food, for firewood, for information. Everyone smuggles something. Eli sent me information about his troop or what he heard the officers say."

"And you passed it to the British," Daniel said from the shadows.

"My share of the money was for Eli. For his future," Carl said.

Becca's stomach swooped. "You weren't the messenger, were you? You *chose* the messengers."

"People are desperate for money. It wasn't hard to find them. Mr. Parcell, the minister, others." His knife hand tilted up and down against her neck as if he were shrugging.

"I'd invite one or two to deliver messages to New York. I'd arrange payment from Mr. Lockwood."

"You said 'we.' You and Mr. Lockwood?" Daniel asked.

"Lockwood already hated Washington. I only had to drop a hint, fan a flame. By the end, he thought it was his idea." Carl's breath was sour on her cheek.

The knife scraped the side of her neck, and she hardly noticed. "You chose my husband to be the messenger. And you told the British that it was time to get rid of him. How could you do that?"

"I saw your husband's letter to General Washington. He left it on his desk. My Eli's name was on it. I couldn't let your husband take away Eli's future," Carl said, as if explaining something obvious to a child. "Not when we were so close to ending the war. All the boys would go home then."

Ending the war. "What have you done?"

"I know you're angry. But it will all end soon. It's better this way." Carl sounded as if he were drifting away from her.

She breathed along with the rhythm of his chest. Would he kill her? To save her from what? A world that didn't contain his son?

Daniel stepped out of the shadows. He must have heard something fatal in Carl's voice, too.

"Eli couldn't make himself kill me or Mrs. Parcell. It tore him up. You didn't count on his conscience, did you, Carl?" Daniel said. "He didn't want to be one of your spies any more. Put the blame where it belongs. Blame yourself for his death."

Carl's arm tightened around Becca's waist, her arms tucked within its embrace. "None of it matters now. Not the Madeira. Not the rest."

Now. Becca crossed her wrists beneath Carl's grip. She used the small bit of leverage she had to drive her arms up and out in a sudden motion. The knife nicked her throat as her arms widened. She lifted her knee and ground the heel of her boot into Carl's instep, then flung herself away from him.

He stumbled back. She heard the crack of metal on bone and, then, a grunt.

Bodies don't crumple all at once. A shoe squeaked as a foot tipped. There was the dull thump of a hip and the sharper knock of a skull striking a dirt floor.

Daniel held a shovel in his good hand. He dropped the tool and reached for Becca. "Are you all right?"

"Yes. Fine. No." She rested against him for a moment, then pushed away.

Daniel crouched. "He's breathing. We'll let someone know he's here." He rifled through Carl's pockets.

"What are you doing?" Daniel's search felt like a violation to Becca.

"You've never been in a tavern brawl, have you?" he asked without looking up. "Always check the pockets. You never know what you'll find."

Daniel stood. He held his left palm out to her, displaying a fistful of gold guineas and Spanish doubloons.

Becca touched one of the coins with the tip of a finger. "Everything Carl did. All the damage. All for Eli."

"No," Daniel answered. "All for himself. All to make himself feel better about abandoning the boy."

She whispered, "This is enough money to buy you a passage on a ship to any country in the world."

"If we leave now, we can be in Trenton by sunrise and Philadelphia by the night after," Daniel said. "You can buy a farm anywhere.

"Or there's a party we might attend." His eyes gleamed. "Carl didn't count on Eli's conscience. He didn't count on ours, either. Shall we?" He swept his arm out.

She ran to the stairs and called back, "Hurry."

Becca thought of Mr. Hamilton and General Washington. They were imperfect men, but they were fighting for the future instead of the past, as messy and painful as that future might be. She had thought she wanted to be left alone, to lock the doors behind her at the farm and keep everyone away but Augusta and Annie. She'd been wrong.

Chapter Forty-Nine

Daniel and Becca barreled across the porch toward the door that led to the ball. The sentry took a tentative step to block their path. He seemed to notice that neither of them was dressed for the evening's festivities.

"Hamilton's orders. Have to keep moving," Daniel called as he passed to the sentry's right. Becca passed to his left.

"There's an injured man in the rooms below. Tell Major Gibbs." Becca pulled her skirts up and took two stairs at a time.

The crowd was a blur of jewel-colored dresses, a sea of dark blue uniforms and white-powdered wigs. There were more men than women, more officers than townspeople. But the best families of Morristown were represented as well as Washington's senior officers.

Becca searched for General Washington and sagged in relief. There, at the far end of the room, on a raised platform next to the refreshment table, he stood surrounded by aides and the redcoat delegation of officers.

She pressed a hand against the pocket where Philip's list of spies lay. A bead of perspiration fell between her breasts. *Not too late. Not too late*, she repeated silently.

One of the redcoats lifted a heavy walking stick and, to focus the crowd's attention, struck it repeatedly against the platform, a dull drumbeat.

"That's Captain Maguire. Been a real gentleman," a local merchant said, his chest puffed with pride.

"You mean, he spent real silver at your store, not that worthless American paper," his companion said.

The crowd surged toward the platform and the general.

A glass broke. Becca craned her neck to follow the sound to its source. Thomas Lockwood stared at her. Ale dripped from his hand.

He spoke to two men in the uniform of Washington's Life Guards, who started toward Becca and Daniel.

"We hardly would have anticipated...." Captain Maguire drew out the word "hawwwwdly," until it practically lost its meaning. "...being greeted with such hospitality." The beginnings of a double chin jiggled slightly as he spoke.

Becca and Daniel pushed forward but were blocked by soldiers, merchants and women in their wide skirts.

A boot kicked Becca's shin. Daniel grabbed her arm to prevent the fall.

Was it on purpose? She thought so. *How did I ever let these people bother me?*

The two Life Guards that Thomas set in motion wove through the crowd, drawing closer.

Captain Maguire snapped his fingers. One of the other British officers handed him a dark bottle and a corkscrew. "And in honor of our common ancestors, we present a bottle of the finest Portuguese Madeira. Your favorite, we understand."

General Washington's eyebrows rose in appreciation as he inspected the bottle. "A very choice Madeira," he said.

"And so." Captain Maguire uncorked the bottle with a twist of his hand. "A toast to Mr. Washington."

The crowd echoed the chant. "Huzzah. A toast to General Washington."

The British officer poured a slow stream of the liquor into a tall cut crystal glass and presented it to Washington, then rested the bottle on the refreshment table near the punch bowl.

The light from a nearby candelabra glittered off the goblet raised in Washington's hand. It glowed like amber.

"It's the Madeira." Becca grabbed Daniel's arm, then released it. In a rush, she said, "Carl mentioned the Madeira. We saw a bottle of it in Thomas' wine cellar. Carl must have added the belladonna to it, then got the bottle to the redcoats."

She felt a tug, and a rough hand pulled her back. One of the guards gripped her elbow as if helping her maintain her balance. His face was impassive. But his grip tightened when she tried to shake him off. The second Life Guard stood next to Daniel, a hand clamped to his neck.

Snippets of conversation surrounded them.

"Did she sleep in that dress?"

"Who let her in?"

"Must be drunk to appear like that."

"Don't let her near the punchbowl, then. She might fall in," a woman tittered.

Don't let her near the punchbowl. A fine idea, Becca thought.

"Don't drink the Madeira!" she bellowed. "Poison."

Time didn't slow. It flattened. Everything seemed to happen at once.

The guard's hand lifted in surprise and Becca, freed, careened forward, aiming for the refreshment table. She swept the large, heavy punch bowl toward the bottle of Madeira and, beyond it, unavoidably, toward His Excellency General George Washington, the goblet still raised in his hand.

For the briefest moment, Becca thought she caught a look of surprised amusement on his face. Then his hands opened as the ruby red punch drenched his uniform, and the goblet tumbled in surrender to the ground.

* * *

The guard's grip tightened round Daniel's neck.

A woman screamed. Officers barreled through the crowd toward Washington and the redcoat delegation.

Daniel struggled to turn again, to find Becca, but he was whipped around until he faced the back of the room. Against the back wall, a red-faced servant poked Thomas Lockwood in the chest with one finger. Which made no sense. No servant would touch one of his betters like that.

Even dressed as a servant, Daniel recognized William Cunningham. Which also made no sense.

He tracked the two men as the crowd and the guard pulled and pushed. Cunningham shoved Lockwood, and they ran, disappearing through a door at the back of the room.

They were heading down to the storeroom. Daniel was certain of it.

With all of Washington's senior officers watching, Becca would be safe here. He jammed his good hand into his pocket and felt the weight of the gold coins. He could run, keep going until Cunningham haunted him only in dreams, then, regretfully decided that Santa Fe could wait a little longer.

He scythed his elbow back and up into his jaw. The impact sent the man flying.

He was no Alexander Hamilton, no hero. He would sound the alarm when he saw which direction Cunningham and Lockwood were heading. That was all he intended. He'd leave their capture and all the glory to Gibbs and his men.

He sped toward the front of the ballroom and down the stairs.

* * *

Hands grabbed Becca as she was jostled through the crowd. Someone spit on her cheek. She angled her head back to search for Daniel and to make sure General Washington was safe. He came into view for just a moment. His gaze followed her as she was pushed from the room.

Servants and officers surrounded him. White napkins rose and fell as the officers apologized and dabbed at Washington's ruined uniform. Several of his guards surrounded the redcoats.

Becca was turned forward and back. Her view of them disappeared, reappeared.

A small plump woman wearing a plain brown gown, the color of the ill-fated madeira, came forward to protect him, as if such a small woman could.

She only had time to think, *so that's Mrs. Washington.* The general's wife curtsied—just the smallest bob—in her direction as Becca was hustled out of the room to the landing above the stairs.

Major Gibbs stood there, grim-faced. Three of his soldiers stood with him.

The hands didn't loosen their grip easily. Someone shook her. Others pushed her toward the wide, steep stairs as if hoping she'd trip down them.

Becca didn't blame them. Her behavior was scandalous.

Gibbs caught her as she tumbled into him. He stepped away, seemingly embarrassed to touch a woman he hardly knew.

Two fiddlers struck up music in the ballroom, something with a quick tempo. Footsteps began to stamp out the strong beat. Morristown was covering its embarrassment with music.

The men slowly retreated, leaving Becca, Gibbs and his soldiers alone on the stairs.

Becca's knees trembled with the aftermath of fear. "I'll go. You needn't follow me," she said to Gibbs.

His voice was soft. "That was well done, m'lady. General Washington wants to thank you. He told us to escort you to the Widow Ford's mansion and wait there until he arrives."

"You knew I wasn't drunk?" she asked.

"Not at first, no." His face warred between outrage and sadness. "We suspected there were turncoats among us. And now we know, thanks to you."

"What about Carl?" she asked.

"We found him alive." Gibbs accompanied her to the front door.

She nodded. Becca didn't hate Carl yet, but she guessed that she would. She was still relieved that he was alive.

"And is Mr. Alloway well?" She gripped the banister with one hand as they descended. She still wasn't certain her legs would hold her.

Major Gibbs frowned. "He rushed down the stairs towards the storeroom. I thought he was feeling poorly again, after this afternoon and all. I thought you knew."

"No. I didn't." She recalled the gold in the palm of his hand. *He's gone.*

Gibbs opened the door for her and she stepped through it, wincing at the cold. They had succeeded. They'd found Philip's list of turncoats. Daniel could travel as far as he wished with Carl's money. And she had earned her farm back.

But he was gone.

Chapter Fifty

A curtain of falling snow separated the ball from the rest of the world. Daniel couldn't even see to the far side of the Morristown Green. He dashed across the porch and stopped at the top of the narrow staircase that led to the cellar. The floor had been swept clean but for an empty tin pail resting nearby.

"Two more. Quickly," he heard Cunningham say.

Barrels scraped the floor.

"This isn't part of the plan." Lockwood's voice was tense.

"It should have been the plan all along," Cunningham growled. "All that planning with the Madeira for nothing. All because you had a *tendresse* for the woman. You couldn't kill her yourself. You had to send someone too weak to do the job. What a mess you made."

Someone too weak? Lockwood—not Carl—had sent Sergeant Bartlett to kill them both.

Daniel stretched and loosened his right hand, which shook with the need to smash something. To smash Lockwood.

Behind him, the sound of two sets of footsteps.

He knew it was Becca before he turned. He guessed she heard what Cunningham said. Major Gibbs stood behind her.

Her mobcap was gone, her black hair loose and disheveled. One sleeve of her gown was ripped from shoulder to elbow. Pale skin peeked through the gap in the cloth and glowed like a soft sliver of moon in the porch's lantern light.

Guilt lodged in Daniel's throat. He thought she would be safe upstairs with Washington's guards. He'd apologize for leaving her in the morning, if they lived through the night. He pointed to the stairs, mouthed the names, "Cunningham and Lockwood."

"Done," Lockwood said. "It's past time to leave."

"Over there. Isn't that yours?" Cunningham called.

"I am...why did you...why?" Lockwood's voice shattered. Then silence.

Becca jammed a fist against her mouth. Her eyes squeezed shut.

Daniel imagined the flash of Cunningham's blade. He tried and failed to swallow past the clenched muscles of his throat.

Then they heard it. A faint sound, barely louder than a sigh. The scratch and hiss of a match. The whoosh of air that accompanies a fuse being lit.

"Can you think of a quicker way to end the war?" Daniel whispered. "Washington and all his officers are upstairs. How much gunpowder is stored below?"

"Not much right now, but enough." Gibbs blinked, then spoke rapidly. "I'll bring out the General and Lady Washington. We'll evacuate as many as we can without causing a panic. Get as far from here as you can."

"Leave me with a pistol. Or a knife. A knife will do." Daniel held out his good hand, palm up.

Gibbs hesitated.

"In case Cunningham leaves this way." Daniel's own sorry life wasn't worth a song on his father's penny whistle. But the men upstairs were different. An explosion here tonight would end the war. It was as simple and devastating as that.

Gibbs unsheathed a long steel knife from its case at his belt, handed it to him and sprinted back to the party.

Two steps brought Daniel to the dark cellar entrance.

"Mr. Alloway? Is that you?" Cunningham stood at the base of the stairs. Half of his broad, pale face was lit by a single candle. The other half was in darkness. "And the delightful Mrs. Parcell." Cunningham laughed. "How charming. Send her down, Alloway." His tongue flicked out, caressing his top lip.

Blood roared in Daniel's ears. "Go. Now."

"No," Becca said.

"Then stay back," Daniel said to her. He stepped out of Cunningham's sight line, swept one arm around Becca's waist and pulled her in. He meant his kiss to convey all he hadn't told her, might never have a chance to say. She leaned in, and he felt the weight of her breasts against his chest, the shape of her against his chest, his legs.

She left behind a jangle of heat, a sonnet of touch. Daniel stepped away and turned to Cunningham.

"Time is short, Mr. Alloway." He bared his small, widely spaced teeth into what might have passed for a smile on someone else. His eyes flicked right where Daniel estimated the powder kegs sat.

"Challenge me or run. It's the same to me. But I can see that it's not all the same to you, is it? There is one reason that men come to me. And you have come to me three times. On the *Jersey*, then, the mayor's house, and now here."

The first step creaked as Daniel placed his weight on it.

"The world's a cage, is it not, for men like you?" Cunningham's knife hand rose, swinging in small circle eights. "I can give you the freedom you crave.

He's right. Daniel thought. Finish it here. The next step creaked and the next. The roar in his ears crescendoed. There was anguish and anger in the sound, warning and lamentation.

"Come, Mr. Alloway. End the struggle." Cunningham's voice was intimate, almost dreamy, as if he understood the darkest of Daniel's thoughts since Amelia's death and his son's.

Struggle. The sound in Daniel's head thrummed, swooped and disentangled into voices that called that one word. He knew the voices were imaginary. Just the after effect of poison, he told himself.

He thought of Becca, of Mr. Rivington's secrets, Alexander Hamilton's confidence and Washington's sad eyes. Struggle was heartbreak and joy and pain and hope. It was life. Becca had taught him that. So had the others. Cunningham's "freedom" was a lie.

Daniel stopped on the dark, narrow staircase, transferring the knife to his injured hand, barely managing to make a fist around it. He braced his good hand on the banister and snapped his legs forward, slamming them feet first against the man's chest.

Cunningham's arms windmilled. He stumbled and fell back, his head striking the earthen floor with a dull thump.

The banister splintered beneath Daniel's weight. His spine hit the sharp edge of a step. Stars exploded beneath his eyelids. He bumped down the stairs, scrambling to stop himself, losing the knife as his palm opened.

Cunningham was on the floor and still, for now. It was worth the risk to recover the knife. Daniel turned his back on the man, sliding his hands along one rough tread then the next until his fingers hit something solid. Scooping up the knife handle, he clambered to his feet.

Angry sparks climbed the fuse along the side of the powder keg in the midst of the almost-empty storeroom. They seemed to float about a foot above the floor.

Daniel's eyes scanned the space for something he could use to snuff out the flame. Transferring the knife to his bad hand, he stepped over Cunningham to reach the kegs.

A hand clasped Daniel's right ankle. There was no thought after that, only time to react. He teetered and kicked out. Cunningham rolled away and rose to his feet. The two men circled each other, tipped, turned and swerved. Cunningham rushed him again, swinging his blade up this time.

Daniel twisted left. The momentum of Cunningham's swing left him within arm's reach, his right side exposed. In his bad hand, the knife rose then fell with strength and certainty he should not have had.

Cunningham roared. He pulled an arm in to his chest, then grinned his eerie, childlike smile at Daniel.

The hissing grew louder, and Cunningham's head jerked toward the sound. Cradling his arm, he sprinted toward the storeroom's rear exit.

Daniel turned to the powder keg as the fuse climbed to the top of the barrel. He lifted the blade he still held. In the weak candlelight, it shone with Cunningham's blood.

Daniel's arm slashed downward, the edge of the knife shearing through a strand of the thick, short fuse. Without a way to keep it taut, the fuse was almost impossible to cut.

He was out of time. He hoped Becca had moved off the porch but knew in his bones she'd be waiting for him at the top of the stairs. He sawed as the flame nicked the back of his hand, the image of her face fixed in his mind.

Footsteps careened down the stairs.

The third cut severed the fuse, and Daniel batted the tiny shard of rope away from the barrel. A wisp of smoke rose as the flame's life hissed out.

Becca ran to him. Her hands shivered across his chest and arms, as if to assure herself that he was uninjured. She inhaled a sob and began to laugh, one hand still splayed on his chest. He dropped the knife and brought his forehead down to hers, wrapping his arms round her.

Eventually, he took her arm, and, together, they climbed the stairs. Daniel turned back in the doorway just for a moment. Facing Cunningham at the base of the dark stairs, he had smelled the dank sea off the Brooklyn shore, felt other hands guiding his knife. He thought they belonged to the prisoners who died on the *Jersey*. He thought they were pleased with him. Perhaps they could rest now.

He would tell Becca about it someday, but not tonight.

Chapter Fifty-One

The cold spell broke the next morning, and the entire town came out to the Green. Women with large baskets rushed in and out of stores, their day dresses pinned just high enough to avoid the snow. Groups of men blew smoke rings from clay pipes and caught up on news in front of Arnold's tavern. The snow sparkled as if delighted by the unexpected sunlight.

They all bowed and curtsied as General Washington passed on his horse. Then their heads lifted. The wind carried the buzz of their surprise.

Washington nodded to each passerby, then leaned toward Becca. "Just a little longer. They need to know you're under my protection. You must smile to me when you speak."

Becca hoped her smile didn't look like she was ready to bite someone. "I don't mean any disrespect, Your Excellency." She shifted in her saddle. "But they never take their eyes off you. How do you stand it?"

General Washington held his horse's reins relaxed in one hand. The corners of his lips twitched with amusement. "It's unsettling at times but useful as well."

"I can't thank you and Mrs. Washington enough. I think I would have been run out of town if it weren't for the two of you."

"Is General Washington *really* escorting that woman through town?" one man asked just loudly enough for Becca to hear.

Mrs. Biddle's mouth opened in shock at the sight.

At last night's ball, some of these men would have pushed her down the stairs. They'd all thought she was drunk.

Becca's shoulders tensed at the insults, then relaxed. *What does it matter?*

This ride should put to rest most of the rumors about her loyalty. And even if the rumors didn't die entirely, not many people would dare to cross someone close to General Washington. That's what Mrs. Washington told her after the ball last night. At the Widow Ford's mansion, she'd grasped Becca's hands, then curtsied to Daniel, and thanked them for saving her husband's life.

"Mr. Washington," the older woman said, her kind, intelligent eyes searching Becca's. "You will find a way to make sure that Mrs. Parcell is safe when we leave, won't you? I have no doubt that you have a plan in place?" She turned the last statement into a question.

"Why don't you tell me your plan first, and we'll see if it's the same as mine," he responded with a wry smile.

Soft lines deepening at the edge of Mrs. Washington's hazel eyes. She nodded at him with approval.

Now Becca and the general were the center of the town's attention, although no one was close enough to overhear them. She had so many questions.

"What will you do with the redcoat delegation?" she asked.

"I'll send them back to New York City, once we've had time for a discussion," he said. "New Jersey's Governor Livingston is pressing me to send them to his prison camp in Princeton. But then the British will retaliate with even worse treatment for our prisoners in New York. I won't have that on my conscience.

"The British officers said they didn't know of Mr. Cunningham's intentions. I believe them. The delegation would have been killed along with my senior officers if the gunpowder had exploded." He hesitated. "They wouldn't hesitate to attack me on the battlefield. But this? Poisoning? It isn't honorable."

"The gentleman's code?"

"Mmmm," he answered. "

"Mr. Cunningham is no gentleman," she prodded.

Washington's face darkened. "No. And he has not treated our men with the dignity they deserve. We will see him again."

It sounded like a vow.

He bowed to three men who stood in front of Arnold's tavern. Becca heard her name whispered over and over.

"There were two other guards on my husband's list of turncoats. What will happen to them?" She thought of Sergeant Bartlett, who hadn't been able to bring himself to kill her.

"They will be tried, and if found guilty, they will be punished." He didn't need to specify the nature of that punishment.

She glanced at the Baptist Church. It had been converted into a hospital earlier in the war. Thomas and Carl were being held there. "And what will you do with Mr. Lockwood and Carl?"

Washington's normally stern expression deepened. "I've told my officers that Lockwood was hurt protecting me from Cunningham. It's better for morale if they think so."

"But Mr. Lockwood knew about the plan. He assisted," Becca said.

"I didn't drink the Madeira, thanks to you," he continued. "The bottle was destroyed. And so there is no proof that he tried to kill me. These events will go unrecorded."

"Aren't you angry?" Becca nodded at another neighbor who curtsied to her and the general.

Washington didn't answer directly. "I stepped away just before the bullet hit Lockwood's father in the war with the French. Did you know that? It is one of the stories that follows me, as if Providence saved me." His voice faltered. "I didn't know that Lockwood blamed me and not Providence for his father's death."

"But you supported his family."

His voice softened. "I deprived him of his father. That's how he saw it. My funds could not return what I took from him. What he thinks I took."

Washington followed her gaze to the small Baptist Church. "There's little point in examining what can't be changed." His voice was wistful.

"What will you do with him? With them?"

Becca watched Washington tuck away his regrets. "If they were soldiers, they'd be subject to court martial. But as it is, they will be banished. They can travel to Nova Scotia with the other Loyalists."

Chapter Fifty-Two

A drop of melting snow smacked Becca's forehead as she walked through into the front hall of the tavern. She wiped away the moisture. Finally. A thaw. Winter was almost over.

The invitation to join the Washingtons for a small dinner came later that afternoon, after her ride with the general. For the occasion, she wore her favorite navy velvet dress with its tight sleeves. They expanded at the wrist to highlight crisp white lace.

Hopper stomped toward her. "General Washington is here. He said to bring you." His hand twitched toward her awkwardly, as if to pull her upstairs.

She turned to the tavern owner. "Are they all upstairs, Colonel Arnold?"

He nodded and continued to rub down the bar with yet another dirty towel.

Conversation stopped when she entered the whitewashed dining room. General and Lady Washington, her mother-in-law, Augusta, and John Mason sat at a large round table covered in a white tablecloth and set with fine blue and white china.

Mrs. Washington and Augusta sat next to each other and beamed at Becca.

John Mason winked at her, and she tightened her lips to avoid laughing. His presence at this dinner proved what she surmised. The most famous thief in the Mid-Atlantic was another one of Mr. Washington's spies.

Mr. Hamilton half sat on the windowsill along the far wall of the private dining room. He held a rolled parchment in his hand. Daniel leaned over the back of a nearby wing chair and spoke intently to Hamilton. He stopped and stood slowly when he saw Becca.

Daniel and Hamilton rushed forward at the same time to pull out her chair. They danced out of each other's way so that she could sit.

A thin stoop-shouldered servant stepped into the room holding a massive tray. He placed it on a sideboard and set down dishes of roast venison, parsnips, and carrots on the dining table. Then he bowed himself out again.

General Washington raised his glass. "To Mrs. Parcell and Mr. Alloway, to whom we owe a debt that can never be fully repaid. Freedom takes courage, which you have both shown in abundance."

As if that were a signal, Hamilton bowed to Becca. He brandished the parchment in his hand as if it were a sword and held it out to her.

She flushed. She had only done what was necessary.

"I spoke to Governor Livingston last night," General Washington said. "Your hearing before the Council of Safety is cancelled, of course. The proclamation confirms your loyalty to the new republic. You can go home now, madam."

Washington looked to Daniel. "And you, sir, are free to find a new home in a place more to your liking."

Daniel lifted his glass in response.

Becca pressed her lips together and stared at the empty dish before her. Daniel would leave now. It was what he wanted all along. The farm was hers. She was happy. Thrilled, she told herself.

Mrs. Washington cleared her throat. Something sorrowful passed between her and the general.

His goblet thumped on the table. "There is less fortuitous news. Lockwood's servant, Carl, woke sometime last night and left his bed wearing only a shift. We found him this morning.

"He froze to death near the Powder Mill, near where Sergeant Bartlett was killed," Washington said. "I am sorry, Mrs. Parcell. I heard you were fond of him."

Becca's knuckles whitened, bones clear beneath the skin. What was she supposed to feel? Carl helped raise her. He was the only person left alive who'd known her as a child. But he had betrayed her husband. Then he almost killed her and the general. She hoped to forgive him one day.

"Carl was trying to rewrite his past," Daniel said, and Becca relaxed at the sound of his voice.

"How, exactly?" Augusta asked.

Daniel's eyes fixed on Becca. "He was trying to be the good father he'd never been. He spent his life looking backward at his own history."

"And he didn't want to live once his son died, once he'd failed him again," Mrs. Washington said quietly.

Becca wondered if she was thinking of her own children. She'd heard the first two died before they reached their fifth birthdays.

The table was silent.

Becca inhaled sharply. Philip also held too tightly to the past. No matter how many plans he made, he couldn't recreate his family's grand history. Mr. Washington was right. Freedom took courage. Freeing yourself from the past took courage, too.

Washington raised his glass again. "This is a celebration. We will speak of more pleasant things."

"In that case, I have excellent news." Hamilton's face lit as he looked round the table.

"It's my news to tell," Daniel interrupted. "I don't know that it is possible to build the kind of country you and Mr. Hamilton talk about." He nodded to General Washington. "The right to set your own direction in life is worth defending. I know I'm not as eloquent as Mr. Hamilton."

"Mr. Hamilton does tend to go on," Mrs. Washington said to Daniel and smiled at Alexander with pride.

Becca almost laughed when Hamilton blushed at the teasing.

Daniel grinned at Becca.

Her stomach tightened.

"And what direction do you choose, Mr. Alloway?" Washington asked.

"I'm throwing in my lot with you." Then Daniel quickly added, "But you still owe me the reward for finding your turncoats."

Becca lifted the wine glass to her face to hide the pleasure she felt. "You won't be travelling to Santa Fe?"

"Mr. Hamilton is threatening to put me to work in Philadelphia."

Becca felt his gaze on her as she lowered her own. *He's not leaving,* then corrected herself. *He's not going far.*

"The British are flooding Philadelphia with false currency, counterfeit money. The price of food is rising, and the people are growing even more disaffected. He'll be looking into it for us," Hamilton said.

"We haven't quite come to an agreement about my compensation." Daniel pointed the tip of his butter knife toward Hamilton.

Hamilton nodded.

"Which will be in silver," Daniel added.

Mason laughed. "And Mrs. Rebecca, after all your adventures, will you be satisfied counting your seeds and waiting for planting time? You could join me and Lady Augusta in Bergen County. You'd make a fine bandit." He gazed at Augusta as if she were the greatest of all the treasures he'd captured.

"You and Lady Augusta?" She wasn't surprised. Mr. Mason and Augusta fit together as if they'd spent years, not months, together.

"I'll only be a day's ride away." Augusta smiled tentatively.

"I am happy for you." Becca was surprised to find that she meant it.

Washington tapped his fork absentmindedly on the side of his plate, then leaned forward. "Might I call on you again if the need arose, Mrs. Parcell? You have a cunning combination of skills."

Becca looked from her mother-in-law to Daniel and watched a kaleidoscope of expressions cross his face.

"No," Daniel interrupted. "Mrs. Parcell has put herself in enough danger. She's earned her freedom...from you, General Washington."

Becca felt her back stiffen. "There was danger. But I quite enjoyed the problem-solving aspect of it all." She brushed a crumb on the tablecloth in Daniel's direction. "Lady Augusta and I can hire someone to take care of the farm until I return. And Annie will be there, of course."

"One or two of my men can help with the planting," Mason offered. "Perhaps Amos."

"Say, 'yes,' Rebecca," Augusta said quietly. "There's more to the world than a farm in Morristown."

"That small matter in Philadelphia might benefit from Mrs. Parcell's skills," Washington said.

"Capital idea. Send them both." Hamilton looked from Becca to Daniel.

"I really must introduce her to Mr. Adams' wife, Abigail," Mrs. Washington said to Augusta.

Becca lifted the cool goblet to her lips and felt the warmth of the wine at the back of her throat. Daniel was right. If she clung too hard to the past, there would be no room for the future.

She just might join him in Philadelphia. There was a whole world to explore and freedom—the country's and her own—still to be earned.

The Turncoat's Widow

An Early American Cocktail

- **8 ounces Hard Apple Cider (Ironbound)**
- **4 ounces Bourbon, (Widow Jane's)**
- **2 teaspoons Honey**
- **2 dashes orange bitters (Fee Brothers)**
- **2 tablespoons Raw Sugar**
- **1 tablespoon Cinnamon**
- **Lime wedge to coat rim**
- **Cocktail Shaker**
- **Apple Slices for garnish**
- **Ice cubes**
- **Cognac glasses suggested.**

Instructions For Two Servings

- Place sugar and cinnamon on a plate and mix well.
- Cut a lime wedge and rub the rim of your serving glass.
- Drag edges of glass through cinnamon and sugar coating.
- Set aside.
- Place Cider, Bourbon, honey, orange bitters and ice in a cocktail shaker.
- Shake until ice cold.

- Strain cocktail mixture into two serving glasses.
- Garnish each with an apple wedge and serve!

Notes

Any hard apple cider will work just fine. As well as any bourbon.

Acknowledgements

There are many people who transformed *The Turncoat's Widow* from a rough draft into a real book, and I am thankful to them all. I am especially grateful to my publishers, Level Best Books' Harriette Sackler, Verena Rose, and Shawn Simmons for their guidance and insight. And without The Writers Circle's Michelle Cameron, Judith Lindbergh, and Vinessa Anthony Sousa, this book wouldn't exist, of that I am certain.

Encouragement from authors Lyndsay Faye, Erica Obey, Lizzie Foley, and the Mystery Writers of America-NY also kept me going through rough patches. So did an off-the-cuff remark author Jeff Markowitz flung in my direction years ago: "If you're not having fun writing, don't do it." Words to live by.

I owe a debt of gratitude to Jude Pfister, Chief of Cultural Resources at the Morristown National Historical Park, who sparked the idea that became *The Turncoat's Widow*, then, more recently, read a draft and pointed out historical errors. Mistakes that remain are entirely my fault.

Author Tina deBellegarde has been my partner-in-crime from the earliest days of writing our respective mysteries. I can't imagine this journey without her kindness, support, and friendship.

A special thanks goes to fellow writers and boon companions at The Writers Circle, including Eileen Sanchez, Connie Fowler, Andrea Stein, Karla Diaz, Suzanne Moyers, Mary Rahill, Laura Romain, and Niv Miyasato for their honest critiques and friendship.

And here's a shout-out to the librarians at the Warren Township Library, where part of *The Turncoat's Widow* was written.

Finally and forever, all my love and gratitude to my wonderful family, especially to my husband, who keeps me grounded and laughing, and to our son, who believed before I did that this day would come.

About the Author

Mally Becker was born in Brooklyn and began her professional career in New York City as a publicist and freelance magazine writer, then worked as an attorney for more than 20 years and, later, as an advocate for children in foster care. She and her husband raised their wonderful son in New Jersey where they still live.

Mally thought she'd be clearing trails when she volunteered at the Morristown National Historical Park but found herself instead sifting through the Park's archival collection of letters. That's where she found a copy of an indictment for the Revolutionary War-era crime of traveling from New Jersey to New York City "without permission or passport." That document became the spark for *The Turncoat's Widow*, her debut novel.

She is a winner of the Leon B. Burstein/MWA-NY Scholarship for Mystery Writing and a member of Sisters in Crime and the Historical Novel Society.